EVE'S DAUGHTERS

LYNN AUSTIN

EVE'S DAUGHTERS

BETHANY HOUSE PUBLISHERS
MINNEAPOLIS, MINNESOTA 55438

Published by Bethany House Publishers
A Ministry of Bethany Fellowship International
11400 Hampshire Avenue South
Minneapolis, Minnesota 55438
www.bethanyhouse.com

Printed in the United States of America by
Bethany Press International, Minneapolis, Minnesota 55438

Library of Congress Cataloging-in-Publication Data

Austin, Lynn N.
    Eve's daughters / by Lynn Austin.
      p. cm.
    ISBN 0-7642-2195-7
    I. Title.
PS3551.U839 E94   1999   99-6517
813'.54—dc21   CIP

"... for I, the Lord your God, am a jealous God,
punishing the children for the sin of the fathers
to the third and fourth generation of those who hate me,
but showing love to a thousand generations
of those who love me
and keep my commandments."

EXODUS 20:5–6 NIV

PROLOGUE

"All right, what are you two arguing about this time?" Emma Bauer knew her daughter and granddaughter had been quarreling the moment they walked through her apartment door. Her daughter's carefully groomed eyebrows were creased in a frown, her mouth pinched like the drawstring of a sack. She held her arms and shoulders rigid, clutching her purse to her side. Emma inhaled the pungent scent of French perfume as Grace kissed her cheek.

"We weren't arguing, Mother."

Emma chuckled. "Well, I can see plain as day that you were. Honestly, it's only a thirty-five-minute drive over here. Can't you two last longer than that without squabbling?"

"Suzanne and I came to help you move, not to air our dirty laundry."

"My dear, if you could see the thundercloud hanging over the both of you, you wouldn't be talking about doing laundry."

"You're imagining things, Mother." Grace smiled briefly at Emma, then turned to Suzanne with a withering look that clearly said, *Not in front of Grandma.*

Suzanne rolled her eyes. "Grandma's going to find out sooner or later." Her features and gestures were loose and careless, like the faded jeans and oversized blouse she wore. Suzanne was thirty years old, but she tossed her shoulder bag onto Emma's sofa and dropped beside it like a pouting teenager. "You're afraid to tell her because you know Grandma will be on my side."

"I know nothing of the sort." Grace's flushed cheeks served as a barometer for her rising temper, just as her father's always had. "Our discussion is finished, Suzanne. We've come here to work."

"To work?" Emma repeated. She examined her daughter with mild amusement. Grace wore pale blue linen slacks and a matching cashmere sweater with her trademark string of pearls fastened around her neck. At fifty-five she was still slim and fashionable, her reddish gold hair and lacquered nails fresh from the salon. "Well, Gracie, I'm glad to see you wore your old work clothes today."

"Those *are* Mom's rags," Suzanne said, scornfully. "The pearls are fake."

Emma laughed, but when Grace's prim expression didn't change, she gave a shrug of resignation. "All right, if you're determined not to tell me what the feud is all about, come pour yourselves some coffee and let's start packing."

Grace tossed her car keys to Suzanne. "Here, go get the rest of the empty boxes out of my car, please." Grace followed Emma into the kitchen and looked around in dismay. "You haven't done any packing! I thought . . ."

"I know, I know, I promised I would sort through things. But when the time came, it was very hard to get started. I've lived here thirty-five years, you know, and the memories keep crowding in around me. I can't seem to get anything done."

"Now, Mother, it was your decision to move to a retirement home. You said you wanted to get out of the city and move closer to Suzanne and me. We discussed this months ago."

Emma covered Grace's hand with her own. "I'm not changing my mind, dear. I'm just mourning all the losses—the old neighborhood . . . all my friends . . ."

"I hate to spout clichés, but you'll have dozens of new friends in no time. People always seem to flock around you wherever you go. Stephen calls you a people-magnet."

"Well, if I don't weed out some of this junk, there won't be enough room for *me* in my new suite, let alone flocks of people." Emma opened one of her kitchen cupboards and stared at the jumble of mismatched dishes, then closed it again. "I just can't seem to decide what to keep and what to toss."

"Then why don't we move all of it and you can weed it out once you're there?"

"Oh no, you don't," Emma said, laughing. "I may dress like a bag lady, but I'm not going to start living like one. I couldn't fit all this junk in Birch Grove if I used a trash compactor."

Emma heard the familiar jingle of chimes on her front door, then the hollow, empty sound of cardboard boxes dropping to the floor. "We're in here," she called.

Suzanne wandered into the kitchen and sank onto a chair as if she had already done a day's work. She was usually so animated, her blue eyes sparkling with life as she talked, her expressive hands adding energy and shape to her words. She was a career woman, editor of a magazine for career women, and she usually charged into a room and took control. She was decisive, organized, assertive—some would say hard-edged if they didn't know her as well as Emma did. But something had dimmed Suzanne's vibrancy. Her dark hair fell across her face as if she were trying to hide behind it.

"Where do you want us to start, Grandma?" Her tired voice lacked enthusiasm.

"Well, that's the problem, you see. I can't seem to decide where to begin. When I started setting aside all the things I wanted to give you, I was surprised to find there's very little worth giving. I never really thought about it before, but I guess when I divorced Karl years ago I left my own heritage behind." She took a sip of coffee, remembering Karl's bitter words as clearly as if he had spoken them yesterday. She shook herself to erase them from her mind, then exhaled. "We'd better start packing if I'm going to be out of this apartment by Wednesday."

Emma led the way into the living room and stopped in front of her antique curio cabinet. She opened the curved glass doors and gestured to the shelf of pink and green depression glass.

"Let's start with these. Do you want them, Gracie? They're yours, you know."

"Mine?"

"Yes. Don't you remember where you got them? Tell Suzanne."

"Oh yes . . . They gave them away at the movies as premiums during the depression." Grace's voice betrayed her impatience at Emma's rambling excursions into the past.

"If you and Grandma were so poor during the depression, how could you afford the movies?" Suzanne asked.

"I don't know . . . you gave me the money to go, didn't you, Mother?"

"You mean you don't remember?" Emma asked in surprise. "All those books you read, Gracie?"

"Oh, that's right. The parish priest paid all the children in the neighborhood five cents for every book we read." Grace almost smiled. "That's when I first learned to love books so much. I used the money I earned to go to the movies every Saturday. I'll never forget what a big heart Father O'Duggan had. I wasn't even Catholic, but he paid me just like all the other kids."

"But you were the only one who cleaned out his pockets," Emma said. "None of the other children ever did much reading as far as I remember, even for a nickel."

Suzanne examined a green, etched-glass dessert bowl. "They really gave these away for free? They're so pretty."

"Do you want them, Gracie?" Emma asked again. "Get some newspaper and we'll wrap them up. Phew, they're dusty!"

"No, I'd better not take them," Grace answered slowly. "Stephen hates little knickknacks like this cluttering up his house."

Suzanne's reaction was swift and angry. "Mom, it's your house too!"

The tension Emma had first noticed between them snapped as taut as a rope as their secret tug-of-war resumed. She placed an empty carton on the floor between them, hoping to ease the strain. "Just wrap up the dishes and put them in a box, then," Emma said. "If neither of you wants them, I'll let the antique dealer buy them. It doesn't matter." She hoped her voice hadn't betrayed the disappointment that knifed her heart.

The room was quiet except for the rustling of paper as they removed each piece and carefully wrapped it before placing it in the cardboard box. A knobby pink sugar bowl rattled as Suzanne took it down from the shelf.

"There's something inside here, Grandma. Oh look . . . is this coal?" Suzanne held up a shiny black lump the size of a walnut.

Tears came to Emma's eyes as she remembered words heard long ago. She repeated them to her granddaughter. "That's not coal, honey, that's a diamond-in-the-making. God will use pressure and stress to turn it into something beautiful."

"Sometimes we ran out of coal during the depression," Grace explained to Suzanne. She was wrapping dishes with her back to Emma and didn't notice her tears. "Coal was almost as precious as diamonds to us in those days. I remember one winter it was so cold your grandmother caught pneumonia and nearly died. But after that we never ran out of coal again. It was like the miracle in the Bible—the widow with her jar of oil that never ran out. Our bin always had a couple of pieces of coal in it. Did you ever find out who was filling it for us, Mother?"

"I always knew who was filling it."

Grace whirled to face her. "Who?"

Emma realized that the truth would lead to more questions—questions she wasn't willing to answer. She smiled faintly. "You wouldn't make me break a promise by telling, would you, dear?"

"But that was ages ago. What difference could it possibly make now? I'll bet the mystery person isn't even alive anymore."

"What is it about moving that dredges up the past so vividly?" Emma asked. She stared at the dusty cabinet shelves as if they were a window into her own past. "Lately I've been thinking so much about all our old friends and neighbors from King Street, I've almost expected one of them to pop through my door—like Crazy Clancy or those dreary Mulligan sisters. Remember them?"

Grace folded her arms across her chest. "You aren't going to tell me who filled our coal box, are you."

"No, dear, I can't. But take the coal home with you. Keep it to remember how much we were cared for back then, even in hard times."

As Emma reached to take it from Suzanne's palm, she noticed that her granddaughter wasn't wearing her wedding ring. A paler band of skin marked the place where it had once been. Their eyes met. Suzanne quickly shoved her left hand into the pocket of her jeans as if to hide an ugly scar, then bit her lip, struggling to hold back her tears. The room fell silent except for the drone of traffic in the street below, the distant wail of a siren.

"What's wrong, Suzanne?" Emma asked gently.

Suzanne glanced at her mother, then sighed. "Jeff and I are getting a divorce."

"Oh, honey, no!" Suzanne's words were so unexpected, so devastating, it was all Emma could manage to say. She had invested all her failed hopes and dreams in Jeff and Suzanne, trying to redeem her own mistakes through their marriage.

Behind her, Grace's trembling voice broke the silence. "You are *not* getting a divorce, Suzanne! You can't do that to your children. You and Jeff need to see a counselor and talk about this. If it's a matter of money, your father and I—"

"I already told you it's not the money. And we have talked about it. Endlessly. I'm sick of talking about it."

"But a marriage counselor could . . ."

"Could what? Make Jeff change his mind? I don't think so, and right now that's the only thing that can save our marriage."

Emma watched them both, hating to see the two people she loved in such pain, unable to imagine what had triggered such a drastic decision on Suzanne's part. Could Jeff be having an affair? She recalled Suzanne's earlier comment that Grandma would be on her side of the argument and wondered why she would think such a thing. Was it because Emma herself had divorced years ago? She took Suzanne's hand in her own.

"Why, Sue?"

Emma waited as Suzanne gained control by drawing strength from her anger. "Jeff's company offered him a promotion if he transferred to Chicago. He accepted the job, Grandma. He didn't even discuss it with me first—he just told them yes, he would move halfway across the country. But I'm not going to move. I've worked too hard to build my own career, and if I sacrificed it for Jeff, I'd end up hating him. There's nothing for me in Chicago."

"You don't know that," Grace said. "You haven't even looked for a new job there."

"I don't want a new job, Mom. I want the job I already have. I love my work. Our families live here. The girls have their schools and their friends. How can he ask us to give up everything?"

"It's so strange how history repeats itself," Emma said. "My mother had to leave her family and her home in Germany to immigrate to America for my father's sake. That was . . . what? More than eighty years ago. She never saw her family again." Emma wondered what Louise would say to this great-grand-daughter of hers if she were alive. Would she tell Suzanne she was making the right decision? Would Louise agree that no marriage was worth such a staggering sacrifice?

"Women didn't have much choice in those days," Suzanne said. "But I do." She finished wrapping another dish and shoved it into the box.

Grace pushed past Emma, taking Suzanne by the shoulders. "If Jeff wants this job, if it's important for his career, how can you stand in his way? He's the head of your house and—"

"No, Mom. I don't believe all that Bible stuff about wives submitting to their husbands." She twisted free. "I'm not like you. My entire life doesn't revolve around my husband and the church. I would never allow Jeff to tell me I can't work, like Daddy tells you." Her eyes met Emma's. "Did Mom tell you about that, Grandma?"

"Tell me what, dear?"

"She's been working so hard to set up a crisis pregnancy center, but when the board asked her to serve as their first director, Daddy made her turn it down."

"He didn't make me—"

"He did so!" Suzanne interjected.

"No, I hadn't heard about that," Emma said. She rested her hand on Grace's arm. "Is this the place you were telling me about where girls who don't want an abortion can get help?"

Grace nodded. "But I didn't refuse just because of Stephen. What would I know about directing an organization like that? I'm a housewife. I can't—"

"Mom, you created that entire center from scratch," Suzanne said. "You assembled a board of trustees, raised funds, renovated the vacant building, planned the advertising campaign—all as an unpaid volunteer. You're a registered nurse, a doctor's wife. You'd be perfect for the job and the board knows it. That's why they asked you. But you turned it down because Daddy doesn't want you to work. That's insane!"

"We're not talking about me," Grace said with carefully controlled anger. "We're talking about you and Jeff."

"But you're the reason I made this decision! I refuse to live the way you do. I'm like Grandma. I don't need a husband to take care of me; I can take care of myself and my daughters. I've always admired you for that, Grandma—for raising Mom alone after your husband deserted you."

In one terrible instant, Emma realized that the house of lies she had so carefully constructed was on the brink of collapse, trapping the people she loved beneath its weight. She had built it to protect and shelter them, thinking that she alone would be hurt if it ever fell.

"This is my fault. . . ." Emma mumbled to herself. She lowered herself onto the nearest chair, feeling every one of her eighty years.

"No, it's Jeff's fault. He doesn't care about his family, only himself. He already decided what's most important to him—his job. So I'm going to do the same."

"Oh, Sue . . . where did all the love go?" Emma asked softly. "Remember when you thought Jeff would have to fight in Vietnam? Remember how you were going to follow him to Canada if you had to? You were so in love with him then. Where did it all go?"

Suzanne looked away. "I don't know, Grandma. I honestly don't know. Our lives just got so busy. We both have careers. . . ." She lifted a cut-glass candy dish from the shelf and idly wrapped it in newspaper. "Now we've grown so far apart that Jeff just accepted the job without even asking me what I thought."

"What about your children?" Grace pleaded. "Aren't they as important to you as your careers? They're so young. How can you ruin their lives like this?"

Suzanne heaved a tired sigh as she placed the last bundle in the box and folded the flaps. "Mom, times have changed since Grandma got divorced. Half the kids in Melissa's kindergarten class come from single-parent homes."

"But your girls need their father! You have no idea what it feels like to be abandoned by your father!" Grace shuddered, as if her entire body felt the impact of her words. "If you did, you would never do this to Amy and Melissa."

"I'm not the one who is—"

"No, you listen to me. I shoved my needs and my career aside to please your father so that you would never have to live through what I did. My father left his family. And all my life I've felt forsaken—unworthy of his love!"

"Oh, Gracie, no. You were precious to him. Your father loved you more than life itself." Living alone as she did, Emma often spoke her thoughts aloud. She didn't realize that she had done so this time until the room grew utterly still.

Grace stared at her in astonishment, her mouth hanging slack. "What did you say?" she whispered.

Emma felt the earth tremble beneath her and saw her structure of lies teeter and sway. She could prop it up with more lies, but she was deluding herself if she thought it would shelter her loved ones from further pain. The anguish in Grace's words had revealed the depth of her wounds. And Emma knew firsthand the devastating loneliness Suzanne would face in the years ahead, even if society was more tolerant of divorce in 1980 than it had been in 1925. The falsehoods Emma had fit together so carefully had silently caved in, pinning Grace and Suzanne beneath the wreckage.

Emma stood and reached for her daughter's hand, taking it in hers. "Gracie, why did you work so hard to set up that clinic? Why are you so passionate about fighting abortion?"

"Mother, I want you to explain what you just said about my father."

"Answer my question first."

"You know why—because my father didn't want me to be born. When he tried to force you to have an abortion you had nowhere to go, no one to help you."

"Then why would you turn down the directorship of a place you've worked so hard to build? Especially when it's for a cause you care about so deeply?"

"Mother, please . . ."

"Is it because you're afraid your husband will abandon you too, Gracie?"

She didn't answer. Instead, she covered her face and wept without making a sound. Grace had cried that way ever since she was a child, as if her sorrow wasn't worth disturbing anyone. Her silent weeping moved Emma to tears, as it always had. Suzanne wrapped her arms tightly around her mother.

"I'm sorry, Mom. I'm hurting so much right now, but I never meant to hurt you."

Emma longed to pull out all the fallen joists and timbers one by one, to untangle the thousands of lies, to free her loved ones from the rubble of their destroyed lives. But after more than fifty years, the truth might cause more confusion and suffering than it cured. They would have to discover a way out by themselves.

"Suzanne, I want you to listen to me," Emma said. "It was my own fault that my marriage ended in failure and that Karl left me. Please don't say you admire me for that. You have an image of me as a strong, independent woman, someone you want to imitate, but that's false. I've brought a lot of this on both of you by making the wrong choices years ago."

Grace dried her tears and carefully raised her shield of poise and dignity once again. Her eyes met Emma's. "Tell me why you said that about my father."

He did love you, she longed to say again. Instead, Emma took refuge in another lie. "The words came out all wrong, Gracie. I'm getting old. I was trying to say that Karl doesn't matter. I love you. I only wish that my love could have been enough for you, that you didn't long so for your father."

Grace stared hard at her as if challenging the explanation. Unable to bear the scrutiny, Emma bent to retrieve a tattered photograph album from the bottom shelf. "I want you to have this. There's one picture in here of Karl, our wedding picture. You've seen it before. I've kept it so you'd always know what he looked like."

Grace folded her arms around the book without opening it. "I don't think I can . . . not right now. . . ."

"May I see it, Mom?" Suzanne asked. Grace didn't resist as she took the album from her and began leafing through it. "Which one is he, Grandma?"

Emma peered over her shoulder. "Right there. That's Karl and me."

"Did you love him, Grandma?"

"When I married him? No. Our families were old friends. I married him to please my parents. That's the way things were done back then. Love was supposed to grow once you were married. This is my mama and papa, right here." When Suzanne turned the page without asking more questions, Emma breathed a sigh of relief.

"Who are all these people?"

"Most of them are old friends from when we lived in the apartment on King Street. These are our landladies, the Mulligan sisters."

"The 'dreary' Mulligan sisters?"

"Yes. Aren't they horrible old crows?"

"Oh, Mother, they weren't that bad," Grace said. "They watched out for me when you had to work."

"And this is Crazy Clancy with Father O'Duggan."

"The priest who paid Mom to read? He's young. Good-looking too."

Grace moved to peer over Suzanne's other shoulder. "Where? Let me see. Yes, that's him. You know, whenever I hear an Irish brogue I always think of him."

Emma pointed to another picture on the same page. "Here's you, Gracie, when you were about four years old."

"That was taken at Mam's house. I stayed with her when you caught pneumonia. She was so good to me. Oh my, and that's Booty Higgins who ran the store."

"What kind of a name is 'Booty'?" Suzanne asked.

"It was a nickname," Emma said. "I don't remember his real name anymore, but he was a bootlegger during Prohibition."

Grace stared in surprise. "Was he? I never knew that."

Emma simply smiled.

"Who are these three guys in the white dinner jackets and black bow ties?" Suzanne asked.

"Oh, let me see!" Grace said. "That has to be Black Jack, Slick Mick, and O'Brien! Yes, that's them."

"Who are they?" Suzanne asked. "They look like gangsters."

"Yes, but they were lovable gangsters," Emma said, laughing. "What a crazy collection of characters we all were. Nowadays I suppose we'd be locked in a lunatic asylum. But we looked out for one another back then, took care of each other. They were the only family we had."

She gently eased the book from Suzanne's hands and closed it. "Do you realize that it's almost ten o'clock and we've barely packed one box? The photo album is for you, Gracie. And I want Suzanne to have this."

She reached into the cabinet and removed a white bone china cup, trimmed with gold. A delicate painting of a little girl in a faded pink gown and bonnet decorated the front. "I'm sorry that I don't have very many heirlooms to pass along to you children, but the piece of coal is one of them, and this cup is another."

"Oh, Grandma, I remember that! It's the 'crying cup.' "

"Do you remember how it worked?"

"Whenever I was sad about something, you would let me drink from it and all my tears would magically disappear."

Emma pressed the cup into her hands. "If only it still worked, Suzy. If only I could fill it with something that would make all your tears disappear."

"I know, Grandma."

"Wasn't it your mother's cup?" Grace asked. "Didn't she bring it with her when she immigrated?"

"Yes, it belonged to Mama's grandmother in Germany. *Oma* was the one who first named it the 'crying cup' years earlier. When my mother left her family to come to America, Oma gave it to her. Mama said she filled it to the brim with tears on the boat to America."

"How did you end up with it, Mother?"

Emma didn't answer. Instead, she opened a cabinet drawer and lifted out a worn cigar box. "Do you remember these, Gracie?" Inside were three hemmed strips of cloth—green velvet, purple satin, white brocade—trimmed with elegant lace and fringe.

"The miniature vestments I made! Oh, Mother, I can't believe you saved those silly things all these years."

"You made these, Mom? What are they?"

"Vestments . . . you know, it's a kind of shawl that clergymen wear over their robes on special occasions. Only these are doll-sized. I made them when I stayed at Mam's house."

"You'd better not let Amy and Melissa see them, or they'll swipe them for their Barbie dolls."

Grace laid the cigar box aside and reached for another empty carton, filling it with books from Emma's shelf. Emma caught her breath when a worn, pocket-sized leather book fell out from where she had hidden it behind the others. The black leather cover curved slightly from the years it had spent inside a breast pocket, conforming to the swell of a man's broad chest.

"Is this a Bible?" Grace asked. Before Emma could stop her, Grace opened the cover and read the inscription on the front page. " 'Presented to Father Thomas O'Duggan, June 5, 1923.' " She gazed at Emma in astonishment. "Mother, why on earth do you have Father O'Duggan's prayer book?"

"I . . . I have no idea where it could have come from. Let me see it . . . I suppose I should give it back to his family or someone from his church." The book seemed to burn in her hands like the lies burning in her heart. The pages rustled like dry leaves as Emma fumbled through them, searching for the place marked with the faded purple ribbon.

Have mercy upon me, O God, according to thy lovingkindness: according unto the multitude of thy tender mercies blot out my transgressions. Wash me thoroughly from mine iniquity, and cleanse me from my sin. For I acknowledge my transgressions: and my sin is ever before me. When the page blurred, Emma closed the book.

The doors and drawers of her curio cabinet stood open, ready to be emptied so that she could move on to the next stage of her life. Emma longed to do the same with her past—to empty it of all its secrets so that Grace and Suzanne could move on with their lives—but that was impossible. If only she hadn't made such a mess of things. She carefully laid the book down and picked up a framed photograph of Suzanne and Jeff with their two girls.

" 'For I the Lord your God, am a jealous God,' " Emma recited, " 'punishing the children for the sin of the fathers to the third and fourth generation . . .' "

Suzanne gazed at Emma curiously. "What did you say, Grandma?"

"Nothing . . . just something Papa once told me years ago." She turned the photograph around so Suzanne could see it. "Your mother is right," she said softly. "What you and Jeff do will affect these children for the rest of their lives. Don't base your decision on the choices your mother made. She was influenced by the wrong choices I made. And my decisions were based on my own mother's mistakes. And so it goes, on and on. We're like those wooden dolls that nest inside one another, each taking the shape of the one that came before it. Someone has to open the last one, someone has to break the pattern. Learn from the past, Suzy, don't repeat it."

"But Grandma . . ."

"Did you ever hear my mother's story?"

"I don't think so. Maybe years ago."

"Then perhaps it's time you did."

PART ONE

Louise's Story
1894 ~ 1904

ONE

THE RHINE VALLEY, GERMANY, 1894

It had seemed like any other Christmas Eve at first, with laughter drifting through Papa's sturdy farmhouse along with the aroma of roast goose and apple strudel. I was home again, spending Christmas with my family after becoming Friedrich Schroder's bride only four months earlier. My sisters, Ada and Runa, had come home with their families, and our brother Kurt, who farmed with Papa, had crossed the fields from his cottage with his wife, Gerda, and their children. Emil, who still lived at home, bounded around all of us like a puppy dog, delighted to have the farmhouse bursting with loved ones once again.

I spent all morning in the kitchen, of course, bumping elbows with three generations of Fischer women as we hurried to put the finishing touches on dinner. Toddlers balanced on my sisters' hips or clung to their skirts as we worked, adding their sniffles and whines to the clamor of banging pots and bubbling kettles. I reveled in every noisy, chaotic moment as I sat at the table peeling potatoes. The four miles of pastures, farmland, and forests that lay between Papa's farm and my new home in the village hadn't broken the link that forged me to these other women. That bond was the "three k's"—*kinder, kuche*, and *kirche*. Those three—children, cooking, and the church—defined the life of every good German wife. Like all the other women in my family, I found my duty, my identity, in them.

"You're risking a swat with this wooden spoon," Ada warned as her two children scampered through the kitchen with their cousin, trying to steal a sweet gherkin from the dish on the sideboard.

"Oh, let them be," Mama said. "One little pickle isn't going to spoil their appetites. Besides, it's Christmas." As she held the forbidden relish tray within their reach, I marvelled at how my mama, who had raised five children with stern discipline and rules, had transformed into another woman altogether once she became a grandmother.

"That's all now! Stay out of the kitchen!" Ada shouted as the children skipped away, licking sweet pickle juice from their fingers. "At least the men have sense enough to stay out from underfoot," she grumbled.

"Where did they all disappear to?" I asked.

"They're in the parlor," Mama said, "discussing politics and farm prices, I suppose."

Runa shook her head. "Don't believe it, Louise. They're in there smoking fat cigars and drinking schnapps. And I'll bet my egg money they're teaching your Friedrich all their bad habits too."

"Uh oh," Oma said, "I'd haul him home fast if I were you, Louise." Everyone laughed. Being teased by the other women was the price I paid for being the newest bride. I was probably in for a lot more of it before the day ended.

My grandmother, Oma Fischer, presided over the kitchen full of women, her gray eyes shining in her wrinkled face, a strand of wool-white hair sliding loose from its hairpins as she bustled around the hot stove. She finished basting the Christmas goose and closed the oven door, then paused beside the table to caress my cheek. I loved the touch of her soft, plump hands. They smelled of cinnamon and cloves.

"How pretty you look today, *Liebchen*," she told me. "And so grown-up with your hair fixed in a French bun." I had never thought of myself as pretty until Friedrich began telling me I was. And even though I was nineteen and married now, I barely thought of myself as grown-up. Whenever I studied my face in the mirror, hoping to see a woman gazing back at last, I was always disappointed to see the full, innocent face of a young girl, with freckles on her nose and lips that pouted like a child's. Instead of the slender, high cheekbones I yearned for, my cheeks dimpled and blushed like a schoolgirl's when I smiled.

Oma bent to kiss my forehead. "What gives you such a rosy glow and sweet smile?"

"It must be her handsome new husband," Ada said with a wink. "She and Friedrich are still newlyweds, you know." I felt the color rise to my cheeks against my will.

Runa, who was eight months pregnant, smiled knowingly. "Could it be the glow of motherhood, baby sister?"

I attacked the potato skins as I felt my blush deepen, wishing I could run away and hide with the children. I was fairly certain that I was expecting, but Friedrich and I had agreed not to share the news with anyone yet. It was still our own special secret, to be savored and treasured for a while between the two of us.

"Don't listen to my silly sisters, Oma," I said. "If I have a glow, it comes from the coal stove. The goose isn't the only one who's roasting." I chopped the last potato and dropped it into the water with the others, then carried the pot over to the stove to boil. The kitchen was steaming hot, and I wiped the moisture off the window to gaze outside.

Beyond the foggy glass, the farmyard lay beneath a covering of fresh snow, Papa's cattle a stark contrast against it as they huddled together beside the creek. I smiled to myself, remembering how those witless animals had brought Friedrich and me together—his father owned the butcher shop where Papa sold his beef. As lifelong friends, Papa and *Herr* Schroder thought it only natural to arrange a match between the butcher's fourth son and Papa's youngest daughter.

I turned away from the window as Mama paused from her labors to gaze around the cluttered kitchen. "Now, what have I forgotten?" she murmured.

Everyone laughed. Mama prepared so many different dishes at family gatherings that she always forgot to bring one of them to the table. We would invariably find it long after the meal was finished, still sitting in the pantry or the warming oven.

Our laughter transformed to murmurs of sympathy as Runa's three-year-old daughter stumbled into the kitchen in tears. "She pinched her finger in the door," an older cousin reported. Tired and overexcited, the girl wailed loudly. Runa couldn't console her.

"I know just what she needs," Oma said. She reached up to the shelf in the crockery dresser and fetched the white porcelain cup that I remembered so well from my own childhood. Painted on the front, the delicate girl in the pink dress hadn't aged a day. Oma filled the cup with thick buttermilk from the pantry.

"There, now," she soothed. "A few sips from Oma's crying cup should put things right, eh, little one?"

I watched the cup perform its magic. By the time the milk was gone, all of my niece's tears had disappeared as well. Laughter and tears . . . then laughter again. The words embroidered on Oma's favorite sampler were true: *Joy and sorrow come and go like the ebb and flow.*

"It's time for the presents," Mama whispered to me. "Since you're not busy, go light the tree candles for me. Get Friedrich to help you with the highest ones. Tell Papa to ring the bell when everything's ready."

I felt a shiver of excitement as I untied my apron and slipped from the kitchen. Not too many years ago, I had been among the children who would soon enter the parlor, gaping in awe at the glittering tree, wondering how all the presents piled beneath it had magically appeared. Now I was one of the adults, helping to create the enchantment. I couldn't have said which role I preferred.

The parlor door was closed to keep out the curious children, but I could hear the men's voices on the other side, even before I opened it. Unlike the laughter and harmony in the kitchen, the atmosphere in the parlor was tense, the voices loud and strident. Embroiled in their argument, the men barely noticed that I had entered the room.

"No, I can't agree with you," Friedrich was saying. His brow furrowed as he pushed his sandy hair off his forehead. "It isn't necessary at all."

Papa gestured forcefully, using his cigar for emphasis. "Russia and France are allies now. We would be forced to fight a war on two fronts. Our military must be stronger than their combined armies."

"But where will it end?" Friedrich asked. "If we increase our military forces, they will also increase theirs. Europe is already an armed camp, waiting for a spark to set off a war."

"A strong military is the best deterrent against war," Kurt insisted.

I crossed to the freshly cut pine tree in the corner and began checking the candle clips, making certain they were firmly in place, the candles not touching any other boughs. As I listened to the argument, I was horrified to discover that Papa, my brothers, Kurt and Emil, and my two brothers-in-law, Ernst and Konrad, all agreed that Germany needed a strong military. And they all agreed that it was both a duty and an honor to fight and die for the Fatherland. My husband did not agree.

Glancing at them, I saw that he looked different as well, standing among my brawny family members. He was the only one wearing a vest beneath his suit coat instead of braces, the only one sporting a neatly trimmed Belgrave beard instead of a handlebar mustache and muttonchops. But then, Friedrich *was* different from the others, the only one with a university education. My father had been so proud to have a man of learning in the family—a schoolteacher, no less. Now Papa struggled out of his armchair to stand and join the argument against his new son-in-law.

"You expect Germany to wait helplessly," he asked, "while France starts a war on one front and the czar starts one on the other?"

"I'm only saying that the money the *Kaiser* is spending to arm Germany would be better spent fighting the poverty in our own industrial centers."

I had never heard Friedrich raise his voice before. I stopped what I was doing to stare at him. He was taller than my brothers but leaner; Kurt's and Emil's muscles were the product of years of farm work. When I first learned that Papa had made a match for me with the butcher's son—who had been away at the university for four years—I was terrified that Friedrich had changed, that he might now resemble his father, who was as fat and pink as the sausages hanging in his shop window. I had been relieved to find that Butcher Schroder's son, who was five years older than me, was slender and fair-skinned, with deep-set eyes as pale blue as the winter sky. His eyebrows and beard, a shade darker than his sandy hair, were the color of nutmeg, with brown and auburn and golden hairs all mixed together. His features were too angular to be considered handsome, but his quiet strength and the way he took an interest in people had attracted me to him immediately. After only three months of courtship and four months of marriage, I still barely knew him. And I had never really noticed the stark contrast between him and my family members before. Now it worried me. Why couldn't he be more like Papa or Kurt?

"Are you against all wars, young man?" Papa asked. "Because the Scriptures are filled with battles fought in the Almighty's name, you know."

"That's true, sir. But when it finally comes, this war will be fought in the name of greed, not justice. Christ always put the needs of people ahead of governments and institutions. Hatred and violence aren't acceptable among His followers. He said, 'Blessed are the peacemakers: for they shall be called the children of God.' "

Kurt rested his hand on Friedrich's shoulder. "If the Kaiser approves the new enlistment scheme, you won't have a choice. You and I will both be included in the draft, married or not."

Friedrich lowered his head. "Yes, I know."

My brother Emil, who was only seventeen, seemed excited by the prospect. "We could be shipped to China . . . the African colonies . . . anywhere!"

"Your religious convictions won't mean a thing to the Kaiser," Papa said. "You'll either serve in his army or go to jail."

"I will never serve in his army."

I dropped the box of matches I was holding. "Is that true, Friedrich? Would they force you to choose between joining the army and going to jail?"

The men turned to me in surprise, as if seeing me for the first time.

"Yes, it's true," he said as he bent to retrieve the matches.

"But . . . but you're a schoolteacher, not a soldier."

"Louise," he said quietly, "let me help you with those candles." He struck a match and began lighting them, easily reaching the highest ones on top. I watched him as if he were a stranger.

Papa cleared his throat. "Listen now, the Kaiser's grand plans have fizzled and died many times before. There's no need to start worrying about something that might never happen. It's Christmas, after all."

His words broke the tension, and a few minutes later the men were laughing and helping Friedrich with the candles as if nothing in their lives would ever change. But I knew that my own life had changed. I gazed at all the men I loved, gathered around the glimmering tree, and felt as if I were watching them from a great distance.

When the last candle was lit, Papa retrieved the little silver bell from the mantel. "All right, stand back," he said with a broad grin. "I wouldn't want anyone trampled to death."

At the sound of the bell, the children flooded into the parlor with shrieks of excitement, followed soon afterward by the mothers and grandmothers. The youngsters squirmed restlessly as Papa read the familiar Christmas story from the family Bible, then ripped into their presents at last. Mama had made rag dolls and new mittens for the girls. Papa and Emil had carved toy boats and spinning tops out of wood scraps for the boys. From the village store came a silver baby's rattle, a doll-sized tea set, and a shiny red coaster sleigh.

Friedrich smiled his shy smile as he handed me a beautifully wrapped present. "This is for you. Merry Christmas."

Beneath the wrappings, in a box from a fancy shop in Stuttgart, lay a sterling silver hand mirror. Engraved on the back, amid swirls of flowers and leaves, were my new initials, L. S. The sight of them jolted me, reminding me that I was no longer Louise Fischer but Louise Schroder. I belonged to Friedrich.

"Do you like it?" He smiled as he tenderly brushed a wisp of hair off my forehead. His caress would have seemed natural in the privacy of our own home, but it embarrassed me here in Papa's house. The other men never made such intimate gestures. In fact, as I glanced around the room, all the men sat at stiff, safe distances from their wives. The gifts they gave them were practical things like a new shawl or a pair of gloves, not something as extravagant and personal as a silver hand mirror.

"It's . . . beautiful," I murmured. I felt the heat rush to my cheeks. I didn't know how to tell him that I was pleased with his gift in front of my family. I wished that Friedrich and I could treasure it all by ourselves instead of exposing it to everyone's scrutiny. An odd sensation shivered through me as I felt myself more a part of Friedrich's life than my family's. Then it passed as Mama and Oma stood to return to the kitchen. I quickly excused myself to help with the food.

Christmas dinner was a boisterous affair with everyone crowded around the dining room table, passing platters of roast goose and smoked pork, bowls of creamy potatoes and sauerkraut, and dishes of pickled onions and *blutwurst* and herring. By the time we had eaten our fill, dusk had fallen. The other women and I hurried to wash the dishes before the Christmas Eve church service, while the men wrapped themselves in their warmest clothes to do their chores and harness the sleighs.

The little stone church in the village looked the same as it had every Christmas Eve of my life. The candles, the carols, the story of the baby born in a cattle stall, all reinforced the comforting belief that my life was part of an unbroken tradition that would never change.

"All is calm . . . all is bright," we sang. There would be no military draft, no war. I would live my life exactly as all the other women in my family had. Tonight and every night until I was as old as Oma I would sleep beside my husband in peace.

When the service ended, Friedrich and I said good-night to my family and walked the short distance home from church to our cottage in the village. It was cold inside our house, with the cast-iron stove left unattended all day. I kept my jacket and cape on, shivering as I waited for Friedrich to shake out the ashes and add coal and kindling to restart the fire. His lean hands were quick and competent in their work, his mind intent on his labor. I watched him and felt a thrill of happiness that I belonged to him, with him. I carried his child.

When he finished he turned to me, brushing the soot from his hands. "You're cold. Come stand closer. The fire should catch in a minute." He wrapped his arms around me to warm me.

Suddenly a knot of resin in the firewood popped like a gunshot, shattering my happiness as I remembered the threat of war. I lifted my head from Friedrich's shoulder to gaze up at him.

"Friedrich . . . what you and Papa and Kurt were talking about today in the parlor . . . When might the military draft happen? When will you know for sure?"

"I'm so sorry you had to hear that, Louise. It may never happen, and then we've worried you for nothing." He tried to draw me close again but I pushed away. I knew better than to question my husband, but I couldn't stop myself.

"What will you do if you're drafted?"

The wood inside the stove crackled and snapped as it caught fire. Bright flames flickered behind the grate. Friedrich took a long time to answer. When he spoke, his words were slow and careful, his eyes sorrowful.

"I could never aim a gun and kill a man just to help the Kaiser win a chunk of someone else's land. Maybe if we were attacked I could fight back, but even then . . . even then the Bible says we must love our enemies."

"But Papa said they would send you to jail if you don't go. You'd lose your job and they'd never let you teach again if you had a criminal record. And the baby—"

"Louise . . . Louise . . . that isn't going to happen." He gathered my icy hands in his and held them against his chest. I could feel his heart pounding strong and steady beneath them, and I began to cry.

Friedrich came undone at the sight of my tears. He stood beside me, wringing his hands. I could tell that he wanted to hold me, to console me, but he hesitated, unsure what to do. I had never wept in front of him before.

"Louise, don't cry. . . . I'm so sorry . . . please don't cry. I don't want to go to jail, but . . . if the teachings of Christ ever come into conflict with the laws of men, I have to obey God."

His reasoning seemed so strange to me. The men in my family rose before dawn to do their chores, not to read the Bible by lamplight. Never in my life had I seen Papa on his knees in prayer as I often saw Friedrich. My brother Kurt was a deacon in the village church and he didn't want to serve in the Kaiser's army either, but he would choose that alternative before going to jail.

"I don't understand," I said, weeping.

"I know you don't, I see that now, and I wish I could find a way to explain it without upsetting you." He pulled a handkerchief from his vest pocket and handed it to me awkwardly. "Here, use this. It's clean."

I quickly dried my eyes and blew my nose, embarrassed that I had become so emotional in front of him. "I'm sorry . . . it must be my condition. And it's been a long day. . . ." As I battled to control my emotions, Friedrich drew a deep breath.

"Louise, God has blessed my life in every possible way—providing me with an education, giving me a good job, sending you into my life. I know He's going to continue to provide what's best for us and for our baby. We have to trust Him and not worry about tomorrow. We're in His hands."

Friedrich always talked so strangely, so intimately about God, as if the Almighty spoke to him the way He spoke to people in the Bible. I believed in God, of course. I had attended church with my family all my life. But Friedrich's faith was different, somehow. It was one more thing about him that I didn't understand.

The fire had finally begun to heat the small room. I unfastened my cape and went to hang it on the peg by the door. Friedrich hurried to help me with it, then laid his hands on my shoulders and made me face him again.

"Louise, I don't want you to worry any more about the draft. Promise?" He was so concerned for me, so distraught, that I allowed him to take me into his arms again. I wanted so much to trust him, to have unquestioning faith in my husband, but that was such a difficult thing to do.

"All right, Friedrich," I lied. "I promise I won't worry."

TWO

By the end of February I had convinced myself that nothing would change after all. Friedrich and I would always live in this village by the river, our duties and routines as comfortable as old shoes. He would dash off to school each morning, eager to teach his students, and I would walk the three blocks to the village square on market days to shop with the other women. The only change was my name and social status; Herr Schultz the grocer, *Frau* Braun the baker, Reverend Lahr and his wife, and all the other townspeople who had known me from childhood now greeted me as Frau Schroder, the young schoolteacher's wife. Because of Friedrich, I was highly respected in all the shops as I made my rounds, gathering goods and gossip.

While I may have had little knowledge of the larger world and its problems, I knew all of the other villagers' joys and struggles intimately—who was up-and-coming and who was down on their luck; who was expecting a baby, and whose husband drank too much; who was ailing, who was needy, who was dying.

The village itself never changed. The brick and stone *Rathaus* on the village square, the tidy shops that supplied all our needs, the narrow row houses with their steep roofs and gables, all had an air of permanence that I loved. Even the towering church spires, like the ancient beech and pine trees beneath them, seemed deeply rooted in the soil of my homeland. Flowing through all of our lives was the river, its course wide and steady and deep. And if its level sometimes changed with drought or flood, it was only to remind us that "joy and sorrow come and go like the ebb and flow."

For two months I kept my promise not to worry, forgetting all about the threat of war, until I happened to meet my sister Runa while shopping in the village one morning.

"Is your house in as big an uproar as ours is?" she asked.

"Why would we be in an uproar?"

"Well, because of the news. You know, the Kaiser's new draft plan?"

It was a beautiful, clear morning, the snow crisp and clean on the shrubs and pine boughs, but I suddenly felt as if the sun had died. I pulled my sister into the café to talk, but I was much too upset to eat the apple strudel we ordered.

"Friedrich hasn't said a word about it," I told her.

"Maybe he hasn't heard the news yet. Ernst only told me about it yesterday. Under the new plan, even married men with families will have to serve two years in the army."

"But why? Is there going to be a war?"

"No, of course not." She waved her hand as if to dismiss my fear. Her voice had an overly patient tone, my wise older sister explaining why I needn't fear the monsters under the bed. "Ernst said that General von Schlieffen wants to build a bigger army, that's all. Just as a precaution."

"What's Ernst going to do?"

"I think he'd rather join the army than the navy," she said, misunderstanding. "But he says he won't have to decide until his draft notice comes." Ernst would serve his country. There was no question of him going to jail.

I wanted to question Friedrich about the news the moment he walked through the door after school, but of course I didn't dare. Nor could I ruin our meal by raising the subject during dinner. If we had been married for a few years, he might have sensed that something was wrong, but we were still so new to each other, so unsure of what went through each other's mind.

After dinner I curled in my chair beside the fire with my feet tucked beneath me, listening to the angry February wind as it circled our tiny cottage. How could I talk to Friedrich without revealing that I had broken my promise not to worry? I finished another row of knitting and smoothed the gray, woolen sock flat on my lap.

"I'll need your foot when you get a minute," I told him. He looked up from the bookshelf he was building and grinned.

"Why? Did you forget what Limburger cheese smells like?"

I couldn't help laughing as I held up the unfinished sock. Before we were married, I never would have imagined that a man as quiet and serious as he was could make me laugh. I smiled as I watched him work, his sandy hair bright in the lamplight. He had his vest unbuttoned, his sleeves rolled up, a fine layer of sawdust on his beard and forearms.

Usually he sat at our little wooden table in the evenings, frowning slightly as he corrected papers or looked over his lessons, and I would study his lean hands and long fingers as he scrawled with his fountain pen or turned the pages of his books. I wanted to learn everything there was to learn about him—his likes and dislikes, the way his eyelashes drooped when he was tired, the way the muscles of his back moved as he stretched his broad shoulders when his work was finally finished. Watching him labor over the simple wooden bookshelf these past few evenings, I'd learned that he wasn't very handy with tools and lumber. After each evening's work, I had to dig the splinters out of his fingers and doctor all his nicks and scrapes with iodine.

"I'm going to hang a shelf on this wall to give us more space," he had told me when he arrived home with the lumber. "It'll keep my books out of your way . . . and out of the baby's reach." He always smiled, so pleased with himself whenever he mentioned our baby, still a barely perceptible bump beneath my apron.

Now as the wind howled outside, rattling the windowpanes as if looking for a way inside, I rehearsed the words I had longed to blurt out ever since Friedrich arrived home from school. My stomach fluttered uneasily as I prepared to speak.

"I ran into Runa today while I was shopping," I began. "Her new baby has the colic and she's about worn-out from being up all night with him." While Friedrich murmured sympathetically, I drew a deep breath, feeling as if I was about to plunge into icy water. "Runa also told me what her Ernst said about the military draft." I watched closely but Friedrich didn't look up.

"Oh? And what did he say?"

"That Kaiser Wilhelm approved the new draft plan. Now even married men with families will have to serve two years." I waited for him to respond but he seemed intent on his work. "Ernst said that General Something-or-Other is trying to—"

"General von Schlieffen?"

"Yes. That he's trying to build a huge army."

"The Schlieffen Plan," Friedrich said, and I heard the bitterness in his voice. "He wants enough men to fight a war on two fronts."

"You know about all this, Fritz?"

"I've been following the news," he said quietly.

"Doesn't it upset you? I can't stand all this uncertainty about our future, especially with the baby coming and everything. How can you be so calm about it?"

He finally looked up. "I'm very concerned, Louise. I've been praying about it for months. But I've learned that it's wiser to leave things like this in God's hands. There's really nothing you or I can do about it anyway." He returned to his work. I could tell that he didn't want to discuss it. I also knew that I shouldn't question him, but I couldn't help myself.

"If you pray hard enough, could God keep you from being drafted?"

"That's not what I'm saying. But whatever does happen, I know He'll get us through it."

He might as well have said, "Amen," the way Reverend Lahr did when he finished reading the Scriptures—Friedrich's words had the same ring of finality to them. But I didn't know Friedrich or God well enough to trust either one of them with my future.

"Oh, Friedrich, if worse comes to worst and you are drafted, can't you just serve your two years and be done with it? That's what Ernst is going to do. We're not at war with anyone. You wouldn't have to kill people."

He shook his head. "This race to arm all of Europe, this insane escalation of military firepower, goes against everything I believe in. I can't possibly be part of it."

"But the Kaiser already approved the new law and—"

"Just because the conscription laws have changed doesn't necessarily mean I'll be drafted. The *Reich* always needs teachers, even in wartime."

"You mean, you might be excused from serving? And you wouldn't have to go to jail?"

He looked away. "It's possible, yes."

Friedrich would never lie, but when he hesitated, I knew he had left something important unsaid. "What if they don't excuse you?" I asked. "What if you are drafted?" I knew by the expression on his face that he didn't want to answer me.

"We can always leave Germany," he said at last. "We could go to America. I have a cousin there."

"Leave? Oh, Friedrich, no!" America was a huge, wild, unknown land across the sea. I would have to leave behind everyone I loved. I would never see my family again. "Please don't make me move to America! How can you even think about leaving Germany, leaving our families, our home?"

I waited, certain by the sorrow in his eyes that there was more. He laid the hammer he had been tightly clutching on the table and wiped his palms on his trousers.

"I applied for immigration papers last month at the consular office. I pray we won't need them, but I was afraid that if the new draft law went through and my teacher's exemption is denied, they would deny the visa too."

I suddenly felt terribly alone, as if Friedrich had already left. I knew it was irrational, but hadn't he already taken the first step? I couldn't even imagine leaving Germany, but my husband had not only imagined it, he was preparing for it.

"Please don't make me leave Germany," I begged.

"I can't promise that we'll stay. Our future is in God's hands."

The idea of leaving my fate to God didn't comfort me. Surely there was something I could do to control the direction of my life. I felt like a rudderless boat on the Rhine, tossed about at the current's mercy, floating downstream to a destination I couldn't predict. Life wasn't that way for Friedrich. He could make choices and plans. But he was a man.

"Louise, I didn't tell you about the immigration papers or the Kaiser's decision because I didn't want you to worry. You promised me you wouldn't, remember? It's not good for the baby. We're going to take this one step at a time . . . and trust God. It could be another year or more before the new draft plan goes into effect, and maybe by that time I'll be too old to serve. Or maybe I'll get a teaching exemption."

I laid down my knitting and crossed the room to where he stood. I wanted to cling to him, plead with him, but I knew that I lacked the power to change his mind. Besides, I didn't want to believe that Friedrich would make me move to America. It was just crazy talk. "I'm trying to keep my promise," I said. "I'm trying not to worry."

He met my gaze. His eyes were tender, trustworthy. "I know you are."

I had pushed him further than any good wife should have pushed. I had no right to question my husband, and he had no obligation to answer me. Papa always walked away from Mama when she crossed the line. The fact that Friedrich had answered me, that he hadn't become angry with me, drew me to him in a way I didn't fully understand yet. His patience made me want to be a better wife, to do what he asked and forget all about the military draft.

Before I could think of something to say, Friedrich pointed to his bookshelf. "Well? How do you like it?"

He was trying to change the subject too. I saw a chance to atone for my behavior. I put worry out of my mind as firmly as I would put an unwelcome animal out of the house.

"It's great! Is it finished?"

"Yes, finally. If you could help me, I think I'm ready to nail it to the wall. It isn't too heavy." He lifted the shelf into position and I steadied one end, while he pounded two nails through the brace on the other end, fastening it to the wall above the table. When he took my place, I stepped back to watch while he finished nailing it.

"How do you know it's level?" I asked.

"I measured up from the floor and marked it." I could tell he was proud of himself for thinking of it.

"What makes you think the floor is level?" I teased. He pounded in one last nail and turned to me with a grin.

"Well, if all the books are on the floor in the morning we'll know the house is tilted. Thanks for your help." He kissed me, a quick peck. When I didn't move away, he took my face in his hands and kissed me again, a slower, hungrier kiss. I felt the uncharacteristic roughness of his hands from the wood. "How am I supposed to get any work done with my lovely wife distracting me?" he asked afterward.

"Sorry. I'll go sit over there so you can work." I backed away from him, feeling shy suddenly, but he pulled me to himself and kissed me until neither one of us could breathe.

"I'm all done working," he said.

"Don't you have papers to grade?"

"Later." He lifted me into his arms and carried me to the tiny alcove off the main room that served as our bedroom.

"Friedrich, it isn't time for bed yet!" He laid me on top of the quilt and stretched out beside me. I enjoyed his affection, but his ardor still embarrassed me at times. Did other husbands carry their wives to bed this early in the evening? It wasn't a subject I had ever heard discussed, nor had my parents openly displayed their affection in front of me when I was growing up. "I'm not even sleepy," I protested.

"That's all right," he said between kisses. "I don't plan on sleeping."

"Oh? And just what are you planning to do?"

"We're going to celebrate."

I laughed, forgetting my shyness, and wrapped my arms around his neck. "Again? What are we celebrating this time? Surely not another wedding anniversary. Didn't we just celebrate our six-month anniversary a few days ago? It can't be seven months already."

"I'll have you know, my dear wife," he said, pretending to be serious, "that tonight we are celebrating the successful completion of my bookshelf."

He kissed me again and I melted into his embrace, like butter in a hot skillet.

"And if the books haven't slid to the floor by morning, will we celebrate that too?" I asked.

"Absolutely."

THREE

As winter's fury yielded to the soothing caress of spring, my brother Emil came to our cottage one evening to ask Friedrich for a favor.

"I've decided to go to university next year," Emil said. "I hear there are some excellent job opportunities in industry for men with engineering degrees. But I'll need to pass the diploma exams first. I was wondering if you'd be willing to tutor me?"

"Certainly, Emil. That's wonderful news. I'll be glad to arrange some extra lessons." A pleased smile spread across Friedrich's face. He'd often told me how much he loved to teach, especially a student who was eager to learn.

I became accustomed to the sight of Friedrich and Emil bent in study over our kitchen table in the evenings—Friedrich's hair as light and fine as a baby's, Emil's hair dark and thick and unruly from tugging on it whenever he grew frustrated. They filled huge sheets of butcher paper from my father-in-law's shop with numbers and diagrams and mathematical formulas too complicated for me to follow, but as I listened, I glimpsed a side of Friedrich I had never seen before. He was a born teacher—patient, creative, dedicated. If Emil had trouble grasping a concept, Friedrich would search tirelessly for a new approach, a different explanation, until the light of understanding finally lit my brother's eyes. I never saw Friedrich lose his temper or grow impatient, no matter how thick-skulled or stubborn Emil became at times.

"You can do this," he would urge. "It's not as hard as it seems, take your time." The satisfaction on his face when Emil finally caught on told me that for Friedrich, the joy of teaching was its own reward. He made the lessons so interesting that I felt a little envious that I hadn't attended the *Gymnasium* or university. Like most rural girls, I had graduated from the *Volkschule* at fourteen, then prepared for marriage and housekeeping.

But Friedrich's tutoring sessions with Emil also brought an end to the privacy we had enjoyed as newlyweds for the past several months. It became a source of much amusement for me—and much frustration for Friedrich—that

Emil chose the most inopportune times to pound on our front door. He arrived early on a Saturday morning as we lingered in bed; he took us by surprise one lazy Sunday afternoon; and several times he returned to the house for something he had forgotten moments after Friedrich had swept me into his arms murmuring, "It's safe . . . he's finally gone!"

"He does it on purpose," Friedrich grumbled one evening. He was helping me clear the dishes off the table so they would have a place to work. "I think your father sends him over here so I'll keep my hands off his daughter."

"Don't be silly, Fritz. Papa likes you. Emil doesn't know he's interrupting anything."

"Well, maybe I'll have to tutor him on the facts of life tonight."

"Don't you dare! I would die of embarrassment!"

Friedrich grinned and traced my flaming cheek with his finger. "You are so pretty when you blush like that." Then he suddenly grew serious as his eyes searched mine. "I think our parents made a good decision when they arranged our marriage, don't you? I've grown very fond of you, Louise. I know that three months of courtship didn't give you much time to get to know me, and I realize that I was a virtual stranger to you when we married, and I recognize that I have certain peculiarities that don't always make me easy to live with, especially considering that I lived here alone before we were married and—"

"Fritz . . ." I covered his lips with my fingers. "I've grown very fond of you too."

He looked surprised. And pleased. "You have? Truly?"

"Yes," I said, though I had never realized it until that very moment.

He drew me close, pressing my head against his shoulder. "I'm glad. I've heard that it sometimes takes years for a couple to adjust to one another, and for . . . for fondness to grow. And I also know that sometimes a husband and wife can live together and raise a family without ever liking each other at all. But sometimes, Louise . . . sometimes their mutual fondness can even mature . . . into love." He spoke the last words so softly I barely heard them above the sound of his heartbeat.

I wondered what it felt like to be in love. Surely it was very different from this quiet contentment and affection I felt for Friedrich. Being in love, I imagined, would make all the colors in the world more vivid, all the stars shine more brightly, all the moments of my life dance and crackle with excitement like flames leaping in a bonfire. I had never heard my parents tell each other "I love you," but did that mean that they didn't? I wished I could ask Mama or my sisters what they felt for their husbands.

"Fritz?" I said suddenly. "Can we tell them now? My family, I mean . . . about the baby?"

"Do you want to?"

"Well, they're certain to notice soon, and I'll need to borrow some clothes from Ada and Runa before too long." I gazed up at him, hopefully. "Maybe we could go to the farm for dinner this Sunday, after church?"

I missed my family terribly, especially Mama and Oma, but I didn't dare ask Friedrich to take me home too often. He had little in common with Papa and the other men in my family, and he grew restless out at the farm long before I was ready to leave.

"I guess this Sunday is as good a time as any to tell your parents what we've been up to here in town."

The way he phrased it made me blush again, but I hugged him impulsively. "Oh, thank you, Fritz! Emil can let them know we're coming."

"Ah yes. Good old Emil. You've been in my arms for a full five minutes now—I imagine he'll start pounding the door down soon. May I steal one last kiss from you before he does?"

I laughed and lifted my lips to his.

———

We went out to the farm the following Sunday, and my family greeted the news that I was expecting with such joy it might have been their first grandchild instead of their eighth. The men lit thick cigars and toasted Friedrich in the parlor with clinking glasses of Papa's best schnapps while the women shared home remedies for morning sickness with me as we washed dishes in the kitchen. Becoming a mother forged a wonderful new bond between Mama and me, strengthening a love that was already strong and deep. It seemed to me that motherhood—even more than marriage—marked the dividing line between being a child and becoming a woman.

Later that afternoon, when Runa climbed the stairs to nurse her squalling baby in the bedroom under the eaves, I followed her, remembering the whispered confidences we'd shared in that room as children. I sprawled comfortably at the foot of the big feather bed with my chin propped on my hand as I watched my sister put the baby to her breast. I wondered what it would be like, nursing my own child like that, but when I finally spoke, my thoughts were on my husband. He always seemed like a stranger to me again whenever we visited the farm. I was at home here, I belonged here—Friedrich didn't.

"Runa, what did you think of Ernst before you married him?"

Runa leaned against the headboard, her baby making contented sounds as he suckled. "I thought he came from a good family, that he earned a good living . . . he would be able to provide a nice life for our children and me."

"Did you think he was handsome?"

Runa smiled, shaking her head. "Ernst isn't handsome. But he isn't Klaus Gerber either." I laughed as I pictured the bedraggled town drunkard.

"Do you love him?" I asked a moment later.

Runa grew flustered, red-faced. She rocked the baby a little faster in her arms. "Goodness, Louise, where are all these silly questions coming from? He's my husband."

"Does that mean that you do love him or you don't?"

"It means that I don't have time to dither about such nonsense. We're married. I do my part—cooking his meals, bearing his children, keeping his home—and he provides a living for us."

"You make it sound like you're his servant and the house and your food are your pay."

"For heaven's sake, that's what marriage is. We're women in a man's world. We're his rib—his helpmate."

"Are you fond of him, then?"

"Of course I'm fond of him. He treats me well, he's a good, hard-working man—what more could I want?"

"I don't know . . . love?"

Runa stopped rocking and studied me curiously. "Are you and Friedrich having problems? It's quite normal the first year or two, but if you give the marriage time . . ."

I sat up and squeezed my sister's hand. "We're not having problems— didn't we just announce that we're having a baby this summer? I'm very happy with Friedrich. He's kind and thoughtful and—" I almost said passionate but changed my mind, too unsure of Runa's reaction to confess how much I enjoyed sharing Friedrich's bed. If women spoke of the marriage bed at all, it was usually in terms of duty or childbearing. And judging by the conversations I had overheard, only immoral women admitted to being eager to sleep with a man.

"I'm very fond of Friedrich," I said, "but sometimes I wonder what it's like to be in love and how you can tell if you are. You've been married five years—I just wondered if it took that long for love to grow. That's all."

"That's all, she says! Do I love Ernst after five years, she asks!" Runa laughed and lifted the baby to her shoulder, patting him gently on the back. "I know what size to knit his socks without measuring his foot. I know the sound of his tread on the stairs, how thick to make his gravy, and how shiny he likes his boots. I could probably pick out his shirt with my eyes closed because it would smell like he does. Isn't that what love is? Knowing everything there is to know about the other person and being content with it?"

"Oh, Runa, that can't be all!"

"What more do you want?"

"Something deeper, more beautiful, more . . . more exciting! I want my heart to be moved. I want to be changed inside from knowing him."

"Romantic love is for fairy tales, Louise. You're married, and that means being content with the ordinary, day-to-day giving and serving. It means giving up what you want and putting your husband's needs first."

I remembered Friedrich's immigration papers lying in his dresser drawer, and the room suddenly seemed colder, the afternoon sky outside the window darker. We would have to start back to our cottage in town soon.

"You're right, Runa," I said, climbing off the bed. "I sometimes forget that fairy tales are just that—fairy tales. I'd better go downstairs so you can get the baby to sleep."

In the kitchen, Oma was shoving her tiny feet, shoes and all, into a pair of Papa's old boots. She had her egg basket slung over one arm. "Time to put my chickens to bed," she said as she wrapped a shawl around her shoulders.

"I'll come with you." I grabbed Emil's jacket off the hook near the door and linked my arm through my grandmother's as we followed the path to the chicken coop. The hens scratching around the yard fluttered toward Oma with a raucous greeting. I watched her fill a bowl with feed.

"How long were you and Grandpa married?" I asked.

"Let's see . . . more than forty-three years."

"Did you love him?"

"Humph . . . that stubborn old man?" she asked with a snort. Then she smiled and her voice grew soft. "Yes, I loved him."

"When did it happen? How long after you were married did you fall in love?" I followed her into the tiny coop and helped her sift through the straw for eggs in each of the roosts.

"I don't exactly know when it happened . . . we never thought about love, years ago. We were too busy, too down-to-earth when we were your age to waste time thinking about such frivolous things."

"But do you remember the day you knew for sure that you loved him?"

Oma set the basket on the roosting ledge as if it had suddenly grown too heavy. Her eyes seemed unnaturally bright in the fading light. "Yes, Liebchen. It was the day that he died. I knew by the measure of my grief what the measure of my love had been. But by then it was too late to tell him."

"He knew, Oma. Don't you think Grandpa knew?"

"Yes, maybe so. But still, it would have been nice, I think, to say the words just once, and to watch his face when he heard them." She turned back to her chickens, gently pushing a plump hen aside to reach into the nest. "Move, *Frau Huhn*. Let me see what you're hiding under there. Ah, a nice brown one. Louise can take it home for Friedrich's breakfast."

"He'll be thrilled. He loves fresh eggs." I carried the basket as we ducked out of the chicken coop. Oma shooed all the stragglers inside and latched the door for the night.

"Your Friedrich is a good man, Louise. And I can tell that he's very content with his new wife."

"What makes you say that?"

"The nice way he treats you and watches out for you. The way his eyes follow you around the room. The way he gazes at you when you're not looking."

I hoped it was too dark for my grandmother to notice my flushed cheeks. "Oma, how will I know when I'm in love?" I asked at last.

"I can't answer that, Liebchen. It's different for each person, I think."

"What was it like for you?"

"I knew I loved your grandfather because when he died, part of me died too. And the part of me that was left felt like something was missing—like apple strudel without the cinnamon. I'll see something he would have liked and I'll turn to say, 'Oh, look at that.' But he isn't there to enjoy it . . . and so I don't enjoy it either."

"I didn't realize you missed him so much, Oma."

"Mmm. I never dreamed that I would."

When we reached the back door, I saw Friedrich through the kitchen window. He was probably ready to leave and had come searching for me. Oma took my arm and paused before going inside.

"When that day comes for you, Louise, when you know that you love him, don't wait until it's too late. Tell your Friedrich. Let him hear the words. That way you'll have no regrets."

I wrapped my arms around my grandmother. "You'll see Grandpa again in heaven, Oma. You'll have all of eternity to tell him."

"Yes, Liebchen, I'll see him again . . . but the Bible says there are no marriages in heaven."

FOUR

Spring edged toward summer. Our baby grew strong and vigorous inside me. As my time drew nearer and none of the men had been drafted, I was almost lulled into believing that nothing had changed except the seasons and my waist size. Then Emil burst through our backyard gate one warm June afternoon as I was removing laundry from the clothesline.

"News, Louise! Have I got news!"

"Don't startle me like that, Emil! Do you want me to go into labor?" He laughed, gripping the clothespole with one hand and swinging in a circle around it.

"So. . . ?" I prompted. "Is it good news or bad?"

"Some of each. Where's Friedrich?"

"He'll be home from school any minute." I folded a linen towel and placed it in the laundry basket, waiting. "You aren't going to make me wait, are you?"

"Of course!" Emil smiled mischievously, and I caught a glimpse of Papa in his wide, lopsided grin.

"I know! You must have heard the results of your university entrance exams!"

"I'm not going to say . . ."

But I thought I saw a glint of triumph in his eyes before he spun away from me and strolled into the house to wait. As the sun disappeared behind a cloud for a moment, I wondered what Emil's bad news was.

By the time I finished folding all of the laundry and hoisted the basket to my hip, Friedrich arrived. He had his usual armload of books and papers, but he transferred them to one hand and took the basket from me with the other.

"Here . . . let me help you. You shouldn't be lifting heavy burdens."

"Is that right, 'Doctor' Schroder?" I said, smiling. "That will be good news to expectant mothers everywhere. We can just lie back with our feet up from now on." He laughed and leaned forward to kiss me but I stepped aside, blushing. "Emil's here."

"Ah. I might have known."

"He has some news," I explained as I opened the back door. "Good news and bad, he says." Emil sat at the kitchen table, a broad grin illuminating his face.

"You've passed the exams, haven't you!" Friedrich guessed. He dropped the laundry basket on the floor and dumped his books on the table so he could pump Emil's hand. "Congratulations, brother!"

"Thanks. I couldn't have done it without all your tutoring."

"Were you accepted into the engineering program too?"

"With flying colors."

"That's terrific news, Emil. I'm proud of you." Friedrich finally released Emil's hand and circled his arm around me, pulling me close.

"What's the bad news, Emil?" I asked. "That you'll be leaving all of us and going away to university next year?"

His smile vanished abruptly. "No, not exactly . . ." He glanced at Friedrich with a strange, worried look.

"Then, let's enjoy the good news," Friedrich said quickly, "and let the bad news wait for another day. Can you stay for dinner, Emil? We should celebrate."

"Thanks, but I can't tonight. I have to get back to the farm. Papa is—" He stopped, the odd look crossing his features once again. He stood to leave. "We'll celebrate another day. I just stopped by for a minute to tell you the news."

I twisted out of Friedrich's grasp and blocked Emil's path to the door. "What happened? What about Papa? Tell me, Emil."

He lifted his shoulders as if trying to shrug off his uneasiness. "Papa's a little upset, that's all." He tried to edge around me.

"Why? Not because you're going away to school. Papa wants you to go."

"No. Not because of me, Louise." He paused, and it seemed to take forever for him to find the words. "Kurt received his draft notice yesterday."

"*What?* Who will help Papa run the farm?"

"Exactly," Emil said softly. "I told Papa I would wait two years until Kurt gets back, but you know how proud Papa is to have a son going to university. He won't listen to reason. He's cursing the Kaiser and the army generals and everyone else he can think of."

"But they *can't* draft Kurt!" I cried. "He has a family and . . . and responsibilities! How can they do such a thing?"

Friedrich gripped the edge of the table and slowly lowered himself into a chair. It took me a moment to realize why the news had upset him so much. He and Kurt were the same age.

Emil exhaled, as if even the air he breathed was weighted with doom. "Some of Kurt's friends received notices too. I'm sorry, Friedrich. I know what this means for you."

"No . . ." I whispered. "This can't be happening." The room felt as if it were spinning. I moved to the stove and stirred the pot of chicken stew that was simmering for dinner. "We're having a baby in two months. They have no right to disrupt our lives this way." My hands shook as I opened the grate and shoved a piece of firewood into the stove. Ordinarily, Friedrich would have been on his feet by now, helping me, but he remained slumped in the chair as if all of his bones had dissolved.

"How long until Kurt has to report for training?" Friedrich finally asked.

"Three months. But don't worry . . . 'Fischer' is near the beginning of the alphabet. It might take a few more months for them to get to 'Schroder.' By that time your baby will be born."

"What about your teacher's exemption?" I asked in a quivering voice. Friedrich lifted his head to meet my gaze.

"It seems there is a surplus of teachers at the moment," he said. "Besides, all the new June graduates will be looking for work soon. . . ." His voice trailed off. He looked shaken, as if he might be sick, and I realized that underneath his calm assurances that God would provide, he was as distraught and unsure about our future as I was. I watched his hands slowly tighten into fists as anger, a rare emotion for Friedrich, gradually replaced his paralysis.

"What a stupid, ridiculous waste!" he shouted, pounding the table. "Why can't they leave Kurt alone to farm the land he loves? Why can't they let Emil study engineering instead of teaching him how to shoot a gun? Why can't I be free to live in peace with my wife and child? Can't any of our nation's leaders see where this insanity is leading us? Can't they see the carnage and destruction that's going to result from their greed? What a waste! What a terrible, tragic waste!"

In the silence that followed Friedrich's outburst, I could hear the crackle of flames in the stove as the wood caught fire. The baby tossed and squirmed in my womb as if responding to the turmoil in our lives. I gently rubbed my stomach to soothe him. Then I noticed Emil, standing by the door like a beaten dog. This should have been one of the happiest days of his life, and we had ruined it for him. I crossed the room and gathered my brother in an awkward hug, the baby an ungainly lump between us.

"I'm so proud of you," I said, "and I know Papa is too. He'll find a way for you to go to school next year, even if it means hiring extra workers or leasing the land for a year or two until Kurt comes back."

"Do you really think so?"

"I know so." I stood on my toes to kiss his cheek.

"She's right, Emil," Friedrich said. I heard a note of forced cheer in his voice. "Maybe you can squeeze in a few years of college before it's your turn."

Emil gave him a puzzled look. "Have you decided to serve after all, Friedrich? I thought you said . . ."

"One step at a time. I haven't been notified yet." He wouldn't look at either of us as he arranged his school books into a pile on the table with deliberate care. "How is Kurt handling the news?" he asked.

"He was upset at first—especially since Papa took it so hard. But now he's more or less resigned to going—as long as they don't ship him to one of the colonies."

"Is that a possibility?" I asked.

"I guess so," Emil said with a shrug. "Personally, I'd jump at the chance to travel."

"What is Gerda going to do when Kurt leaves?" I asked.

Emil sighed, as if weary of all our questions. "Why don't you and Friedrich come out to the farm on Sunday and you can talk to everyone yourselves. Should I tell Mama to expect you?"

"Would that be all right, Fritz?" I looked at him hopefully, but he didn't respond right away. I realized that he was reluctant to go because he would have to answer all of my family's questions, and they didn't understand his strange convictions any more than I did.

"We can go if you want to," he said eventually.

After Emil left, I busied myself with the dinner preparations. Friedrich sat at the table in glum silence, kneading the worried frown on his forehead. More than anything else, I longed to ask him what he planned to do, but a good wife didn't pry into her husband's business. He knew how I felt about leaving Germany, and I had no right to discuss it with him further, much less nag him or plead with him. He would tell me when he was ready to. Besides, I was terrified to hear his answer.

Where is God in all this? I wanted to shout at him as I banged pots and pans on the stove. *I thought you said we could trust Him. I thought we could leave everything in His hands. Now look at this mess!* But I didn't say any of those things. Instead, I silently beat flour, milk, and eggs together to make dumplings, then spooned them on top of the stew.

When I approached the table to set it for dinner, Friedrich reached for my hand. "Everything is moving too fast, Louise. I never dreamed the army would start conscripting men my age so quickly."

"Is this the way it's going to be from now on? Waiting for the mail to come every day? Wondering if you'll be called up next?"

"The Lord taught us to pray, 'Give us *this* day our daily bread.' We're supposed to live one day at a time, not borrow trouble from the next."

I bit my lip, torn between the desire to submit to my husband and the urge to argue the impossibility of fulfilling such a stupid request. In the end, duty lost the battle, and the words rushed out of my mouth before I could stop them. "It's very hard not to think of the future with the baby coming so soon."

He didn't react to my anger but gently touched my bulging stomach, tracing small circles with his fingertips. "I know," he said. "But we never *really* know our future, Louise, only what our hopes for it are. All we can do is put our faith in God, then live . . . just live . . . one day at a time."

———

July grew hot. I grew enormous and miserable. I wasn't sure which was worse—waiting for the baby to arrive or waiting for the dreaded draft notice. I was restless and irritable, especially with Friedrich, who was home on school holidays. He fled outside for most of the morning to labor in the vegetable garden I'd asked him to plant. I knew Papa would give us plenty of produce from the farm, but the sight of my own garden, slowly ripening in the hot July sun—green beans and kale, cucumbers for pickles, cabbages for sauerkraut— offered the illusion that we would still be living here when winter came.

In August, my ankles began to swell and the doctor ordered me to stay off my feet. "Fritz, please take me home to the farm," I begged. "It's so much cooler out there than in town, and Mama and Oma will know what to do better than the doctor does."

"You shouldn't ride that far in a bumpy carriage. I don't want anything to happen to you."

"I always thought my babies would be born on the farm," I said tearfully, "with Mama and Oma there."

"Louise, I promise that the moment your time comes, I'll ride out to the farm and bring both of them back here—after I fetch the doctor, of course." His smile seemed strained, and I realized that he hadn't smiled much lately or tried to make me laugh, as he used to do. Suddenly all my anxiety about the future boiled over. I couldn't stand the uncertainty a moment longer. I unleashed a flood of tears, the only weapon I had against my helplessness.

"Oh, Fritz, please tell me what's going to happen. I can't stand not knowing what you're thinking or what you're going to do if that draft notice comes. Are you really going to leave Germany like you said and make us move to America? *Please* tell me."

"Louise, stop . . . You're upsetting yourself. . . ." He pulled his handkerchief from his pocket and pressed it into my hands. "I haven't told you anything because I was afraid this would happen."

"But not knowing upsets me just as much . . . maybe more!"

"Shh . . . don't cry. Don't cry. . . ." He gathered me awkwardly in his arms, but his skin was hot and sweaty, his shirt damp, his beard itchy against my neck. I pushed him away.

"What are you going to do, Fritz?"

"If the draft notice comes . . ." He closed his eyes. "*When* it comes, I'll have to leave Germany. I would have left months ago, but—"

"But the baby and I complicated your life."

"That's not what I meant to say at all. I want this child more than you'll ever know, Louise." He tried to rest his palm on my stomach, but when I felt the damp heat of his hand through my dress I shoved it away. He looked wounded. "The only reason I haven't left Germany already is because I know you don't want to go. I thought that if I waited something would change—the Kaiser would raise his army without me, or they'd overlook my name somehow and we'd be able to stay after all. . . ."

"Do you really think that might happen?"

"No. Not anymore. Not since Kurt got his notice. I've looked into every avenue of escape I could think of, from a teaching exemption to applying for conscientious objector status, but I've exhausted all of my options."

Tears spilled down my cheeks again. I would have begged at his feet, pleaded with him not to tear me from my home and my family and make me move to America if I thought it would do any good. "When are you planning to leave?" I asked instead.

"Not one moment before I have to. They gave Kurt three months to report, so I assume they'll do the same for me. I hope to have saved enough money for my passage by then."

I had no idea how much money Friedrich had, or even how much money he earned as a teacher, let alone what the boat fare for all of us would cost. It wasn't my place to ask.

"I might have to go to America first and get settled," he continued, "then send for you and the baby after—" He stopped when I started weeping again. "Please don't, Louise . . . this is exactly why I didn't want to tell you any of this." He wore such a pained expression that I regretted asking questions. Friedrich had been right to shield me from the facts. They were upsetting both of us.

"Listen," he continued, "some men I know were going to come here tomorrow night to talk about what's involved in getting across the border, but if you'd rather we met somewhere else . . .."

"What do you mean? I thought you had all the documents you needed to cross the border."

"They may not be valid anymore now that the conscription laws have changed. Once my draft notice comes—"

"You'll be leaving the country *illegally*?"

He tugged at his shirt collar, as if it were suddenly too tight. "I'm not sure. That's what I need to find out at this meeting."

I didn't understand my husband at all. How could he claim to love God, yet be willing to break the laws of Germany to escape the draft? And how could he be so concerned for my welfare one moment, then announce that he was emigrating to America against my wishes the next? I wanted to know and understand him, but now it seemed that what was most important to each of us would be lost if the other got what he wanted.

"I'm sorry, Fritz," I said, wiping my tears. "I shouldn't have forced you to tell me all this. I want you to have the meeting here. I'll be all right."

I allowed him to hold me in his arms in spite of the sticky heat, but I drew no comfort from his embrace.

———

The following evening, I poured glasses of cider for his friends when they arrived for the mysterious meeting. I saw by their clothing and beards that some of the men were Mennonites, including the one named Rolf, who was supplying Friedrich and the others with information. I retired to our bedroom alcove with my knitting as I'd promised, but I listened to every word they said as they huddled around our kitchen table.

"The authorities have begun patrolling the borders for draft dodgers," Rolf warned. "If you haven't received your draft notice yet, I advise you to leave immediately, before it arrives."

"What if that isn't possible?" Friedrich asked. "Our child will be born later this month. I won't leave my wife before then."

"If you wait, you'll have to leave the country illegally."

"Even if I have immigration papers?"

"They're not valid once you're drafted. The army takes priority over the immigration office."

The room grew very quiet. The only sound was the rhythmic clacking of my knitting needles. I stopped, unwilling to disturb the silence. One of the Mennonite men finally spoke.

"In that case, can you advise us how to cross the border illegally?"

Discipline and obedience to authority were solemn virtues to most Germans. I couldn't comprehend why my husband and these other men were willing to risk prison to avoid the law. They bent closer to Rolf, eager to hear his advice.

"You'll need to make a copy of this map. I've circled several border villages and marked some little-known trails into Switzerland that avoid the main roads. I recommend that you cross after dark."

"What about the Swiss authorities?" Friedrich asked. "Will they deport us if we're caught?"

"They'll honor your American visa papers once you make it across. You are fortunate to have them, Friedrich."

I wanted to snatch them from our bureau drawer and toss them into the stove, but I couldn't will my body to move.

"One final warning," Rolf said. "Be very careful as you travel to the border. The authorities are searching any men who look as though they might be draft age. If they find this map or your emigration papers, or see that you're carrying all your personal effects and large sums of money, they can arrest you for draft evasion. I advise you to have your belongings shipped after you've made it safely across. And be ready with a cover story when you travel. You'll need a legitimate destination and a reason for traveling."

"But I won't lie," Friedrich said.

"Then God help you if you're caught."

FIVE

One hot day followed another. There was a terrible drought that summer. When Friedrich stopped watering our garden for fear our well would go dry, our vegetables shrivelled and died beneath the sun. The Rhine River was so low in places you could see great stretches of riverbed along both of its banks. The air stank of dead fish. As more and more men Friedrich's age received their draft notices, my hope and joy ebbed along with the river.

One night a heartrending moan awakened me from a deep sleep. It took me a moment to realize that it had come from my husband.

"Fritz . . . Fritz, wake up . . . you're dreaming." He opened his eyes when I shook him, then lay panting as if he'd run a long distance. Sweat soaked the sheets beneath him. "Fritz, what's wrong? What on earth were you dreaming?"

"It was terrible. There was a flood and the water was rising higher and higher, and I couldn't find you . . . you were lost . . ." Sweat trickled down his face. I pulled him into my arms and felt his heart galloping like a runaway colt's.

"I'm right here, Friedrich. It was only a bad dream."

"There was a horrible war and you . . ."

"I thought you said it was a flood?"

"It was both, somehow—a flood . . . and yet I knew it was a war. I can't explain it. Everything was destroyed—the villages and farms, all the buildings and trees. I called your name over and over, but you were lost to me."

I smoothed his damp hair off his forehead, remembering how irritable I had been with him for the past few weeks. "I'm not lost. I'm right here." But the discovery that it had been only a dream seemed to give Friedrich no comfort. My words, my touch did nothing to soothe the troubled look from his face. "Let's go back to sleep, Fritz."

"I don't think I can. My tossing would only disturb you, and you need your rest." He climbed out of bed and pulled on his trousers, then disappeared into the darkness. Once my eyes adjusted to the gloom, I saw the pale outline of his naked shoulders as he moved ghostlike around the cottage. I waited for him to return, but he never did. Eventually I dozed.

As the light of dawn lit the room, I awoke again and slipped into my dressing gown to go in search of him. I found him slumped on his knees, his forehead on the floor. At first I thought he was ill, then I saw his Bible lying open in front of him. I turned to tiptoe away. When the floor creaked, he lifted his head.

"I'm sorry," I said. "I didn't mean to disturb you."

"It's all right." He slowly pulled himself to his feet, as if stiff from his cramped position. "Come here," he whispered. He drew me into his arms, holding me so tenderly I might have been made of glass and would shatter if he held too tightly. His hands gently caressed my shoulders, my hair, my face, as if trying to memorize my form. I felt him shiver, but when he kissed me, I knew by the delicate brush of his lips that it was from sorrow, not longing.

"Friedrich, what's wrong?"

"I don't want to lose you."

"But you won't. I'm right here."

He rested his cheek against my hair. "Louise, I think my dream was from God."

"You mean like the dreams in the Bible?" When he nodded I almost laughed aloud. "You don't really believe God still speaks to people in dreams, do you? And even if He did, why would He pick you? Maybe you should talk to Reverend Lahr—"

"No, I need to talk to you."

"But I don't understand anything about . . ."

"Then I need to make you understand. Otherwise I might lose you, just like in my dream."

"You're talking in riddles. You didn't get enough sleep last night."

"No, listen to me." He tightened his grip on my arms. "I know you don't want to leave Germany, and I've searched and searched for a way to obey God without moving, but there just isn't one. There's going to be a war in Europe— maybe next year, maybe not for ten years, I don't know—but the fuse has been lit and sooner or later it's going to explode. I can't be part of it. I can't kill and destroy and conquer for the sake of national pride and greed. And I want you and our child to be safe from it. We're surrounded by enemies, Louise— Russia on the east, France on the west, Great Britain . . ."

"It was only a dream, Fritz."

"No, it was more than that. I've been praying about what to do ever since Kurt was drafted, and I think my dream was a warning that . . . You don't believe me, do you? I can tell by your face that you think I'm crazy."

"I think you're upset, that's all. A nightmare can seem very real, but you can't make important decisions based on a dream."

"I'm not. I already knew in my heart what I needed to do. The dream showed me that I need to make *you* understand why we can't stay in Europe."

"Because you think there will be a war."

"I *know* there will be a war. Our leaders know it too. Why do you think they're drafting more men?"

"Then shouldn't our families leave too?"

"Yes, of course, but they don't want to believe it's going to happen any more than you do. I just hope and pray that if we go to America first and get settled over there, I can persuade them to join us later."

"You know they'll never leave Germany. If we move to America, we'll never see any of them again." My knees felt too wobbly to hold me any longer. I had been confined to my bed for more than a week. I pulled away from Friedrich and sat down at the kitchen table. That's when I noticed for the first time that Friedrich's new bookshelf was empty. I glanced around the room, but didn't see his books.

"Fritz, where did all your books go?"

"I sold them."

"*Sold* them? But they were your most precious possessions!" I waited, hoping he would tell me why.

"I needed the money for my passage to America," he said at last. "Besides, it would be too costly to ship them."

I turned my head so I wouldn't have to look at the empty shelf. Was this just the first of many losses we would be forced to endure until we were finally stripped of everything we loved? A moment later he moved behind me, resting his hands on my shoulders. His next words came out in a rush, as if he wanted relief from their awful burden.

"I've decided to go to America alone, to get settled over there, then send for you and the baby when I've saved enough money. In the meantime, I thought you'd be happier living with your family than staying alone here in town, so I've made all the arrangements with your father. He has agreed to move you and the baby back to the farm after I'm gone."

His words seemed unreal, like his nightmare. We were leaving Germany and moving to America. I could no longer deny the truth or pretend it would never happen. Each time I saw the empty bookshelf, I would be reminded. Our departure had begun.

"I'll fix breakfast," I said.

"No, let me. You're supposed to stay off your feet."

"Please, Fritz. I'm sick and tired of staying in bed." I stood and began rummaging in the pantry for potatoes and eggs. My distress was made worse by a nagging pain in my back, and the aching, cramping feeling that usually came with my monthly curse.

We had just finished breakfast when I heard the postman outside, dropping several letters through our slot. Friedrich rose to retrieve them. I watched his face as he sifted through them, then saw his expression change when he came to the last envelope. I knew without being told that his draft notice had arrived. He stared at it for a long time, then laid it on the table.

"Don't open it, Louise." His voice sounded hoarse.

"Is it really worth risking prison for, Fritz? What will become of the baby and me if you get caught? Why would you take such a chance? I still don't understand!"

He opened his mouth as if forming his answer, then clenched his jaw and closed his eyes in despair. When he opened them again he wouldn't look at me, but he snatched up his hat and left the house without a word, closing the door gently behind him.

I glared at the envelope for a long time, as if it were Pandora's box and would unleash disaster upon us if opened. But hadn't disaster already been unleashed when the draft law changed? Friedrich's books were gone. He was leaving for America. There was no way I could stuff everything back into the box.

I left the breakfast dishes where they lay and crawled back into bed, too numb to cry. What if I could go back and change everything? Would I have agreed to marry Friedrich if I had known he would make me move to America? Would I have chosen him before my family, my homeland? No, I decided as the cramping grew worse. No. I would rather have married Klaus Gerber, the town drunk, than move away from everyone I loved.

As I tossed on the bed in misery, it slowly occurred to me why I felt so sick—the baby was coming. And I had no idea where Fritz had gone or when he would be back. I couldn't bear the thought of starting my labor all alone, so I decided to go next door for my neighbor, Mrs. Schmidt. She'd given birth to five children and had offered to help when my time came. But first I would have to get up and get dressed. It all seemed so impossible with my swollen ankles and aching back.

I managed to change into a housedress, but then I saw what a mess the kitchen was, with unwashed pans on the stove and our dirty breakfast dishes still on the table. I couldn't let anyone see my home in such a state. I hobbled to the sink and worked the hand pump but nothing came out. Then suddenly there was water everywhere, running down my legs, soaking my clothing, spreading in a puddle around my ankles. My baby would be born today. Friedrich's baby. She would grow up in America, never knowing her grandparents, her aunts, her cousins. I sank onto a kitchen chair and wept.

It took me a long time to clean up the dishes. I was on my knees with a bucket and rags, mopping the floor when Friedrich returned.

"Louise! What on earth are you doing!" He pulled me to my feet and steered me to the nearest chair. "You're not even supposed to be out of bed, let alone working and . . . and your dress is soaked! What on earth—?"

"Please go get Mama and Oma." I couldn't stop sobbing.

"Is it your time? Should I fetch the doctor?"

"I want Mama. She'll know when to send for the doctor."

Mrs. Schmidt stayed with me while Friedrich rode out to the farm. I don't remember seeing him much after that. Oma probably shooed him out of the way. Delivering babies was women's work. Later I learned that Friedrich had spent the entire day praying. His prayers didn't help.

My labor was very long and difficult—hours and hours of pain with no relief in sight. Everything that was happening to me was out of my control, and now even my body had turned traitor. It seemed to function without my help, possessing some instinctual knowledge of what to do, wrenching my child from me—I was simply along for the ride. But what a terrible ride it was. I vowed never to have another child if it meant going through this agony again, but Mama smiled and assured me that each baby got a little easier. When I screamed that I was being ripped in half, Oma told me that I was close to the end.

Then they laid my daughter in my arms and my joy overflowed. Her tiny, wrinkled face looked so much like Oma's that I decided then and there to name her after my beloved grandmother. The bitterness I felt toward Friedrich was so strong, it never occurred to me to ask his opinion.

"I'll name you Sophie," I whispered. "My little Sophie."

SIX

Friedrich's draft notice lay on his dresser, unopened, for more than a month. He didn't need to read it to know he would have to leave us soon. School reopened in September without him. He had told the headmaster that he'd been summoned for military service, but not that he was fleeing to America. The school authorities were kind enough to allow us to stay in the cottage until Fritz left, and they promised him a job when he returned from the army in two years. I still didn't understand why Friedrich couldn't sacrifice two years in the army for my sake, instead of making me sacrifice the rest of my life for his.

As my resentment festered, I started to pull away from Friedrich the way people pull away from a loved one who is dying, distancing themselves from the pain. I lavished all of my love on Sophie, who grew stronger and prettier every day. But the more I withdrew, the more Friedrich seemed to cling to me, desperate to preserve the fragile bonds that had grown between us during our brief year of marriage. As far as I was concerned, his decision had already severed them.

He was seated at the table beneath the barren bookshelf one evening, writing yet another letter to his cousin in America, when the notion came to me. "Fritz, why don't you just leave now," I said, "instead of prolonging this for two more months? You'll go crazy sitting around the house for that long with nothing to do, and I'll go crazy watching you."

He carefully laid down his fountain pen and blotted the page before answering. "I promised you I'd stay as long as possible."

"I never asked you to make that promise."

"I know . . . but I thought that you would want me here."

Tears stung my eyes. I rocked Sophie in my arms, even though she was sound asleep. "What I want doesn't really matter, does it?"

"It matters a great deal."

I waited until I could look up at him, dry-eyed. "Then I want you to leave.

You're ready to go, I know you are. Why drag it out any longer?"

He didn't answer. I had been nurturing the hope that when the time came to leave, Friedrich wouldn't be able to desert us after all; that the reason he hadn't already left was because he was having second thoughts. But when he returned from posting his letter to America, he spread the map of his escape route into Switzerland on the table. I laid Sophie in her basket and peered over his shoulder at the map, wondering what he planned to do. *Be ready with a cover story when you travel*, Rolf had warned. I pointed to one of the towns circled in red.

"My aunt Marta lives in this village. You could tell the authorities you're going to visit her."

Friedrich exhaled. "I already told you, I'm not going to lie."

"Then why not plan a real visit? It only takes a day to get there by steam ferry. Sophie and I could come too."

"I won't involve you and the baby."

"I think it's a bit late to worry about that," I said curtly. "We're already involved. Wouldn't the authorities be less suspicious if you had your wife and child along?"

"Louise . . ."

"I'll write to Aunt Marta. I'm sure she'd love to meet her new grandniece." I picked up the box of stationery and envelopes that Fritz had been using and sat down at the table to compose my letter. I knew I was being stubborn, but why make it easy for him to desert us? I had it in my mind that Fritz would never be able to take his leave from us if we were in a strange village so far from home.

He exhaled again and rubbed his eyes. "Let me think it over."

———

In the end, Friedrich reluctantly agreed to my plan and allowed Sophie and me to go with him as far as the Swiss border. A bite of frost chilled the air the morning we boarded the steamship that would take us up the Rhine, and as we pulled away from the wharf, Sophie and I took shelter inside with the other passengers. Fritz stood at the stern, watching our village grow smaller and smaller until it finally passed from sight. I knew he was saying good-bye. He had bid farewell to his family the evening before, pleading with them until late into the night to join him in America. "Sell your shop and open another one over there," he had begged his father. "They need good butchers in America too." No one from either of our families had made any promises.

By early afternoon we were more than halfway to my aunt's village. The day turned unseasonably warm, and we sat in chairs on the deck of the ship watching farms and vineyards and church steeples slide past us on shore. I removed my hat to let the sun bathe my face. Sophie was asleep on my shoulder. The afternoon was so lovely I wished we really were on a day trip. If only this steady chugging upstream wasn't taking Friedrich away for good. The fact that this journey was upstream seemed like a lesson in itself—he was fighting the current, taking us with him against the flow.

I closed my eyes, feeling drowsy in the sun's warmth. I had only dozed for a moment when Friedrich gripped my arm.

"Louise . . ."

"Hmm?" I opened my eyes and saw two men in uniform—an officer and a younger soldier—slowly making their way across the deck. They scanned the passengers as if searching for someone, their expressions cold, unsmiling.

"They weren't on the ship earlier today," Friedrich whispered. "They must have boarded at the last stop." We watched as they paused beside the young bank clerk from Cologne we had met earlier. The officer held out his hand, probably asking to see the identification papers, which all men of draft age were required to carry. Then they made the man stand while they searched his pockets and bags. All the color, tinged by wind and sun, washed from Friedrich's face.

"No . . ." he whispered.

With perfect clarity, I saw that I could alter my future. I could keep Friedrich in Germany, cling to the life I loved. I didn't have to be swept away to America against my will. The decision was mine to make, and I wouldn't even have to say a word because Friedrich would never lie. The soldiers would find the packet containing his money, his emigration papers, the map marked with the trail across the border, his cousin's address in America. I felt the power of control as I had felt the power of the ship when it had begun to move, plowing upstream against the current. I could fight the current too.

Now the soldiers were questioning the young medical student Friedrich had chatted with. The student seemed to be making light of the situation, smiling as he showed his identification papers and as he unbuttoned his jacket to be searched. But the soldiers responded with haughty efficiency. They had guns, power, authority. I tried to imagine Friedrich in a uniform, forced to act like these men, forced to aim a gun and kill. Then I tried to imagine him in prison, with real criminals.

My feelings toward Friedrich were like a tangled skein of yarn that I couldn't unravel. I hated the choice he had made, hated his complete power over me as my husband. Yet he was a good man, a hardworking man, tender and affectionate. Part of me wanted to protect him, part of me wanted to punish him.

I cuddled my daughter, asleep on my shoulder, brushing my lips against her soft, sweet skin. Friedrich was her father. She needed him to provide for her, protect her. I had no means of supporting Sophie without him.

What I was unable to decide for Friedrich's sake became an easy choice to make for my daughter. I leaned my head near Friedrich as if to nuzzle his neck, as I had seen lovers do.

"Fritz," I whispered, "give me your papers and the map."

He didn't move. One of the soldiers glanced our way as if scanning the deck for his next victim, while the other continued to interrogate the young student. I caressed Friedrich's hand, lying clenched on his thigh.

"Hurry, Fritz."

I lowered the sleeping baby from my shoulder to my lap. Sophie awoke and began to fuss, but I didn't try to soothe her back to sleep. Maybe her cries would distract the soldiers. Men always seemed unnerved by fussing infants.

"The money too. Quickly."

At last Friedrich summoned the strength to move. He bent over Sophie, speaking softly to her as he reached into his breast pocket for the packet containing all his papers and the money he had saved for America. He had tied up everything with butcher paper and string like a packet of pork chops. Leaning over the baby to conceal it from view, Friedrich slipped the packet to me.

I pretended to check Sophie's diaper and slid everything into her knitted soaker pants. She wailed in protest. She hated lying on her back, and I knew if I lifted her to my shoulder she would stop. But as the officials approached, I wrapped her shawl around her legs again and allowed her to cry.

"Your identification papers, please."

I wondered if they saw the tremor in Friedrich's hand as he gave them over, or noticed the knotted muscle in his clenched jaw. I studied the officer's face as he took his time reading. He was a thin, colorless man with pale hair and skin and eyes. He reminded me of a fish that lives deep inside a cave, far from the warmth of the sun. The touch of his slender hand would be as cold as an underground stream.

"I see that you are eligible for military service, Herr Schroder," he finally said. "Have you received your draft notice?"

"Yes, I have."

"How long ago?"

"It arrived the day my daughter was born. About a month ago."

"Why haven't you reported for duty?"

Friedrich hesitated. I almost spoke for him, but finally he said, "As I'm sure you're aware, the government allows me three months to get my affairs in order before I'm required to report for duty."

The officer stared long and hard at Friedrich, but my husband's gaze never wavered. I prayed that the official wouldn't ask him a more direct question.

"Your ticket, please."

Friedrich fumbled in his coat pocket and produced our two round-trip tickets. Sophie was screaming in earnest now, the sound fraying my nerves. The soldiers seemed deaf to it.

"What is your business in this village?"

"My wife's aunt lives there. We're visiting her with our new baby." Friedrich spoke only the truth, but it sounded stilted. The younger soldier pulled out a small notebook and a pencil.

"Your aunt's name and address?"

While the soldier scribbled down the information, the officer eyed Friedrich as if he were a farm animal he was thinking of purchasing.

"Stand up," he said abruptly.

They searched Friedrich in front of the other passengers, forcing him to raise his arms and spread his legs as they patted him down like a criminal. Their arrogance outraged me. One of them removed Friedrich's wallet and counted his money, while the other leafed through the book he had been reading. His bookmark fluttered away on the breeze.

"Just what, exactly, are you looking for?" I asked angrily.

"Shh . . . It's all right, Louise," Friedrich murmured.

"Where are your bags?" they asked when they finished with him. Friedrich reached beneath his deck chair and pulled out our satchel. The soldier pawed through it, scattering all our belongings on the deck. I fought tears as he tossed my nightgown aside in plain sight.

"Is this all of your luggage?" the officer asked.

"We're only staying the weekend," I said with controlled fury. "But here is the baby's bag, if you'd care to see wet diapers." I shoved it toward him with my foot. They searched it carefully, in spite of the sopping diapers and soaker pants.

When they finished I stood, lifting Sophie to my shoulder. "Would you care to search me, as well?"

The officer's pale eyes bored into mine for a moment. My heart pounded with anger and fear. I wondered if I would go to prison along with Friedrich if they found the packet.

"That won't be necessary," he said at last. The two men turned in unison and proceeded up the deck as if they'd merely inquired about the weather, not searched us like thieves.

When they were out of sight, I sat again. I didn't dare look at Friedrich for fear that my tears would be unleashed. He bent to scoop our rifled belongings back into the satchel, then sat down and opened his book. It trembled in his hand.

I gazed at the tranquil hills floating past, the autumn-tinged leaves that hinted at the winter to come, and rocked my sobbing baby in my arms. For the first time I understood that Friedrich's power to choose my fate wasn't something to be envied. Making a decision was a balancing act, like the acrobat I had seen in the circus, suspended on a wire between two platforms. Once you've chosen, once you've taken the first step, you must continue no matter how terrifying the journey, until you either fall to your death or reach the other side. You can only hope that you've made the right choice, and pray for the strength to follow through.

The baby found her thumb and finally stopped crying. The afternoon turned chilly as the ferry churned into the lengthening shadows cast by the hills. Friedrich slowly closed his book and clasped his hands together on top of it.

"Louise . . ." I turned and saw a tear glistening on his lashes. "Thank you."

We docked in my aunt's village late in the afternoon. During the warmer months it was a favorite tourist destination with pleasure boats anchored in the Rhine and sidewalk cafés dotting the waterfront. Even in autumn the village was picturesque with Swiss-style buildings, painted flower boxes, and a clock tower on the village square that chimed the hour. It was also much cooler here and I was grateful for my shawl.

The fresh air and long journey had made me drowsy, and my legs wobbled feebly on dry land. My skin felt tight and wind-washed, my hair tangled from the breeze. I longed for a hot bath and a thick feather bed. A row of carriages for hire stood across the street.

"Fritz, can we afford to take a carriage to Aunt Marta's? I'm too tired to walk."

"Yes, but I . . . I've been thinking." He searched my face, struggling for words. Was he going to change his mind about leaving us, after all? I held my breath, waiting.

"Louise, I don't want to involve your aunt in this."

"What do you mean? She's expecting us . . . and we gave the soldiers her address."

"I know. That's the problem. I'll need to explain to her that I'm breaking the law when I leave tonight, and then she might have to lie to the authorities. I don't want to put her or you at risk if I can avoid it. I'll hire a carriage to take you and Sophie there . . . but I think I'd better leave you now."

"Fritz, no!" My disappointment was quickly overwhelmed by my rising panic. Until this moment I hadn't really comprehended what his leaving meant. Now a terrible emptiness echoed through me—I felt so light I might have blown away on the breeze if Friedrich hadn't had his hand on my shoulder. I remembered Oma's description of feeling incomplete after Grandpa died. How could I feel so angry with Fritz for leaving me, yet feel such a loss when he did?

"Louise, it's for your aunt's sake. It's bad enough that I involved you."

"But we can't say good-bye like this . . . standing here!"

A row of shops and restaurants faced the wharf. Friedrich steered me across the busy street and into a café. We sat at a table in a rear corner and ordered hot chocolate, but the cups sat untouched. Twice Friedrich started to speak, then stopped, before finally finding the words he sought.

"If there were any other way out of this . . . if I had any other choice . . . I swear I'd never leave you like this, Louise."

I nodded, too close to tears to trust myself to reply.

"Will you and Sophie be all right?" he asked uncertainly. "The journey home?"

I nodded again, biting my lip.

He reached across the table for my hand. "Louise . . . why did you help me today on the ferry? I know you don't want me to go . . . yet you made it possible for me to leave."

I lifted my chin, wanting to hurt him for some reason. "I only did it for

Sophie's sake. How would she survive if her papa went to jail?" When I saw how much my words had hurt him, I quickly relented. "Besides, the soldiers made me angry. They were so arrogant. I was afraid of what they would do to you if . . . and I realized that you could never be like them. And you would have to be, wouldn't you . . . if you joined the army?"

"It's part of their code . . . order and discipline and unquestioning obedience to authority. Do you regret your decision now that the soldiers are gone?"

I felt tears burning. "What difference does it make? It's over and done."

"The Scriptures say a husband and wife will become one flesh. What you did . . . moved me . . . because it was such a loving act. You put my welfare before your own wishes." He was having trouble speaking as he battled his emotions. I felt a knot growing in my own throat.

"I know you felt something for me once, in the beginning," he continued. "I treasure our early days together before . . . this. And I pray that you'll feel the same affection for me again someday." He propped one elbow on the table and rested his forehead on his hand, shielding his eyes. "I know you still don't understand why I'm doing this . . . why I have to leave . . . why I'm making you move away from everyone you love . . ." He paused, then looked up at me. "But do you think you will ever be able to forgive me?"

The tears I had been holding at bay rolled down my cheeks, one after the other. I couldn't answer. I didn't know the answer.

"Louise . . . please say something."

I slowly lowered Sophie from my shoulder and held the swaddled bundle out to Friedrich, across the table. "Do you want to hold her one last time?"

He took her awkwardly, tenderly, nestling Sophie in the crook of his arm. He studied her delicate face for a moment, tracing her cheek with his finger. She rewarded him with a smile. When he closed his eyes and lowered his head, I thought he was weeping; then I realized that he was praying for our daughter. When he finished, he kissed her forehead. We both stood at the same time and Friedrich laid Sophie in my arms again. He gathered our things.

The door to the café closed behind us, cutting off the warmth. Dusk was falling and the air near the river had a frosty edge to it. A carriage and driver stood at the curb, as if waiting for us. I watched as if in a dream as Friedrich told the driver the address and paid him in advance. He lifted our bags aboard.

Friedrich's departure should have been a memorable occasion, marking a new chapter in both of our lives. Instead it would end like any ordinary departure, with a few hasty words, a quick embrace, the impatient stamping of horses.

"It's going to be all right, Louise, I promise you." He enfolded Sophie and me in his arms. "Everything is going to be all right for us in America."

Another tear escaped to race down my cheek at the dreaded word. Clinging to Sophie, I couldn't return his embrace. He bent to kiss my forehead, all he dared to do on such a busy street. It was a stranger's kiss, polite, tentative, and I remembered how he had once smothered me with kisses. He was no longer the same carefree man who had kissed me with playful abandon when we were first married, when our life together held only joy and promise.

"I love you, Louise," he whispered for the first time. "I love you so much."

I heard his words, but I didn't believe them. *No, Fritz*, I thought. *No you don't. You couldn't possibly do this to me if you loved me.*

SEVEN

Three days after I returned home from Aunt Marta's house, Friedrich's first letter arrived. It was little more than a hastily scrawled note. Its brevity confused me after his profession of love, and I wondered if it was because I hadn't been able to say "I love you" in return.

September 23, 1895
Louise,
I have arrived in Basel, Switzerland. By the time you read this, I should be on my way overland through France and Belgium to the Dutch port of Rotterdam. Please have my father ship the trunk I packed to the overseas office of the White Star Lines in Rotterdam.
Friedrich

Mama and Emil helped me pack our remaining belongings, and on a cold October morning a week after Friedrich left, Sophie and I moved back home to the farm. I settled into my old bedroom under the eaves, placing Sophie's cradle beside the big feather bed I had once shared with my sister Runa. Since my brother Kurt had already left for the army, the farm was also a refuge for his wife, Gerda, and their three small boys. We were two "widows" of the Kaiser's war schemes, raising our children alone. Gerda would spend the winter in her cottage, but when spring came she would have to move into the farmhouse with me so Papa could offer the cottage to the tenant he would hire to replace Kurt. Emil had been forced to wait a year before starting university, since Papa couldn't find anyone else to help him with his cattle and dairy herds. My heart ached for all of us. Our lives, our dreams, were in ruins.

Friedrich's next letter was delivered to me at the farm.

October 9, 1895
Dear Louise,
I have arrived in Rotterdam and have purchased a ticket in steerage on the White Star Lines ship, Bristol. *I depart in three days for Liverpool, then*

New York. I'm told it will take about ten days to cross the Atlantic. My trunk arrived safely at the shipping office. Thank you for having it sent. I trust you and Sophie are being well cared for at the farm. I'll write again as soon as I arrive in America. I miss you already.

Friedrich

I tried to imagine Friedrich boarding the ship, to picture the transatlantic voyage as he had described it to me before he left, but I couldn't do it. The only excursions I'd ever taken were on the Rhine, and I shrank in fear from sailing on a body of water so vast I would lose sight of its shores. In my mind, when Friedrich crossed the border of Germany—the only land I'd ever seen— he had stepped off the edge of the earth. The gray cloud of the unknown had engulfed him, as thick and deep and cold as a lowland fog.

His next letter was postmarked *New York.*

October 24, 1895
Dear Louise,

I have arrived at last in New York City. My ship docked yesterday morning, and I was ferried along with the other steerage passengers to the immigrant facility on Ellis Island. My processing went smoothly, as I am in good health, educated, and have pocket money and a sponsor. Many of the others did not fare nearly as well. Tomorrow I will take a train to my cousin's house in Pennsylvania, but for now I am writing to you from a very nice rooming house run by a German couple from Bonn. The Germans here in America are very helpful to their fellow countrymen, especially those of us who don't speak much English. In fact, you would never guess from the food and the atmosphere and the conversation here in the rooming house that I wasn't still in Germany.

I haven't seen much of New York City itself, although I did glimpse the great statue of Lady Liberty as we sailed up the river. It was very foggy when we docked, and today it was still gray and raining. It is quite cold as well. I am already wishing for a warmer overcoat and gloves.

Louise, I thank God that He led me to come over first and send for you and Sophie later. I believe that it was to spare you the ordeal of traveling in steerage. I had heard tales of how bad it was, but having lived through it, I now realize that I need to save more money for a second-class fare for you. I won't put you through what I went through. Most of the other steerage passengers were unbelievably poor and had no concept of cleanliness. I was fortunate to have only caught lice on the journey, and not consumption or cholera or something much worse. Saving the extra money will take more time, however, and it will mean that we'll be separated a little longer than I originally planned. I will work three jobs if I have to, and I promise to send for you as soon as I'm able. I pray that the time will pass quickly for both of us.

You can write to me in care of my cousin and send it to his address. By the time your first letter arrives I should be living there. Please write soon. I miss you both so much.

Love,
Friedrich

Even as I read Friedrich's letters describing America, I wouldn't face the reality of joining him. I'd settled back into my familiar routine on the farm, content with the illusion that my life there would never change. Surely Friedrich would return home to us once he was too old to serve in the army.

But eventually, the village gossip concerning my husband reached me at the farm. They had branded Friedrich a coward, a deserter—running lily-livered from his duty to the Fatherland. He would be unwelcome in Germany now even if he wanted to return. I was both pitied and shunned by the other villagers, many of whom had sons or husbands serving in the army. I was glad when the snow piled high in drifts that winter, isolating me from their cold stares.

November 10, 1895
Dear Louise,

Your first letter arrived yesterday, and I can't tell you how pleased I was to hear from you at last.

The countryside in this part of Pennsylvania reminds me very much of Germany, with farms and villages and rolling hills. In fact, much of it was settled by Germans. You will feel right at home here. I hate living in the city, but that's where most of the jobs are. A university degree from Germany doesn't count for much over here, and teaching is out of the question, even in private schools, until my English improves.

For now I've found work in the coal mines. They will hire almost anyone who is willing. The pay is fairly good, but the work is exhausting—ten hours a day, six days a week. You would hardly recognize me after a day's work, as I am black with coal dust. Later in the winter, I will get up two hours earlier every day to earn extra money cutting ice. The river will freeze solid this time of year, so we'll cut the ice into blocks and store it in sawdust until next summer.

*Please write again soon—and often. It meant the world to me to find a
letter from you after a long day of work. Kiss Sophie for me.*

Love,
Fritz

I felt so detached from Friedrich as I read his letters that they might as
well have come from a stranger. I didn't know this man who cut ice from frozen
rivers and labored in coal mines until he turned black. He lived his life over
there, I lived mine here.

The letters I composed to Friedrich in my mind were entirely different
from the ones I finally mailed to him. In my head I railed at him for sinking
to the level of a common laborer after earning a university degree. I reminded
him of how much he had loved to teach, of how happy we'd been in our cozy
cottage in the village. Sophie was growing up without him, I chided. She
wouldn't know him from a stranger. Was slaving underground in a coal mine
better than serving two years in the army? Was what he'd gained worth more
than what he'd lost?

The letters I wrote on paper were little more than weather reports and a
chronicle of Sophie's progress: her first tooth; her sprouting hair, which was
the same sandy color as his; her attempts to sit up, to roll over, to eat from a
spoon. If he noticed the lack of endearments in my letters he never spoke of
them.

December 5, 1895
Dear Louise,

*I've been attending Sunday worship services at a little mission church
that tries to bring the Gospel to coal miners and their families. The services
are in English because the pastor and many of the miners are Welch
immigrants, but there are a great many Germans in this area too. When
the pastor discovered my interest, he asked me to help him conduct services
in German. Last Sunday I preached my first sermon. It was quite well-
received. . . .*

Friedrich, a preacher? This wasn't the same man I'd consented to marry.
Half a world away, he was changing, becoming someone else. I began to dread
the day this stranger would send for me.

In all the bustle and excitement of Christmas on the farm, I barely had time
to think about Friedrich. It wasn't until Mama sent me into the parlor to light
the tree candles that I remembered the previous Christmas and all the changes
that had been set in motion that day. I found the atmosphere in the parlor

≫ 69 ≪

quite different from a year ago as well. Friedrich and Kurt were gone, Papa and Emil seemed beaten down by all the changes they'd been forced to make in their lives, and Ernst and Konrad seemed on edge, waiting to receive their own draft notices. As I wondered how many more changes would take place in the coming year, and if I'd still be in Germany next Christmas, I was overtaken by a panic so strong I could scarcely breathe.

Later, as we gathered around the tree to open our Christmas presents, we heard the jangle of sleigh bells in the farmyard. Since I was sitting closest to the door, I went to see who it was. It took me a moment to recognize the stranger standing on our doorstep, brushing snowflakes from his uniform.

"Merry Christmas, Louise."

"Kurt! For goodness' sake! Why didn't you tell us you were coming home?" His woolen uniform felt scratchy against my cheek as he hugged me. I caught the scent of bay rum and missed Friedrich.

"They gave me two days leave for Christmas. I wanted to surprise Gerda. Is she here?"

"Everyone's in the parlor, opening presents."

I followed him inside and watched Gerda's face light with joy and surprise when she saw her husband. Kurt couldn't disguise the longing in his eyes as he swept her into his arms and held her close. Then everyone began shouting and cheering all at once. Kurt's three boys attached themselves to his legs, clamoring for his attention. Mama pulled a lace handkerchief from her sleeve and dabbed at her eyes. Papa uncorked a bottle of his best brandy. "This calls for a celebration," he cried.

For the first time since he left, I missed the crush of my husband's embrace, the fervor of his kisses. I imagined Gerda nestled beside her husband tonight and realized how empty my bed felt without Friedrich. How was it possible to be so angry with him, yet to miss him so terribly?

Overwhelmed, I fled upstairs to my room. The sterling silver mirror, Friedrich's present to me last Christmas, lay on my dresser. I traced the engraved initials—L.S.—then turned it over and gazed at my reflection, blurred by falling tears. I didn't know who this woman was. My name was no longer Louise Fischer—the initials reminded me of that. I was Louise Schroder now, but who was she? Where did she belong? Papa's farmhouse wasn't "home" anymore, nor was the schoolmaster's cottage in the village. And I knew I didn't belong in America either.

I heard footsteps on the stairs, then Mama's soft voice behind me. "You miss your Friedrich, don't you, Liebchen."

"Yes," I whispered, wiping my tears. Mama's arms surrounded me.

"It won't be much longer now. He'll send for you soon." I lifted my head from her shoulder.

"But I don't want to go to America. I want Friedrich to come back home, like Kurt did. I want everything to be the way it was."

"I know, Liebchen. I know," she sighed. "But that just isn't going to happen."

March 2, 1896
Dear Louise,

I have wonderful news! I have been praying about finding a better home for us, as I know you would never be happy in the city, and God has answered my prayer in a most remarkable way. I have received an offer to pastor a small country church in a German community called Bremenville, ninety miles from here. The pastorate even includes a modest parsonage on about six acres of land beside the church. I was concerned, at first, that we couldn't afford to live on the meager pay, but construction is scheduled to begin soon on a new textile mill outside Bremenville and it will require hundreds of workers. How perfectly God fits everything together!

Now that the ice in the river has begun to thaw, I've started a new job—delivering the morning newspaper from the printers to newsstands throughout the city. The pay isn't bad for three hours of work, and I can still make it to the mine by 6:30 A.M.—provided the horse cooperates!

I have nearly enough money to send for you, Louise. We can celebrate Sophie's first birthday together this August. I know she is no longer the tiny newborn I kissed good-bye, but that's the way I still picture her. Whenever I see other men spending time with their families on Sunday afternoons, the longing I feel for my own family is more than I can bear.

Soon, Louise. Very soon we'll be together again.

With love,
Fritz

EIGHT

Spring arrived, bringing with it a beautiful, breezy day with sky the color of robins' eggs. Wooly white clouds skipped across it like lambs. Mama, Oma, and I carried the washtubs into the sunshine to launder our winter petticoats, flannel nightgowns, and Papa's woolen union suits. I tied a handkerchief over my nose and mouth and beat the dust from the rugs with a carpet beater, then we hung the feather beds on the line to air. Sophie watched us work from beneath the parasol of her wicker carriage. She was sitting so nicely now, propped up with pillows and bundled in sweaters. Her cheeks were as round and rosy as two apples.

Shortly before noon, Papa and Emil arrived home from the village, where they'd gone to do errands. But instead of driving the wagon into the barn to unload the supplies, Papa pulled into the yard and set the brake. His face was somber as he climbed down from the seat, his back and shoulders rigid, as if he were walking to a funeral. He strode to where I was scrubbing bed sheets on the washboard.

"This came. It's for you." His voice was as thick as the official-looking envelope he held out to me. As soon as I dried my hands on my apron and took it from him, Papa turned and hurried away. I knew without opening it that my tickets to America had arrived.

The sun should have disappeared behind a cloud, the wind should have suddenly blown bitter and cold, the birds should have stopped singing to mark this dreadful moment in my life. But none of that happened. Instead, Oma gave a little cry and covered her mouth with her hand. Mama's arms went limp, leaving the corner of the bed sheet she had been pegging to the line to billow like a loose sail in the wind.

"So. The day has finally come," she said.

I ripped open the envelope and quickly read the information, but later I would have to read it again as I would be unable to recall a word of it. It contained my second-class ticket on the *Hibernia*, departing Rotterdam for

New York on April 21, 1896. I had two weeks to prepare.

Without a word, I swept Sophie into my arms and tossed the envelope into her empty carriage, then set out across the muddy pasture toward the ancient beech tree near the creek. It had been a favorite refuge for Emil and me when we were children. We would scramble up its low-hanging branches like monkeys, fearlessly ascending to the very top for a glimpse of the village church steeples and the distant Rhine, snaking through the valley. One of our favorite games—one we made up—was called *Someday*.

"*Someday* I'm going to marry a handsome baron," I would say.

"*Someday* I'm going to hunt lions in darkest Africa," Emil would say.

Unlike Emil, I had never longed to wander very far from home in my *Someday* dreams. Now my one-way ticket to America had arrived, and I didn't know what to do. How I longed to be a child again, to return to the innocent days when Emil and I shared our dreams of the future. But I couldn't turn back the calendar any more than I could climb the tree wearing a long skirt and carrying Sophie in my arms.

If I stayed in Germany, I could probably apply for a divorce. After all, Friedrich had abandoned us eight months ago, hadn't he? He had broken the law by failing to report for the draft and by leaving Germany illegally. But was divorce the best choice for my daughter?

Sophie gnawed contentedly on my knuckle as she tried to work another tiny tooth through her gum. It was so quiet in the pasture that when someone approached, crossing the field behind me, I clearly heard the sound of footsteps rustling through the grass even before I turned to see who it was. I was hoping it was Emil, but I faced my father instead.

"What are you doing way out here, Louise? Don't you know it's dinnertime? Your mother is calling for you. Everything is on the table."

He looked tired, his broad shoulders sloping as if he wore weights on his wrists. For the first time, I noticed how much he had aged this past year, especially since Kurt and Friedrich had left. Papa hated it when Mama or any of the rest of us fussed over him, but I tenderly brushed wisps of loose straw from his jacket.

"I'm sorry, Papa. I needed to be alone for a while, to think. I'm trying to decide what to do."

"What do you mean *decide*? What's to decide?"

"Well . . . whether I'm going to stay here or go to America."

Papa's mouth worked, his lips pursing and unpursing as if he were chewing on something. It was a habit of his, whenever he battled his emotions. After a moment his back went stiff again, and he lifted his chin in the air. When he spoke, his voice was rigid as well.

"There is no decision to make. You cannot stay here. You cannot live in my house any longer."

"Papa! You don't mean it!"

"Of course I mean it! You are Friedrich's wife. You belong with him. That's the end of it."

"You would force me to leave home?"

"Didn't you hear me? This isn't your home anymore. You're a married woman now. It has been this way all through the ages—Sarah went with Abraham, Rebekah left her family, Rachel and Leah left their home—and you must leave too."

"Papa, no!"

"Oh yes! You stood in God's house and made a vow before Him that you would honor and obey your husband until separated by death. That wasn't just an idle promise, Louise. You vowed before God."

"I didn't know Friedrich would decide to move to America, or I never would have married him. I never would have vowed—"

"But you did vow. For better or for worse, for richer or for poorer. What God has joined can never be sundered."

"You wouldn't force me to leave against my will . . . I'm your daughter!"

"Not anymore." Some of the sternness had faded from his voice, replaced by sorrow. "I gave you away to your husband at your wedding, remember? Just as you and Friedrich must one day give Sophie away."

I clutched my daughter closer to me, unable to bear the thought of losing her.

"Whose child is she, Louise? She isn't mine, she's Friedrich's. He must raise her, not me."

Friedrich had spoken of us becoming one flesh. The union that had produced Sophie linked us together—I had helped him escape from the authorities because of Sophie. Now Friedrich and I could never be separated because of her. I understood all of this in my head, but my heart couldn't accept it.

"I can't leave my home, Papa!"

"Your home is with your husband and that's that. It's time to eat." He turned to stalk across the field toward the house, but not before I saw his jaw tremble, a sign of weakness he needed to hide from me. I knew that his outward anger had been a front to mask his sorrow. With my own heart as heavy as my dragging feet, I followed him.

Dinner was a somber affair. None of us had the strength to make small talk or to pretend that our grief didn't exist. Papa merely pushed his food around on his plate, and Emil bolted his so quickly I wondered if he'd even tasted it, then they both hurried out to the barn. Oma clung to Sophie all through the meal, aware that her time with her namesake was short. When she carried Sophie upstairs to change her, Mama and I were alone with the dinner dishes.

"Papa is making me leave," I finally said. "Did he tell you? He says I have no choice, I must go to America with my husband." Tears rolled down my cheeks and dropped into the soapy water.

"Papa is right," she said quietly. "You don't have a choice." She finished drying a cup and hung it on the hook in the cupboard before continuing. "When you were a little girl you wanted to be like Kurt and Emil, remember? You would put on their old boots and stomp around in the barn behind them. Their chores were more interesting, you insisted, more fun than ironing or mending or plucking chickens. You spent more time scrapping and wrestling with Emil and his friends than you did playing dolls with Ada and Runa." Mama put her hand on my shoulder and made me look at her.

"It's time to stop fighting, Louise. You're a woman, not a man. There is no 'happily ever after' like in the fairy tales. There is no paradise until we die. We're under a curse because of Eve's sin. As Eve's daughters, we will suffer pain in childbearing—as you already know. And the Bible says, 'Thy desire shall be to thy husband'—that's why you miss Friedrich. But God also said, 'He shall rule over thee.' Now and always. That's never going to change. God ordained that your husband make the decisions."

She picked up a dinner plate and slowly dried it, battling her own tears. "Your papa and I both wish that Friedrich had decided differently, but he didn't. He chose America. And now you have no choice but to go to him."

No choice. I had no choice.

For the next week, those words rang through my dreams at night and shaped the course of my days as I packed my belongings for America. Emil followed me around like a lost puppy, with Sophie perched on his wide shoulders. I spent a day in the village with Runa, saying farewell, then another afternoon with Ada, doing the same. I hadn't known when I'd said good-bye to Kurt at Christmas that I'd never see my older brother again.

Long before my heart was ready, I found myself standing beside the wagon as Papa loaded my trunks.

"You will take your leave here, in the privacy of our own home," Papa had informed us the night before I would board the ferry to Rotterdam. "I won't have my wife and children weeping in the middle of town for all the world to see."

Emil clung to me until Papa announced that the wagon was ready. "I can't watch you go," he mumbled, then he turned and raced across the farmyard. As he disappeared into the barn, I caught my last glimpse of his broad, muscled back and flying hair.

Mama, Oma, and I were all crying. They would have let me stay, I told myself, but they lacked the power. "Who will sit with me while my babies are born?" I wept. "Who will I turn to when Sophie has an earache or the colic?"

At the last moment, Oma thrust the crying cup into my hands. "I want you to take this with you to America. Give it to your little ones for their tears . . . and may it soothe away your own sorrow whenever you think of me."

"It won't help, Oma. I'll grieve until the day I die."

"Liebchen, the power isn't in the cup. It never was. The power to find joy again is within your own heart." As I kissed her and Mama for the last time, I didn't think I could ever feel joy again.

Papa said very little as we rode into town. Then he busied himself with the task of unloading my trunks and bags, making sure they were properly tagged for the voyage. As he waited on the wharf with me for the ferry that would carry me down the Rhine to Rotterdam, he kept clearing his throat. I wondered if it ached as much as mine. He didn't find the courage to face me until we heard the signal to board.

"I hope you will forgive me for sending you away," Papa said. "Your Friedrich is a good man—a man I can trust to care for my daughter. If he weren't . . ." He squinted into the distance as if the sun were in his eyes, even though it was at his back. "If he weren't such a fine man, I could never let you go."

He pulled me into his arms, hugging me so fiercely I feared that Sophie would be crushed between us. "May God go with you," he whispered. Then, like Emil, he turned his back and hurried away.

I walked up the gangway as if in a dream. While the other passengers lined the rails, waving handkerchiefs and hats to their loved ones on shore, I carried Sophie to our tiny stateroom, unwilling to watch my village, my home, disappear forever from sight. Life would continue without me—births, deaths, weddings; my nieces and nephews would grow to adulthood—and I would miss all of it.

Inside, my emotions seethed, a blazing cauldron of feelings I could barely control. The sorrow and loss I felt were greater than any I'd ever known, but they were dwarfed by my anger—white-hot rage at my inability to choose the course of my own life; bitter resentment that others possessed the power. The heat and violence of this inner storm frightened me.

I had once watched Papa and my brothers extinguish a grass fire, beating it down with blankets that had been soaked in water. Smoke and steam had encircled them, blurring them from view as the sparks and the flames gradually died. That's what I began to do with my inner fire—blanketing my emotions, obscuring the reality of how I felt, losing myself in the process. Smothering my feelings was safer than allowing them to burn out of control, and I needed to feel safe. I didn't realize until much later what a high price I would pay for extinguishing the flames. A heart that is deadened to pain is also deadened to love.

On the outside I probably looked the same. But inside, like Papa's charred fields, little remained except a blackened wasteland.

———

Friedrich had carefully arranged every stage of my journey to America, from the steam ferry that took me down the Rhine, to the lodging house where I would spend the night in Rotterdam, to the second-class stateroom aboard the *Hibernia*. Sophie and I shared the cabin with a woman from Dusseldorf named Magda Bauer, and her four children, Wilfred, Paul, Stefanie, and Karl. Friedrich had met Magda's husband, Gustav, in America. Sending for us at the same time assured them that we would have companionship on the journey.

Magda was seven years older than I was—I would be 21 next month—and quickly became like an older sister to me. Her youngest child, Karl, was not quite a year older than my Sophie. Magda was a plain, round-faced woman with wide hips and weary eyes; the quiet, hardworking sort of woman who would never be noticed in a crowd. With her drab hair and unadorned gray gown, she was a simple brown sparrow in a world of blue jays and cardinals. But she had a large, warm heart that was willing to encompass me, even though I gave her so little in return.

"Why don't you come up to the deck with us for some fresh air," she urged on our second full day at sea. "It has finally stopped raining, and the air will do both you and Sophie good."

"Oh, Magda, I can't bear the sight of all that water, stretching out in every direction, as far as the eye can see. It makes me feel so lost."

She had been bundling up her children in sweaters for their walk outdoors, but as she paused to study me, her eyes filled with compassion. "You three run ahead," she told her older children. "Wilfred, take Stefanie's hand. I'll be along in a moment." When they were gone, she sat on the bed beside me, her youngest son wailing loudly at being left behind.

"I daresay most of the people on board this ship are looking forward to a new life in America. But you're not, are you, Louise?"

"I've left everyone I loved back in Germany, except for Sophie. I have nothing to look forward to."

"Are you trapped in a marriage you didn't want?" she asked quietly.

"No, I consented to marry Friedrich, but I didn't know he would make me leave home. If I had known, I never would have married him."

"You would rather be a spinster?" Magda asked, smiling.

"No, that's a horribly lonely life, with everyone pitying you. And I wouldn't have had Sophie." I smoothed my fingers through her silky hair.

"Tell me about Friedrich. He treats you badly?"

"Oh no. We were very happy together . . . until the draft law changed. He was very kind to me . . . very affectionate . . . hardworking . . ." My voice trailed off as I realized that I couldn't think of any glaring faults.

"You are fortunate. Many wives are little more than their husbands' slaves. I've known men who were drunkards, men who couldn't hold a job, men who demanded their marital rights, giving little love or affection in return, men who worked their wives into early graves." Something about the haunting way she spoke sent a chill through me.

"Is your husband like those men, Magda?"

She smiled slightly but there was no humor in it. "Gustav is always chasing dreams. That's why he went to America—to chase his dreams. In Germany he changed occupations four times, always searching for something better. None of them ever worked out. Twice he borrowed money to embark on a new business venture, and twice he failed."

"Did he ever mistreat you?"

She sighed, considering the question for a moment. "Failure can rob a man of his dignity and self-respect. I suppose a wife is an easy target for his frustrations. A wise wife learns to keep out of his way."

"I'm so sorry, Magda."

She gave a small shrug, as if to say it didn't matter. "My childhood in Dusseldorf wasn't so nice—my life actually improved when I married Gustav. I believe that America will be better still."

"Has he found an occupation he enjoys?"

"Yes . . . for now." I saw the brief, humorless smile again. "Gus crossed over nearly two years ago. I was pregnant with Karl at the time. He has found a job selling farming equipment and says he's doing well with it. But someday he wants to own his own establishment and sell automobiles—another dream to chase. He thinks the horse and buggy will become a thing of the past and everyone will want a horseless carriage someday."

"What do you think, Magda?"

"I'm not a dreamer like Gustav. I've learned to look no further than to-morrow."

Her honesty lent me the courage to be open with her in return. "I know I've been miserable company, but it isn't because Friedrich mistreats me or anything like that. It's because I love my family and my home in Germany, and I didn't want to leave. Every mile this ship travels takes me farther and farther away, and I'm so afraid I'll never see any of them again."

"My life with Gustav has always been up and down—like the waves on the sea out there. You are down here, just now," she said, motioning with her hands. "And so you think you will never be on top of the wave again. But you will, I promise you."

" 'Joy and sorrow come and go like the ebb and flow,' " I quoted sadly.

"Yes, that's true . . . I like that."

"My grandmother had it stitched on a sampler. I saw it every day when I was growing up, but I never thought about what it meant . . . until now."

"It's the woman's job to adjust to that ebb and flow, Louise, like adjusting the seams of a dress. We take the seams in to make it smaller, we add fabric to make the dress bigger. . . ." She patted her ample hips and smiled. "And when there is nothing left to do with it, we turn it into scraps and make a quilt. Men create the original design and pattern; women can only alter it and tailor it as we go along. We will adapt to America, Louise. You'll see."

―――――

With the comfort of Magda's friendship—and five small children to look after between the two of us—the eleven days it took to cross the Atlantic passed quickly. On the morning that *Hibernia* steamed into New York harbor, the ship came alive with excitement, the decks swarming with jubilant passengers. It reminded me of the inside of one of Papa's beehives when it was time to remove the honey. People craned their necks for the first glimpse of America and to see the famous statue in New York harbor, a symbol of the liberty their new homeland offered. Since the statue symbolized freedom, I couldn't help wondering why "Liberty" was a woman instead of a man.

Horns blasted and gulls screamed as tugboats guided the ship to the pier upriver. Stocky and plain, the hardworking tugboats reminded me, not unkindly, of my friend Magda. As second-class passengers, she and I had our entrance papers processed on board and would be spared the steerage passengers' ordeal on Ellis Island. Clutching Sophie, my satchel in hand, I moved through customs in a daze. I knew that Friedrich would be among the crowd waiting on shore behind the wire netting, and I scanned all the faces for his as I finally made my way down the gangplank. Then, above the sound of cheering and people calling their loved-ones' names, I heard my own.

"Louise! Over here! . . . Sophie! Louise!"

I froze at the bottom of the ramp. A man I didn't recognize pushed his way to the front of the mob, waving and calling my name. At first I thought that Friedrich had sent someone else to fetch me, but as the man drew near I saw that it was my husband after all. The sun had bleached his hair the color of flax, and his skin was deeply tanned. But most shocking of all, he had shaved his beard and mustache. I had never seen him without them.

"Louise! Oh, Louise!" he cried as he lifted me off my feet and twirled me around. He hugged me so hard my wide-brimmed hat slipped off. His arms and chest felt more muscular than I'd remembered, and I thought of the brothers I would never see again. Friedrich's joy overflowed at the sight of us, but I had given up too much to feel any joy at our reunion. My smile felt pasted in place.

Friedrich reached out his arms to Sophie but she drew back in fear, hiding her face on my shoulder. "Give her time, Friedrich. I'm sure she'll warm to you."

"She's grown so big. And she's almost as pretty as her mother. Oh, Louise! I'm so glad you've come at last!"

I searched in vain for something to say in reply.

"Fred . . . Hey, Fred, you ready to go?"

Friedrich turned to answer a nattily dressed man in a straw boater hat. "Yes, any time you are, Gus." When I saw that the man held Magda's oldest son Wilfred by the hand, I realized that he must be Gustav Bauer. Friedrich introduced us.

Gustav looked to be a few years older than Magda, probably thirty or thirty-one, with the ruddy face of a man who likes his drink. Friedrich was dressed conservatively in his best dark suit—the one he'd worn when we were married—but Gustav's clothes were in the newest style: a blue-and-gray-striped suit and tie, a striped shirt with a stiff white collar, a shiny gold watch-chain dangling across his vest, his straw boater hat tilted at a rakish angle. A cigarette drooped from his bottom lip. He spoke very loudly, smiling as he pinched his children's cheeks, but I had the feeling that his temperament was much like a spring day—warm and sunny one moment, clouding over the next. The difference between his appearance and Magda's was so startling that I couldn't help wondering why he would choose such a plain wife. I watched her rounding up her children and their belongings while Gus chatted with Friedrich, and I thought of her words: *Many wives are little more than their husbands' slaves.*

"What did Gustav call you?" I whispered as we walked toward the row of delivery wagons.

"Fred. That's how my name translates into English. It's what all the Americans call me."

I hated it. It sounded so bland . . . like cooked vegetables without any butter or seasonings. "Must I call you that too?" I asked.

He stopped walking to turn and smile down at me. "You may call me anything you like . . . just don't call me late to dinner."

"What?"

"I'm sorry," he said, laughing. "That's just an American expression I picked up along the way."

As he made arrangements with a driver to collect my trunks, it sounded odd to hear Friedrich speaking another language—although when the drayman had difficulty understanding him, I gathered that Friedrich still didn't speak English too well. I listened to the strange babble all around me, and tears came to my eyes at the thought of learning a new language, new customs. I felt like a paper character, cut out of my familiar context and pasted in the wrong place.

On the carriage ride to the rooming house, I saw all that I ever cared to see of New York City. It was dirty and smelly near the wharves and unbelievably noisy as vendors competed with each other, hawking their wares from carts that they pushed through the lanes—selling everything from newspapers to roasted sweet potatoes. I had never seen anything like the tangle of horses and delivery wagons and carriages that jammed the narrow, littered streets.

"Not every part of New York looks like this," Friedrich assured me. "Up on Fifth Avenue, where the Vanderbilts and Carnegies live, there are wide, tree-lined boulevards and magnificent mansions."

But that wasn't the side of New York that greeted me. Most of the buildings were ramshackle wooden structures, called tenements, that looked as though they would topple over on me. Everything in America looked newly built and hastily thrown together, nothing at all like the centuries-old buildings I was used to in Germany.

I spent my first night in the same German rooming house that Friedrich had stayed in months ago. Comforted by the cadences of my own language and the tastes of familiar foods, I clung to the hope that I might survive this drastic transplantation after all. Once we retired to our room, though, I suffered the nervous unease of my wedding night all over again. I felt shy and uncertain with this clean-shaven stranger the Americans called Fred. Friedrich was tender and patient with me, just as he had been the night we were married nearly two years ago. I thought of Magda and her haunting words: *Some men demand their marital rights, giving little love or affection in return.*

I knew that my husband was a good man, as Papa had said. He didn't drink alcohol or abuse me or treat me like a slave. Why, then, couldn't I love him as he so obviously loved me?

NINE

"You were right," I told Friedrich, "this countryside does remind me of home." I gazed out of the window of the passenger train at a green patchwork of rolling farmland—fruit orchards and dairy farms, scattered forests and hills. We had left the ugliness of New York City behind and traveled into the state of Pennsylvania.

"That's one of the reasons I decided to settle here," Friedrich said. "I'd hoped that the familiar surroundings would help you feel more at home."

"I keep thinking we'll ride over the next hill and I'll see Papa's farmhouse. Those could be his cattle grazing in the field . . . his horses pulling that plow. . . ." Friedrich squeezed my hand, then returned to the formidable task of trying to win Sophie's affection. She clung to me as if overwhelmed by all the strange new sights and sounds, refusing to accept even a sweet from her father's hand. But when he enticed her with a game of peekaboo, hiding behind his hat then peeking out again, Sophie's resolve began to weaken. It had been a favorite game of hers, played with Uncle Emil.

Late in the afternoon, the train pulled into the station in Bremenville. The Squaw River, which flowed through town, wasn't nearly as wide or majestic as the Rhine, but the village, nestled at the base of Squaw Mountain, was pleasant nonetheless. I was relieved to see that many of the signs in the store windows were in both English and German. Even so, Bremenville looked very American to me. Most of the buildings were constructed of wood, with roofs that were flat or covered with dark shingles if they were peaked. The houses looked flimsy to me, as if a strong wind would blow them over. The public buildings in Germany had been huge, barnlike structures built of brick and stone, their humped roofs red-tiled. Only the main street of Bremenville was paved, and the sidewalks, when there were any, were made out of wood. I missed the rumbly cobblestone streets of home.

We said good-bye to Magda and her children at the train station. The home Gustav had rented for them was in the village, on one of the steep streets partway up Squaw Mountain. One of the deacons from Friedrich's church, Arnold Metzger, met us at the station with his wagon and drove us to our new home across the river, a mile outside the village. Along the way, Friedrich pointed to a cluttered work site near the river where a wood and brick structure was under construction.

"That's the new textile mill I'm helping to build." I remembered his clumsy efforts with the bookshelf back in Germany and found it hard to imagine. "Of course, I'm not one of the carpenters or masons," he explained. "All I'm good for is hauling and loading, but even that pays pretty decently."

"Is that the church?" I asked when I saw a white, wooden steeple in the distance, poking through the trees.

"*Ja*, that's it," Herr Metzger replied.

The road was little more than a lane, bordered by fields and woodland, following the course of the river below it. I didn't see any other houses.

"Do we have neighbors nearby?" I asked.

"The Metzgers are the closest ones, about a quarter of a mile up the road. I know it seems isolated now, but with the new mill going in, I wouldn't be surprised to see new streets and houses all the way from here to the village someday."

I felt gritty, hot, and weary after nearly two weeks of travel, but I saw boyish excitement in Friedrich's eyes as he swung me down from the wagon in the driveway of the parsonage.

"Well, Louise, this is your new home. What do you think of it?"

I thought that the square, clapboard house, painted a dingy gray with darker gray trim, was one of the homeliest I'd ever seen. I couldn't lie, but I didn't want to say anything insulting in front of Herr Metzger either.

"It . . . um . . . it looks big," I managed. "Much bigger than our cottage back home. What will we do with so many rooms?"

Friedrich laughed and chucked Sophie under her chin. "We'll just have to fill them up with children, I suppose. Why don't you have a look around while we unload these trunks."

I decided to start with the church, thirty yards away, and walked across the weed-choked yard that separated it from the parsonage. Friedrich had explained that the church served about forty families from Bremenville and a neighboring village. The white frame sanctuary was boxy, plain, and in desperate need of a coat of paint. Up close, the steeple looked as if someone had chopped off a third of it, then pasted the belfry back on top.

The arched door was unlocked. I stepped inside to be greeted by a musty odor so disagreeable that even Sophie wrinkled her nose. Simple oak pews flanked the center aisle, facing an unadorned pulpit. The four narrow windows on each of the side walls were made of clear glass. I remembered the rich, walnut woodwork and stained-glass windows in the stone church where I'd worshiped back home and felt cheated. I had been forced to give it up—for this?

By the time I walked back to the farmhouse, Herr Metzger was preparing to leave. I thanked him for fetching me from the train station.

"My wife will pay you a visit in a few days, when you're settled," he promised before he drove away.

I turned back to my new home, staring in dismay at the dingy gray box. There were two large maple trees in the front yard, but nothing else; no bushes or shrubs, no flowers or climbing vines or painted flower boxes.

"Come inside and let me show you around," Friedrich urged. I followed him up crooked wooden steps and across a wide front porch with railings all around it. "This will be a nice place to sit on summer evenings when it's hot," he said.

The walls of the frame house seemed flimsy and thin compared to the thick-walled German farmhouses I was used to. I wondered what would happen when the winter wind blew. The front door opened onto a dark hallway with stairs leading to the second floor. Friedrich opened the door to a small room on the right. "This will be my study someday. Can't you picture it with a desk and some bookshelves?"

The parlor was through the doorway on our left, and beyond it was a formal dining room with a bay window. All of the rooms were sparsely furnished with items donated by the parishioners. Undismayed by the barrenness of the huge, high-ceilinged rooms, Fritz showed me a thick magazine.

"This is the Sears Roebuck catalogue. It has everything we'll need to furnish a house. And the prices are very reasonable too. We just mail in our order with the money, and they deliver it by mail or railroad freight." I tried to feign interest as Friedrich leafed through the pages, pointing to pictures of upholstered sofas, rocking chairs, oak bedroom sets with dressers and nightstands—even pianos and sewing machines. But Friedrich was too excited to linger over the catalogue for very long.

"Wait until you see the kitchen." He led me by the hand into a kitchen so large that Mama, Oma, both of my sisters, and I could have all worked without bumping elbows. It had a cast-iron cook stove that would burn either wood or coal, a pantry lined with shelves, a granitine sink with a hand pump, a well-worn linoleum floor, and wainscoted walls. A gas lamp hung from the ceiling and three extra lamps lined a shelf above a porcelain-topped worktable.

"There's plenty of storage space for your dishes and things," Friedrich said, unlatching the door to one of the two tall cupboards that hung from the wall. "And when we get hungry, there's some chicken and dumplings in the icebox for our supper, courtesy of Mrs. Metzger."

I was weary of forcing a smile on my lips that I didn't feel. For some reason, I felt close to tears. I turned to peer out of the kitchen window to hide them and saw a couple of apple trees, a garden area, a small barn, the privy, and two other outbuildings.

Friedrich took my hand again."Want to see upstairs?" His grin vanished when he saw my face. "Louise, what's wrong?"

"I'm sorry . . . I guess I'm just feeling a little overwhelmed."

He lifted Sophie from my arms and set her on the floor. When she began to cry I reached for her but Friedrich stopped me, pulling me into his arms instead.

"She'll be all right for a moment or two. I've scarcely had a chance to hold you without the baby wedged between us." He gave me a long, lingering kiss, then took my face in his hands. "I love you, Louise. And I'm going to do everything in my power to make you happy here."

Friedrich meant well, but all my joy had been extinguished as I had sailed away from my home and my family in Germany. This was my first day in my new house in America. I should have been content. But I was sure that I would never really be happy again.

———

I soon learned that I had many expectations thrust upon me as Pastor Schroder's wife. In nice weather, Friedrich liked me to go with him on his rounds, paying social and condolence calls on his parishioners, bringing meals to the sick and shut-in. Although I was one of the youngest wives, I was expected to lead the women's missionary society, raising funds in support of overseas missions in China. I was called upon to help prepare meals for all the church functions, such as picnics and weddings and funeral luncheons.

Friedrich was immensely successful and well-liked in the community, but as I listened to the glowing tales of the former pastor's wife, I realized that compared to her, I was a great disappointment in every way—not the least of which was my inability to play the piano. Judging by all the attention and the pitying looks the older matrons gave Friedrich—the gifts of breads and pies and pastries they brought to him—I knew they all felt very sorry for poor Pastor Schroder. What a heavy burden he carried, encumbered with a useless wife like me.

Although I knew a lot of women in the village by name, I didn't feel close to any of them. Magda was the only "family" I had, and I didn't see her very often. She lived more than a mile away on the other side of the river. Gustav traveled a great deal with his work, stranding her at home without transportation. I looked forward to Sunday church services not for the opportunity to worship God, but because I would see Magda.

I blamed Friedrich's God for my losses. Friedrich preached that He was a God of love, and that He'd shown His love by sacrificing His Son, Jesus Christ. But to me He was the God who had told Friedrich not to serve in the army, the God who talked to him in dreams, the God who convinced him to immigrate, and then held me to my marriage vows until death.

The God I'd once known had been left behind in the stone church in Germany where Papa was an elder, Kurt was a deacon, and our lives were held in perfect balance—the church where Sophie was baptized at the walnut font in the nave, and where my grandfather rested beneath a stone marker in the cemetery outside. Having faith in Friedrich's God meant giving up control of my fate. He was one more person who wielded power over my life.

And so I sat in the pew with Sophie on my lap, Sunday after Sunday, too angry to pray. The only control I had was over my emotions, and I chose bitterness and resentment.

Friedrich was jubilant when we learned later that first summer that I was expecting. We both wanted another baby very badly. But in September I suffered a miscarriage.

"It's little wonder that a child can't live in my womb," I told him. "I feel so dead inside . . . like I have nothing to live for."

"Aren't we enough, Louise?" he whispered as he lay in the darkness beside me. "Aren't Sophie and I enough?" But I was afraid to love them, afraid I would lose them too.

My grief and despondency lasted well into December. It was Friedrich who decided we needed a Christmas tree and dragged one into our parlor, trimming it with candles and ornaments from home. It was Friedrich who cut pine boughs to decorate the church for the Christmas Eve service. And it was Friedrich who greeted all the parishioners who stopped by the house, bringing Christmas gifts and baked goods. If the Metzgers hadn't invited us to their home for Christmas dinner, we wouldn't have had a dinner at all.

Friedrich was in the habit of rising early every morning to read the Scriptures and pray before he left for work at the mill. One morning when I was unable to sleep, I found him on his knees before dawn. "What do you need to pray for?" I asked bitterly. "You got your own way. Your prayers were answered. We're here in America where you wanted to be."

I saw the sorrow in his eyes as he pulled himself to his feet. "I pray that you will forgive me for bringing you here," he said softly. "And that you will love me again someday."

Friedrich never stopped trying to show his love and to win mine in return. True to his promise, he filled our home with furnishings from the Sears Roebuck catalogue and stocked my kitchen with blue-enameled cookware and all the latest cooking gadgets. In springtime he brought me bunches of violets and apple blossoms, tucking a flower in my hair or in the buttonhole of my shirtwaist. In summer he presented me with the first ripe tomato from our garden, still warm from the sun. When I stood at the sink washing dishes he would often come up behind me and encircle me with his arms, resting his head against the back of my shoulder. He never begged me to love him or demanded that I return his love. He was never angry or impatient with me, even when I was sunk in despair for days at a time. He simply loved me. But I felt nothing in return.

I learned that I was expecting again the following spring, one year after arriving in America, and suffered a second miscarriage that summer. I had lost so much weight, the doctor said that I was too unhealthy to carry a child to term. I gazed at the hollow-eyed woman I saw in the silver mirror and wondered how Friedrich could still think she was pretty.

My despondency deepened my second winter in America when Mama wrote to tell me that Oma had died. She had suffered a bad fall and had died a week later. I buried Oma's crying cup deep inside a drawer in the sideboard.

Meanwhile, my friend Magda had delivered her fifth child, a son, and was pregnant with her sixth. Gustav had become dissatisfied with his job selling farm equipment. He had worked at the mill with Friedrich for a while, but he had been fired after an argument with his boss. Now he worked as a traveling salesman, peddling patent medicines door to door. Friedrich bought a supply of Dr. Brown's Vegetable Cure from him, hoping it would cure my malaise.

Magda had so little compared with me—a tiny, rented house full of ragged children; a sporadic income; a husband who showed her little affection. Why couldn't I appreciate the bounty Friedrich's labors had produced? His church was thriving, his sermons so popular with the new mill workers that his congregation had doubled to eighty families. With the increase in pay, he no longer needed to work at the mill but was studying books on theology and Greek, preparing to apply for ordination. We'd been given a milk cow and some chickens, we had fruit trees and a garden—all that we could ever need or want. Yet Magda thrived and I was miserable.

———

In July of 1899, I discovered that I was in a family way for a fourth time. Unwilling to lose another child, Friedrich hired one of the Metzgers' plump, teenaged daughters to help me with the cleaning and washing. Sophie, who would turn four the following month, adored her.

That August we learned that my brother Emil had been drafted after completing only two and a half years at university. When he finished his military training he was shipped to the German colonies in the Far East. Emil's letters read like adventure novels. He was so excited by all that he saw and did that he didn't have time to be homesick. He sent me a photograph of himself in his uniform, and it brought a rare smile to my lips. "He's finally seeing the world," I told Fritz. "That was his *Someday* dream."

I was relieved to discover that I didn't need to learn English, since I could talk to Magda and most of the other villagers in German. Friedrich had learned to read and speak English quite well after nearly four years in America, so he would translate the newspaper for me, especially any news that involved Germany or the Far East, where Emil was stationed. I would sit in the rocking chair in the parlor every evening after dinner, or on the front porch if the weather was nice, and listen while Friedrich read me the news of the day.

Then on a rainy day in April of 1900, Emma was born—a child of a new century, a new homeland. As Friedrich baptized her in his musty-smelling church, I realized that unlike her parents and older sister, Emma was an American.

Caring for her brought me more pleasure than I'd known for a long time, and my health was much improved. The only dark cloud on the horizon was the news of the Boxer Rebellion in the Far East and the fear that my brother would be swept into the maelstrom.

———

On a scorching summer evening in late August, the telegraph boy rode his bicycle into our backyard. I had just rocked four-month-old Emma to sleep and laid her in her basket, clad in only her diaper. Sophie, who had just turned five, was cooling off with a bath, happily splashing in the kitchen washtub. I stood by the kitchen door listening to the sound of crickets and katydids, watching the fireflies wink on and off in the tall grass beside the barn.

Friedrich was hoeing a row of pole beans in the garden, stripped to his singlet and trousers in the blistering heat. When he saw the telegraph boy, he propped his hoe against the shed and walked across the yard. I watched him as he studied the envelope and saw his shoulders sag as if he'd just hefted a heavy sack of grain onto his back. When he glanced up at the house, I was gripped by a terrible dread. He dug a coin from his pocket for a tip and the boy wheeled away. I saw Fritz glance at the house again before ripping open the envelope.

I couldn't watch. I turned away and pulled Sophie from the water, wiggling and protesting. "No, Mama . . . wait! I want to play some more."

"It's time for bed." I towelled her dry, none too gently.

"But it isn't dark yet. Can't I catch fireflies with Papa?"

"No. Put your nightgown on. Now." I was immediately sorry for speaking sharply, promising to read *Hansel and Gretel* to make it up to her. I moved through the routine of bedtime—unplaiting her braids, brushing her hair, reading the fairy tale, saying her prayers—as if slogging through deep water.

I was upstairs when I heard the screen door slap shut. Friedrich's work boots echoed on the linoleum floor as he paced around the kitchen. I hugged Sophie so tightly she squealed. After tucking her in, I slowly descended the stairs. Friedrich waited for me in the kitchen, his face white with pain.

"Is it Emil?" I whispered.

He nodded. "The Chinese rebels attacked a train carrying allied troops to Peking. Emil . . . Emil was killed." He held his arms out to me, waiting to comfort me, but I couldn't run to him. I didn't want his comfort. He and God were all wrapped up in one package and I felt betrayed by both of them, abandoned and angry.

I took refuge in the parlor. It was dark and gloomy in the waning twilight, the curtains drawn against the heat. Emil's photograph beckoned me from the mantel shelf. He looked so different in his uniform, his square jaw set, his posture a stiff military pose. He had plastered his dark hair flat across his forehead, but I could imagine his cowlick sticking up beneath his hat just the same. His wide mouth wore the faint curl of a smile, as if laughing at some private joke, and I had a sudden memory, crisp and clear, of Emil's unfettered laughter—of all of us laughing a lifetime ago. If only we could have remained safe in that happy world.

"Louise, are you okay?" Friedrich asked from the doorway. He had followed me into the parlor.

"Well, you were right," I said bitterly. "Right about all of it—the war, the destruction, death . . . It all happened just as you said it would."

"It gives me no pleasure to be right." Friedrich's voice sounded strange. I looked up from my brother's photograph and saw tears glistening in his eyes. "Emil was so bright, Louise, so talented, so eager to embrace life. He could have been anything he wanted to be." He crushed the telegram in his hand as he wiped his tears with his fist.

I couldn't weep. In my mind I saw myself beating down the flames of rage and despair once more. Clouds of smoke and steam engulfed me, blocking my husband from sight.

"Louise?" Friedrich's voice sounded far away. He stood with his arms outstretched to me again, his eyes pleading. I shook my head, rejecting his embrace, but his next words surprised me.

"I need you, Louise. Please hold me."

TEN

"Look, Mama! A sunbeam, a sunbeam!"

I turned from the sink full of dishes I was washing and saw Emma, who was four years old, standing in a beam of sunlight. It slanted through the kitchen window like a theatrical spotlight, illuminating the floor where she stood.

"Isn't it beautiful, Mama?" She lifted her face and stretched out her arms, dancing and twirling to a song that only she could hear. The sun illuminated the fine tendrils of hair that had escaped from her braids and bathed her head in a golden halo. It was a dance of pure joy, performed by a child who was happy simply to be alive.

"The sunshine won't last," eight-year-old Sophie told her. "There are too many clouds in the sky. See? It's disappearing already." She was so different from Emma, so serious and practical. Friedrich called her his little worrywart.

"Come on, Eva, you'll dance with me!" Emma grasped two-year-old Eva's chubby hands and pulled her to her feet. The baby giggled until she hiccuped as her sister twirled her around the kitchen floor. From the time she could walk, Emma had skipped through life with a song, dancing among the fireflies in summer, catching snowflakes on her tongue in winter, embracing mounds of colored leaves in fall. Where had it come from, this optimism of hers? Had being born an American given her this nature, just as being born a German had given Sophie hers?

"Eva and I are doing an Indian rain dance," Emma announced.

"No, Emma. You do a rain dance if you *want* rain," Sophie said. "We have too much rain already, right, Mama?"

"Yes, I'm afraid we do."

It had rained for the entire month of April that year, 1904, and showed no sign of stopping. Added to the snowmelt from an unusually heavy winter, the rain had swollen the Squaw River to its highest level on record, twenty feet above flood stage. From our front porch, I could almost watch it rising steadily, hour after hour. The grassy bank along the river was now submerged, bringing the rushing, chocolate-colored rapids nearly level with the road. The trees alongside it waved their branches out of the water like drowning men. If it didn't stop raining soon, the river would spill across the road and into our front yard. There were already huge puddles in all the low spots by our barn, and the churchyard where the wagons parked every Sunday was flooded halfway up the hitching posts.

I heard Friedrich's boots clumping up our cellar stairs and watched him duck his head as he emerged through the door with a crate of potatoes in his arms. Winter-long tendrils sprouted from the potatoes like pale worms. "This is the last load," he said. "Is there room for them in the pantry?"

"I'll make room." I was weary after the long morning's work, but since the water was slowly seeping into our root cellar, the perishables had to be moved.

"Ugh! What's that white stuff in your hair, Papa?" Sophie asked.

"Probably cobwebs. The rafters are covered with them."

Emma tugged on her father's pant leg. "What do they feel like, Papa? Can I touch them?" Friedrich had to be tired after countless trips up and down the steep steps, but he crouched beside his daughter, still cradling the box of potatoes, and bent his head toward her. Emma's eyes shone with delight as she combed them from his hair with her fingers. "Ooo, they're real sticky! Come feel them, Sophie."

"No, I hate spiders."

"Do you know why cobwebs are so sticky?" Friedrich asked as he rose to his feet. "It's so that when an insect flies into them, they'll become trapped. Spiders eat insects, you see." He deposited the crate on the pantry floor and returned to the kitchen. "Louise, I think I'd better go over and check the church basement too. There are some old hymnals and church records stored down there. I should move them to the belfry."

"You'll need a rowboat to get there," I said. "The churchyard has turned into a lake."

"Can I go with you, Papa?" Emma begged. "I want to play in the puddles."

"It's pouring rain!" Sophie said. "You'll catch your death!" She sounded much too fretful for an eight-year-old.

"We'll take a humbrella, won't we, Papa."

Friedrich smiled down at Emma and gently tugged one of her pigtails. "Not this time, Liebchen. It isn't safe to play in the water when there's a flood like this. It might carry diseases from all the flooded outhouses. It can make you very sick."

"See, Emma? I told you you'd catch your death." Sophie looked too smug. Quick as a flash, Emma wiped her hand on Sophie's head, then stuck out her tongue.

"Now you got cobwebs in your hair!" She raced from the kitchen with Sophie close behind, wailing and scrubbing her head with the dish towel. I thought their behavior shameful, but Friedrich could barely keep from laughing out loud.

"That Emma's a regular imp, isn't she? Who do you suppose she gets it from?"

"Emil used to tease Ada and Runa with snakes and spiders and things like that all the time," I said without thinking. A huge lump suddenly caught in my throat. I hadn't spoken Emil's name in nearly four years.

For a moment, I could see my brother so clearly in my mind—his crooked grin, his wild tangle of dark hair—then a flash of pain scorched my heart when I remembered that he was dead. I dried my hands and turned away from the sink to tackle the job of reorganizing the pantry. I would beat down the flames of sorrow with hard work.

"Louise . . ." Friedrich's voice was gentle as he stood in the pantry doorway behind me. "Tell me what else you remember about Emil."

I shook my head. I couldn't talk about my brother. I couldn't talk about my family in Germany at all. I read their letters in silence, wrote back to them in silence. My daughters had never heard tales of my childhood in Germany.

"I thought you were going over to the church," I said without turning around.

"It can wait. Louise, if you would only talk about him, maybe it would help you grieve."

When I didn't answer, Friedrich sighed. A few minutes later the kitchen door closed behind him.

———

Late that afternoon it was still raining hard. I could tell by the way Friedrich gazed through the window of his study at the muddy river across the road that he was worried. The wind had begun to blow so violently that when Peter Schultz, one of Friedrich's parishioners, banged on our back door, I thought at first that it was a loose shutter or a tree branch striking the house.

"Pastor Schroder, I'm terribly sorry to bother you," Peter said, "but it's my father. The consumption is about to take him, and he's asking for you to come and pray with him."

"Of course, Peter. Let me get my coat. Should I follow you in my wagon?"

"No sense risking two wagons getting stuck in the mud. I'll bring you home again after supper."

"All right, if you're sure . . ."

"It's the least I can do for troubling you like this."

Peter appeared to be drenched to the skin, and as I watched Friedrich put on his hat and coat, I knew he would probably be just as soaked by the time they reached the Schultz farm three miles upriver.

The three girls were lined up like stairsteps, watching. Friedrich caressed each of their heads briefly, then kissed my cheek. "Bye. I probably won't be back until after dark. How were the roads, Peter?" he asked on his way out the door. "Is there much flooding?"

"The water was almost up to my wagon hubs in some of the low places . . ." That was all I heard as the door closed behind them.

"Will Papa be home in time to tuck us in?" Emma asked as I helped the girls get ready for bed later.

"I don't think so."

"He has to wait for old Mr. Schultz to die," Sophie said. She sounded very matter-of-fact, but when I looked at her, I saw that her eyes were brimming with tears.

"What's wrong, Liebchen?" I asked.

"It's spooky here all alone, without Papa." The rain drummed hard against the slanted ceiling of their bedroom. I understood how she felt.

"Papa will come in and give you a good-night kiss, even if you're asleep," I said.

Tears spilled down her cheeks. "Peter Schultz said that his papa was going to die. I couldn't bear it if . . . I would be so sad if . . ."

"Shh, Sophie. Don't cry. . . ." I pulled her tightly to me, muffling her words before she could speak them. Her sisters watched us, wide-eyed, not quite understanding what was going on. "Mr. Schultz is an old man with grandchildren. He's lived a long, useful life already." I dried her tears, and because of the stormy night, I tucked all three of them into the big double bed in Sophie's room, promising to stay with them until they were asleep.

I was in the parlor, pacing, when the mantel clock Friedrich had bought from Sears Roebuck struck nine. My ears had been straining to hear the sound of a horse and wagon outside, and I jumped in fright when the clock broke the silence. Once again I pressed my face to the window and peered out. It was too dark to see if the flood had crossed the road, but it had been raining steadily since Friedrich left five hours ago, so I could well imagine that it had. I decided to wait another half hour for him, then go to bed. Perhaps he had judged it best to wait until morning to return home.

At twenty past nine I finally heard a wagon pull up out front, and I rushed to open the door. But it wasn't Friedrich who stood dripping on my porch.

"Herr Metzger! What's wrong?" He appeared wild-eyed and dishevelled, as if the hounds of hell had been pursuing him through the wind and rain. My heart began to race.

"Where's Pastor Schroder?" he asked breathlessly.

"He went to pray with old Mr. Schultz earlier this evening and he hasn't come back yet."

Herr Metzger groaned and clutched his forehead. "The Schultzes live even farther upstream!"

"Yes . . . Won't you please tell me what's wrong?"

"The old earthen dam on Squaw Lake is threatening to give way. They're warning everyone who lives near the river to evacuate. Grab your children quickly and come with us. We can make room for you in our wagon."

"I'm sure Friedrich will be home any minute," I said, forcing myself to remain calm. "He has likely heard the warning by now, since the Schultzes live near the river too."

"There's no time to wait for Friedrich. You must get your family to higher ground before the dam breaks!"

"Yes, of course . . . I understand," I said. "But I think Friedrich would want us to wait for him."

"There isn't time! When that dam goes, all the water in Squaw Lake is going to come rushing down this valley faster than any of us can possibly run. The force of it could wash your house away. The river is almost on your doorstep now, as it is. Please come with us. Write the pastor a note. Tell him we're going up to my brother's house across the river, where it's safe."

I drew a deep breath, then exhaled slowly to prove I was calm. "Thank you for your kindness, Herr Metzger, but I want to wait for Friedrich."

"But, Mrs. Schroder—"

"I appreciate your concern," I said, "but I'm sure your own wife and daughters must be anxious to leave." I planted my hands on his chest and began pushing him firmly toward the door. I wanted Friedrich to come back and take us to safety, not Herr Metzger. He gazed at me sadly, shaking his head.

"I tried . . . God knows, I tried. . . ." he mumbled, then hurried away.

I stood on the porch, shivering, watching the wagon until it disappeared from sight. The road was so flooded that his horses appeared to be walking on water, while the wagon plowed downriver like a boat. I turned to gaze in the opposite direction, hoping to see Friedrich coming to save us. But after watching for twenty minutes or more, there was still no sign of him.

Then, above the drumming of the rain on the porch roof, a steady roaring sound gradually grew in my consciousness like a mighty crescendo until it seemed to fill the night. *The river*. Swollen and angry, it prowled in the darkness just beyond my doorstep, stalking my family. Any moment now, it might rise up like an angry monster and devour us all. I finally understood what Herr Metzger had been desperate to make me understand.

My family. I had to get my family to safety.

I had always depended on Friedrich to make the decisions and decide on a course of action, but this time I couldn't wait for Friedrich to save us. For once in my life I was responsible for my own life—and for my daughters' lives. They were depending on me to make the right decision. *What a heavy burden of responsibility Friedrich carries every day*.

As quickly as I could, I laced on my sturdiest high-top shoes, then put on my winter coat. Kerosene lantern in hand, I waded across the flooded yard to the barn, the rain lashing my face. On my left, the church floated like an island in the middle of a lake, completely surrounded by water. Inside, the barn smelled of hay and manure and old wood, reminding me so strongly of Papa's barn that I nearly called out his name. Then I remembered where I was and what I needed to do.

The animals squirmed nervously in their stalls as the wind howled through the cracks and rattled the doors of the barn. The mare was usually the calmer of our two horses, but even she whinnied fearfully, the whites of her eyes gleaming in the lantern light as I opened the door of her stall. I spoke soothingly to her as I fastened on the bridle and buggy harness, then hitched her to our carriage. She balked as I tried to lead her out into the storm, so I decided to let her stay in the barn until the girls were dressed.

I retraced my steps to the kitchen, my skirts wet and heavy around my legs. I quickly pulled off my petticoats and apron to make walking easier, then hurried upstairs to bundle the children in their warmest coats. They stood whimpering in the kitchen doorway, sleepy and bewildered, as I drove the buggy up to the back door. One by one, I carried them outside, and they huddled together on the carriage seat in the dark. Even with the flaps drawn, the buggy roof offered little protection from the drumming rain.

"I want Papa. Where's Papa?" Sophie wept.

"We can't wait for Papa, Liebchen. We're going to spend the night at the Bauers' house."

I had to crack the buggy whip hard before the mare would leave the relative safety of our yard and head out onto the flooded road. She heard the ominous rumbling of the river and flattened her ears against her head, nostrils flaring. My arms soon ached with the strain of keeping her on course while all her instincts urged her to flee back to her stable. Rain pelted the leather carriage roof like a drum roll. The wind whipped it against our faces.

Cold, wet, and miserable, the children cried for their papa and pleaded with me to take them back home. I didn't want to frighten them even more by mentioning the dam.

"I know you don't understand what I'm doing or why you had to leave your warm beds, but you must believe that this is for your own good—because I love you." My words seemed hauntingly familiar. They were what Friedrich had tried to tell me over and over again about leaving Germany and moving to America. I had to deliver my children to safety, just as Friedrich had felt compelled to deliver us to safety in America. I remembered the dream he'd had in Germany about a flood, and I shuddered. I finally understood.

The wind had uprooted dozens of trees and knocked down branches all along the road. When one loomed ahead of us like a twisted wraith, the mare balked and no amount of whipping could get her to move forward. I had to leave the girls huddled in the carriage and climb down to lead her, pushing the branches aside so we could pass. The water was knee-deep in the road, the current swift, and I felt the mud sucking against my boots. Our progress seemed agonizingly slow. If Herr Metzger was right, the dam could give way any moment and sweep us all to our deaths.

I suddenly realized where Friedrich was. As soon as he heard of the danger, he would have gone to the lake to try to prevent disaster. Instead of fleeing in panic, he would be laboring with the other men to shore up the dam with sandbags, and trusting his family to God's care. I knew he was praying for us—probably this very moment—but my fear for Friedrich's safety suddenly welled up like the floodwaters around me.

At last we reached the bridge. I could see the wooden trusses outlined against the night sky, but the roadbed itself lay somewhere beneath the river's roiling surface. A huge mound of branches and what looked like debris from a house or a shed had piled up against the bridge's central support, creating a logjam and turning the bridge into a dam. As the force of the dammed-up water increased, it sloshed across the flooded roadbed in waves.

I yanked hard on the mare's bridle and started across the bridge, wading through water that reached to my thighs. The sound of the river's fury roared in my ears, and I felt the bridge rumble and vibrate beneath my feet with the force of the raging river.

When we were a quarter of the way across, something struck the bridge with a jolt. The roadbed shuddered and swayed.

"Mama!" Sophie screamed. "I'm scared! Go back! Go back!"

The horse reared, yanking the bridle from my grip. As she bucked and snorted in terror, I knew I could never make her continue forward to the other side. But how could I get the wagon turned around on the narrow span to go back?

The bridge began to pitch and rock. I heard the hideous squealing sound of wood against metal as it twisted with the force of wind and water. It was breaking apart. We had to get off.

"Mama!" Sophie screamed again.

"Grab the reins!" I yelled. "Pull back on them as hard as you can!" I ducked beneath the harness and began to push against the carriage with all my might, trying to roll it backward off the bridge.

"I can't! I can't!" Sophie wept.

"Just pull, Sophie. You can do it. The horse wants to back up, let her know it's all right, I'm helping her."

I heaved. At first I couldn't tell if the carriage was really moving or if I was just feeling the motion of the water and the bridge. Then the wheels slowly began to turn. Inch by inch, the carriage rolled backward. The mare followed. All the while, the bridge twisted and writhed beneath my feet.

I heard Emma mumbling something and realized she was reciting the Lord's Prayer. Sophie joined her, between terrified sobs. I didn't dare turn around until I felt mud beneath my feet instead of the wooden planks of the bridge. When I did, it was a horrifying sight. We'd barely made it to shore when the bridge began to collapse. Support timbers splintered and cracked like matchsticks, disappearing beneath the angry torrent as the logjam finally gave way. In a matter of moments, the bridge washed away in the churning rapids without a trace. I shuddered with horror. We might have been on it.

I couldn't think what to do next. Our escape route to higher ground had vanished before my eyes. I leaned against the carriage, my knees too weak to support me, and trembled from head to toe. I felt alone—truly alone—with no one to help me, no way to save my daughters.

"What are we going to do?" Sophie wept, echoing my terror. Baby Eva hadn't stopped weeping since I'd pulled her from her bed, what seemed like hours ago.

"Papa would tell us to pray," Emma said solemnly, "or maybe sing a song."

"Can you think of a song, Liebchen?" I asked in a shaking voice. When she didn't answer, when the only sound was the river's deafening roar, I knew the deluge was going to defeat me. We would all be swallowed alive.

Then, against all hope, Emma began to sing, her voice shining like a thin ray of light against all the darkness and fear.

" 'A might-y for-tress is our God . . .' " she sang, " '. . . a bull work never fail-ing . . .' "

I began to weep. I knew she couldn't possibly understand the words, but I felt their power lifting me, just the same.

"No, that's not a good song," Sophie said. "Sing something happy."

"But it *is* a good song," Emma insisted. "It has a part in it about a flood." She began to sing again. " 'Our help-er He-e, a-mid the flood . . . of more tall hills pre-mail-ing . . .' "

Slowly the words surrounded my fear, bringing it under control. *Our helper He, amid the flood.*

I closed my eyes as she sang and silently prayed to Friedrich's God. "Lord Jesus, you always show Friedrich what to do. Please help us now . . . please show me what to do."

When the mare snorted and backed against me, I opened my eyes. Down-river, silhouetted against the night sky, was the dark outline of another bridge truss. The railroad bridge. The tracks crossed the river by the mill, a little farther downstream.

With a great deal of pushing and shoving, soothing and coaxing, I got the horse and carriage turned around. We followed the main road along the river until it crossed the tracks, then we veered onto the raised railbed. The wheels thumped rhythmically as the carriage bumped along the crossties. I heard the roar of the river grow louder as we neared the railroad trestle. The horse heard it, too, and dug her hooves into the cinders, refusing to budge. I knew she could never cross the trestle in the dark, with only the railroad ties—spaced two feet apart—to balance on. It was useless to try to force her to go farther.

I looked between the ties and saw the dark water swirling beneath me only six feet away—boiling, debris laden, swift. I closed my eyes for a moment to halt the sensation of falling. If the dam gave way, this bridge would be swept aside in moments, too, like the other one.

"We'll have to walk from here," I told the girls. "The horse can't cross this kind of bridge." I unhitched her and set her free, hoping she would eventually find her way home. She trotted down the embankment and disappeared into the darkness. The rain was still pouring down in sheets.

"But these are railroad tracks," Sophie said. "What if there's a train?"

I almost laughed out loud. A train was the least of our worries. Before I could reply Emma said, "There won't be. Papa says to pray whenever we're afraid, remember? And the angels will fly down to watch over us."

"Jesus will never leave us or forsake us," Sophie echoed shakily. The girls had Friedrich's faith. He had done a good job of teaching them—in spite of me.

I gazed across the narrow, fifty-yard span to higher ground on the other side. We would have to keep our balance in the gusting wind, leaping from tie to tie in the dark, with no railing to hang on to. I shuddered at the thought of one of my girls slipping, falling between the ties, disappearing into the raging water below. I couldn't ask them to walk across. I would have to carry them, one by one.

"Sophie, give the baby to Emma. That's it. I'm going to take you across first, then I'll come back for the others. Hold on to Eva tightly and wait right here, Emma."

I gathered Sophie in my arms and left the two younger children huddled together on the carriage seat, clutching each other. As I started forward, Emma began singing a new song, her voice high and thin. " 'Fair-est Lord Je-e-sus . . . Ruler of all na-ture . . .' "

Child of the sunbeam, I thought. Able to sing even in the rain and storm.

It wasn't until I was halfway across that I began to fully realize what a difficult, dangerous trip this was. And I would have to do it four more times. I needed to look down to watch my footing, but when I did, the rushing water made me sick and dizzy. I had to pause every few feet and close my eyes until it passed. My knees trembled so violently they could barely support my weight, much less Sophie's. She clung to my neck, whimpering softly.

"I can't breathe, sweetheart," I gasped. "Don't hold so tightly."

The roar below me grew louder until I could no longer hear Emma singing behind me. I prayed to Friedrich's God for strength, begging Him with all my heart to spare my children. Then, glancing up, I saw the other side.

When I left Sophie standing alone in the rain alongside the tracks, she looked so forlorn that it nearly broke my heart to turn away and leave her there. But I had to go back for the other two. I hurried across the span, the trip somewhat easier without a child's added weight. I would carry baby Eva across next.

" 'Fair are the mead-ows . . .' " Emma sang. " 'Fair-er still the wood-lands . . .' "

"I'm going to take Eva next," I told her. "Can you be very brave, Liebchen, and wait here all alone until I get back?" She nodded valiantly, but her eyes shone with tears.

Eva wrapped her arms and legs around me, clinging like a vine to a wall. "Mama . . . Mama . . ." she cried, unable to stop.

The railroad ties were slick with rain, the leather soles of my shoes slippery. If I fell, there would be nothing to grip for balance. The baby could easily tumble between the ties and plunge into the flood below. I made my way with agonizing slowness—balancing, praying, stepping from one tie to the next by rhythm.

I had to pry Eva off my neck when I reached the other side. She didn't want me to leave her, but I had to go back for Emma. Gritting my teeth, I left my baby, screaming, in Sophie's arms. One more trip across the slick ties—hurrying, mindful that the dam might burst at any moment. In my haste I stepped too far, and my foot slid through the crack between two ties. I fell down hard, banging my knee painfully against the rail. For a moment I lay stunned, then I crawled to my feet and hurried on, grateful that my arms had been empty. What if I had fallen with one of my children?

"I'm coming, Emma," I called out. "Keep singing, sweetheart."

I saw her outline in the distance. She sat perched on the buggy seat, bravely starting another song. The words soothed my trembling limbs like balm. I wanted so badly to believe they were true.

" 'I do not know how long 'twill be . . . or what the future holds for me . . . but this I know, if Jesus leads me . . . I shall get home someday.' "

When I finally reached her she hugged me tightly, shivering. Then, with hands as cold as ice, she wiped my wet hair from my face and pressed her cheek against mine. I started back across the bridge for the last time—slowly, carefully, my throbbing knee a reminder to gauge each step. If we lived through this, I knew that I would hear the roar of the river in my dreams for years to come.

I heard Eva crying in the distance and knew I was almost there. Her little voice was hoarse. I set Emma down and lifted her in my arms. "Shh . . . shh. It's all right. Don't cry, Eva. Mama's here."

While I soothed her, I planned what to do next. We were still much too close to the river to be safe. But the railroad tracks would lead to the mill yard, and from there we could follow the road up the hill to Magda's house. How far? It had to be at least half a mile.

"You'll have to walk from here," I told the older girls. "I can only carry Eva."

"I'm cold, Mama," Emma said. She was soaked and shivering. We all were.

"Maybe walking will warm us up. Hold Emma's hand, Sophie." We started forward in the driving rain, Eva riding piggyback, Emma clutching my skirts with one hand and Sophie's hand with the other.

"Is this a flood," Emma asked, "like Noah and the ark?"

"Yes, darling, this is a flood."

"But Papa said God would never send another flood to destroy the earth," Sophie said.

"Your Papa's right. This flood doesn't cover the whole earth like Noah's flood did."

"God sent a rainbow, remember?" Emma added. "That means He will keep us safe."

"Where is Papa?" Sophie asked. "Is he safe?"

I remembered that Friedrich was farther up the valley, closer to the dam, and felt a deep, soul-shaking fear for him. I began to talk, saying the first words that came into my mind, hoping that a long, rambling explanation would serve as a distraction to keep all of us going.

"Back home in Germany there was a terrible drought the year you were born, Sophie. A drought is the opposite of a flood—when there is no rain for a long, long time and the river dries up. Floods and droughts are just part of the normal cycle of life. God promised not to destroy the earth, but sometimes He causes the river to flood and we're so afraid it's going to destroy us but it doesn't, you see, because . . ." I had to stop as the flood of sorrow I'd been holding back all these years threatened to let go.

"Did we live by a river in Germany?" Sophie asked.

I cleared the lump from my throat. "Yes, it flowed through the little village where you were born, where your papa was a schoolteacher. When I was a girl I could see the river if I climbed my favorite tree in Papa's pasture. My brother Emil and I would climb it together and play a game called *Someday*."

"How do you play it?"

"Well, you take turns saying: 'Someday I'm going to . . .' Then you fill in whatever you'd like to do. It's kind of like wishing on a star. My brother Emil wanted to see the world for his *Someday* dream."

"Did he get his wish?"

"Yes. He traveled all the way to the islands in the Pacific Ocean and even to China."

"What did you wish for, Mama?" I paused to rest a moment, shifting Eva to my hip. I was puffing from our uphill climb, so I knew we were probably high enough to be safe now if the dam broke.

"Oh, lots of things . . . but what I wished for the most was to marry a handsome baron."

"What's a baron?"

"A very rich man who owns a mansion and lots of land."

"Papa is handsome, isn't he," Emma said.

I thought of Friedrich's broad shoulders, his sandy hair, his gentle blue eyes. "Yes, darling. Papa is very handsome."

We walked and walked, and for the first time in almost eight years, I began to talk about my family in Germany, telling stories my daughters had never heard before. I told them about Mama and Papa, my brothers Kurt and Emil, my sisters Ada and Runa, and finally my precious grandmother, Oma. A flood of words and memories poured out, held back for much too long.

I talked, and Eva stopped crying and fell asleep on my shoulder. I told about opening presents in the parlor on Christmas Eve, and for a while Sophie and Emma forgot that they were wet and cold and frightened.

An hour later, tired and drenched to the bone, we arrived at Magda's door. Only then did I realize that the rain had stopped. And that my face was wet—not with rain, but with tears.

ELEVEN

In the morning, Gus Bauer left with one of the rescue parties to look for survivors—and to help bury the dead. We learned that some homes along the river had washed away during the night and several people were missing. We didn't know yet if our home was among them. Gus made no mention of Friedrich, but when he tipped his hat to me in farewell, I knew it was his promise to find him.

"Be careful, Gus," Magda pleaded as she said good-bye. I saw something in her eyes that I'd failed to notice before—she was in love with him. It didn't matter that he couldn't hold a job or that they had very little money or that she was pregnant again with their eighth child. She loved him. For better or for worse. For richer or for poorer. Until death parted them.

Later, as I stood at Magda's sink washing the breakfast dishes, I remembered how Friedrich would sometimes wander up behind me and encircle me with his arms, resting his head against the back of my shoulder. I wondered if I would ever feel his arms around me again, and I couldn't stop my tears.

"I know it's probably useless to tell you not to worry," Magda said as she wrapped her sturdy arms around me. "I'd be worried sick if I were in your place."

"All I've ever thought about for the past several years was how much I hated it here in America . . . how much I wanted to return to Germany. And now . . . if my house is gone . . . if Friedrich is gone—"

"Don't even think such a thing! Friedrich will be fine. Gus will find him, you'll see."

I stared out of the grimy kitchen window at the rain that continued to fall. "But what if he isn't fine? I've been trying to imagine my life without him and I can't do it. I suppose I could move back home to Germany again with Mama and Papa and my sisters and Kurt . . . but there would be a huge hole in my life. Part of me would be missing . . . like apple strudel without the cinnamon." I glanced at Magda, afraid she might think I was rambling crazily, but I saw that she understood perfectly. "I love him," I whispered.

"I know," she said simply.

"But I've never told him."

She pulled me into her arms again and held me tightly. "Then I'll pray that you will get a chance to tell him."

Gus returned at noon without Friedrich. "We haven't been able to get much news from your side of the river, since the bridge was washed away," he told me. He spoke quietly so that the older children, who were eating picnic-style on the floor in the parlor, wouldn't overhear us. "But if he went to the Schultz farm, he should be okay. They live a little ways back from the river."

"Any news about the dam on Squaw Lake?" I asked.

"The dam is still holding, but I guess we won't be completely out of danger until the water levels go down. Some men worked all night long sandbagging it. And I heard that two volunteers were drowned in the process. One of them lost his footing and fell in, and the other jumped in to try to save him. They haven't found the bodies yet."

"Did you hear who they were?" I could barely force the words out.

"No, I didn't, but—" Gus stopped chewing. A stunned look froze on his face. "You . . . you don't think Fred would have gone to help out at the dam, do you?"

I could only nod.

Gus groaned. "You're right. He would do some fool thing like that."

And Friedrich, who was a strong swimmer, would also leap in to save a drowning man. Gus pushed his chair back with a loud scrape and shoved his arms into his oil slicker.

"I'll be back just as soon as I find something out for you . . . one way or the other."

I sat stitching beside the parlor window all afternoon, helping Magda catch up with her endless mending. Baby Eva was sick and cranky, having caught a cold in the wind and rain, so I laid her down on Magda's bed for a nap after lunch. Sophie disappeared somewhere with two of the Bauers' daughters, but Emma sat on the floor by my feet with a pencil and a scrap of used butcher paper, drawing a picture.

"All done," she finally announced. I laid the mending aside as she crawled onto my lap to show me. Five stick figures of varying sizes stood beneath the arch of a rainbow, holding hands. "That's Papa, that's you, that's Sophie, that's Eva, and that's me," she explained, pointing. All of the figures wore curving smiles on their round faces except me. My mouth was fixed in a short, straight line, giving me a vacant, dazed look.

"Why aren't I smiling?" I asked. Emma looked at me and shrugged. The gesture spoke for her—my daughter didn't understand why I never smiled.

"Do you like my picture?" she asked.

"Yes. It's beautiful."

"You can keep it forever," she said, sliding from my lap to go in search of the other children.

Emma had never seen me hold Friedrich's hand either, but I was clasping it tightly in the picture, linking myself to him and to our three children. I could picture Friedrich's hands so clearly in my mind—broad and strong and tanned, with veins like cords of twine. I saw them raised in benediction over his congregation, glistening with water as he baptized a child into God's covenant family, folded in prayer as he knelt in his study every morning. I had loved Friedrich's hands ever since we were first married, when I had watched him grade papers each night in Germany.

The clamor and commotion of children continued in the other rooms, but for the moment I was alone in the parlor. I folded my own hands together like Friedrich always did and closed my eyes. I wanted to pray like I had last night during the storm—to the God Friedrich talked with every day and preached about on Sunday, the God he loved and worshiped, the God I'd been angry with. But without my children to lead the way, I scarcely knew how to begin.

Almighty God . . . That's how Reverend Lahr back home began his prayers, and it had seemed right in the hush of that quiet sanctuary with its carved wood and stained glass. But that wasn't how Friedrich prayed. I began again.

Heavenly Father . . . Tears sprang to my eyes as I remembered running to my father's arms when I was a child. It was the way my girls ran to Friedrich. Now I ran to God.

Heavenly Father, I pray that you would spare my husband's life. Fritz loves you and serves you and obeys you. I know I don't deserve to ask anything of you. I've been angry with you and with him for so long. But please . . . if our house is still there, I promise I'll plant flowers, I'll make it a home, I'll be the wife Fritz deserves.

I wanted to do and to be all that the Bible asked of a wife. The Scriptures listed those requirements somewhere. I opened my eyes and took Magda's huge old family Bible from the shelf where she kept it and began to page through the New Testament, searching for the verses that would tell me what to do. I knew from my childhood catechism classes that the verses were in there.

The Bible was in German but was very old, the faded Gothic lettering hard to read. I persevered, scanning all the headings, page after page, with the same will to succeed that had helped me survive last night's storm. I found what I was looking for in the book of Ephesians, under the heading "Christian Duties."

Wives, submit yourselves unto your own husbands, as unto the Lord. For the husband is the head of the wife, even as Christ is the head of the church: and he is the saviour of the body. Therefore as the church is subject unto Christ, so let the wives be to their own husbands in every thing.

I was surprised to find only three verses. But as I continued reading, I discovered that the duties of a husband were much longer—nine verses.

Husbands, love your wives, even as Christ also loved the church, and gave himself for it. . . . So ought men to love their wives as their own bodies. He that loveth his wife loveth himself. For no man ever yet hated his own flesh; but nourisheth and cherisheth it. . . . For this cause shall a man leave his father and mother, and shall be joined unto his wife, and they two shall be one flesh.

Those words described my husband. Friedrich had labored in a coal mine and cut ice in the river so that I wouldn't have to travel in steerage. He had hauled loads of lumber and bricks at the mill for two years to furnish my home with everything I needed. Husbands were to give their very lives—a much greater sacrifice than what was required of their wives.

Friedrich had shown Christ's love to me through his own, and I knew instinctively that God had heard my prayer, that He loved me just as Friedrich did, even though I had treated Him so coldly. God was patiently waiting, just as my husband was, for me to return His love. Friedrich's God was a Father who loved me. And as I prayed for His forgiveness, I found I could also believe in Jesus, who loved me enough to lay down His life for me.

———

Gus still hadn't returned when Magda and I fed the children their supper. Later, we tucked all but her two oldest boys into three overcrowded beds and turned a deaf ear to their whispers and giggles. Together, we waited for our husbands in the parlor.

It was dark when we finally heard voices outside. I peered through the parlor window and saw a knot of men moving toward the back door—gray, hunched figures without faces. A shrouded form lay in the back of a wagon. I heard their stamping boots and muffled voices as they came through the kitchen door and felt the same fathomless dread I'd felt the day the telegraph had arrived with news about Emil. Magda got up quietly and hurried into the kitchen, but I couldn't move. I would wait in the parlor for the news to come to me. Even when I heard footsteps approaching in the hall, I couldn't face the door.

"Louise . . ." I whirled around at the sound of Friedrich's voice. He stood in the doorway, hat in hand, as if unwilling to enter the parlor in his muddy boots. I ran to him, clung to him. He was soaking wet and coated with mud— reeking of it. I didn't care.

"Oh, Louise! I was so worried about you! Thank God you and the children are all right . . . I don't know what I'd ever do without you!"

We were one flesh, our arms encircling, our lips joining. One. I thanked God for my husband.

"I'm getting you all wet!" he said when he could finally speak.

"It doesn't matter. I want to hold you forever."

"I know. Me too. But I have to go back out again for a little while. Do you mind? I want to offer what comfort I can to those who have lost loved ones. I won't be long."

As I brushed a streak of mud off his forehead, the dam I'd built to hold back my emotions suddenly burst, flooding my heart, bringing the burnt stubble to life.

"I love you, Friedrich."

He went utterly still. "What. . . ?" he whispered.

"I do. I love you."

He went limp, staggering against me as if he lacked the strength to stand. He buried his face on my neck. Then, clutching each other tightly, Friedrich and I both wept.

———

It took more than a month to clean the muck and debris from our yard so that I could plant flowers in front of our house and around the church. The floor of the sanctuary had been ruined by the flood and would have to be replaced. Maybe the musty smell would finally go along with it.

I was rinsing my hands in the sink after planting some rosebushes when

Sophie came into the kitchen with Eva in tow. The baby was wailing loudly and I could see that they'd had more than enough of each other.

"Eva is crying for no reason, and I can't get her to stop, Mama," Sophie said with a sigh.

I scooped Eva up in my arms. "Ja, little one. I know just what you need to make your tears go away." I dug Oma's cup out of the drawer in the sideboard where I'd hidden it four years ago.

"What is that, Mama?" Sophie asked, trailing behind me.

"It's my grandmother's very special crying cup. Whenever you drink from it, all of your tears will magically disappear." I filled it with milk and held it to Eva's lips. "I used to drink from this cup when I was a little girl in Germany. You're named after Oma, Sophie. She loved you very much, and she wanted you and your sisters to have her magic cup so that you would always be reminded of her."

As I watched Eva gulp the milk I wished I could talk to Oma one last time and tell her all that I'd learned in America. I would tell her that I'd finally learned not to smother my feelings to avoid being hurt but to embrace life and love, giving and forgiving. I'd learned that having faith doesn't mean giving up my life, but putting it into God's hands, allowing Him to mysteriously weld two together into one. I'd learned that true power doesn't lie in making the outward choices, but in making the inward ones—choosing to love and to nurture, choosing to trust God. I'd tell Oma that she was right when she gave me the crying cup—the power to find joy isn't in the cup, but within my own heart. But maybe Oma knew all of these things, after all.

Eva finished drinking her milk and pointed to the little girl painted on the cup. "Baby!" she said with a grin. A creamy band of milk spread across her lip.

Sophie stared in surprise. "It worked, Mama! She stopped crying!"

"Of course, sweetheart. Oma's crying cup always works."

Outside the kitchen window I heard the creak of a rope against a tree branch as Emma played on the swing that hung from one of the apple trees. She was singing a hymn in her sweet, clear voice—the hymn I'd come to think of as my own:

> *I do not know how long 'twill be, nor what the future holds for me,*
> *but this I know, if Jesus leads me, I shall get home someday . . .*

TWELVE

Suzanne closed the flaps of the box she had just packed and stacked it against the living room wall with the others. "That was a great story, Grandma, but what does it have to do with me?"

"Honestly, Suzanne!" Grace was trying to dry her tears without smearing her makeup, while Emma searched in vain for the box of tissues.

Suzanne ducked into the bathroom and retrieved a roll of toilet paper. "Here, use this. I don't want to start another fight, Mom, but if you think about it rationally, you'll see that there are several important differences between Great-grandma's situation and mine."

Grace blew her nose. "Maybe, but the point is the same."

"Right. And what is the point? Great-grandma adjusted to her new life and so will I? Humbug! Great-grandpa and Jeff both had to make a tough decision? Double humbug! Great-grandpa was following his conscience, but Jeff's decision was just plain selfish! Maybe husbands didn't have to consult their wives in the nineteenth century, but this is the twentieth century, and they should know enough to consult us today! We're not just another possession anymore! And you're forgetting another big difference too—Great-grandma's identity was defined by 'children, cooking, and church.' I'm the assistant editor of *New Woman* magazine. I love my job! I have an identity apart from my husband and children, and no one has a right to make me give that up!"

"Suzy, Suzy . . . why are you shouting at us?" Emma said. She caressed Suzanne's back to soothe her. Suzanne stopped, surprised by her own outburst. Why was she so angry? Had Louise's story affected her more than she cared to admit?

"Let's face it," Suzanne finally said, "times change, roles change, expectations change. What's right for one generation isn't necessarily right for the next one."

"But there are some things that shouldn't change," Emma said quietly. "You told me you didn't want to be like your mother. She chose to give up her career for her husband's sake, and so you've decided not to make the same mistake. But don't you see? You're still reacting to the choices she made. That's what I did. My marriage to Karl was a mistake because I was reacting to my mother's choices. We're supposed to learn from our mother's mistakes, not react to them. That's the pattern you have to change."

"I gave up my career because my marriage was more important," Grace added. "Isn't yours important? Marriage involves sacrifice. Your great-grand-mother's story should have told you that, if nothing else."

Suzanne rolled her eyes. "Well, in my case, all the sacrifices are one-sided."

"But that's the definition of a sacrifice," Grace said. "Think of Christ's sacrifice—"

"Oh, please don't drag theology into this conversation," Suzanne said, groaning. "It's getting maudlin enough as it is."

"She's right, Gracie," Emma said. "We don't need a sermon. But, Su-zanne, just suppose for a moment that my mother had the same choices you do. Suppose she'd had a career back in Germany and had decided to divorce Friedrich and stay there. What then?"

Suzanne gave a flippant laugh and raked her dark hair from her eyes with one hand. "Then none of us would even be here arguing about this."

"Yes, exactly." Emma smiled knowingly and Suzanne saw she had been trapped. "If you don't heal this rift—if you let Jeff walk out of your life—you might lose something very, very precious that you can never retrieve again."

For a moment the room was silent. Suzanne was aware of the many sounds of life outside her grandmother's apartment—doors slamming, children squealing, the hiss of air brakes at the bus stop, the steady mumble of traffic and airplanes like a distant river. Unable to bear the scrutiny of her mother and grandmother, she glanced at her watch.

"You know what? We need to leave. I promised to pick up the girls before supper, and the expressways are going to be jammed if we don't get going."

She practically fled to the car, using the excuse that she wanted to load the items that Emma had given to her and Grace—then she decided to wait on the sidewalk for her mother to tie up all the loose ends in the apartment.

The warm spring day had turned chilly by late afternoon, and Suzanne shivered as the sun disappeared behind the apartment building. Signs of the season were harder to find here in the densely populated city, but as she waited she spotted dandelions on a small triangle of grass across the street and budding green leaves on a scraggly tree near the corner. She thought of the changes her great-grandmother had endured coming to America and wondered if God had devised the seasons as a reminder that nothing in life remains the same.

She looked up at the square brick building and found Emma's living room window on the third floor. Would moving to the suburbs be difficult for her grandmother after so much time? Then she thought of the changes that lay ahead in her own life after the death of her ten-year-old marriage, and she shivered again.

A few minutes later her mother and grandmother emerged through the doors of the apartment building. How different they were—from head to toe! Grace's curly hair was beautifully styled; Emma wore her straight, silver hair short and casual. Grace's feet were shod in expensive Italian leather pumps; Emma's feet sported cheap canvas deck shoes. How different their personalities were too! Grace was so much more cautious and conservative than her uninhibited, fun-loving mother. But then, Suzanne and her mother were very different women as well. Suzanne never would have worked her way to the top at *New Woman* magazine if she had been as passive as Grace.

Emma gave Suzanne a hug and kissed her good-bye. "Thanks for all your help, dear. And please don't fight with your mother on the way home, all right?" She said it with a smile, and Suzanne couldn't help smiling in return.

"That's one of the things I've always loved about you, Grandma—you don't give long lectures."

Grace was unusually quiet on the drive home, deeply withdrawn into her own thoughts. Suzanne wondered what those thoughts were and if she was upset about something, but she decided not to ask. She really didn't feel much like talking either. Almost against her will, she found herself thinking about her great-grandmother's story again.

There was another important difference between her and Louise, one she hadn't wanted to mention. While Louise had barely known her husband when they'd married and had later learned to love him, her story was the opposite—she and Jeffrey had started out deeply, passionately in love. They had begun their marriage as "one flesh," but those bonds had long since died, along with the sparks and the flames.

Jeffrey had made his choice, she had made hers. And although she would never admit it to her mother, she was already seeing the consequences of those decisions in her daughters' lives. Amy had been unusually disobedient and rebellious lately, Melissa overly emotional and clingy. They were both reacting to all the tension at home. Maybe things would improve once Jeff left for good.

Suzanne glanced at her mother and saw her surreptitiously wiping a tear. She was probably still crying over the happy ending to Louise's story. Grace always cried at happy endings. Sue remembered her own reaction to the story and wondered why she hadn't allowed herself to cry. Was she smothering her emotions as Louise had?

She sighed and merged the car into the racing freeway traffic. There was no room in her life for mawkish sentimentality. Like Louise wading out into the flood, she would have to be very strong in order to survive her new life alone.

———

A week after her mother gave her the photograph album, Grace sat alone in her kitchen leafing through it, brooding about the mysteries of her past. The black-and-white photos, faded and brittle with age, offered no hints to help her unravel Emma's riddles, and the unanswered questions revolved endlessly in Grace's mind like a carousel. She would grab hold of one and ride it for a while until the journey to nowhere made her dizzy, then let it go to ride the next one.

She turned each page of the album slowly, careful not to loosen the glue on the old-fashioned corner-mounts. Emma's elaborate script, scrawled in white ink on the black pages, was nearly illegible, so she studied the mute faces instead. Some, like her father's and her grandparents', were known to Grace only by these photographs. What other expressions had animated their features besides this one, frozen forever by the camera?

Grace sat by the bay window in her breakfast nook, the only cozy spot in her sleek, echoing kitchen. Earlier that day her entire house had been polished to perfection by her weekly maid service, and she hated to disturb the vast, gleaming rooms. She could think of plenty of other things to do besides wasting her time with this scrapbook, but the paralyzing lethargy she felt seemed soul-deep.

When the kitchen doorbell suddenly rang, she was tempted to ignore it until she peered through the window and saw that it was Suzanne. She was dressed in a business suit, and Grace realized with a start how late in the afternoon it was. Suzanne was on her way home from work already. How had the empty day flown by so swiftly? Grace planted both palms on the table and wearily pushed herself to her feet.

"Why do you always ring the bell?" she asked as she opened the door. "Didn't I give you a key?"

"I didn't feel like sorting through all these to find it." Suzanne held up an enormous key ring jammed with at least two dozen keys.

"Are all those really necessary? What on earth are they all for?"

"I have two locks on each door of my house," she recited. "I need an ignition key and a trunk key for both of our cars, one key is for your house, one's for my mother-in-law's house, one's for my post office box—and the other dozen are all from work."

"I'm glad my life isn't that complicated."

"And I'm glad I don't have to sit around in an empty house all day." The mumbled words were loud enough for her to hear, but Grace chose to ignore them.

Suzanne handed her a manila file folder. "These are the design samples for the crisis pregnancy center logo. I've been reminding Jeff that he promised to do them for you weeks ago, and he finally scribbled them off last night—in between his endless calls to Chicago. If you don't like any of them, don't feel you have to use them. You won't hurt Jeff's feelings because he doesn't have any feelings. There's a new art director at my magazine who does great work—I can commission her to design a few."

Jeffrey had sketched six designs in a variety of styles from modern to ornate, all beautifully and professionally rendered. Grace couldn't help admiring her son-in-law's creative talent. "Tell Jeffrey these are wonderful, thank you. The board will have a tough time choosing."

Suzanne took a mug from the cupboard and poured herself a cup of coffee. "Speaking of choices, has the board had any luck finding a director yet?" There was a nasty edge to her voice that made Grace sink into her chair in the breakfast nook and rub her eyes.

"Don't start on me, Suzanne. It's been a trying week, moving your grandmother."

Suzanne's voice softened as she refilled Grace's cup, then took a seat across from her. "I'm sorry. I just wish you'd listen to your heart and not to Daddy." Grace didn't answer. She felt so inexplicably close to tears, she didn't dare. "You look a little down, Mom. What's wrong?"

"I don't know . . . exhaustion from the move . . . these photographs . . . I never imagined that moving my mother would stir up such a cloud of memories. Every time I look at these I feel pressured to sort through the memories and deal with them too, whether I want to or not." She turned one page in the book, then another, without seeing any of the photos. "I can't stop thinking about what my mother said the other day when we were packing. *'Your father loved you more than life itself.'* Do you remember that, Sue? Didn't it strike you as odd?"

"Grandma explained what she meant, didn't she?"

"She attributed it to old age, but you and I both know she isn't senile. I had the distinct feeling she was hiding something."

"Actually, I did too. But if that really was the truth—if Karl Bauer really did love you more than life itself—then everything else she's told you about him was a lie."

"I know. That's why I've been in such a muddle the past few days. It's very unsettling to have holes suddenly poked in the fabric of your life. I wish I could mend them, but how? Sue, the truth couldn't possibly be worse than this terrible uncertainty, could it?" When Suzanne simply shrugged, Grace turned to the back of the album where there were several blank pages. She removed a folded piece of gray writing paper and handed it to her. "Read this. I found it stuck in the back of this scrapbook."

Suzanne unfolded it and read the handwritten words aloud:

" 'To my beloved Emma,

> When you are old and gray and full of sleep,
> And nodding by the fire, take down this book,
> And slowly read, and dream of the soft look
> Your eyes had once, and of their shadows deep;
>
> How many loved your moments of glad grace,
> And loved your beauty with love false or true,
> But one man loved the pilgrim soul in you,
> And loved the sorrows of your changing face;
>
> And bending down beside the glowing bars,
> Murmur, a little sadly, how Love fled
> And paced upon the mountains overhead
> And hid his face amid a crowd of stars.' "

"Wow . . ." Suzanne breathed.

"I don't recognize the handwriting," Grace said, swallowing.

"I could be wrong, but I think this is a poem by Yeats. I'll look in one of my anthologies when I get home."

"I know that my mother bought this photo album when we lived on King Street, but for the life of me, I can't imagine who would give her a love poem."

Suzanne refolded the page and handed it to Grace. "If I were you, I'd search out the facts and deal with the past head on. Have you ever gone back to the town where Grandma came from and talked to her family—*your* family?"

"I didn't think it was a good idea to rake up the past."

"Closure, Mom. Don't you ever wonder what really happened between her and your father?"

"Of course I do. I've wondered about it all my life. When I was a child the other girls would hound me about him. Who was he? Where was he? Why didn't he live with us? Was he in jail? Divorce was a rare and scandalous event back then."

"Did you ever confront Grandma and ask her to tell you more about him?"

"It didn't occur to me to question her until I became a teenager. Then when she refused to answer my questions, I decided to run away and find Karl Bauer myself. I even bought a bus ticket to Bremenville, but the man who ran the bus depot knew my mother, and while I was waiting for the bus to arrive, he sent for her. She and I had a terrible fight. The more I insisted on going, the more upset she became until finally, for the first time, she told me that my father didn't want me—that he had tried to make her abort me. By the time she finished the gruesome story, she had me convinced that if I went anywhere near him he'd want to kill me all over again. That was also the first time I learned what he did for a living—that he owned a drugstore in Bremenville."

"You're an adult, not a teenager. Surely you're mature enough to handle your father's problem for what it was—*his* problem, not yours."

"It took a huge toll on my mother to have to tell me the truth that day. And there was something else. A sense of . . . I don't know . . . a sense that I was hurting her by wanting more love than she could give me. She always insisted that she and I were a family, complete in ourselves. I think it would still hurt her if she found out I was looking for my family somewhere else."

"Then don't tell her. Besides, I'd like to know more too. He is my grand-father. We have a right to know the truth."

"We went to Bremenville once to find him. Do you remember?"

"No, when was that?"

"We had driven up to the state park for a picnic one Saturday, all four of us. You and your brother were in grade school at the time. On the way home I saw the signs for Bremenville, only twenty miles or so off the main road, and I asked your father, please . . . couldn't we at least just see the town? It was summertime and beastly hot riding in a car without air conditioning, so I was amazed when he agreed to stop. You know how your father hates to change his plans."

Suzanne made a stern face. " 'Let's stick to the plans, here,' " she said, in an uncanny imitation of Stephen. " 'No need to change well-laid plans.' "

"That's him," Grace said, smiling. "Anyhow, Bremenville turned out to be a quaint little town, nestled in a valley in the mountains. I imagine it's a tourist trap by now, with the lake and all, but back in the '50s it was relatively undiscovered. You could tell it was settled by Germans because the village looked as if it had been plucked right out of the old country and transplanted to America. Even the names on the stores and the mailboxes were German. The Squaw River divides the town in half, and although it looked peaceful enough when we were there, I couldn't help remembering Grandma's story about the big flood when she was a child. Especially when it started to rain as soon as we pulled into town."

Suzanne twirled her hand impatiently. "And the point is . . ."

"The point. . . ?"

"Did you find your family or not!"

Her impatience irritated Grace. "You're your father's daughter, Suzanne. Don't let anyone tell you otherwise. And I *am* getting to the point. We stopped for gas on the outskirts of town and it seemed to take forever for a fill-up, especially since I'd been waiting all my life to find my father. So when Stephen rolled down the window to pay for the gas, I asked the attendant if there was a drugstore in town. 'Sure,' he says. 'Bauer's drugstore, straight down Main Street about four blocks. Can't miss it.'

"There's no way to describe how it felt to be so close—thrilling and terrifying at the same time. I was in Bremenville, four blocks from my father's drugstore! Stephen asked the attendant if the Bauers still owned it, and I was afraid I'd never be able to hear his answer above the drumming of the rain on the roof and the hammering of my heart.

" 'Yes, sir,' he said. 'Karl Bauer has run that store for as far back as I can recall.'

"We pulled out of the gas station, but only drove about a block down the street when all of a sudden the sky opened up in a tremendous cloudburst. The rain just poured down. I'd never seen anything like it before—or since. Stephen had to pull over and stop because we absolutely could not see a thing."

"I remember now!" Suzanne said. "That was unbelievable! I thought for sure the car was going to fill up with water and we were all going to drown."

Grace took a sip of coffee. "I was getting worried too. The rain went on and on—probably for a good ten minutes. When it finally let up, we started inching our way down the street again, but about a block later the entire intersection was flooded. Stephen didn't dare drive through it, so he took a detour around the block, and by the time we dodged all the flooding on the side streets we ended up lost."

"So you never found his store?"

"Oh, we eventually found it. Stephen was a man on a mission, you know. The store looked like something out of a bygone era . . . striped awning out front, ornate soda fountain with those little wire chairs, a row of old-fashioned glass medicine bottles with stoppers. But Bauer's drugstore was closed."

"No!"

"It was ten minutes past six by then, and the store had closed at six o'clock. Evidently on Saturday night, the entire town closed up at six o'clock. By the time we got back to the gas station, that was closed too. There wasn't a soul we could ask for directions to Karl Bauer's house—not that I would have dared go to his house! Getting up the nerve to go into his store was one thing, but going to his house? No, it just wasn't meant to be."

Suzanne rolled her eyes. "You know, I really hate it when you start all that 'Divine Destiny' stuff. Name one good reason why God wouldn't want you to meet your father? Aren't you curious about him? Don't you *want* to know more?"

"Aside from curiosity, what would be the point? Besides, he was several years older than my mother, so he must be long dead by now."

"What about Grandma's family . . . whatever happened to her sisters?"

Grace paged through the scrapbook to find the old-fashioned studio portrait of four little girls in starched white dresses and high-button shoes. "That's her older sister, Sophie, who was born in Germany; that's Mother; that's Eva; and that's the baby, Vera. As far as I know, when my mother left Karl, she never saw her parents or her sisters again."

"Doesn't that strike you as terribly strange, Mom? Avoiding Karl is one thing, but turning her back on her own family? It doesn't make sense."

"I know. Grandma would never even talk about them. I was very surprised when she told us her mother's story last week."

"I'll go to Bremenville with you if you want to play detective. This time we'll check the weather report first," Suzanne added with a grin.

Grace slowly closed the photo album. "No, let's just leave things the way they are, Suzanne."

Long after her daughter left, Grace remained at the kitchen table, too weary to move. At last she opened the scrapbook again to the only picture she'd ever seen of Karl Bauer. He stood behind her mother on their wedding day, only slightly taller than Emma, but his vast shoulders and thick-set build seemed to dwarf her slender frame. His hair and full beard were dark, his flowing mustache hid all but a sliver of his mouth from view. His broad face was dramatically handsome with high, well-defined cheekbones and dark, curving eyebrows. Grace stared longest of all at his eyes, studying them for a glint of cruelty that might have forewarned Emma of her future. But no matter how long she gazed, Grace couldn't read any emotion in them at all.

She remembered her youthful determination to go to Bremenville and find him, how she had studied the bus schedule, traced the route on a map, counted her rumpled dollar bills and loose change. Then she recalled the chill that had frozen her heart when she'd learned that her father didn't want her, that he'd conspired to abort her. Why would he do that if he "loved her more than life itself"? She tried to read the mystery behind his silent face, but it seemed obscured by a driving sheet of rain and a row of glass bottles in the window of a closed store.

———

The following Saturday afternoon, Grace knocked on the door to her mother's new suite, then turned the knob. "Anybody home?" she called as she and Suzanne stepped inside. No answer. "We probably should have phoned and warned her we were coming."

"Wow! What a spectacular mess!" Suzanne exclaimed as she followed Grace through the door. "If Grandma is in here, we'll never find her!"

"It's just as I thought . . . Mother hasn't unpacked a thing." The cardboard boxes were no longer stacked neatly against the walls where the movers would have left them, though, but haphazardly torn open, their contents partly strewn on the floor or piled on the chairs, the table, the sofa, and every other available space. The weariness Grace had been battling struck with renewed force. "Why don't you get started, Sue. You've got a gift for organization. I'll go track Mother down."

Leaving the door to the suite open, Grace walked down the hall to the activity lounge in the center of the complex. As she drew nearer, she heard the unmistakable sound of singing and laughter. When she recognized a rollicking piano rendition of "Alexander's Ragtime Band," she knew she had found her mother.

A dozen senior citizens were gathered around the baby grand piano, clapping and singing as if it were party night at the campus fraternity house. Emma sat in the middle of it all, pounding away on the keyboard, the life of the party. Her cheeks were nearly as bright as her crimson sweat shirt, and she wore her silver hair tied back with a shocking pink scarf. How could she possibly be eighty years old when she looked as alive and youthful as a sorority girl?

Suddenly Emma spotted her. "Why, here's Gracie!" she cried, and her face lit with love, just as it always did. Grace had never doubted for a single day in her life that her mother loved her utterly, yet Emma's love had never been smothering or possessive.

"Hey, everybody, I'd like you to meet my daughter, Grace Bradford."

Grace was instantly engulfed by well-wishers introducing themselves and pumping her hand.

"I'm Lester Stanley. You have no idea how much we enjoy your mother."

"Oh, I can well imagine," Grace murmured.

"She's more fun than an open fire hydrant on the Fourth of July," a tiny sparrow of a woman added.

"I tell you, honey," drawled a woman in a wheelchair, "I just don't know what we did for laughs around here before your mama came."

Still seated at the piano, Emma smiled up at Grace. "What brings you here today, dear?"

"Must be something special," Lester said. "She's all dressed up like Sunday-go-to-meetin' day."

Grace glanced down in dismay at what she'd thought was a casual outfit—gray linen slacks, a peach blazer, and matching sweater, a silk scarf knotted around her neck.

"No, Gracie always dresses up like that," Emma said with a wave of her hand.

"I came to see if you needed some help settling in."

"Settling in!" Lester shouted. "Why, Emma is already a permanent fixture!"

Emma rested her hand on his arm. "Thank you, dear, you're very sweet to say so, but I think she means my suite. You didn't happen to peek in, did you, Gracie?"

"I did."

"Oh dear. I'm in trouble now." She played a few bars of a funeral dirge on the piano, then stood. "Sorry, folks, but I guess I'm grounded until I clean my room." When everyone hooted with laughter Grace felt old and prudish.

"Honestly, Mother."

"Hey, do you need help, Emma? We can all pitch in." There was a chorus of assents.

"No, it's kind of you to offer, Lester, but I'm afraid you'd never get through my door. It is a mess, isn't it, dear?"

"Well . . . yes. . . ." Grace smiled weakly.

"Don't worry, everybody," Emma said cheerfully. "I'll dig my way out in time for the canasta championships."

It took several minutes for Emma to pry herself away from all her admirers, but eventually she and Grace made their way back to the suite.

"I told you you'd make friends in no time, Mother."

Emma linked her arm through Grace's. "Those sound like my words to you on your first day of school."

"Sorry, I didn't mean to be condescending."

"I'm glad, dear. Now, where shall we begin? Why, Suzanne! How did your mother rope you into this?"

Suzanne was on her knees, sorting through a box of sheet music from the 1940s. She shrugged. "I needed to get out of the house. Jeff took the girls to a Saturday matinee. He's trying to prove he's an ideal father now that I'm divorcing him."

"That's such an ugly word," Emma said with a sigh.

Suzanne stood, dusting her hands on the seat of her blue jeans. "Grandma, I was also wondering if you'd be willing to talk a little bit about your divorce. You said the other day that it was your fault Karl left you—but I always thought you left him because he didn't want Mom."

"Oh dear," Emma murmured as she sat down on the arm of her sofa. "And here I thought you came to help me unpack."

Grace eyed her mother with alarm. Emma no longer looked as young and carefree as she had a few moments before in the lounge. Why did Suzanne have to upset her by dredging up the past? Yet at the same time, if Emma did share the story of her divorce, giving a realistic portrayal of the heartaches a single mother faced, maybe it would help heal the rift in Suzanne's marriage.

"Can't we talk and unpack at the same time?" Suzanne asked.

"Of course, dear. Just give me a minute while I think where to start. . . ."

"Why is everything in such a mess?" Grace asked. She meant her mother's suite, but her question seemed weighted with a double meaning. "Wouldn't it have been simpler to empty one box at a time instead of rummaging through fifteen of them?"

"Probably. But I was looking for things, you see, and I was in a hurry.

Freida wanted to borrow one of my crochet books, and Stella Grabinsky needed some wrapping paper, and Lester couldn't find his knife sharpener, so I said he could use mine, and—"

"That's why everyone loves you so much, Grandma. You're generous to a fault. I think you'd even give away your heart of gold if someone needed it."

Emma frowned. "I'm not the saint you girls think I am. That's what I meant the other day when I said that I shared some of the blame for my divorce. It wasn't black and white, you see. And Karl wasn't the evil villain. He was a generous, hardworking man, and even if what he wanted me to do was wrong, he had his own reasons for it." She picked up a pile of dish towels lying on the back of the sofa and carried them across the room to the kitchenette. She opened one drawer after another, discovered they were already full, then carried the towels back to where she'd found them.

"And your divorce won't be all Jeffrey's fault either, Suzy," she continued. "You two were once deeply in love. I know you were, I saw you together. What you had was very rare and precious, but somehow or other you let it die. The problem with Karl and me, right from the start, was that we were so very different. And without that common ground to water and till, our love never had a chance to grow. . . ."

PART TWO

Emma's Story
1906 - 1924

THIRTEEN

I clearly recall two events from my childhood, growing up in Bremenville. The first was the night we escaped from the flood when I was four years old, and the second was the warm July day when I was six that Papa's surprise arrived. He had ordered it, like everything else in our house, from the Sears Roebuck company in Chicago. Papa was always one of Mr. Sears' best customers. In fact, the company could have photographed every room in our house, pasted the pictures together, and called it their catalogue. If Sears had sold proper Christian husbands, Papa probably would have ordered four of them for us from the catalogue too. He trusted Mr. Sears.

This day turned out to be almost as exciting as the Fourth of July, which we had just celebrated the week before. Around ten o'clock, the stationmaster's son rode his bicycle out to our farm to tell Papa that a huge crate addressed to Reverend F. Schroder had arrived from Chicago on the morning train.

Papa's grin stretched ear to ear. "Pack a picnic lunch," he told Mama. "We're all going to town."

"What is it, Papa? What did you buy this time?" Eva and I jumped around him like two grasshoppers in a hayfield.

"Can't tell you," he said. "It's a surprise."

"Is it something for the farm, the church, or the house?" Sophie asked. She was nearly eleven and much better at guessing games than Eva and me.

"It's for the house, Liebchen," Papa replied.

That really stumped me. I couldn't imagine what else we could possibly need for the house. As far as I could tell, every room was already stuffed to the brim with gewgaws and gimcracks. Then I remembered all the books piled on the floor of Papa's study. Maybe he had finally bought a new bookcase to hold them all.

"Who is the surprise for?" I asked, hoping to show up Sophie with my cleverness.

"It belongs to all of us," he said, laughing, "and that's all I'm going to say! No more hints!" Although we begged and pleaded with him, he wouldn't relent. He waded through the kitchen toward the back door with the three of us attached to his legs like leeches. "Do you girls want to come with me to borrow Mr. Metzger's wagon?" he asked.

Of course we did! That was part of the ritual whenever a crate arrived at the station from Sears. We would ride our two horses bareback across the fields to the Metzger farm—Papa and Eva on the big gelding, Sophie and me on the mare, hanging on to her mane and to each other for dear life. Then we'd hitch the horses to the Metzgers' farm wagon to fetch Papa's latest prize home from town.

By the time we returned to the parsonage with the borrowed wagon, Mama had packed a lunch and changed from her everyday cotton wrapper into a long summer skirt and shirtwaist. "You girls come in the house and get ready too," she called from the back door.

Ready? I was ready! But Mama made us all come inside and wash our faces and tie clean pinafores over our dresses and, worst of all, put on shoes. Accustomed to going bare, my feet felt hot and pinched, imprisoned in Sophie's cast-off high-buttons. Sophie fastened a Sunday ribbon in her hair, but I couldn't be bothered. I wet my hands and slicked back the loose tendrils that had escaped from my braids, then raced out to the wagon again. I pitied baby Vera, who had just celebrated her first birthday. With only thin tufts of hair on her round, pink head, she was forced to wear a scratchy, starched bonnet to protect her scalp from the sun. She tugged on her bonnet strings and grunted like a baby pig, desperate to free herself.

When we arrived at the train station, it seemed as though the whole town had gathered to ogle Papa's enormous crate. A half-dozen ragged Bauer children crawled all over it, trying to peer through the planks to see what was inside. It had huge arrows and warnings painted on all four sides that said *This End Up!* Whatever it was, it obviously had a bottom and a top that couldn't be mixed around.

The crowd parted to let Papa through, just as I imagined the Red Sea had once parted for Moses. Papa shook the stationmaster's hand. "Do you have a pry bar I could use, Amos?" he asked.

"Are you gonna open it up here?" old Amos asked in astonishment. I held my breath with the rest of the crowd.

"Yessir. It says on the guarantee that I'm supposed to inspect it at the depot, and if I'm not completely satisfied with the quality or the tone, I can return it to Chicago and they'll send me my dollar back."

"A *dollar?*" Amos cried. "They sent this all the way from Chicago for only a dollar?"

"That's right," Papa said proudly. "It's called the 'no money in advance' plan. The balance is on deposit at the Bremenville bank until I see whether or not this instrument is as good as the advertisement claimed."

Everyone stared at Papa in awe. He had to be just about the smartest, most well-educated man in Bremenville. A prickle of excitement scampered down my spine at his words: *this instrument.* It was no ordinary bookcase after all, but something truly wondrous!

Wood creaked against nails as Papa carefully pried off the front of the crate. I glimpsed a dark, reddish form beneath wads of excelsior. Then a hush fell over the crowd as Papa removed the packing material and we all caught sight of his latest surprise. It was a full-size, American Home upright parlor grand piano, with a twenty-five-year guarantee. The wood, beneath a layer of dust, was rich mahogany with recessed panels, engraved with swirling leaves and vines. Fancy carved pillars held up the keyboard—and it even came with a stool and an instruction book. It was so magnificent that for a moment, no one could speak.

"That's a mighty fine-looking piano you have there, Fred," the station-master finally said in a hushed voice. Everyone nodded in agreement. I almost said *Amen.*

"Let's see what it sounds like." Papa wiped his hands on the seat of his pants and carefully lifted the keyboard cover. Ivory and ebony gleamed in the sunlight. His long fingers found the keys he wanted—and out came music! I hadn't even known that Papa could play! Several familiar hymns eventually took shape—liberally sprinkled with wrong notes and false starts. Even so, it was clear to me that this was the finest piano in the whole world.

"Are we going to keep it, Papa?" I asked when he finished a stumbling version of "Ein Feste Burg."

He rubbed his chin thoughtfully. "I don't know, Liebchen. It sounds to me like they left an awful lot of wrong notes in it at the factory."

My heart froze, then I saw the corners of Papa's mouth twitch as he suppressed a grin. Sophie caught on a few seconds before I did.

"You're teasing us, Papa! Those wrong notes are in your fingers, not in the piano!"

He laughed out loud, and I knew that the piano was mine. "*It belongs to all of us,*" Papa had said, but in my heart it was mine. I wormed my way between everyone's legs so I could touch it and claim it. In an instant, I fell in love with the feel of the cool, smooth keys beneath my fingers. I sounded one note, then another and another. I heard rollicking music in my head—hundreds and thousands of notes and melodies—and I vowed that one day they would spring magically from my fingers.

We ate our picnic lunch in the park beside the train station while Papa and the other men nailed the crate shut again and loaded it onto the wagon. The four Bauer boys—Wilfred, Paul, Karl, and Markus—came home with us to help unload it. Not trusting any of them—especially Markus—I rode in the back of the wagon to guard my precious cargo. Markus was three years older than me and, according to Sophie, a renowned prankster at school. He had dark, shaggy hair that hung in his eyes, and he wore a smirk of superiority on his wide mouth as if laughing at the whole world and everyone in it. I couldn't imagine what he could possibly find to laugh about—his clothes were little more than rags and his bare feet were always stained three shades darker than the rest of him with ground-in dirt. Shopkeepers would suddenly grow more alert whenever Markus wandered into their stores, and I felt the same way every time he came around.

Papa drove the wagon slowly, carefully, all the way home. After a while, I discovered that if I pressed my ear to the side of the crate I could hear faint, chiming chords whenever we hit a bump. I closed my eyes and listened, imagining that I heard angels playing their harps in heaven.

"What in the world are you doing, *Katze*?" Markus asked. He called me Katze because I loved to chase the cats that lived in our barn.

"Nothing. I'm just resting my head." I didn't want to share my secret, but before I could stop him, Markus pressed his ear against the crate and discovered it for himself.

"Hey! You can hear music!" he announced to all his brothers. "Put your ear on it and listen!" If it hadn't been such a terrible sin to hate someone, I would have hated Markus.

When we pulled into the yard, I didn't see how the four scrawny Bauer boys could ever heave that huge piano up the porch steps and into our house. But Papa—wonderful, wise Papa—had figured everything out already. He pried loose a section of porch railing, then backed the wagon up to it. Once the crate was opened, the piano simply rolled off the wagon, across the porch, and right into our parlor on its own little wheels. He paid each of the Bauer boys for helping him—even Markus who, to my mind, hadn't done much of anything. He allowed them to plunk the keys and spin around on the piano stool a few times as part of their reward, then gave them each a couple of Mama's apple fritters and packed them off to town on foot.

At last—and forever—the marvelous Sears Roebuck American Home upright parlor grand piano was mine!

———

Because she was the oldest, my sister Sophie was allowed to take piano lessons with the organist from church. At first I was green with envy—another terrible sin—but it soon became obvious to me and everyone else that Sophie would never find her way out of Book One. She couldn't carry a tune if you put it in a bushel basket for her, much less play one on the piano. When her square, chunky fingers hit the ivories, it sounded as if a herd of Holsteins had stepped on a bees' nest and were stampeding across the keyboard. She was supposed to practice for half an hour every night, but she would ask every five minutes if her time was up. And the way she squirmed on the piano stool, you would have thought it was crawling with fire ants.

I would hide in the parlor during Sophie's lessons, listening to every word the teacher said about whole notes and quarter notes and arching my wrists, then I'd play all my favorite songs later, by ear. I caught on quickly—unlike Sophie, who took so long to find each note that it was like waiting for stalactites to form in a cave, one slow drip at a time.

One afternoon Papa heard me playing a hymn and decided—to everyone's great relief—that I was the one who should take lessons. I can't say who was more thrilled, me or Sophie. I practiced for hours on end, progressing all the way through Book Three in no time. Mama would have to come into the parlor and tell me to stop practicing and go outside to play.

I was content playing hymns and practice exercises until the world-famous Redpath Chautauqua came to Bremenville when I was twelve. I had walked into town with Eva, who was ten, on an errand for Mama one sunny June day, to discover posters in all the shop windows announcing the great event. More posters had been nailed to all the tree trunks, banners draped from Main Street's lampposts, and a Redpath hawker stood in Lincoln Park urging the crowd to purchase advance tickets to be sure of a seat—even though the show itself wouldn't arrive for several weeks.

Bursting with excitement, Eva and I ran all the way home to ask Papa if we could buy tickets too. We knew what the Chautauqua was, of course. A girl in my class at school named Hilda Lang had seen one in the city last summer and told us all about the week-long event with live music and magical wonders and famous orators. But I had never dreamt that the "inspirational tent show" would come to Bremenville.

Eva and I raced up the porch steps, all out of breath, and slammed into the front hallway—only to find Papa's study door firmly closed. That meant he was writing a sermon and couldn't be disturbed. Panting and gasping, we sank down on the floor to wait, leaning our backs against his door.

"Do you think there will really be a Red Indian at the show, like the one on the poster?" Eva whispered.

"Oh yes," I whispered back. "Hilda said she saw Indians with feathers and war paint and everything."

"Was she scared? I'd be terrified!"

"Don't worry, I'm sure they're all friendly Indians. They wouldn't dare send any other kind."

"What else did Hilda see?"

"A real Hawaiian crooner with a ukelele, and a magician who made stuff disappear, and a yodeler . . . and she said it was the most magnificent music she'd ever heard in her life! And Hilda said—"

Suddenly Papa opened the door and we fell backward at his feet. "What in the world is all this running and panting and whispering about? Did some great tragedy just occur that I should know about?" He had his vest unbuttoned and his shirt sleeves rolled up as if he had been working very hard. He planted his hands on his hips and frowned, but I wasn't fooled. Gentle, patient Papa had never laid a hand on any of us, unlike the Bauers' papa who took his belt to them sometimes. I scrambled to my feet to hug Papa's waist.

"It's not a tragedy at all. It's the most wonderful news I ever heard! The Redpath Chautauqua is coming to town on July seventh, and we have to hurry and buy tickets or the man said they'd all be sold out and we'll miss the chance of a lifetime to hear the brass band and the opera singers and a real live orchestra and—"

"And Red Indians!" Eva added.

"Can we go, Papa? Please, *please*, can we go?"

Papa stared at me as if he hadn't understood a word I'd said. I thought I would have to repeat the whole explanation in German, and I was trying to translate it in my mind when Mama hurried out from the kitchen, drying her hands on her apron.

"What's wrong? What happened?"

"Well, Louise, it seems that the Chautauqua is coming to town," Papa said with a wry grin.

"Oh, is that all?" Mama said. "Where's the sugar and baking powder I asked you girls to buy?"

Eva and I stared at each other in horror. We would have to walk a whole mile back into town! When Mama saw that we had forgotten them, she threw up her hands and disappeared into the kitchen, mumbling beneath her breath in German. Papa covered his mouth, and I knew he was trying not to laugh. I decided to take advantage of his good humor. "Hey, Papa! Since we have to walk back into town anyway, could you give us some money for the Chautauqua so we could buy the tickets now . . . while they last?"

"Hay is for horses," he said, "not proper young ladies. And I can't promise that we'll go until I look into it and see if it's a respectable show. I won't allow my daughters to watch a bunch of show girls or anything else that's indecent."

It took a long time to walk into town and back. And it took longer still for Papa to investigate the Chautauqua and learn that the women who traveled with the show weren't racy show girls at all, but wholesome college students. And that the climax of each show was an inspirational lecture on such beneficial topics as the glories of hard work or achieving personal success. A week before the big day, Papa bought tickets for our whole family. I hugged him so hard he claimed I'd nearly broken his ribs.

When the Chautauqua arrived in Bremenville on a special train, the entire town came out to watch. Sophie, Eva, Vera, and I finished our chores quickly so we could walk into town and see the huge canvas tent go up. A brass band, dressed in white uniforms with gold braid, marched in a parade from the train station to the tent grounds. I could scarcely get to sleep that night.

The show was everything I had dreamed of and more. We sat in the same row as the Bauers, who had somehow managed to scrape together enough money for tickets. Markus Bauer planted himself in the seat beside me, but I refused to let his oily presence spoil my rapture.

"Who'd you steal your ticket from?" I whispered during intermission. Markus stuck out his tongue at me.

That night, the Chautauqua changed my life. Eva said it changed hers too, but that was only because she had nightmares about Indians chasing her for months afterward. But my life was *really* changed because for the first time I realized what a huge, exciting world existed beyond Bremenville, a world filled with exotic people and dazzling music—a world where large-bosomed opera divas sang magnificent arias in Italian; where orchestras played soaring overtures; where magicians in black silk tuxedos performed for queens and kings; where the sound of yodeling echoed through the mountains; and where Hawaiians with broad, honey-colored faces strummed ukeleles beneath palm trees.

I fell in love with all kinds of music that night when I was twelve years old. The four-part hymns I used to coax from my Sears Roebuck piano seemed like dull noise in comparison. I bought my first piece of real sheet music after that—a popular tune called "Alexander's Ragtime Band," composed by a man named Irving Berlin—and I practiced it over and over whenever Papa left the house.

"Come and play dolls with me under the apple tree," Eva would beg.

"You'll have to play with Vera. I'm practicing."

"How come all you ever want to do is *practice*?"

"Because I'm going to see the whole world, Eva. And this piano is my ticket out of Bremenville."

"That's stupid!" Eva exclaimed. "You can't carry a ticket as big as a piano!"

I saw what she had imagined and smiled. "No, silly. What I mean is, I'm going to join the Chautauqua someday. And then I'm going to travel all over the world."

"Did Papa say you could go?"

It was the one flaw in my plan. How could I explain to Papa that I wanted to play something besides hymns? Or that I wanted to play music in a concert hall, not a church?

I spent the next two years trying to figure out a way.

FOURTEEN

A month after I celebrated my fourteenth birthday, Archduke Francis Ferdinand was assassinated and war broke out in Europe. The news devastated Papa. The sound of his warm laughter no longer filled the parsonage as it used to, but a cloud of gloom fell over all of us, as thick as the cloud of smoke that would soon blanket Europe. Papa paced the floor of his study late into the night.

"God showed me it was coming, Louise," he moaned as he read the newspaper, "but I never imagined it would be this bad." He gazed solemnly across the dinner table at his wife and four daughters and murmured about how thankful he was that he'd left Germany when he did. Each time a letter arrived from Germany he would get angry, raging on and on about how he wished his relatives had listened to him and moved to America too. He favored neutrality for the United States and preached sermon after sermon about peace and about Jesus, the Prince of Peace. I prayed for the war to end too—so I would have my old papa back.

Mama had always been high-strung, but now her nerves seemed about to snap from the constant worry about her family back in Germany. Five of her nephews fought on the western front—three of Uncle Kurt's sons, one of Aunt Runa's, and one of Aunt Ada's. As the war spread, disrupting and eventually halting the telegraph and mail services, Mama's fear for their safety escalated.

I looked for any excuse to escape the suffocating atmosphere at our house. Eva and I fled to the movies to watch Fatty Arbuckle in *The Keystone Kops* every chance we got. Papa had always been very mindful of where his daughters went and what they did, but the war so distracted him that he didn't notice how much time we spent at the movies. I saw this as a good sign as far as my plan to join the Chautauqua was concerned.

It was a welcome diversion from all the doom and gloom when Mama and Papa decided it was time to find a husband for Sophie, who would turn nineteen in August. Everyone always said how pretty Sophie was, with her round face and blue eyes and fair hair the color of Papa's. She had a nice round figure too—the kind that drew idiotic attention from all the boys—with a narrow waist and a matronly bosom like Mama's. I was still such a scrawny sack of knees and elbows that I despaired of ever having proportions like Sophie's.

My sister was all for the idea of marriage—but then, she didn't have a future on stage to look forward to like I did. Sophie actually liked to cook and sew and things like that, so Papa had no trouble at all arranging a match between her and Otto Mueller, who was twenty-two and helped his father run the feed store. Otto was okay to look at, I suppose—a lot cleaner and better dressed than any of the Bauer boys Mama was always raving about. Otto was going to fix up a couple of rooms in the back of the store for them to live in. I didn't know how Sophie could stomach the idea of living with a boy, much less living behind the feed store. The smell of feed always made me sneeze, and the idea of sharing a double bed with any of the boys I knew from school didn't bear thinking about.

Sophie's wedding plans rolled forward like a carriage without a hand brake—slowly at first, then gathering speed and momentum until we were all running in a hundred directions at once and the whole affair was out of control. I vowed to die a spinster before I would get carried away with such nonsense. By the time the day of the wedding arrived, I think we all felt as though we'd been run over roughshod by a team of horses.

"What a beautiful bride you are, Sophie!" Mama exclaimed on the big day. "If only my oma could see you! You were named after her, you know."

Yes, Mama. You've told us a hundred times, I thought, rolling my eyes. I didn't dare say it out loud. Mama carried on like that all day, and her eyes leaked so many tears I thought I was going to have to put some punch in the crying cup to make her stop. Magda Bauer said they were tears of joy, but I wasn't so sure. Sophie helped Mama around the house a lot more than Eva and I did—without even complaining—so I figured Mama had to be a little upset about losing her best helper.

Sophie did make a beautiful bride, though. Eva and I spent the afternoon before the wedding gathering huge bunches of wild flowers and roses from parishioners' gardens all over town to decorate Papa's church and all the food tables. Everything looked beautiful, and smelled beautiful, too, as the scent of roses filled the air. The reception on the church lawn turned out to be so lovely that I even heard Papa laughing like he used to do. His sorrow ebbed for a little while as his joy overflowed, just as the sampler in Mama's parlor said it would.

"Did you see how pink Sophie's cheeks got when Papa said, 'You may kiss the bride'?" I asked Eva. We were supposed to be making sure the guests had plenty of punch, but we were giggling behind the hydrangea bushes instead.

"She looked like a scalded pig!" Eva said, laughing. "Do you suppose that was the first time Otto ever kissed her?"

"No, I saw him sneak a kiss once in our parlor. She turned red then too."

"Why?" Eva asked. "She never turns red when Mama and Papa kiss her."

"That's because when a boy kisses you it's disgusting and embarrassing!" I shuddered at the thought.

"How do you know it's disgusting?" a deep voice behind me asked. "Have you ever been kissed, Katze?" I whirled around to face Markus Bauer. I didn't know what made me angriest—the smirk on his face, the fact that he'd been eavesdropping, or his outrageous question. I tackled his question first.

"It's none of your business if I've been kissed or not, Markus Bauer!"

"That must mean you haven't been," he said, laughing. He moved a step closer and fastened his dark eyes on mine. "Want to try it?"

For the space of a heartbeat I forgot that he was disgusting Markus Bauer and noticed instead how long his lashes were and what a rich shade of chocolate brown his eyes were. He had beautifully shaped lips, too, even if they were always curled in a sneer, and I wondered what they tasted like. Everyone always commented on how handsome his father, Gus Bauer, was, but for the first time I noticed that Gus's seventeen-year-old son was just as good-looking. Then I came to my senses and realized that it was only Markus.

"I'd sooner kiss a mule," I said.

"Be my guest," he laughed. "Come on, I'll even drive you over to the Schultzes' farm in my Model T. They've got two mules. You can take your pick." He took my arm and propelled me forward a few steps toward the street. I pictured myself flying down the winding river road in his motorcar with my hair streaming and the wind in my face, laughing for joy as the trees rushed past us. Then I stopped walking. I shook off his hand.

"No, thank you."

"Suit yourself, Katze," he said with a shrug. "There are plenty of other girls who'd love a ride . . . *and* a kiss." He winked and strolled across the grass like a lanky tomcat to talk to Hilda Lang. For some reason, the sight of them laughing together made me furious.

"He almost kissed you," Eva said breathlessly. "His lips were this close. . . ."

"Oh, go soak your head!" I told her and stomped away.

Two years before, Hilda Lang wouldn't have given any of the Bauers the time of day. But somehow or other Gus had scraped together enough money to go into partnership with Arno Myers on a Ford motorcar dealership just as the Model T became the working man's car, and the Bauers had been respectable ever since. Markus had quit school to work in the Ford garage, and everyone said there wasn't an engine in the world that Markus couldn't fix. He'd already earned enough money to buy his own Model T and a decent set of clothes for himself. I wondered if his feet were still three shades darker than the rest of him.

When I heard a cheer go up from the church lawn, I wandered back to join the party again. I was just in time to see Sophie and Otto say farewell to their guests as they prepared to leave. As I watched them drive away in Mr. Mueller's buggy, I got a funny hollow feeling inside. Markus left in his car shortly afterward, giving Hilda Lang and her brother Peter a lift into town. I didn't know why, but as I helped clean up after the wedding, I felt angry with all five of them for deserting me. I was outside, scraping plates and slamming dishes around, when Mama and Magda Bauer's voices drifted out to me from the kitchen where they were washing dishes.

"Such a beautiful day," Magda murmured, "and such a happy couple."

"Yes, I pray that Fritz and I can find a fine young man like Otto for each of our girls."

Mama's words brought me up short. I didn't need her and Papa to find me a husband! I knew they had arranged Sophie's marriage, but I wasn't at all like Sophie. She was five years older than me and very old-fashioned. Besides, she had been born in Germany where everything was done differently. I was an American.

"The Muellers are a wonderful family," Magda agreed.

"You and Gus have always been like family to us," Mama continued. "And we'll become a real family someday, if the match works out between Emma and Markus."

Me and Markus? I dropped the plate I was holding and ran. I didn't know where I was running to or who I was running from, but I had to escape from their terrible words. I didn't want to believe they were true. I wanted no part of the life they were planning for me, but it sounded as though I had no choice. I would have to obey my parents as the Bible commanded and marry Markus, wouldn't I? My life would slowly roll toward that future as inevitably as Sophie's had.

I ran toward the barn, searching for Eva, then decided I didn't want to talk to Eva, so I kicked off my Sunday shoes and ran in the opposite direction, barefooted. By the time I reached the churchyard, I was out of breath. I slipped into the sanctuary to rest and think, but I wasn't alone. Papa was puttering around the nave, gathering up wilted garlands from the wedding.

"What's wrong, Liebchen?" he asked as I flopped into a pew, breathless and shaken. I decided to come straight to the point.

"Are you and Mama going to arrange a marriage for me like you arranged Sophie's?"

Papa looked puzzled. "Of course," he said after a pause.

"Why can't I pick my own husband?"

"Well, because it's been done this way for generations and . . ."

"Why?"

Papa steepled his fingertips together the way he did when delivering a sermon. "For several good reasons. When you're young, it's much too easy to look for qualities in a mate that are superficial and unimportant to an enduring marriage. Parents who understand the commitment involved are better able to judge someone's maturity and stability."

"But what if I don't want to marry the man you choose? Are you going to make me marry him anyway?"

"No, of course not. But I would hope that you'd give the young man a chance and not dismiss him before you get to know him." He bent to pick a flower off the floor, then sat down in the pew beside me. "What's this all about, Liebchen?"

"I wasn't eavesdropping on purpose, honest I wasn't, but I heard Mama and Aunt Magda say that I'm supposed to marry Markus. Is that true, Papa?"

When he sighed wearily I was sorry I had quelled what little joy he had found that day. "I've known Gus Bauer since I first arrived in America. Your mother traveled on the boat with Aunt Magda. They're our oldest and dearest friends, and we share a great deal in common. Family traditions and a common background provide a good basis for marriage. And Markus is a bright, hard-working boy who—"

I clapped my hands over my ears. "No! I can't stand Markus! I've known him since we were little kids!"

"But you aren't children anymore, and if you give Markus a chance, I think you'll see how much he's changed since he's grown up. Neither one of you will be ready for marriage for several years, but when the time comes, I hope you'll be as fair to Markus as you would be to any other suitor."

"I don't want any suitors at all! I don't want to get married and live in Bremenville!"

Papa stared at me in silent confusion. I saw lines around his eyes and gray hair at his temples that I'd never noticed before. He looked so bewildered that I felt I had to explain what I meant. Before I could stop myself, my secret tumbled out.

"I'm going to join the Chautauqua, Papa. I'm going to travel all over the country and play the piano."

"Emma," he said quietly. "God didn't give you such a fine musical talent to waste on the Chautauqua."

"Oh, Papa . . . I knew you wouldn't understand."

"But I do understand." His tired eyes met mine and I saw a well of wisdom and sorrow in them. "You feel like there's a fire burning inside you that could light up the night with its brilliance if only you could release it. Making music gives you such joy that you want to share it with everyone you meet so that others can sing the songs you hear in your heart."

"How . . . how did you know?" I felt as though Papa had looked into my heart and read its secrets.

"Because that fire comes from God, Liebchen. Whether you burn to play the piano or to preach the Gospel, He plants the desire inside each of us to be used for His purposes." Papa reached for my hand and took it in his. "On the night of the Chautauqua, you experienced the power of music. But you don't have to travel the show circuit to unleash that power. There are other means of expressing the song God has put in your heart."

"Then you'll really let me play the piano, Papa? You won't make me marry Markus and live in three rooms behind the Ford garage?"

"Let's not get ahead of ourselves," he said with a sigh. "Finish school first, Liebchen. Then we'll pray about what comes next."

———

In 1916, a group of Germans blew up a munitions arsenal in New Jersey, and the attitude of most Americans toward the war in Europe began to shift out of neutral. A year earlier I'd learned to play the popular tune "I Didn't Raise My Boy to Be a Soldier," but now many Americans were eager to send their boys over there to kill those "filthy Huns." Such talk wasn't common among our own church members, of course—we were still a mostly German congregation. But after two more factories moved into Bremenville several years earlier, the town's population had grown to include a large number of

Irish immigrants. They had even built their own church—St. Brigit's Catholic Church—across the river from ours. They hated Germany and all things German.

By the time I was seventeen, my figure had finally begun to fill out in all the right places. I wasn't as pretty as Sophie and Eva, who had Mama's upturned nose and Papa's clear blue eyes, but I was passable. I had inherited Papa's oval face and long, straight nose, and some unknown relative's gray eyes. I would never be as petite and curvaceous as my sisters, but I liked my tall, willowy shape the way it was. It was my hair that I hated. It wasn't blond and curly like all three of my sisters', but plain and straight and the bland color of wheat toast. I didn't have the patience to pin it up on my head and make it look good, so one day I had it bobbed, like all the city girls were doing.

"What on earth will Papa say?" Eva worried all the way home. "You look like a suffragette!"

"Good! I had to do something different to prove to him that I don't belong in Bremenville."

"Don't say such things. Where else would you belong but here with your family?"

"Listen, Eva. It's fine for you and Sophie to get married and live here, but I'm not getting married. I'm going to play the piano all over the world."

As it turned out, Papa had just learned that morning that thousands of women and children were starving to death in Germany because of a terrible famine, so he and Mama wouldn't have noticed if I had shaved my head bald. All the boys from church noticed, though, and they fought over my basket at the annual church picnic the following Saturday. Hilda Lang's father auctioned off the picnic baskets to raise money for missions that year, since Papa didn't think he could cope with a lot of foolish fun and festivities.

My basket fetched the highest price, but when the winner came to claim the privilege of sharing it with me, I was surprised to discover that Markus Bauer had bought it. I shook my head in disbelief.

"What's wrong with you, Katze?" he asked with a crooked grin. He was tall and muscular and twenty years old, with the swarthy good looks of a movie idol.

"You could have had your pick of any girl in town!"

"I know."

"So why did you pick *me*? We're practically cousins, for goodness' sake."

"I saw the way all the boys fluttered around you like moths, and I made up my mind to beat them all to the flame."

"I don't know why they were acting like that," I said as I bent to spread my picnic cloth on the grass beside the church. "I didn't do anything to encourage their attentions. I don't care one fig about any of them."

"Not here, Katze," Markus said, snatching up the cloth. "Follow me." He headed toward Papa's orchard away from all the other picnickers.

"Wait . . . where are you going?" I had to hurry to keep up with his long-legged stride.

"Considering the outrageous price I paid for this lunch, I deserve a little privacy when I eat it," he said. He spread out the picnic cloth behind an apple tree and flopped down beside it, stretching out like a hound dog before a fireplace. "I expect to be hand-fed, you know," he said with a lazy smile.

"Then you bought the wrong girl's basket," I replied. "Maybe Hilda Lang or one of your other adoring fans would be willing to feed you, but not me." I knelt down on the opposite side of the blanket from him and began laying out plates and food from the basket.

"That's what makes all the boys flock to you, you know . . . that saucy attitude of yours. You don't flirt and sigh like all the other girls or act as though your main concern in life is to trap some poor fellow into proposing."

"Of course not! I don't intend to get married until I'm much older. In fact, I'll be leaving Bremenville one day soon."

"Is that right?" he said with a grin.

I threw a piece of fried chicken onto his plate. "Why do I always get the feeling that you're laughing at me, Markus Bauer?"

"I'm not laughing, Katze . . . honest I'm not." But no matter how hard he worked to pull down the corners of his mouth, he couldn't disguise the laughter in his dark eyes.

"You are too. You've been laughing at me ever since I was a kid."

The laughter in his eyes suddenly died. "You're Pastor Schroder's daughter," he said quietly, "not Gus Bauer's. You have no idea what it's like to be really laughed at." He picked up his piece of chicken and began eating. I was afraid that I'd ruined the afternoon and hurt his feelings, but as he took a second bite he said, "Mmm, this is good. Did you make it yourself?"

"No, Eva did. I'm a terrible cook. If those boys who bid for my picnic basket knew the truth about me, they'd all run in the other direction."

"They're not after you for your cooking," he said, swallowing a bite of his dinner roll. "They're intrigued with the challenge of winning your cold, cruel heart."

"Ah, so that explains it! I knew it wasn't my looks."

He swiped his napkin across his mouth, then laid it beside his plate. "You honestly don't know, do you?" he murmured. I was astounded to see that Markus was even more handsome when he was serious than he was when he was smirking.

"Don't know what?"

"That you're beautiful, Emma."

"I am not." But I saw by his expression that he meant it. I looked away, afraid that I was blushing like a foolish schoolgirl. He took my face in his hand and turned it toward him again. His fingers felt rough as he caressed my cheek.

"Beauty is more than perfect features, Emma. You have an inner fire that draws everyone to you, the way flowers turn toward the sun. You walk into a room and the place comes alive at last. You sit down at the piano and there's laughter and song. You don't need anyone or anything because you know exactly who you are, and you're complete all by yourself. You *are* beautiful, Emma. All the more so because you don't even realize it."

I felt as though I should say something in return, but I didn't know what to say. I had known Markus all my life, but for the first time I caught a glimpse of how vulnerable he really was. For all his outward swagger and handsome charm, he was a hurt little boy inside, hiding his pain and his family's shame behind pranks and laughter.

When he finally lowered his hand, my cheek felt hot where his fingers had been. Then a careless grin spread across his face as he hid himself again. "So did Eva bake me something good for dessert too?"

For the next hour, we laughed and talked like the good friends we had never been. We were comfortable with each other, our conversation flowing easily, and we shared so much in common, it surprised me. Then I recalled Papa's words about common traditions making a good basis for marriage, and I remembered Mama's plans for a match between Markus and me, and I became so panicky I wanted to run. When I heard Mr. Lang rounding up all the children for the games and foot races, I quickly began packing away the picnic things. Markus stopped me, covering my hand with his.

"Can I ask a favor, Katze?"

"You want to take the leftovers home, right?"

"No," he said, laughing, "it has nothing to do with leftovers. I was wondering if you'd write to me." His face was serious again.

"Write to you?"

"Yes. It's only a matter of time before President Wilson declares war on

Germany, and I'm going to enlist in the army as soon as he does. Will you write to me when I'm over in France and tell me what's going on back here at home?"

"Sure, Markus . . . that is, if I'm home myself. I'm hoping to get out of Bremenville someday soon."

"I'd be glad to hear from you wherever you are." He released my hand and helped shove plates and napkins back into the hamper. When we were finished we stood, and I shook the crumbs off the tablecloth. Markus stared at his feet, suddenly shy.

"Can I ask another favor, Katze?"

"What now?"

"Will you give me a kiss to remember you by when I'm slogging through the trenches?" He turned his head and pointed to his cheek.

What's the harm? I thought and stepped toward him, closing my eyes. But at the last second he whirled to face me, kissing me full on the lips! He caught my bobbed hair in his hand and held my mouth against his until he had taken his fill. When he finally released me, my head spun. I was too stunned to remember to slap him.

"I've been wanting to do that ever since your sister's wedding three years ago," he said as he sauntered away, laughing. "Now I can die a happy man."

———

When the United States declared war on Germany, Markus Bauer enlisted along with millions of other American men "to help make the world safe for democracy." He came home for a brief visit before Uncle Sam shipped him overseas, and every girl in Bremenville except me swooned at the sight of him in his uniform. The Bauers invited our family to his going-away dinner. I found myself conveniently seated beside him at the table and knew that our parents hadn't abandoned their matchmaking plans. Mama gazed across the table at us throughout the meal, her head tilted dreamily to one side. I felt like a fly under glass. When Uncle Gus lit a fat after-dinner cigar, I used the smoke as an excuse to flee to the Bauers' front porch. I might have known Markus would follow me.

"Don't forget, you promised to write," he said as he settled down on the porch steps beside me. I moved to keep a good, safe distance between us, wary of being tricked into another heart-stopping kiss.

"I'll write . . . but don't expect a lot of sentimental mush. You'll have to write to Hilda Lang if you want that kind of nonsense."

He leaned back on his elbows and laughed, stretching his long legs straight out in front of him. His army boots were brand-new and spit-shined to such a high gloss I could almost see myself. They seemed out of place on Markus, who had always run all over Bremenville barefooted.

"Would it bother you if I wrote to Hilda Lang?" he asked.

"Not in the least," I said with a wave of my hand. "I wouldn't care if you wrote to every girl in town."

"Brr!" he said, feigning a shiver. "You're still as cold and cruel as ever, Emma. Promise me you won't change while I'm away, okay? I'll look forward to thawing your frozen heart when I get back."

"You'll have to find me first," I said. "I'm planning to leave Bremenville as soon as I finish school and the war ends."

"Where will you go?"

"I don't know yet . . . but far away from here!"

"You'll be easy to find," he said with a lazy grin. "I'll just follow the music to where the fun is. You'll be right in the middle of it all."

The next day I waved good-bye to Markus and a whole trainload of local boys as they set off to "kill the Kaiser." It gave me a funny feeling to think about them shooting at my German cousins. I only knew my relatives from photographs, but they didn't look any different to me than the American boys who were so intent on killing them. No wonder the war had shattered Papa. If he could have stood in no-man's-land between the two armies and shouted at them to stop the slaughter, he would have done it gladly.

Every time they published pictures of the war in the rotogravure section of the newspaper, Papa would shut himself up in his study alone. The pictures horrified all of us—hospitalized soldiers, blinded by mustard gas; a landscape of blackened stumps in what was once a German forest; mangled corpses lying heaped in a muddy trench. For some reason, I never worried about Markus. I knew he could take care of himself. He'd done it all his life. I envied him for traveling so far beyond Bremenville, even if the journey had taken him away to war. He wrote to me faithfully, describing the queasy voyage across the Atlantic on a crowded troop ship; the frenzied greeting the doughboys received in Paris; the blood-chilling sound of mortar shells exploding at close range. I answered barely one out of every three of his letters.

After most of Bremenville's work force left, I wanted to apply for a job at the woolen mill to do my part like all the other girls my age. But when Papa learned that the mill had a government contract to make Army uniforms, he refused to let me work there. He was so adamantly against the war, he even forbid twelve-year-old Vera to buy liberty stamps because the money went toward the war effort. "I'm the only girl in school," she complained, "who can't 'lick a stamp and lick the Kaiser.' It's unpatriotic!"

Papa did allow us to participate in voluntary rationing programs, such as "wheatless" Mondays and "meatless" Tuesdays. On "gasless" Sundays, all our parishioners hitched horses to their cars for the ride to church. When the Red Cross converted an empty storefront by the train station into a canteen, Papa reluctantly allowed Eva and me to do volunteer work there, since the Red Cross had a reputation as a neutral organization. We decided not to tell him that all the socks we volunteers were busy knitting were sent to our American troops.

Along with knitting, another of our jobs was to collect peach pits, which the army used to make charcoal filters for gas masks. It took seven pounds of pits to make enough charcoal for one mask, and since Uncle Sam needed one million masks, gathering pits kept Eva and me pretty busy. I held the record for collecting the most pounds in a single week—three-and-a-half. Hilda Lang tried to beat my record, foolishly eating an entire bushel of peaches herself, and spent a day and a night in the outhouse with dyspepsia. I remained champion.

But my favorite job at the canteen was entertaining the soldiers who came through Bremenville on the train from all over the country. If I couldn't travel to interesting places, meeting interesting people would have to suffice. While the soldiers ate free sandwiches and cookies and drank gallons of coffee, I played popular tunes on an old upright piano to boost their morale. Sometimes their spirits soared so high we would push all the tables and chairs against the wall and start dancing. Of course, Papa knew nothing about this side of Red Cross work.

I was on my way home from the canteen alone one afternoon when I came upon a commotion in the street. In the center of the gathering crowd I heard the dull thuds and grunts of a fistfight. Curious, I peered over heads and between shoulders for a better look. Three middle-aged factory workers from the Irish part of town had ganged up on a fourth man, who lay on the ground like a heap of used clothing. My stomach lurched. Something about that clothing looked horribly familiar.

"You're a spy for those filthy Jerries, aren't you, man! Aren't you!" Every time the fallen man moved, one of the others would kick him.

"Tell the truth, Fritzie. We know you're one of them."

"If you're not, then let's hear you say the Pledge of Allegiance."

When the man crawled to his knees and tried to stand, they knocked him down again. But not before I caught a glimpse of the man's bloodied face. It was Papa.

"Stop it! Stop it!" I screamed. "Leave him alone!" I ran into the street with my fists flying. I had no intention of turning the other cheek to these bullies like my father was doing. The ringleader grabbed my arm. "Well, then, and who might you be, girlie?" He had the florid face and reddened nose of a man who drank too much. I kicked him hard in the shins.

"Aye! You must be a bloody Hun too," he said, grunting. "You surely fight like one!" He let go of my arm to rub his leg.

"I was born in America, not in an Irish bog like you!"

The other two bullies laughed as they circled around me, teasing and baiting me. I had become the center of their attention now, but I was too angry and too worried about Papa to be afraid for myself. I could hear my father moaning softly on the ground behind me.

"How dare you attack an innocent man! One who won't even fight back!"

"Sure, and he's not so innocent, missy," the red-faced man said. "He talks just like the Kaiser."

"Vee vill vin dis var!" a short, apelike man cried, mimicking Papa's accent.

"We don't tolerate spies," the leader said. "We believe in America for Americans."

"We're more American than you are, you stupid Micks!" I shouted. "Just because you're too old and decrepit for the army doesn't give you the right to start your own private war!"

They were no longer laughing. I had made them mad. Monkey-man grabbed me from behind, pinning my arms. "Let me go, you ugly ape!" I kicked and struggled to free myself, but he was too strong. I despaired of anyone helping me, when a man suddenly pushed his way through the crowd of bystanders.

"Leave them alone! Let her go, Liam! What's the matter with you?" I could tell by his accent that he was Irish like the other three.

My captor jerked roughly on my arms. "We've caught us a couple of spies, Paddy. And a feisty one, at that."

"Aye, this one here refused to buy liberty stamps." The florid-faced leader gave Papa another kick in the ribs.

Before I had time to cry out, the newcomer grabbed the bully by the front of his shirt, nearly lifting the man off the ground. "You want to fight someone, Kevin, fight me!" he said in his face. "Not a harmless man of the cloth."

"But he's a Protestant—"

"This isn't Ireland! Haven't you had enough hatred for one lifetime? Isn't that why we came to America? To get away from prejudice and fighting?" My defender was in his early twenties, much younger than the other three men, but he wielded a mysterious power over them that caused them to back away in respect.

"Now, I'm thinking you owe these people an apology," he said, releasing the man.

The leader straightened his clothes. "I'm not apologizing to Huns," he said sullenly.

"Then don't you dare show your face at St. Brigit's until you do, Kevin Malloy."

"Aw, now Paddy, what are you taking their side for? They're Jerries . . . and Protestants to boot."

Paddy took a step toward him, fists clenched. "Help the man to his feet, Liam."

"But he—"

"I said, help him to his feet!"

They quickly obeyed, hauling Papa to his feet none too gently. I couldn't understand the magnetic authority the young man had over men who were twenty years his senior. After they got Papa off the ground, Paddy coaxed a reluctant apology from the three bullies.

"I forgive you," Papa said, holding a handkerchief to his split lip. I was furious.

"How can you forgive them? Look how they've hurt you!" He'd been beaten so badly he couldn't even stand up straight, and I feared by the way his left arm hung that it was broken. Papa held up his hand to silence me.

"I forgive them because the Bible says that we must."

"Well, I'll never forgive them for hurting you. Never!"

The young Irishman and I helped Papa to a chair inside the canteen. "You ought to see a doctor, Reverend," he said. "I'd like to help you. Who is your doctor? Let me fetch him."

"Thank you, but I'll be fine." Papa allowed me to clean the blood off his face with a wet cloth, but he insisted that we forget the matter and go home. We went home, but forgetting the matter didn't turn out to be so simple.

News of the attack quickly spread all over town, and a group of elders and deacons came to the parsonage that night to talk to Papa. I stood in the hallway outside the closed parlor door and listened to every word.

"We need to arm ourselves, Pastor! If they would do this to you, what would stop them from attacking our women and children next?"

"He's right, Friedrich. These incidents aren't happening just in Bremenville. Anti-German hysteria has spread all over the United States. We need to fight back!"

"Listen to yourselves," Papa said. His voice was soft, his phrases clipped, as if it hurt him to draw a deep breath. "We cannot stoop to their level. Those who live by the sword die by the sword. Is that what you want for your families?"

"We want our families safe, not beaten to a bloody pulp!"

"There's something else we need to say, Pastor Schroder." I recognized Mr. Metzger's voice. He was the head of the consistory. "There are new laws . . . the government is inflicting heavy penalties for criticizing the war. We think you should stop preaching sermons about peace."

"Am I now taking orders from you instead of the Holy Spirit?" Papa asked angrily. "Are you telling me what I can and cannot preach?"

"We are asking you to consider what happened today. It could have been any one of us. Until this war ends, we dare not draw attention to ourselves or to our German ancestry." He paused, and when he spoke again his voice was calm but firm. "The board has decided to cancel the German-speaking service and to hold English-only services until the war ends. The elders and deacons will be warning our members to speak English in public and to avoid all contact with the Irish-Catholic population. We need to stick more closely together as a community to protect ourselves and our children. . . ."

Disgusted, I didn't wait to hear the rest. I hated Bremenville and my cloistered life here more than ever, and I renewed my determination to flee as soon as the war ended. I was sure my chance could come soon. The news from Europe was good; we were winning the war. The steady stream of letters I received from Markus were optimistic that victory was close at hand.

Markus's letters were also filled with his dreams for the future—dreams which, in his mind, included me. He knew about our parents' scheme to match the two of us and thought it was a good one. But I had no intention of sharing my future with Markus Bauer.

Papa had promised me that he wouldn't make me marry against my will, but the war had altered him so much that I feared he wouldn't remember. I loved my family, but I didn't want a life like Mama's and Sophie's. I wanted one that was filled with music and laughter—I wanted to travel to new places and see new things. As restless as the geese flocking in the Metzgers' field near the river, I waited for the day I could mount up on wings and fly away.

Then in the fall of 1918, just as the Allies stepped up their offensive on the western front, the Spanish influenza epidemic hit. The flu swept through army camps and service ports first, and thousands of soldiers fell ill and died. The outbreak spread to the civilian population next, paralyzing cities as thousands of workers became infected.

"I don't want you girls to work at the Red Cross canteen until this epidemic runs its course," Papa announced at the breakfast table one morning. "Stay away from all public places."

I thought he was being much too overprotective. "What about church?" I said sullenly. "That's a public place."

Papa's face was uncharacteristically stern. "Dr. Strauss has already warned me that the church will need to close if any cases are diagnosed here in Bremenville."

"I feel like a prisoner in this stupid town as it is," I mumbled as I pushed eggs around on my plate.

"You are young, and you imagine that you are invincible, but I assure you that you are not." Papa rose from his seat at the head of the table and laid the newspaper in front of me. "Read this, Emma. Read about the tens of thousands of people who are ill and dying. In some cities, the authorities have gone door to door heaping the corpses on carts, like they did during the Dark Ages when the bubonic plague struck. I'm making you stay home for your own good."

After I'd endured several weeks of being confined to the house, I rebelled. Using the excuse of visiting my sister Sophie in town, I made arrangements to meet a boy at the movies. Eva came with me. We did stop at Sophie's house briefly, as I'd told Papa we would, then I hustled Eva off to the show.

Bremenville's main street was unusually quiet for a Friday night. Even the Irish pubs along the riverfront seemed to be doing a poor business, judging by the stillness of the town and the absence of the bars' noisy ruckus. The ticket lines for the movies stretched to barely half their usual length, but it was the large public warning sign posted outside the theater that stopped Eva in her tracks:

INFLUENZA
frequently complicated with
Pneumonia
is prevalent at this time throughout America.

This theater is cooperating with the Department of Health.
YOU MUST DO THE SAME!
If you have a cold and are coughing and sneezing,
do not enter this theater!
GO HOME AND GO TO BED UNTIL YOU ARE WELL!

"I don't like the sound of that," Eva said. "Let's go home. I don't want to see this stupid movie anyway."

"But if you go home, I'll have to go home too, and I'm supposed to meet someone here. Please, Eva," I begged. "Do me a favor . . . just this time? You may need a favor someday too."

I could tell she was afraid, but I pressured her until she gave in. It was the worst mistake I ever made in my life. There wasn't a thing wrong with my sister that night, but three days later she was burning with fever and gasping for every breath. Papa sent me to fetch Dr. Strauss. I waited in the parlor with Mama and Papa while he examined Eva.

"It's the Spanish influenza," he said when he'd finished examining her. He pulled off the gauze face mask he wore and shook his head. "There's very little we can do except wait for it to run its course."

I went cold all over with dread. It didn't occur to me to be worried about catching the flu myself, even though Eva and I shared a bedroom. But the thought that my disobedience had endangered my sister's life shook me to my core.

"It's very important that we locate the source of infection," Dr. Strauss was saying, "as well as isolate anyone Eva may have infected since then. Can you tell me what her movements were for the past four or five days? Did she attend church yesterday?"

"No, she wasn't feeling well enough to go," Mama said. Her voice was hushed with fear. Papa took her hand in his and held it tightly.

"The only time in the past week that Eva left the parsonage was when she and Emma went to our daughter Sophie's house Friday night," he said.

Everyone turned to me. I didn't wait for the inevitable questions but quickly confessed the truth, hoping that God would have mercy on Eva if I did. "It's all my fault. We did go to see Sophie, but then we went to the movies afterward. It was my idea. Eva didn't want to go inside the theater when she saw the health notice, but I talked her into it."

Dr. Strauss closed his eyes for a moment. "In that case, I don't see how we can possibly stop it from spreading now." He stood and shoved his arms into the sleeves of his overcoat as if it was made of lead. "At this point, you can do much more than I can, Pastor. You can pray."

As soon as the doctor was gone, I fell to my knees in front of the sofa and began to plead with God, my face buried in the cushions. Papa must have seen that my tears of guilt and remorse were genuine because he was surprisingly gentle with me. He knelt beside me a few minutes later and rested his hand on my back.

"Emma . . . I don't make rules to spoil your fun. I make them for the same reason God does—to protect the people I love."

"But why is God punishing Eva?" I cried. "Tell Him to punish me! I'm the one who disobeyed!"

"It's not a punishment, Emma. It's a consequence. God isn't punishing Eva. Sin always carries its own consequences. You both walked past the warning sign. That's what God's laws are—warning signs. We ignore them at our own peril."

My parents wouldn't let me go into the bedroom for fear that I would get sick too, so I stood outside the door, pleading with Eva for forgiveness. I don't know if she heard me or not.

Papa and I nearly wore holes in the floor of the empty church where we knelt and prayed for Eva, but God didn't listen to either one of us. Eva died a week later. Mama and Papa were both at her side in the end. The look on their faces when they closed the bedroom door and came downstairs to tell Vera and me the news haunted me for years afterward.

No one from our church was allowed to come to her funeral and mourn with us because the Department of Health feared that the epidemic might spread. Even my sister Sophie, who was expecting her second baby, didn't dare to come. But Gus and Magda Bauer defied caution to stand in the cemetery behind the church with us that cool fall afternoon and help lower Eva's coffin into the ground. As brilliantly colored leaves drifted to the ground all around us, it seemed impossible that Eva's life, like the leaves', had ended.

My grief and guilt were beyond measure. I felt responsible for Eva's death as surely as if I'd put a gun to her head and pulled the trigger. I couldn't face Papa, who sat in his study the rest of the day, refusing to eat. I couldn't face Mama, who wept and grieved for her daughter upstairs in their bedroom. I couldn't face my sister Vera, who eyed me as though I might somehow cause her death too. And I couldn't face being alone in the room I'd shared with Eva all my life, staring at her clothes and dolls, remembering her, missing her.

I sat shivering on the front porch that evening, wishing with all my heart that I had died instead of Eva.

As twilight fell, I heard a car coming down our road. When it slowed near the church and turned into our yard, I was surprised to see that it was Uncle Gus. He and Aunt Magda had just gone home a few hours ago after the funeral. He turned off the engine and sat in his car for several minutes, unmoving. I wondered if he'd been drinking, but he finally got out and slowly walked toward the house. He looked disheveled, his eyes red, his face streaked with tears he hadn't bothered to wipe.

"Where's Fred?" he asked in a hoarse voice.

"In his study. . . . What's wrong, Uncle Gus?"

He trudged past me into the house as if he hadn't heard my question. I followed him as far as the door and saw Papa come out of his study to meet him in the hallway.

"Gus?"

"It's too much to face in one day, Fred," he wept. "It's too much. . . ."

Papa gripped Uncle Gus by the arms as if they could hold each other up. "Tell me," he whispered.

"Magda and I just received word . . . Markus is dead."

"No!" I cried out. "No, he can't be dead, he can't be! When did he die, how long ago?"

Uncle Gus gazed at me, bleary-eyed. "He died in a tank explosion last week."

I covered my face and wept. I had written to Markus to say that I did not want to marry him when he came home. Now he was dead at the age of twenty-one on a battlefield in Germany—the very soil his parents had left a year before he was born. For the second time, I felt the rod of God's punishment and wrath strike me to my core.

The third blow came a week later when Magda Bauer became ill with influenza and died. She and Eva were only two of the twenty million influenza fatalities worldwide, but we mourned as if they were the only ones.

After the armistice was signed in November of 1918, terrible news began to pour in from Germany too. The nation had been devastated by the war, then ravaged by disease and famine. One after another, my German grandparents had all died. Aunt Runa's son and all three of Uncle Kurt's sons had been killed in battle. Aunt Ada's son had been wounded. The war was finally over, but neither of my parents was ever the same. Nor was I.

FIFTEEN

"Karl Bauer is back in town and has asked permission to court you," Papa told me in the spring of 1919. I hadn't even realized that Karl had left town. He disappeared when he was eighteen and I was twelve, but there were so many more ragged little Bauers running around that I don't think anyone even noticed he was gone. He had been sick shortly before that, laid up in bed for almost a month, but no one ever said what the illness was. Now he was back in Bremenville.

"I'll go out with Karl," I said. It didn't matter to me who I dated. Eva had been my best friend, and I was so lonely after she died that I would have agreed to be courted by any boy who asked just to dull the pain.

Karl arrived a few nights later in a brand-new car to take me to the movies. He was twenty-five, three years older than his brother Markus, six years older than me. If I had never known Markus, I might have described Karl as handsome—he had many of the same facial features as his younger brother. But Markus's looks had been extraordinary; Karl couldn't compare. He had a dash of Aunt Magda's plainness, including her short, squat frame—which on a man translated into "stocky" and "barrel-chested." He had Markus's chocolate-brown eyes, but without the spark of laughter, and he hid his mouth behind a bushy dark beard and mustache.

"So where have you been hiding the past few years?" I asked as we bounced down River Road, headed into town. He gave me a peculiar look, as if he thought I might be mocking him. Markus would have made a joke of it, but Karl seemed to have a much more serious nature. He smoothed his mustache with his thumb and forefinger, then stroked his dark beard.

"I served in the army during the war," he finally said.

"Your parents never mentioned . . ."

"They didn't know."

"I see. Well, where were you stationed, what did you do?" I was just trying to make conversation. The other boys I dated talked endlessly about their exploits during the war. Karl was very different.

"I'm not at liberty to say," he told me. "My work for the government was classified. They made use of the fact that I'm fluent in German and English."

I didn't know if he was telling the truth or not. No one I knew had ever seen him in a uniform.

"What did you do before the war?" I asked, still trying to make conversation. "You've been away from home a long time."

"I was in college."

"Lucky you! Where did you go? What did you study?"

He didn't reply. I might have posed the question to a deaf man. By the time he parked the car near the movie theater I'd forgotten I'd asked, but he turned to me after shutting off the engine and said, "I'm an educated man, Emma. I graduated from college before the war."

His stern demeanor made me feel like a chastened schoolgirl. "Sorry. I didn't mean to be nosy," I said. "It's just that I'm envious of people who have left Bremenville and seen other places. I can't imagine why you'd ever want to come back."

"I plan to open a pharmacy on Main Street."

"A pharmacy! So did you earn a science degree or a business degree?"

Karl didn't answer, but one thing became very clear after only a few dates with him: Karl Bauer had money. Lots of money. Where it had all come from was a mystery.

After we'd dated for about a month, he drove me downtown one day to show me the storefront he'd purchased. A construction crew, hard at work on the renovations, practically stood at attention and saluted when they saw Karl.

"Bauer's Pharmacy will be open for business in another month," he told me. He proudly stroked his beard, a peacock freeing his feathers. "I am outfitting the store with the finest mahogany shelves and display cases. And over here I'm installing a soda fountain with an imported marble counter top." He pointed to where his name had been painted on the front window—*Bauer's Pharmacy*, and in smaller letters, *Karl D. Bauer, Proprietor.* "That's genuine gold leaf," he said, as if I might be tempted to contradict him.

When it came to spending money, Karl had to have the very best of everything, no expense spared—not only for his store, but also for the house he was having built. He drove me up the hill to the most fashionable area of Bremenville to show me the rambling Victorian home.

"Karl, it's huge! What will you do with so much space? Will your father and sisters be moving in too?" Gus had lost heart after Markus and Magda died, drinking so heavily that he'd lost his home and his share in the Ford garage. He and Karl's four youngest sisters lived on charity. I asked the question without thinking, and Karl answered it with silence.

Much later, after we'd walked all around the site and had returned to his car, Karl said in a voice as cold as the grave, "My father will never set one foot in my house." I knew better than to ask about his sisters.

Karl lavished lots of money and charm on me during our four-month courtship. Mama lit up like a Roman candle every time he appeared on our doorstep. "Such a fine young man," she would murmur. "Magda would be so proud of her son if she were alive." My sister Vera adored him—and his pocket full of peppermints. And though I never knew quite how he did it, Karl made Papa laugh. It was a welcome sound in our home after all the years of gloom.

"May I sit with you in church tomorrow, Emma?" he asked as he brought me home one Saturday night. I knew it would serve as a signal to the congregation that we were officially courting, but I lacked the will to refuse.

"You must stay for Sunday dinner," Mama insisted after the service ended. I saw where Karl's and my relationship was headed, but like a boat without oars, I allowed the current to sweep me along, knowing that our marriage would bring my parents some much-needed joy. It seemed like the least I could do for them.

It was at another Sunday dinner, a few months later, that our courtship reached its inevitable destination. Without preamble or declarations of undying love, Karl took advantage of a pause in the conversation to say, "Reverend Schroder, I would like to ask you for Emma's hand in marriage."

Mama uttered a little cry of happiness. A pleased smile spread across Papa's face too, but he turned to me first. "What do you say, Emma?"

"Yes, Papa . . . I'll marry Karl."

I had several reasons for saying yes to him. I knew our marriage would make Mama and Papa happy. I still felt so guilty for causing Eva's death that in my confusion I thought I should take her place. She would have married a local boy and lived in Bremenville, not traveled all over the world playing the piano. And then there was the guilt I felt over Markus. The memory of what I'd done to Markus bled my heart dry.

I had caused three deaths: Eva's, Markus's, and Aunt Magda's. There were no Bauer sons for Vera to marry, so I owed it to Aunt Magda and Markus to marry Karl and keep their memories alive. When Karl and I had children, they would become the family that Mama had lost in the war. I didn't love Karl, but he treated me kindly, and I figured love would grow between us, as it had between Mama and Papa.

Karl orchestrated every detail of our wedding with the same efficient precision he'd used to build his home and his business. "I have picked out the wedding dress I'd like you to wear, Emma. You have an appointment with the seamstress tomorrow. . . . I've hired a photographer from the city to take our picture. I'm not happy with the quality of the local studios. . . . I've arranged for our wedding dinner to be held at the hotel rather than outdoors. . . . We will be married on the twenty-first of this month. . . ." Again, I floated along with the current, without opinion or dissent. It was as if my will had died along with Eva.

Papa beamed with delight as he read us our vows. Well-wishers and friends packed the church, and Uncle Gus managed to stay sober until the ceremony ended. That night, Karl and I moved into his stately Victorian home.

I soon discovered that I was nothing but Karl's trophy, a prize he had pursued and won. He should have shot me with a double-barreled shotgun, stuffed me like a moose, and hung my head on the wall. It would have been less painful for me in the long run.

I didn't dare complain to Karl, but my life as the wife of a wealthy entrepreneur bored me to near paralysis. Karl hired a German woman to cook our meals, and a maid to come in during the day to wash our clothes and clean the house and polish all the massive European furniture he had imported— no Sears Roebuck catalogue for Karl Bauer! The maid was an Irish-Catholic girl from across the tracks, and I was surprised he'd hired her, knowing how much he disliked Irish-Catholics. He required her to wear a black dress with a white apron and made her call him "Sir." But while she was busy confirming his sense of superiority, I was left with nothing to do.

"Let's take a vacation, Karl," I suggested one evening after dinner. I had waited for him to finish the section of newspaper he was reading and lay it down, then I'd quickly planted my hand on top of the next section before he could pick it up and hide behind it again. "How about Niagara Falls? We could drive your car . . . or take the train."

"Out of the question."

"Please . . . I've always wanted to travel, Karl, but I've barely been out of Bremenville."

His eyes narrowed with suspicion. "Why are you so eager to leave town?"

"Because Bremenville never changes! The last exciting thing that happened here was when the Chautauqua came to town when I was twelve! Can't we go to Philadelphia some weekend and see a show or hear a concert?"

"My business cannot run itself, Emma." He eyed his newspaper, frowning as if commanding me to lift my hand.

"Well, if we can't go anywhere, how about letting me work in your store a couple of days a week. I'd love to get out of the house and talk to people for a change, help them find what they need. . . ."

"No."

His cold, unyielding tone made me angry. "I'm not stupid, Karl. I know the difference between witch hazel and Bromo seltzer. I think I can figure out when to prescribe Castoria and when to prescribe corn plasters. I can count out five penny candies for a nickel."

"You are my wife, *not* an employee. I work hard six days a week so that you don't have to."

"I know I don't *have* to work," I pleaded. "I *want* to work. We could be together all day." I tried to drape my arm around his shoulder, but he brushed it away.

"Enough, Emma! I will hear no more about it!"

"But why—?" I had pushed him too far. He turned on me like a dog on a short chain.

"Because I cannot forget how my father lay drunk in bed all day while my mother worked like a peasant, scrubbing floors and emptying other people's chamber pots just to put food on our table! What was her reward for all her hard work? She had the privilege of bringing him pleasure every night, then she'd give birth to another scrawny, unwanted brat nine months later. She would have had thirteen children, Emma. Thirteen! Just like a filthy Catholic, but four of them had sense enough to die and avoid being beaten senseless whenever our old man came home in a drunken rage!"

Even in his anger, Karl was cool and controlled, his words clipped and precise. They pummelled me like a rain of hailstones.

"I don't want to hear this, Karl."

"No? Well, maybe you should hear it." He rose to his feet, his face inches from mine. "Then you can explain to me why the good Reverend Schroder looked the other way all those years while his best friend Gus Bauer treated his family like garbage."

"Papa never knew—"

"He *chose* not to know, Emma."

"How dare you accuse my father of such a thing! Papa put food on your table from his own garden countless times! Mama brought you milk and eggs—"

"How I hated their pity!" His hands bunched into fists and he took a swing at a Chinese vase I'd filled with gladiolus. It crashed to the floor.

Karl's violence terrified me. I'd rarely seen Papa lose his temper, and even then he'd never resorted to smashing things. I needed to soothe Karl before he turned on me.

"Let's not fight, Karl. It doesn't matter—"

"It matters to me!" he said, waving his finger in my face. "Don't ever forget it!"

————

"The Bremenville Women's Exercise and Dramatic Club is accepting new members," Karl told me one night at the dinner table. "You must join."

"But why? You know I hate that sort of thing."

"The mill owners' wives and all the other high society ladies belong. It will help my standing in the community. Do it for me."

I reluctantly agreed to go to the next meeting. I was the only woman who didn't arrive dressed in a toga. "Why don't you let me play the piano for you," I offered. "You can dance or exercise or whatever it is that you do, and I'll play."

I plunked away on the piano while the other ladies twirled around the dance floor like fat cows, pretending they were Grecian urns. They looked ridiculous to me. I deliberately speeded up the tempo as they danced, but I did it gradually, so that no one noticed it until they were whirling like crazed dervishes, the sweat pouring down their faces. When they tried to halt their own momentum, they began tripping over each other's togas until they finally toppled like a row of plump dominoes. I played a chorus of "Alexander's Ragtime Band" for an encore as they struggled to untangle themselves. They never invited me back.

Shunned by polite society, I spent more and more time out at the parsonage—the very place I'd wanted so badly to flee. I worked hard to disguise my misery so my parents would have no idea how unhappy I was. Restless and discontented, I eventually lost the will to play the piano.

One gorgeous spring day, the urge for excitement became so strong I went to our garage and sat behind the wheel of Karl's car. "How hard can it be to drive?" I asked myself. I started the engine. I felt the latent power of the purring eight-cylinder engine, and my mind was made up. I stole Karl's car.

By the time I reached the farm, I was already managing the clutch without jerking and hopping like a startled rabbit. My sister Vera had the day off from school. "Do you feel like having an adventure today?" I asked her.

"Emma! I didn't know you could drive!"

"Nothing to it. Climb in and I'll show you."

We flew down River Road like two sparrows set free from their cages, bouncing on the stiff velvety seats and laughing like a pair of lunatics escaped from the asylum. When we got to the neighboring village we went on a shopping spree—or I should say, a trying-on spree. Karl would never allow me to wear such outrageous hats and brightly colored frocks in a million years. We had a glorious time.

If I hadn't scraped the car's fender along the garage door when I tried to sneak it back inside, Karl never would have known what I'd done. I was in a hurry though, since he would be arriving home for dinner any minute, and I didn't take the time to prop open the garage doors like Karl always did. The wind blew one of them shut as I drove inside, leaving a neat, vertical dent in the rear fender.

Karl discovered the dent that same evening. "Do you know anything about that dent in my car?" he asked with icy calm. I'd grown to fear that tone of voice.

"I'm sorry, it was my fault, Karl. The garage door blew shut on it—"

"How could that happen if the car was inside the garage?" I could tell he knew the truth. He was torturing me the way a boy might toy with an insect.

"The car wasn't in the garage. I borrowed it to go out to the farm."

"You took something that didn't belong to you, Emma?"

"Well, yes . . ."

The first blow of his palm across my face took me by surprise. The ones that followed seemed inevitable. It was a simple matter of cause and effect—I'd damaged his car, he beat me in return.

"I'm sorry," Karl said as I huddled on the kitchen floor afterward. "But since you aren't the submissive wife I thought I married, this is the only way to teach you."

I didn't want our maid or anyone else to see me until my bruises healed, so the next day I banished myself to a tiny island in the middle of Squaw River that I had often explored as a child. The wooded islet was privately owned but rarely used, and it even had a small fishing lodge on it. I sat on the front step of the cabin and listened to the melody of bird song and lapping water, dreaming of the music I'd forfeited the right to play.

For a long time I sat wondering what my life would have been like if I'd obeyed Papa and stayed away from the movies with Eva that fateful night. When I realized the futility of such thoughts, I wondered for the hundredth time why I hadn't died instead of Eva, or why Karl hadn't died instead of Markus. When I tried to imagine being married to Markus I remembered the passion of his kiss . . . and mourned the lack of passion in my husband's kisses. But it was useless to rail against the hand of God. Karl was the punishment I deserved. As the pine trees cast long afternoon shadows across the little clearing, I rowed the borrowed rowboat back to shore—back to Karl.

Karl and I slept in separate bedrooms with a small dressing room in between. If he wanted to sleep with me, he would politely ask permission first, as if we were strangers at a fancy ball—"May I have this dance, Milady?" "Yes, Milord." Then he would remove his dressing gown and lay it neatly on the chair beside my bed. Karl called it "The Marital Act," as if the words were written with capital letters, but it resembled a Japanese tea ritual more than an act of passion.

"I want to make an appointment to see the doctor," I told him after three years of marriage. "I don't understand why I'm still not pregnant." I had followed him into his den after dinner, knowing that the best time to talk to Karl was when he was relaxed and mellow after a good meal. He had already made himself comfortable in his leather armchair and lit his cigar. I leaned against the mantel, attempting to appear casual, but I was always on my guard around Karl.

"You're not pregnant because I am preventing it."

His words stunned me. I stared at him, but his dark eyes were as unfathomable as two lumps of coal.

"But, Karl, why?"

"I will decide when to begin a family." He flicked the ash off his after-dinner cigar like a gentleman and picked up his newspaper. To Karl, that was the end of the discussion.

"Well, when might you decide to start one?" I asked. "I need something to do all day besides sit in this cold, polished house, listening to the clock tick. I'm going crazy." When he turned the page of his newspaper without answering me, I lost my temper.

"You need to arrange everything, don't you, Karl? You always have to be in control! You get to decide when we eat, what we eat, when we sleep together, even when we'll have children! You're so afraid of being poor again, so afraid I'll end up like your mother with nine children and you'll be like your father—"

Karl threw down his newspaper and leaped from his chair so swiftly that I didn't have time to step back. His face, just inches from mine, twisted with icy rage. "Don't you ever say another word about my mother," he breathed. "And don't you ever, *ever* mention my father and me in the same breath again!" I was terrified of another beating, but it never came. He turned and walked back to his chair as if nothing had happened.

But late that night, Karl came to my room. There was no question of consent or polite formalities. Karl claimed his marital rights, delivering a message clearer than any beating. I would remember it well for the next two years. I was Karl's possession. I was powerless. He was in complete control.

SIXTEEN

"You have eaten nothing, Emma. Aren't you feeling well?" Karl removed his napkin from his lap and laid it on the table, then pushed his plate forward an inch to signal that he was finished eating.

I hated the clock-ticking silence of dinnertime. Karl insisted on eating in the formal dining room, even though there were only two of us. The scent of furniture polish hung heavy in the air, filling the hush between us.

Karl wasn't one to converse unnecessarily. At home he was so quiet and self-contained that I heard little more from him at mealtimes than the sound of his silverware clinking against the plate. He was very different in his store, of course—much warmer and friendlier with his customers, almost gregarious. I often thought about disguising myself as a customer so that he'd talk to me.

"Emma? Did you hear me?"

Tonight I was the one who didn't feel like talking. It was October 1924, and I knew that I was pregnant. I was terrified to tell him.

"I'm fine, Karl."

"Then eat something."

I stabbed a piece of roast pork with my fork and lifted it to my mouth. I couldn't get it past my lips. As my nausea rose, I bolted outside to the privy to be sick. We had an indoor bathroom, of course—one of the first in Bremenville—but I didn't want Karl to hear me being sick. Afterward, I sat on the back porch step, letting the cool fall air revive me. It was filled with the scent of rain. I was surprised when Karl came outside and stood behind me.

"When were you planning to tell me?"

My stomach turned over with fear. "Tell you what?"

"You don't need to hide it from me, Emma. I know you are in a family way."

I didn't reply. I couldn't.

"You forget, sometimes, that I am an educated man. I know about such things."

"I don't *forget* that you're an *educated* man. How can I possibly forget? You won't let me forget!" My tongue invariably got me into trouble, but I couldn't help myself. I cringed, waiting for one of Karl's bitter lectures, but it never came.

"How far along are you? One month?"

"Almost two."

He paused to light his after-dinner cigar. As the smoke curled around my head, I had to sprint to the outhouse again to be sick. He was waiting for me when I returned.

"It's senseless to continue like this, Emma."

"I can't help it if I'm sick. You make it sound as if I enjoy it." I might have known he'd be unsympathetic. Stoic, disciplined Karl would put wheels on his deathbed so he could roll himself to work.

"There is a woman who comes into my pharmacy who was a midwife back in Germany. She knows things. Home remedies and such."

"I'll be all right. The nausea will probably go away in another month or so."

Karl grunted a word in German that I didn't understand and turned to go inside. "When you have cleared away the dinner things we will go to her."

"Tonight? I told you I'm all right now."

"Do as I say, Emma." He disappeared into the house.

I often wondered if he really meant to sound so cold and dictatorial or if it was just his odd German-style phrasing of English. He didn't have an accent exactly, but whenever Karl spoke, his consonants all seemed to have sharp, pointed edges.

I knew it was useless to argue with him, but I took my time clearing the table, washing the dishes, and drying them instead of leaving them for the maid. Maybe he would change his mind if he saw that I felt better. When I went out on the back porch to shake the crumbs from the tablecloth, I saw that it had begun to rain. The air smelled of wet earth and ozone. It was such a gentle, cleansing rain that I lingered on the porch to watch it. I loved the way each drop glistened in the grass, the way it turned all the muted evening colors a darker shade.

"What is taking you so long?" he asked from the doorway.

Karl hadn't changed into his smoking jacket but stood in the kitchen doorway dressed in his suit, tie, and waistcoat as if he were going to work. He twirled his hat in his hand, a sure sign that he was impatient with me.

"Emma."

"It's raining, Karl. . . ."

"I'll fetch my umbrella."

The engine purred as the car glided through the streets as slow and heavy as a well-fed cat. We drove through our own neighborhood of vast gingerbread houses with wide verandas and tall trees, then left the gaslit part of town to turn down darker, narrower streets. I heard the bells on the Catholic church strike eight. When we crossed the river, we entered a section of town near the docks with crumbling warehouses and dark alleyways. Mangy dogs moved in the shadows behind barrels and crates. The air stank of dead fish.

"Where are we going? Where does this woman live, for goodness' sake?"

Karl didn't answer. A few minutes later, he stopped in front of a tenement house, set the brake, and turned off the engine.

"This is ridiculous," I said. "The place doesn't even look sanitary. Why can't I just make an appointment with Dr. Strauss?" He ignored my question.

Karl got out of the car, walked around the front, and opened my door. Always a gentleman, he took my elbow as he guided me to a set of rickety wooden steps that led up the outside of the building. They were open-backed, and I felt slightly dizzy as we climbed to an apartment on the second floor. I heard the sound of a baby crying and frantic, scratchy music coming from a phonograph that had been wound too tightly. The hallway smelled of burnt potatoes and cigarette smoke.

The woman who answered Karl's knock looked like a gypsy from the old country, complete with dangling earrings and a babushka on her head. Was she going to read my palm and tell me when the nausea would stop? Maybe she would dangle a pendulum over me to see if the baby was a boy or a girl. What was Karl—an educated man—doing here?

"Good evening, Herr Bauer."

"Good evening."

That was it—no introductions, no pleasantries. Maybe Karl didn't know the woman's name. She ushered us in as if she was expecting us, and I was relieved to see that her kitchen was clean, even though it was a bit shabby. There was no cauldron in the corner or mysterious bunches of roots hanging from the ceiling. I peeked through an open doorway into a poorly lit parlor with very little furniture. Business must be slow these days for former mid-wives selling home remedies, I thought. Overall, the apartment gave the impression that it had been knocked askew and was listing dangerously to one side. I would have loved to have put a marble on the floor and watch it roll across the room.

"My wife says she is two months along," Karl said as he twirled his hat.

The gypsy grimaced. "Not as simple, but still possible. This way, please."

She led us down a dark hallway to a small room that appeared to be used mainly for storage. Crowded along one wall was a narrow iron bed with only a sheet and a mattress, and beside it a washstand draped with a towel. A row of apothecary bottles with labels from Bauer's Pharmacy lined a wooden shelf above it. A single bare light bulb hung from the ceiling. Karl moved behind me and slipped my coat from my shoulders.

"Sit here, Mrs. Bauer," the gypsy said. She indicated the bed.

"Should she undress?" Karl asked.

My heart began to pound. "Undress? Why on earth would I need to undress? It's just a little morning sickness."

The woman answered Karl, not me. "Yes. There's a gown on the back of the door."

"Karl, what is this? What's going on?" He planted his hands on my shoulders. His dark eyes seemed to bore into mine.

"Emma, you know this child can never be born."

"What?" I grabbed his wrists and pulled his hands off me.

"You don't have to be afraid, Mrs. Bauer," the gypsy soothed. "This won't take long. You can go home again in a few hours." She lifted the towel, and I saw a tray of medical instruments on the washstand. Karl took an unmarked bottle from his pocket and slipped it to the woman.

"I brought something to ease her pain."

"Karl, *no!*" I couldn't catch my breath, as if I'd just run up a steep hill.

"You will do as I say, Emma. Sit down on the bed." He reached for me, but I twisted away. "Emma . . ."

He was powerfully strong, and I knew I could never get away from him once he caught me. I waited until he lunged for me, then brought my knee up as hard as I could into his groin. It was the only way to save my child. Karl groaned and bent double. I leaped past him through the door.

I hurtled down the tilting hallway, threw open the back door, and crashed down the rickety stairs, tripping, stumbling, clumsy with terror. My leg scraped on the rough wooden planks, tearing my stockings. The narrow, thin-soled shoes I was wearing were never meant for running, but I ran just the same.

"Emma! Emma, come back here!"

I heard him calling behind me but I didn't look back. I ran past the car and down the street, wishing I had paid more attention to where the woman lived. It was very dark now, and raining hard. I had no idea where I was or where the road led, but I didn't care.

I ran, unheeding, until the street came to a dead end at the river. I nearly wept for joy at the familiar sight of the dark ribbon of water. It was my sign-post, pointing me to safety. If I headed upstream, I would eventually come to my father's church.

I had just slowed to catch my breath, too tired to run anymore, when I heard the purr of Karl's car, like heavy breathing, behind me. There were no sidewalks, and only a narrow strip of land between the road and the river. He pulled up beside me and leaned out of the open window.

"Where do you think you are going, Emma? You don't even have a coat on."

"I'm going home to my parents. You can't stop me, Karl." I walked faster but the car kept pace.

"Aren't you ashamed to do that? Under the circumstances?"

"You're the one who should be ashamed—plotting to kill an innocent baby! Papa would never condone an abortion, and you know it!"

"I don't understand. What is this abortion you are talking about?"

I saw then that Karl would deny ever going to the gypsy's apartment. He would convince Papa that we had simply had a lover's quarrel—that my preg-nancy had made me overly emotional. Papa would side with Karl. Wives were supposed to obey their husbands. Mama had obeyed at the cost of everything she loved. I would get no sympathy from my parents. Wet and cold, I felt as though even nature had turned against me.

"You are shivering. Why don't you get in the car, Emma?" His voice was as icy as the rain streaming down my back.

"Never. I'll never go back to that house with you." I walked for another half a block before I felt the heat of the engine as the car slowly crept up behind me again.

"Perhaps we could compromise," Karl said. "I will agree to let you give birth if you'll agree to give it away."

"You can't be serious."

"Certainly I am. I will arrange a private adoption. We will tell everyone there were complications. That it was stillborn."

I started to run, ducking between buildings and sprinting along the muddy riverbank so he couldn't follow me in the car. I was terrified that he would get out and come after me. I ran blindly—running, dodging, hiding. I had to get away from him.

When I could run no more, I peered out from behind a parked truck and saw his car in the distance, slowly cruising up and down the streets as he searched for me. He hadn't left the comfort of his car to pursue me. He must have judged me not worth the bother of getting wet.

I couldn't decide where to go. Karl would be watching for me at the farm, and besides, I knew Mama and Papa wouldn't help me. I wandered aimlessly until I came to the railroad tracks and saw the trestle bridge in the distance. I remembered how it had saved my life on the night of the flood when I was a child. Karl would never expect me to cross such a precarious span in the dark—I wasn't convinced that I could do it, myself. But it was my only hope of escape.

As I started across, gingerly stepping from tie to tie, I realized that my motivation was the same as my mother's had been—to save my child. No matter what, I would never let Karl Bauer within a hundred miles of my baby.

The area on the other side of the bridge near the mill was a notoriously bad part of town, filled with speakeasies and bootleggers, but it seemed much less dangerous than going home with Karl. I huddled in an alley beneath an empty wooden crate until I was so cold that I began to worry about catching pneumonia. I couldn't spend the night outside in the rain. For my baby's sake, I needed to find shelter. My sister Sophie lived on this side of the river, about half a mile up the hill from the mill. I prayed that she would take me in.

"Emma! You are drenched!" she cried when she saw me. "Where's your coat?"

"I left it behind," I said, shivering. "Please . . . let me stay with you tonight, Sophie."

"But what's wrong? What are you doing here?"

"Karl and I had a fight."

"Shall I send Otto over to talk to him?"

"No! Please . . . just let me stay the night."

"Won't Karl be worried about you?"

"A night apart might do him some good. Give him a chance to cool off, think things through."

"But surely—"

"If you love me, Sophie, *please* don't send for Karl . . . please let me stay!" My teeth rattled from cold and fear.

In the end, Sophie agreed. It was clear that she had misgivings, and that her husband, Otto, had even more of them, but since they didn't own a car, he was reluctant to go out on such a terrible night. My plan was to get up early in the morning, before anyone else awoke, and hitch a ride out of town.

I spent a restless night on their sofa, filled with nightmares of evil people who were trying to kill my baby. When I awoke the next morning to find Karl standing over me, I thought it was part of the same dream. Then I saw Otto in the doorway and knew he had gone to fetch him.

"Let's forgive and forget, shall we, Emma?" Karl smoothed his mustache and beard like a cat licking its whiskers. "As the Good Book says we must do?"

Otto and Sophie hovered anxiously, watching. Karl would deny everything that had happened. No one would believe me. A good wife obeyed her husband.

In the end there was nothing I could do but go home with him, playing the part of the dutiful wife. Neither of us mentioned the baby.

"All is forgotten?" he said as he pushed his chair back from the breakfast table. I nodded mutely, unable to look at him. "Good. I must go and open the pharmacy. We will talk tonight."

But the moment Karl left, I packed my bags and bought a one-way train ticket for as far out of town as my hoarded grocery money would take me.

SEVENTEEN

Hours later, Emma's tiny apartment in the retirement home looked nearly settled. Grace felt exhausted, but it was more from the emotional strain of listening to Emma's story than from the work of unpacking. For the first time, Grace realized the full depth of her mother's love. What Emma was afraid to risk for her own sake—leaving an abusive husband—she'd done without hesitation for her daughter's sake.

"That's the most you've ever spoken about my father in my entire life," Grace said.

"Don't be silly," Emma said, waving airily. "You must have forgotten, that's all."

"No, if you had told me he'd beaten you, I'm sure I would have remembered."

Suzanne flattened another cardboard box and stacked it by the door with the others. "You said he wasn't the villain, Grandma, but he certainly sounds like one to me."

"Does he? I'm sorry if I've portrayed him that way. I don't see him as a villain. He was a victim of his own tragic childhood. It left him deeply scarred. A more contented woman could have helped him overcome his past, but I wasn't the wife he needed—or expected."

Emma pulled off the pink scarf and ran her fingers through her silver hair. As Grace studied her mother, she saw that even at eighty years of age, Emma was still an attractive woman. Fifty-five years was a long time to have remained single. The wounds Karl Bauer left on her soul must have been very deep as well.

Grace wanted to ask her mother a question, but she waited until Suzanne took a load of empty cartons to the dumpster and they were alone. "Do you have any plans for tomorrow, Mother?"

"I don't think so, dear, but I can check. The weekly schedule is around here someplace. Why do you ask?"

"Well, tomorrow is Sunday. Now that you live nearby, I was hoping you'd come to church with Stephen and me once in a while."

"Ah, Gracie, don't start with that again," she said wearily. "I'm too old to change. If going to church helps you, then I'm happy for you. But we're very different."

"You've been turning me down all my life, and I've never understood why. Won't you at least explain to me why you won't go?"

Emma smiled mischievously. "You just want my reasons for ammunition—so you can argue with me and show me the error of my ways. Papa used to do the same thing with his reluctant parishioners."

"Look, I don't care if you attend services or not, but I care very much that you're estranged from God. You never want me to talk about Him, you don't read the Bible, you never go to church unless there's a wedding or a baptism . . . I've never seen you take Communion in my entire life. What I don't understand is, why? Why won't you have anything to do with God?"

"You don't know for certain what goes on between me and God."

"That's the point. I need that certainty. I need to know where you'll be for eternity. Can't you please give me some assurance?"

Emma walked to the window, silent for a moment as she looked out at the beautifully landscaped lawns. "Papa baptized me as a baby, you know, and I used to go to church with my parents when I lived at home. Then Karl and I went to Papa's church after we were married. I know what the Bible says, but . . ." Emma didn't finish. It was as if she'd reached a locked door that she refused to open.

"Something must have happened. Why won't you tell me? Does it have anything to do with my father? Or with your sister Eva's death?"

Emma finally turned to face her again. "I can't go to church with you Grace, I'm sorry. But if you give me time . . . maybe I can find a way to answer some of your questions, okay?"

"All right." It would have to be. There had always been doors her mother refused to open, and no amount of coaxing would change her mind. But what of Suzanne's suggestion that they play detective? After all these years, was it possible to find the keys and unlock the secret doors herself?

She pondered the idea as she unpacked a box of kitchen utensils, stuffing them into an already jammed drawer. Then she wandered into her mother's bedroom to set a picture of Amy and Melissa on her mother's nightstand. The stand had a small drawer, and Grace opened it to see if it was as crammed as all the others. It was empty, except for an aged sheet of gray writing paper with the now-familiar handwriting, printed with the same blue fountain pen.

To my beloved Emma,

> *I am haunted by numberless islands, and many a Danaan shore,*
> *Where Time would surely forget us, and Sorrow come near us no more;*
> *Soon far from the rose and the lily, and fret of the flames would we be,*
> *Were we only white birds, my beloved, buoyed out on the foam of the sea!*

Grace's hand trembled as she put the poem inside the drawer and closed it again. She thought she had known her mother well, but she really didn't know her at all. How many hidden drawers and closed doors were there in her life? What other secrets was she hiding?

Back in the living room, Grace studied her mother as she would a stranger. Emma hummed to herself as she searched in vain for a place to store the same stack of dish towels she had tried to put away earlier. Finally, she opened the lid of the garbage can and dropped them squarely into the trash.

"Mother!"

"Oh, who needs them. I never dry my dishes anyway."

"But you can't just throw away a perfectly good set of dish towels!"

"I'm eighty years old, dear. I've earned the right to be eccentric."

"Maybe Suzanne can use them." As Grace fished them out of the garbage she spotted an unopened carton, forgotten beside the broom closet. "Oh no. What's in this one?" She opened the flaps and unwrapped a pink sugar bowl—it was the box of depression glass. "I thought you were going to sell these to the antique dealer."

"Please don't be angry, dear, but I just couldn't bear to part with them." Emma took the sugar bowl from Grace's hand and held it like a priceless heirloom. "Remember how you and I used to have tea parties with these dishes? We called them our 'good china,' and we'd make butter and sugar sandwiches, and pretend we were eating caviar."

Tears sprang to Grace's eyes before she could stop them. "I used to think our tea parties were more wonderful than any held by the king and queen of England."

Emma wrapped her arms around her and held her tightly. "Oh, but they were, Gracie! They were!" When she released her again, Grace carefully wiped her eyes.

"Would you mind if I changed my mind, Mother? I think I'll take the dishes home after all."

"Any idea where I can put these?" Grace asked with a sigh. She stood with Suzanne in the middle of her chic, contemporary dining room, trying to find a place to display the depression glass. Spread out on the marble tabletop, the gaudy pink and green dishes looked like painted prostitutes among her home's carefully coordinated neutral tones. Stephen would never allow her to display the thick pressed glass in the china cabinet beside her Royal Doulton china and Waterford crystal.

"Put them anywhere you want, Mom. And don't you dare let Daddy talk you out of them."

Grace smiled ruefully. "I don't suppose you'd care to stick around and watch the fireworks when he sees them?"

"No thanks. I get all the fireworks I want at my own house."

"What on earth was I thinking when I took these silly things?" she said, sighing again. "I guess finding that second love poem turned my brain to sentimental mush."

"You found another poem?"

"Didn't I tell you? It was in Grandma's nightstand, written on the same gray paper, in the same handwriting as the first one."

"Let's see it!"

"I left it in the drawer where I found it."

"Oh, thanks a lot! Was it signed or anything?" Grace shook her head. "Well, from the way Grandma described him, we know Karl Bauer didn't write them."

"Mother did say she had a lot of suitors before she was married, remember? It must be from one of them."

"I had dozens of boyfriends too, but I wouldn't keep their old love poems for fifty years. You know, Grandma's story raised more questions than it answered. Did she ever explain exactly why Karl didn't want any children?"

"He probably never gave her a reason. I gather he was a man of few words and strong opinions."

"And I still don't understand why she ran away from her own family as well as her husband."

"I guess because she knew they would take Karl's side. That old-world, nineteenth-century concept of a wife being her husband's property died a slow, hard death."

Suzanne gestured to the depression glass. "I'm not so sure it's dead."

"I'll ignore that last comment." Grace scooped up the empty carton and carried it out to the kitchen. Suzanne followed her a moment later, looking at her watch.

"I think I'll head home. Jeff hasn't spent this much time with the girls in their entire lives. He's probably fed up with fatherhood by now and is letting them watch horror movies on cable TV."

"Here, don't forget these dish towels. You know, I just don't understand my mother at all. She throws out a dozen brand-new towels and keeps fifty-year-old love poems . . . not to mention these silly things." Grace brandished the cigar box containing the miniature vestments. "Can you imagine? I made these when I was four years old!"

"It makes perfect sense, Mom. You wanted the depression glass because the pieces have very special memories for you. Obviously, the poems and the vestments must mean something special to Grandma. The question is, what?"

"Well, unless she decides to tell us, we'll never know."

"Not necessarily. I've been thinking . . . you and I will both be on our own the last weekend of this month, with Jeff leaving for Chicago and Daddy going to his medical convention. Why don't we drive to Bremenville and play detective?"

"Have you given any thought at all to going with Jeff and at least *trying* to look for a job?"

"No, so let's not get into it." Suzanne's lips clamped tightly shut, as if that was the end of the discussion. Then, unable to keep her anger inside, it spewed out a moment later like soda pop from a shaken bottle. "He brought home job listings from all the Chicago newspapers the last time he went there, with *possibilities* for me circled in red ink! Can you imagine the nerve? I didn't speak to him for days!"

"He's trying to salvage your marriage, Sue."

"Why should I give up *my* career at a magazine I love, *my* seniority, *my* retirement benefits—just because I'm the woman and he's the man? That's so Victorian it's obscene!"

Grace thought of her two little granddaughters, growing up as she had without a father, and her eyes filled with tears. If only she could find a way to make Suzanne change her mind. Grace knew she was partly to blame; she had sacrificed too much of herself for Stephen's sake and now Suzanne was determined not to make the same mistake. Her mother was right—they were like wooden nesting dolls, each woman shaped by the choices her mother had made. The only way to break that pattern, Emma had said, was to study the past and learn from it.

"Suppose I agreed to go on this fact-finding mission of yours up in Bremenville?" Grace finally said. "How would we go about it?"

"Are you serious? You'd really go?"

"I would love to find Mother's sisters, if they're still alive, and help her make peace with her family. Do you suppose we could locate them after all this time?"

"Sure. There are books that tell you how to go about tracing your roots. We could look up our Bauer relatives too, along with the Schroders. We'll have to leave on a Friday, though, so the government offices will be open. Then we can stay overnight and snoop around some more on Saturday."

"Fridays are out. That's when I get my hair done." The scorching look Suzanne gave her said more to Grace than a twenty-minute lecture on priorities. "All right, all right, I *could* change my appointment. But will you be able to get Friday off?"

"I'll turn it into a writing assignment. Genealogy is a hot topic at the moment, and it would make a great feature article—minus our family secrets, of course."

"What about the girls? Would we take them with us?"

"Jeff's mother would love to get her hands on them for the weekend. He has her convinced that we're all moving to Chicago as soon as school is out and she'll never see them again. So are we going or not?"

Grace hesitated, suddenly unsure if she really wanted to learn the truth about the past. But when she remembered the locked door between Emma and God, she knew she had to find the key.

"This is crazy, Suzanne."

"I know. That's what makes it so much fun."

———

"What's the plan?" Grace asked, yawning, "or are we just winging it?" Five-thirty in the morning seemed a dubious hour to be launching into uncharted territory. She stowed her suitcase in the trunk of Suzanne's car and sank into the passenger's seat beside her.

"Here, I bought you some coffee," Suzanne said as she started the engine. "According to this great book I've been reading, we can find all sorts of records—divorce papers, marriage licenses, death certificates—at the county courthouse. It'll be easier to find Grandma's sisters if we know their married names. My plan is to arrive at the courthouse as soon as it opens and try to find what we need before noon. That will give us time to drive to Bremenville and poke around there for the rest of the day."

Grace sipped her coffee slowly as they drove to the expressway and headed north, allowing the over-boiled brew to nudge her into consciousness. The sun hadn't risen yet, but streaks of red smudged the sky on her right. It seemed an ill omen, like bloody handwriting on the wall.

"Remind me again why we're doing this?"

Suzanne smiled playfully. "Want a little heat on your feet, Mom? Are they feeling a bit cold? . . . Take a look in that folder on the backseat. I wrote up a list of objectives so we'd stay focused."

"You are just like your father," Grace said as she reached into the backseat. "I'm surprised it isn't labeled *Battle Plans*."

The top sheet in the folder had the word *OBJECTIVES* typed in capital letters. Grace read the list to herself.

(1) Find Grandma's sisters: Sophie Schroder Mueller (husband Otto)—born 1895—??

(2) and Vera Schroder   ? born 1905—??

(3) Locate information about Louise and Friedrich Schroder—church in Bremenville.

(4) Find out why Grandma was estranged from them.

(5) Information about Karl Dietrich Bauer—born in Dusseldorf, Germany 1894—??

(6) Divorced from Grandma c.1925?—*Why?!*

(7) Why didn't Karl Bauer want children?

(8) Information about Grandma—Emma Schroder Bauer—b. 1900 in Bremenville.

(9) Who sent her the love poems?

(10)

Mentally, Grace added two more objectives of her own: (1) Find the reason for Mother's estrangement from God, and (2) Demonstrate to Suzanne what a mistake it would be to divorce Jeff. But what if their findings caused an ancient, crumbling skeleton to topple out of the closet? Grace closed the folder and shuddered. The fact that she was searching for answers implied that she suspected Emma's version of the past was incomplete or misleading. Did she really want to risk uncovering an unpleasant truth? She flipped on the radio to drown out these nagging thoughts.

They reached the county courthouse just as it opened at nine o'clock. The huge nineteenth-century brick building sat on the town square in a grassy, tree-shaded park. The clock in the tower, like the sleepy town itself, had come to a halt more than a decade ago. The fact that it had stalled at five minutes to midnight seemed another ill omen to Grace, although she couldn't have said why.

"Corinthian columns," Suzanne informed her, pointing to the pillars that framed the entrance.

"See? Aren't you glad you took that art history course in college?" Grace had intended it as a joke, but when Suzanne frowned and hurried up the steps without answering, she realized her mistake—Suzanne had met Jeff while taking that art history class.

By eleven-thirty, with the help of a clerk, they had unearthed a marriage certificate for Emma and Karl, and for Emma's two sisters, learning that the youngest one, Vera, had married Robert Schultz in 1927. They found death certificates for Eva, who had died in the 1918 influenza epidemic; for Karl Bauer, who had died of cancer in 1969; and for Emma's older sister, Sophie, who had died of heart failure in 1970.

"But there doesn't seem to be a death certificate for Grandma's youngest sister, Vera," Suzanne said when she'd finished searching the most recent files.

"Good!" Grace smiled. "Maybe there's a glimmer of hope that Vera is still alive and can be reunited with Mother. Maybe all this digging will yield sweet fruit, after all. How about a coffee break to celebrate?"

"In a minute." Suzanne's dark head was bent over a file containing divorce records.

Grace pulled a moist towelette from her purse and carefully wiped the dust and ink from her fingers. She had forgotten her earlier misgivings and was beginning to feel euphoric when Suzanne suddenly looked up from the file, her eyes wide with surprise.

"Oh boy. You'd better sit down, Mom."

"Why? What did you find?" Grace was afraid to ask, certain from the expression on Sue's face that she'd see a leering skull or a pile of old bones.

"I found Grandma's divorce certificate, granted in 1926. Are you ready for this? It was Karl, not Grandma, who petitioned the court for a divorce."

"That's not so surprising. She deserted him."

"But the stated grounds for divorce, attested to by two witnesses, was marital unfaithfulness. According to Karl Bauer, Grandma committed adultery."

"That's ridiculous!" But Grace had a horrible, sick feeling in the pit of her stomach, nonetheless. "What a horrible thing to do, slandering my mother's reputation like that!"

"Mom, according to this, she never contested the charges."

Grace's stomach turned over again. Against her will, she pictured the woman who had been caught in the act of adultery and brought before Jesus. A crowd of leering, self-righteous men gathered around to accuse her, pointing fingers. "I wonder who the two witnesses to this alleged adultery were?"

"No offense, Mom, but your father sounds like a real jerk."

"If he was spreading lies like this around Bremenville, it's no wonder my mother left town and never returned."

Suzanne stared at the document as if it contained encoded secrets. "I don't understand why it took two years, though. Grandma left him in October of 1924, you were born in May of 1925, but the divorce wasn't finalized until November, 1926."

"Do you suppose he tried to coax my mother to move back in with him all that time?" Grace mused. "Could he have seen me as a baby and changed his mind about not wanting children? Maybe that's why my mother said he loved me."

Suzanne closed the file. She gathered all the photocopied documents they'd requested and stuffed them into her folder. "Well, we can congratulate ourselves," she said. "We've managed to answer one question on our list—who your aunt Vera married—and we've raised about two dozen new ones."

EIGHTEEN

"I can't believe our luck!" Suzanne replaced the receiver on the motel phone. "Not only is Great-aunt Vera alive and well and living here in Bremenville, but she has just invited us to come and see her in half an hour. She sounded as spry as Grandma on the phone. I'll bet she can answer our questions."

"Wonderful," Grace said flatly. She was lying across one of the motel beds with her arm draped over her eyes, wondering again why she had agreed to come. She had pursued the truth, hoping to restore order to Emma's and Suzanne's lives, but her own life was being thrown into chaos instead. Still reeling from the discovery that her mother had been accused of adultery, Grace wasn't sure she was ready to face any more surprises.

"What's the matter?" Suzanne said. "Do I sense some waning enthusiasm for our 'Magical Mystery Tour'?"

"I've decided that we're never really going to learn the truth. We're just going to hear several different versions of it, depending on who's doing the telling."

"Then let's think of ourselves as the jury. We'll weigh the evidence and see which version is the most credible."

"You're actually enjoying this, aren't you?"

"Yes," Suzanne replied, "and if we hurry, we can stop off at your grandfather's church on the way to Aunt Vera's house. The desk clerk told me how to get there."

They had no trouble finding the church Friedrich Schroder had once pastored, but the small white-frame sanctuary that Grace had expected to see was gone, replaced—according to the cornerstone—in 1953 by a large brick building with white pillars. The barn and the gray farmhouse that had served as the parsonage were both gone too, making room for an addition that housed Sunday school classrooms. Her grandfather had been right when he'd predicted the town's growth—the church no longer stood a mile outside of town but nestled in a subdivision of twenty-year-old ranch-style houses.

When Suzanne explained who they were, the church secretary immediately called the pastor from his study. "So you're one of Fred Schroder's grandchildren! I'm honored to meet you. Reverend Schroder is legendary in this community, remembered as a truly godly man. He didn't exactly found the church, but I understand that he was responsible for helping to make it what it is today . . . but you surely must know all this. You must be proud of him."

"I never met either of my grandparents," Grace explained. "My mother moved away from Bremenville before I was born." She hoped he wouldn't ask for a reason why. She didn't know the answer herself.

"I never had the privilege of meeting him, either," the pastor said. "He died in the early 1940s, I believe, but you might find a couple of old-timers around here who still remember him. He married, buried, baptized, and shepherded this flock for over forty years. I can give you a few names. . . ."

"Please don't trouble yourself. We've taken enough of your time. In fact, we're on our way to see my mother's sister Vera—"

"Yes, of course, Vera Schultz. One of our oldest members—and one of my favorite members too."

They thanked him for his time and went outside to search the cemetery behind the church. Alongside Louise and Friedrich Schroder's double tombstone was a much older one—their daughter Eva's, who had died in October of 1918. The graves had been lovingly tended. Pots of tulips and hyacinths bloomed in a rainbow of color.

Grace stared at the date on her grandparents' grave marker and felt a surge of anger toward her mother. "I was eighteen when they died," she said aloud. "I grew up never knowing a single blood relative besides Mother, and all that time my grandparents lived just a few hours away!"

Suzanne looked up from where she knelt. She had brought a large pad of drawing paper with her to make rubbings of both grave markers. "You need to ask her why, Mom. She owes you an explanation."

But as Grace glanced at the thriving church behind her and recalled the pastor's words of praise for her grandfather, the bigger question in her mind was why Emma had rejected her godly father's faith.

———

The Schultzes' farm was a short drive down the winding river road from the church. The barn and stone farmhouse looked old but well kept, and Grace imagined that it looked much the same as it did seventy-six years ago when her grandfather went out in the flood to pray for the present-day Schultzes' great-grandfather. Aunt Vera was waiting for them on her front porch. Grace was barely out of the car when Vera pulled her into her arms as if they'd known each other all their lives.

"Emma's daughter! Oh, what a thrill it is to finally meet you at last." She gave them such a warm, tearful welcome that even Suzanne, who was usually brisk and businesslike, succumbed to her warmth and returned her embrace.

When she finished hugging Suzanne, Aunt Vera couldn't resist embracing Grace once again. "My, you look just like him. . . ." she murmured.

"Like my father?"

"Why . . . yes . . ."

"The only photograph I've ever seen of Karl Bauer is Mother's wedding picture," Grace explained. "I've never been able to see a resemblance, myself . . . with his hair and eyes so dark and my hair so fair. Do you have any more pictures of him I could look at?"

Aunt Vera's cheeks flushed rosy pink. "Goodness! I don't know . . . Come inside and we can look." As Grace followed her into the house, she felt the irrational urge to cling tightly to Aunt Vera's hand, as if unwilling to lose sight of the first blood relative she'd ever met aside from her mother.

The farmhouse kitchen was as bright and sunny as Vera herself. It looked as though it had been decorated in the 1940s—with white metal cupboards, speckled gray counter tops, yellow walls, red polka dot curtains—and hadn't been remodeled since. Aunt Vera poured coffee into mismatched mugs, and they sat in red vinyl chairs around a porcelain-topped table to drink it.

"My sister Emma was sunshine and laughter and song," Aunt Vera said. "Everyone loved Emma. But, oh, that girl could get into mischief! It was like she just couldn't help herself."

Grace smiled. "You'll be happy to know she hasn't changed."

Aunt Vera laughed. "Good. I'm glad. Oh, what grand fun she was!"

Grace studied Aunt Vera as she talked and saw the resemblance to Emma in her gestures and in the shape of her nose and jaw. Vera was seventy-four, and so round and jolly and white-haired she might have been a stand-in for Santa Claus's wife. She had lived in this farmhouse since she'd married Robert Schultz, and now she shared it with her son Bob Jr. and her daughter-in-law Marilyn. Grace's cousin-in-law was in her late forties, with short cotton-candy hair that was dyed a startling shade of tangerine—a mute testimony against do-it-yourself hair care products. Her makeup looked as though it had been applied with a tablespoon. Marilyn puttered sullenly around the kitchen as

Aunt Vera talked, eyeing Grace and Suzanne as if they'd come to contest someone's will.

"Emma used to call our escapades 'adventures'," Aunt Vera was saying. " 'Hey, Vera, do you feel like going on an adventure today?' she would ask. I remember one time we went on a joyride in Karl's car. Emma had never driven a car before in her life, but she just climbed behind the wheel and took off. Every time she changed gears the transmission sounded like a meat grinder. Poor Karl had his hands full with that girl!"

"What was Karl Bauer like?" Suzanne asked.

"Karl? I always liked Karl. I was only thirteen when they married, but he would bring me penny candy sticks from the store when he came courting Emma. And after they were married, he always treated me to a free lemon phosphate or an ice cream sundae whenever I went into his pharmacy. He was a friendly, outgoing man, always taking time to joke with his customers or inquire about their health. At the time, I was only vaguely aware that Emma was unhappy."

"Why did she break so completely with your family?" Suzanne asked. "It seems odd that after the divorce Grandma Emma never came back to Bremenville to visit and never brought Mom back."

"What did she tell you the reason was?" Aunt Vera asked carefully.

"She wouldn't give me any reason at all," Grace said. "That's what's so frustrating. I'd love to get to the bottom of it if I can so that you and Mother can be reunited someday."

Vera seemed to consider her words before replying. "I believe Emma had an argument with Papa. Of course, no one would tell me the truth about what was going on, but I gathered that Papa wanted her to return to Karl and she refused. I think she stayed away after the divorce because she was afraid the disgrace of it would hurt our family. Respectable Christian women simply didn't run off on their husbands—especially not a pastor's daughter. Papa was so devastated by the whole mess that he resigned from the pulpit."

"Did my mother know about that?" Grace asked.

Aunt Vera shrugged. "I don't know. Of course in the end, the congregation refused to accept his resignation. They begged him to stay, so he did. But losing Emma grieved him as much as losing Eva had. Afterward Papa drew even closer to God and closer to his congregation. It was as if his own suffering helped him better understand their suffering. I remember him reading the Scriptures one Sunday, and he nearly broke down and wept right in front of everyone." Vera stared sadly into space.

"Do you remember what the Scripture was?" Suzanne asked softly.

"Oh yes. I've never forgotten." She paused, and for a moment it seemed as if she might weep too. "It was the verse in John where the woman had been caught in adultery and Jesus said, 'Let he who is without sin cast the first stone.' "

The word *adultery* flew at Grace like a hot potato, suddenly tossed into her lap. She wanted to fling it far away, before it had time to scorch her heart, but it was too late.

Aunt Vera sighed. "Of course, there were so many horrible rumors flying around town about Emma that I suppose if I heard about them, Papa and the rest of the church must have heard them too."

Suzanne sat forward in her chair. "What kind of rumors?"

"I won't say," Aunt Vera said with a quick shake of her head. "It isn't Christian to repeat gossip and rumors. Especially concerning my own sister."

"Aunt Vera, the rumors are fifty years old," Suzanne said. "Besides, we already saw the divorce papers. We know that Karl claimed marital infidelity as the reason for the divorce. He must have been the one spreading the rumors."

"Oh no, you have it all wrong. Karl would never do a thing like that, in spite of how much Emma hurt him when she left. He respected Papa too much to do such a thing. The Bauers were old family friends, you know. I don't know where the rumors started, but they didn't come from Karl."

"Then why did the divorce papers say . . ."

"Well, he had to put something, didn't he?" Aunt Vera was indignant. "They wouldn't grant divorces for any old reason like they do nowadays."

Grace glanced at Suzanne, but she wouldn't meet her gaze. She drew a deep breath and plunged into the conversation. "My mother told me she left my father because she was pregnant with me and he didn't want a baby. Do you know anything about that? Can you think of a reason why he wouldn't have wanted me?"

Vera took a moment to refill their coffee cups before answering. "I didn't even know Emma was wearing her apron high until Mama and I went to see her at Christmastime. That visit was one of the few secrets my mama ever kept from Papa. He had forbidden us to contact Emma, hoping that being cut off from everyone would bring her to her senses and back to Karl. But we took the train into the city to go Christmas shopping, and of course Mama went to see Emma. I was shocked when I saw that she was in a family way. I remember thinking, surely now she'll go back to Karl. But she didn't."

"Do you know if my father ever saw me when I was a baby?"

"Karl? I don't know. He's the one who gave us Emma's address and paid our train fare, so he obviously knew where she lived."

"Was that the last time you saw my mother? That Christmas?" Grace asked.

"No, she came home when Papa died."

"I don't remember that at all," Grace murmured.

"You were away at nursing school. Emma came alone. She was distraught because she and Papa had never reconciled. I remember how she wept and wept, saying she was sorry she had arrived too late."

"What did your father die from?" Sue asked.

"A heart attack, but it was really God's mercy that he died. It was 1943, you see, and right in the middle of the Second World War. He was a pacifist all his life, and the news of all the injustice and brutality killed him. He would read the reports of what was happening in Germany—he and Mama still had relatives there—and he just couldn't bear the news. But God took him home before he could learn the full truth about Hitler's atrocities. It would have broken his heart. He was seventy-four."

"But Emma wasn't feuding with her mother," Grace said. "Why didn't she come home after her father died? Why didn't she bring me home?"

"Emma promised that she would, but then Mama died four months after Papa. The last time I saw Emma was at Mama's funeral."

"What did she die from?"

"That was God's mercy too. He allowed her to go home with her husband. Before she died I remember asking, 'How are you, Mama?' and her eyes filled with tears and she said, 'How do you think I am with my Friedrich in the grave?' She loved him deeply. And he loved her."

They all fell silent for a moment. Suzanne seemed to have run out of questions. Grace remembered her own two objectives and searched for a way to frame her next question.

"Aunt Vera, can you tell me anything at all that will help me understand why my mother left Karl and never went back?"

"No, I'm afraid I can't help you. Emma and Karl are the only ones who really know what went on between the two of them, and he's been dead for ten years now. Lung cancer. After that, Karl's wife sold the drugstore. It's an ice cream parlor and—"

"Wait a minute," Suzanne said. "His *wife*? You mean Karl remarried?"

"Yes, he married a widow woman with a little boy. The boy later died when he was in his teens. Drowned in the river in a boating accident. A terrible tragedy." Her gaze grew unfocused as she stared into the past. Suzanne's next question brought her back.

"Does his wife still live around here?"

"No, I believe she moved down by Harrisburg, where her youngest son lives."

"Karl Bauer had *other* children?" Grace asked in astonishment. For some reason, she'd always imagined her father as a child-hater, living alone all these years, as she and her mother had.

"Karl and his wife had two sons—well, three counting the boy who drowned. It was a shame that neither of them wanted the drugstore, though. Leo Bauer works for the phone company in Harrisburg, but Paul Bauer still lives here in town. He's the principal of our grade school, in fact."

Grace slumped in her chair. "I can't believe it. I have brothers?"

———

Later, as they drove away from Aunt Vera's house, Grace still struggled to absorb all that she had learned. "It seems almost miraculous to finally meet my relatives!" she said. "I spent my entire life with only a mother. Other kids had sisters and brothers, aunts and uncles, cousins and grandparents, but I had no one—until today."

Aunt Vera had shown her photographs of her relatives—ancient ones of Friedrich and Louise and their families in Germany, Aunt Vera's children and grandchildren and great-grandchildren, pictures of Aunt Sophie Mueller and her family. But they'd found none of Karl Bauer.

"I still can't believe I have brothers," Grace murmured.

"Which means I have uncles," Suzanne added.

"Do you suppose my mother didn't know about them, or she just didn't want me to know?"

Suzanne looked at her watch. "It's only three o'clock. Let's go to the elementary school."

"Oh, Sue, I couldn't."

"Why not? Isn't this what we came here for? To find your family? You can ask Paul Bauer about your father, find out what he was really like."

"If I didn't know he existed, chances are he doesn't know anything about me, either. It's hardly fair to waltz into this man's life and say, 'Hello, I'm your long-lost sister.' What if he never knew about Karl's first wife?"

"In a small town like this? That's highly unlikely."

"I really don't think we should bother him. I already regret opening this Pandora's box even a crack. . . ."

They had paused at a stop sign, and Suzanne smacked the steering wheel with her fist. "You know, all this family secrecy garbage is really frying me! I want to meet Paul Bauer. Are you coming with me, or shall I drop you off at the motel?"

"I knew this trip was a mistake."

"Mom, why are you so afraid of the truth? Would you rather live with a lie?"

The word *adultery* floated, unwelcome, through Grace's mind again. "I'm fifty-five years old. I'd much rather live with what I've always known as the truth."

"But I'm dying of curiosity. We can't come this close to finding your father and turn back now. Let's just drive over to the school and look for his son, all right? If it isn't meant to be, then he'll be home sick with the flu or something. If he is there . . ." She shrugged.

Grace met her daughter's gaze. "Yes, Suzanne. . . ? If he is there?"

"Then let's meet him."

It was a short drive to the one-story brick school building. It perched like an island on a sea of grass, separated from the cramped middle-class neighborhood of aging bungalows by a wide swath of green. Just as Suzanne and Grace pulled into the parking lot, hundreds of kids flooded out of the doors, squealing and shoving as they ran to board a long line of yellow school buses. Grace watched the pandemonium with a sick feeling, remembering her own daily walks home from school, enduring the taunts and jeers of her classmates. *"Where's your father, Grace?" "How come he doesn't live with you?"* Nearly fifty years later, she was still trying to answer that question.

They waited until the last bus pulled away, until the flag was lowered and folded for the night. Except for a few stragglers with bulging backpacks, the school grounds were quiet once again.

"Do you want to wait in the car, Mom?"

Grace shook her head, smiling faintly. "I always wanted a baby brother. I used to beg my mother endlessly for one. She rarely lost her temper, but that was a surefire way to make her do it."

Inside, the school smelled of sweaty children and leftover lunches. The empty halls were strewn with the flotsam and jetsam of departure, like a deserted beach after a storm. Grace halted outside the main office where a sign read *Paul A. Bauer, Principal.*

"Cold feet again?" Suzanne asked.

"No, it's just so odd to see someone else with my name. I grew up in 'little Ireland,' remember? Surrounded by Mulligans and Murphys and O'Sullivans."

Suzanne pulled open the door and strode up to the secretary's desk. "Hi. Is Principal Bauer available? My name is Suzanne Pulaski."

The secretary was a round, bustling woman in her sixties who looked as though she probably hugged every child who walked through the door. Her smile was warm and genuine. Grace liked her immediately.

"Pulaski?" the secretary asked. "Does this concern one of our students?"

"No," Sue replied, "my mother and I are tracing our ancestry and it turns out there is a Bauer in our family."

The woman inhaled with delighted surprise. "Really? I took a course in genealogy last winter over at the high school! It was so fascinating! And guess what! I found out that one of my ancestors was related to William Penn! You know, the founder of Pennsylvania."

"Imagine that," Suzanne said. Grace heard the sarcasm in her tone and hoped this friendly woman didn't. "We'd really like to meet with Principal Bauer if he's free."

"Let's see . . . he's around here somewhere . . ." She glanced around the office as if he were a misplaced memo. "Mr. Bauer always supervises our dismissal, you know. He should be back any minute, now that the buses have left."

"Great. We'll wait in here." Suzanne strode past the woman and into the principal's office, seating herself in one of the chairs facing his desk.

Suzanne's assertiveness astounded Grace. Women from Suzanne's generation seemed poorly mannered to her—not to mention unladylike. Did such confident behavior come with having a professional career?

Grace turned to the secretary. "Is it all right if we wait in his office?" she asked, then waited for permission before going inside and taking a seat beside her daughter. "You were very rude," she whispered to Suzanne.

"Oh, Mom, please. Spare me the lecture. Besides, this gives us a chance to check out the family photos before he arrives." Two picture frames were lined up on his desk, facing the other way; Suzanne picked up one of them and turned it around.

"Suzanne! Don't—!"

"He wouldn't leave pictures out in the open if he didn't want anyone to see them. Here, have a look—could they be relatives of ours?"

She thrust the picture into Grace's hand—a studio portrait of a man and woman in their mid-forties, surrounded by three fluffy, over-painted, teenaged girls. Grace looked closely at the unsmiling man, searching for a resemblance to the grainy black-and-white image of Karl Bauer in her scrapbook.

Paul Bauer's hair was thinning above a high forehead and round face. What was left of his hair was dark and straight like Suzanne's, with none of the unruly waves and kinks of her own fair hair. But his swarthy complexion was very unlike Suzanne's milky white skin. His most prominent features were his gray eyes, which glowered as if he'd been forced into the studio at gunpoint and photographed against his will.

"No. I don't see any resemblance at all," Grace said. "But look how different you and I are." She quickly replaced the photo on the desk, peering nervously over her shoulder. Suzanne snatched up the other photo—one of Paul Bauer's brightly rouged daughters in a cap and gown.

"She would be my half cousin, wouldn't she?"

Grace massaged her temples. "Do you have any aspirin? I'm getting a monstrous headache." She heard voices in the outer office and swivelled around in time to see the beaming secretary pointing Principal Bauer toward his office. He wore the same expression as in the photo, clearly displeased to discover uninvited guests waiting for him. He was so stern and unsmiling, in fact, that Grace felt a wave of empathy for any student who had ever been dragged in here to face him.

Sue casually replaced the photo and rose to her feet, confident and poised. "Hello, I'm Suzanne Pulaski and this is my mother, Grace Bradford."

"They're tracing their ancestry," the secretary added, "and they think they might be related to you!"

"Oh? How so?" His tone reflected suspicion, not curiosity.

Grace cringed at the thought of springing unwelcome news on this unhappy man, especially in front of his motherly secretary. But before she could think of a way to handle the situation, her capable daughter took over once again.

"It's rather complicated, Mr. Bauer. Could we possibly have a few minutes of your time, or should we make an appointment for another day?"

He took a long time to reply—a practiced move, Grace guessed, to force anyone in the hot seat to squirm a little longer. She was beginning to believe she had been better off without a younger brother when he finally looked at his watch. "As long as it isn't much more than that."

"Would anyone like coffee?" his secretary asked, plainly looking for an excuse to linger and hear more.

Grace was dying for a cup, the stronger the better. Before she could reply, Suzanne said, "Not for either of us, thank you."

"No. And close the door." Paul Bauer waved the woman away, then sank into the chair behind his desk. An uncomfortable silence fell after the door clicked shut. Paul Bauer wasn't going to make this any easier. Thank God for Suzanne, who possessed the courage to plunge right in.

"As your secretary mentioned, we're tracing our family roots and they've led us here to Bremenville. Specifically, we're looking for information about Karl Dietrich Bauer. I understand that he was your father?"

"Yes."

"And that he owned his own drugstore here in Bremenville?"

"It was a pharmacy."

"Excuse me—*pharmacy*. He was born in Germany in 1894?"

"Yes."

"And he died about ten years ago?"

"Almost eleven."

Sue gave a noisy sigh. "Look, I'd rather not have to play Twenty Questions, Mr. Bauer. We would really be very interested to learn anything you could tell us about him."

"Why?"

Grace decided she'd better enter the skirmish. "This is very awkward, but were you aware that your father was married briefly and then divorced before he married your mother?"

Another long pause. Grace marvelled at his control. She couldn't guess what his answer would be from his stoic expression.

"Yes," he finally said. "I was aware of that fact."

Grace's stomach flipped over, as if she'd crested a hill at high speed and was about to race down the other side. She spoke the next words quietly to disguise the tremor in her voice. "My mother—Emma Schroder Bauer—was his first wife. Karl Bauer was *my* father too."

Dead silence. The deeply annoyed expression never left his face.

Grace tried to smile. "I guess that makes me your half sister."

Paul Bauer leaned forward, resting his forearms on his desk, his hands clasped together. This man had mastered the body language of intimidation and power. "You are mistaken," he said. "My father had no children by his first wife."

"What an absurd thing to say!" Suzanne cried. "She's sitting right here in front of you!"

"I can show you my birth certificate if you don't believe me." Shaken, Grace fumbled in her purse, then laid the photocopy on the desk in front of him, angry that her hand trembled as she smoothed it out. "See? Father: Karl Dietrich Bauer. That is your father's name, isn't it?"

"We've already established that fact. But he isn't your father, Mrs. Bradford."

His arrogance astounded Grace. "Listen, I'm well aware that my father wanted nothing to do with me—"

"Mrs. Bradford—"

"I came to Bremenville to learn whatever I could about my family—the Schroders as well as the Bauers. I assure you, I don't want anything from either side. I simply came to satisfy my curiosity and maybe answer some of the questions that my mother could never answer."

"I understand, Mrs. Bradford." His icy control made her angrier.

"No, I don't think you do understand, or you wouldn't be sitting there telling me that I don't exist and that we're not related."

"Technically speaking, Mrs. Bradford, we are *not* blood relatives. Karl and Frieda Bauer adopted me when I was five days old."

"I see." Grace felt all her anger collapse like a half-baked cake. She might have felt a loss at learning that she didn't have a brother, after all, if it had been anyone other than this ungracious man. Before she could recover, he suddenly went on the offensive, leaning even farther forward, his gray eyes commanding her to hold his gaze.

"And now you will listen to me," he said. There was no heat in his anger, only piercing shards of ice.

She suddenly remembered how amused her mother had always been by Grace's fiery temper. When Grace had asked if it came from Karl, she'd replied, "Karl's anger was ice, not fire—and far more deadly. You can extinguish a fire as quickly as it flares, but how do you survive a chill that freezes your very soul?"

Paul Bauer had learned this behavior from Karl. For the first time in her life, Grace was grateful that she hadn't grown up with her father. Nor could she imagine Emma married to a man like this.

"I said that I understood your disappointment," Bauer continued. "When my secretary informed me that you were tracing your ancestry I thought you might be from my birth parents."

"What about your brother?" Suzanne asked calmly. "The one who lives in Harrisburg? Is he Karl Bauer's natural son?"

"Leo is adopted as well. There really is no delicate way to say this, but you can't possibly be Karl Bauer's daughter. My father contracted mumps as an adult. He was sterile."

Suzanne shrugged. "Well, obviously, he must have had the mumps after my mother was conceived."

"He was eighteen."

Grace picked up her birth certificate and waved it at him. "But it says right here that my father is Karl Bauer."

"Mrs. Bradford. My birth certificate says the same thing. But he isn't my real father any more than he is yours."

Grace felt limp, paralyzed. It required an enormous effort to speak. "You must be misinformed . . . about when he had the mumps, I mean. My mother . . ."

Suzanne stood, shouldering her purse. She tugged Grace's sleeve. "Come on, Mom. I think we've used up our allotted time. Thank you for *all* your help, Mr. Bauer. And good luck finding *your* family." She yanked open the door and added, "You might check out Iceland!"

Grace extended her hand to shake Paul Bauer's, aware that the closest she might ever come to touching her father was shaking hands with his adopted son. "It was nice meeting you," she said. He merely nodded.

Once she was back in the car, Grace replayed all the questions she had longed to ask . . . what was Karl Bauer like, what kind of a father was he, what kind of a man. Did he laugh easily, joyously? Did he lavish love on his children, read stories to his grandchildren? She would never know, but Paul Bauer had certainly given her a few clues.

Suzanne slid behind the wheel but didn't start the engine. "Are you all right, Mom?"

"I'm fine. And quite relieved to know I'm not related to that horrible man."

"No kidding. I wouldn't even put Amy and Melissa in his school, let alone call him Uncle Paul!"

"Can you imagine what a bitter, vindictive woman his mother must have been? Just because she couldn't have children, she convinced her son that my mother never had any, either."

"Um, actually . . . she wasn't the one who was sterile. She had a son by her first husband, remember? The boy who drowned?"

"Oh, let's just forget it, all right? I need a gallon of coffee and a fistful of aspirins."

Suzanne made no move to start the car. "Mom . . . you always assumed Karl Bauer wanted to abort you because he didn't want any children, didn't like children . . . right?"

"Yes . . . so. . . ?" Suzanne was leading her down a path she didn't want to explore.

"He couldn't have *hated* children. He adopted *three* of them."

"People change, I suppose. Maybe he felt guilty for the way he treated my mother and me."

"But think about it, Mom . . . what would motivate a man to pressure his wife to have an abortion, especially in an era when back-alley abortions were so dangerous, not to mention illegal? The obvious answer . . . the only answer that makes any sense . . . is that Karl didn't think you were his."

"What a terrible accusation to make against your grandmother!"

"*I'm* not making it. *Karl Bauer* did. You read the divorce papers; he claimed marital unfaithfulness as the reason. Maybe he really did have mumps when he was eighteen and he assumed he was sterile."

"And so when my mother got pregnant, he refused to believe her! Good heavens, it all makes sense now. But what a horrible ordeal for Mother! No wonder she wanted nothing to do with him. Nowadays a blood test could prove her innocence, but back then it must have been like a witch hunt. And that would also explain her estrangement from her own family. Karl Bauer must have convinced them that she was guilty too."

Suzanne didn't answer. She started the car and slowly drove past the school's athletic field, past the tiny lawns and shuttered bungalows, turning onto the main square by the firehouse and village library. As they parked in front of the diner, Grace was still venting her outrage.

"I heard about a situation like this at another crisis pregnancy center. The husband had a vasectomy and claimed the baby couldn't possibly be his. It was horrible for that poor woman to be falsely accused. Both families turned against her, too, until the counselor told her that a simple blood test could prove he was the father. I can't imagine my poor mother going through such an awful ordeal all alone!"

Suzanne was very quiet. Something was wrong. "What are you thinking, Suzanne?"

"Suppose you really aren't Karl Bauer's daughter?"

"Suzanne!"

"But it would explain so much—why Karl wanted to abort you, why Grandma's parents wouldn't help her, why she left and never came back. If she were innocent, don't you think she'd try to defend her reputation?"

"I refuse to believe that my mother would lie to me all these years, much less have an affair! If she had a mystery lover, why not marry him once the divorce was final?"

"It's obvious, isn't it? He must have been married to someone else."

"I can't believe you'd accuse your grandmother of . . . of . . ."

"Adultery? That's what the divorce papers said. And remember how restless and unhappy Grandma said she was?"

"Impossible! I don't believe it! We've seen enough of Karl Bauer's son to get a glimmer of what Karl must have been like. My mother was falsely accused. Besides, why saddle me with his name if he wasn't my father?"

"Mom, it was 1925. Single motherhood was hardly in vogue back then. And Grandma was still legally married to him when you were born. The divorce wasn't finalized until 1926, remember?"

Grace rubbed her throbbing temples. "I'm tired of this whole mess. If my mother says Karl Bauer is my father, then he is."

"But what about Grandma's strange words? They're what started all this in the first place. She said, *'Your father loved you more than life itself.'* Does that sound like Karl Bauer to you? And I heard Aunt Vera say that you looked like your father, but I don't see any resemblance between you and Karl Bauer—do you?"

"Suzanne, please. Let's call the whole thing off and go home."

"It sounds like Grandma was describing a father who knew you and loved you. Maybe he was the mystery person who filled your coal box."

"I do not want to pursue this one step further, and I want you to stop pursuing it as well."

"But there is a way we could find out the truth. . . ."

"How?"

"We could ask Grandma."

"Absolutely not! You can't confront an eighty-year-old woman and ask her if she's been lying all these years."

"Mom—"

"No, Suzanne. I forbid it. Make up your mind that we'll never know the truth."

Grace spent a restless night trying unsuccessfully to get comfortable on the lumpy motel bed. As sunlight edged past the curtains, she rose and retrieved her Bible from her suitcase to read her daily devotions. But the selected passage from Isaiah 28 made her feel even more unsettled, especially verse twenty which accurately described her own state of unrest: *"The bed is too short to stretch out on, the blanket too narrow to wrap around you."*

Digging and probing into the past had disrupted Grace's comfortable life. Disquieting truths poked through like bedsprings, and a wash of doubt had shrunk her blanket of certainty until she could no longer wrap herself up in it. Cold reality seeped in around the edges—the divorce records accused her mother of adultery; her father had not believed that she was his child. As she stood in the shower beneath a feeble spray of water, Grace found herself weeping.

"Where do you want to begin today's explorations?" Suzanne asked later as they ate a greasy breakfast of bacon and eggs in the Bremenville Diner.

"To tell you the truth, I'd like to go home."

Suzanne's lips pursed in annoyance as she scraped jam across her toast. "Just like that? You're giving up and running home?"

"What more can we possibly accomplish here? We've answered as many questions as we could." She pulled Suzanne's file folder over to her side of the table and paged through it until she found the sheet marked *OBJECTIVES*. Grace ran her finger down the list.

"One, we discovered that Aunt Sophie is dead. Two, we found Aunt Vera and promised her we'd bring my mother back for a visit. Three, we found my grandfather's church and learned that he was highly respected in Bremenville. Four, we learned that my mother was estranged from her parents because they sided with Karl. Five, we met Karl Bauer's adopted son and got an unsettling glimpse of what my father was probably like. And, I might add, it confirmed everything my mother told us about him. Six, Karl divorced my mother because he thought she had committed adultery, and seven, he didn't want me for the same reason. He *assumed* he was sterile from the mumps, but we have no proof that he was. Since he's dead, we'll never know. Eight, all the information we've gathered about Mother points to the fact that she always was a nonconformist and always will be. Nine, I concede that we still don't know who sent her the love poems, but I don't see how we can find the answer by hanging around Bremenville."

When Suzanne signalled the waitress for more coffee, Grace nearly groaned aloud. Just like Stephen, Suzanne would not let go of this until she had crossed every "t" and dotted every "i."

"The love poem was written by Yeats, an Irish poet," Sue began. "Maybe the man who sent it was Irish too."

"I love spaghetti—does that make me Italian?"

Suzanne ignored her. "When Grandma left Bremenville and moved to the city, where did she get the money to live? How did she find a job? It was the 1920s, remember. 'Working woman' had a whole different meaning, and I assume that Grandma wasn't one of those. Who supported her after you were born?"

"I have no idea," Grace answered wearily.

"How did she end up living in the all-Irish section of town? Did she have friends there?"

"A few . . . but I have no idea why she picked Irishtown."

"Your neighbors were all strict Irish-Catholics too, weren't they?"

"Look, it wouldn't have mattered if they were Irish-Hindus. My mother never went near a church. Ever. If you want to unravel a mystery, maybe you can figure that one out. Her father was a minister—why did she turn away from her upbringing and her faith? And while we're at it, why did you turn away from yours?"

"My, my! Someone's in a crabby mood this morning!" Suzanne abandoned her coffee and began gathering her things to leave. "If you insist on going home, I suppose I'll have to drive you." She had twisted Grace's words, but Grace decided to keep her mouth shut and let it pass. Years of experience with Stephen had taught her that it was the safest course.

They loaded the car and took one last driving tour of Bremenville before heading out to the highway. The factories had long been abandoned, including the old woolen mill by the railroad trestle. Much of the population had apparently left with them. The rebuilt dam on Squaw Lake had turned Bremenville into a resort town, and when summer arrived, the population would likely swell with the season.

The shops on the village square had been converted into country boutiques and trendy galleries that catered to the tourist trade, including the store that had once been Bauer's Pharmacy—now an old-fashioned ice cream parlor and candy shop. There was no trace of Mueller's Feed Store, where Sophie and her husband had first lived, but the Ford dealership where Gus and Markus Bauer had worked was still selling cars. Grace and Suzanne never discovered which stately Victorian home Karl Bauer had built. It had likely been made into a bed-and-breakfast, like all the other old homes in that neighborhood. None of them had opened for the season yet.

Grace couldn't have said why, but she felt a sense of relief as they finally drove out of Bremenville. She wondered if her mother had felt the same way when she left more than fifty years before.

As soon as the car merged onto the freeway and headed south, Suzanne began raking the ashes of their earlier conversation, looking for a spark—just as Grace had feared she would.

"I can't help wondering why Grandma never remarried. She was an attractive woman, and she had plenty of suitors before Karl. Did she ever have any serious boyfriends while you were growing up?"

"Not that I recall. She had a few male friends, but she never dated any of them. In fact, if anyone started to get a little sweet on her she would nip it in the bud."

"Why?"

"I never understood how much of a social outcast my mother was until I was a teenager and none of the boys I knew would date me. Divorced women were considered loose and immoral in those days, and married women kept their husbands—and their sons—as far away from them as possible. No matter how carefully a divorced woman lived, she was considered a harlot if she entertained any male friends."

"Do you remember who some of Grandma's male friends were?"

Grace exhaled in exasperation. "I know what you're after, Suzanne. You're on a fishing expedition because you're convinced Karl Bauer isn't my real father."

"I'm not convinced, but I am suspicious. And you have to admit that it makes sense that Grandma would run to your real father for help after Karl tried to abort you."

"What *real* father? You want to make a grand mystery out of this, but there isn't one. Having mumps may have made it unlikely that he would ever father a child, but it probably wasn't impossible."

"Why didn't his second wife ever get pregnant?"

"I don't know . . . maybe . . . maybe . . ." Grace was too tired to come up with a plausible reason.

"And another thing. Why didn't Grandma stay in town and defend her reputation? If you resembled your father as much as Aunt Vera claimed, wouldn't that have been proof enough?"

"Mother told us she was miserable with Karl. She wanted out of the marriage and out of Bremenville long before she ever got pregnant. She probably jumped at the opportunity to do both. Why defend your reputation in a town you want to leave behind?"

"But wasn't it hard for you and Grandma during the depression? Wouldn't it have been easier for her to go home to her family?"

"Certainly. But that was probably sheer stubbornness on her part. You know Grandma. And I think she wanted to shield me from Karl so that I wouldn't be hurt by his rejection."

"But you still felt rejected by him."

"Yes . . . It took me a long time to come to terms with my absent father and to deal with the abandonment so that I could get on with my life. That's why I want you to stop all this useless speculation about whether or not Karl was my real father. It isn't going to change anything. It's only going to upset Grandma . . . and me."

Suzanne was quiet for a moment, then said softly, "So how did you come to terms with not having a father?"

Grace closed her eyes and leaned against the headrest as her thoughts drifted into the past. "Well, when I think back on my own childhood, I can see how God was faithful to send some men into my life who were father figures to me. . . ."

PART THREE

Grace's Story
1929 – 1945

NINETEEN

When I first met Father O'Duggan, I was four years old and staying with our landladies, the Mulligan sisters, while my mother worked as a waitress in a diner. He was a golden-haired giant of a man who seemed to light up the gloomy apartment when he walked through the door. He came to visit old Mrs. Mulligan, who lay dying in a bed in the spooky back room of their apartment. The old woman terrified me. She looked like a storybook picture of a witch, with her chalky face and spidery hands. I thought Father O'Duggan was very brave to go into that room alone with her and close the door—even if he was dressed all in black like all the Mulligans.

Of course, Kate and Aileen Mulligan went into her room sometimes too, but they were almost as witchlike as their mother. They had black hair, which they wore pulled back from their stern faces, and they dressed in long black skirts, and narrow pointy-toed black shoes. I was more than a little afraid of them as well.

What intrigued me the most was the fact that the spinster sisters called him "Father"—which I took to mean that he must be married to old Mrs. Mulligan, their mother. Yet he seemed much too young and handsome to be their father and his name wasn't Mulligan and he didn't live with them and, most mysterious of all, old Mrs. Mulligan called him "Father" too. At four years of age, I couldn't untangle it.

I was already aware that something was missing from my life; other children had a mother *and* a father, I had only a mother. "You have a father. He just doesn't live with us," my mother explained whenever I asked about him. Perhaps my father was like Father O'Duggan, who didn't live with his family either.

As Father O'Duggan stood at the door saying good-bye to Miss Aileen, I tiptoed out from the kitchen and tugged on the hem of his black clerical coat. "Why don't you live here?" I asked. I hoped it might explain why my father didn't live with me. I was so timid, my voice barely rose above a whisper.

Father O'Duggan crouched down so his eyes were level with mine. He rested a black leather book on his knee.

"What did you say, Grace?"

I don't know how he knew my name, since the Mulligan sisters hadn't introduced him to me. Whenever he arrived, they usually hustled me off to the kitchen as if I were an eyesore. I swallowed back my fear and asked again.

"If you're their father, why don't you live here?"

His smile went all the way to his eyes, which were very blue. "Because I'm not their real father, you see. 'Father' is a title given to men who do the work I do. I'm a priest . . . which makes me a 'father' to the people in my parish."

"Are you my father too?"

"Certainly not," Miss Aileen said sharply. "You're not Catholic."

Father O'Duggan laid his hand on my unruly nest of hair and caressed my head. "Now, now, Miss Mulligan, surely I can be 'Father O'Duggan' to wee Gracie too. Remember our Savior's words? 'Suffer the little children to come unto me, and forbid them not: for of such is the kingdom of God.' "

I didn't understand what his words about suffering children meant, but I loved the sound of his deep voice with its lilting Irish brogue.

"Her people have their own priests to go to," Miss Aileen said in a huff. "Didn't you tell me her grandfather was a priest?"

"Aye, he's a minister, Miss Aileen. They're called ministers in the Protestant faith."

"Well then, she—"

"I should be going now," he cut in, then stood and tucked his black book into the breast pocket of his jacket. "Good day to you, Miss Aileen, Miss Grace. God bless you both."

After that, the Mulligan sisters still marched me into the kitchen whenever he came, but I would peer through the crack in the door and call him "father" in my heart.

————

That winter my mother became very ill. She'd had a terrible cough for days, but one morning she didn't get out of bed at all. I crawled up beside her, shaking her and calling her name, but she didn't open her eyes. Her arm felt as warm as a loaf of bread from the oven, and she mumbled words that didn't make sense to me. I decided to let her sleep and fixed myself some bread and jam from the cupboard. She didn't get up when it was time for work either.

As the day passed, our apartment grew colder and colder. Even if I'd known how to keep the fire going in the stove, our coal box was empty. By suppertime, I was so cold I had to put on my coat. I covered my mother with both blankets. When it grew dark, I turned on the light and opened the door to the hallway like my mother always did to catch some warm air from the other apartments. The sound of Father O'Duggan's voice drifted upstairs to me.

"The bishop is spending a few days at the rectory, so that's where I'm likely to be if you need me. . . ."

I crept down the stairs, drawn toward the warmth of his voice. He was still inside the Mulligans' apartment with the door opened just a crack. I couldn't hear what they said to him in reply.

" . . . All right. I'll be on my way then, Miss Aileen. Your mother will be in my prayers." He opened the door wide and nearly tripped over me as he came through it. "I'm sorry," he said, reaching out to steady me. "I didn't realize you were there."

"Grace Bauer! What on earth are you doing down here this time of night?" Aileen Mulligan asked.

"My mama is sick."

"Sick?" Aileen repeated. "Has she been drinking?" I didn't know how to answer because I didn't know what she meant. Father O'Duggan frowned at her.

"Maybe we should go upstairs and see if we can help." He took the creaking stairs two at a time, not waiting for Aileen Mulligan, who plodded slowly behind him, resting both feet on every step, gripping the wobbly bannister in her hand.

I hurried to keep up with him and heard Mother's wracking coughs even before we reached the top step. She lay curled on the bed, shivering beneath the blankets. Two bright red patches flushed her cheeks. Father O'Duggan sat beside her and smoothed away her damp hair to feel her brow.

"Mrs. Bauer . . ." he said, shaking her slightly. "Mrs. Bauer, are you all right?" She mumbled nonsense in reply. I heard the squeak of Miss Aileen's shoes on the wooden floor, and Father O'Duggan and I both turned to her. "She's burning with fever," Father O'Duggan said. "I fear she has pneumonia." When my mother began coughing again, Miss Aileen froze in the doorway as if afraid to come farther.

"Shall I send Clancy for the doctor?" she asked.

"No, she needs to go straight to the hospital. Send Clancy to Booty's store to ask if he'll drive her there." Aileen waddled away, seemingly unhurried, and Father O'Duggan turned to me. "We need to wrap your mama up nice and warm to drive her to the hospital. Can you fetch me her shoes and her coat?"

As I hurried to obey him, I saw him glance around our apartment. It was the first time he'd ever been inside it. We had very little furniture besides a dresser, our two beds and a kitchen table and chairs, but my mother kept the two rooms clean and cozy, decorating the walls with my colorful drawings. I wanted to tell him I'd made the pictures and ask him if he liked them, but his face was angry-looking. I laid Mother's coat and shoes on the bed and backed away.

Father O'Duggan rubbed his hands together to warm them. When he exhaled I could see his breath. Each time the wind squealed outside the window, the curtain moved in the breeze. Mother coughed again, and I felt it like a blow to the pit of my stomach. I wanted her to wake up and be better.

It seemed to take forever for Booty Higgins to arrive with the car, but I finally heard a man's heavy tread ascending the stairs. Crazy Clancy, our elderly next-door neighbor, ducked his head in the doorway, his face flushed with cold and whiskey.

"The car is out front, Father," he said. "I left it running. Booty says to drive Mrs. Bauer yourself. His missus doesn't want him to."

"Thanks, Clancy. God bless you for going out on such a cold night." Father O'Duggan shoved Mother's limp arms into the sleeves of her coat, then pulled the two threadbare blankets off the bed and wrapped them around her as well.

"Will Mrs. Bauer be all right?" Clancy asked.

"I don't know." The priest buttoned his own coat before lifting Mama into his arms. "Don't these apartments come with any heat, Clancy?"

"No, Father. We pay the Mulligans extra for coal and keep warm as best we can."

"Dear Lord, have mercy . . ." he mumbled. "Run ahead and get the downstairs door for me, would you, Clancy?"

It seemed to take the old man a moment to comprehend the question. He looked from Mother to me, then patted my head with his quivering hand. "Don't you be getting sick on us, now," he said. I smelled the rich, buttery scent of whiskey on his breath. Clancy tottered down the stairs, leaning on the rail as if on board a tossing ship, then swayed across the hall to open the front door.

"Open the car door too, Clancy," the priest called.

I saw a sheen of ice on the sidewalk and held my breath, hoping Clancy wouldn't slip as he lurched toward the car. When he'd made it to the curb, he opened the door with a small bow. Father O'Duggan ducked his head as he bent to lay my mother on the backseat. "Thanks, man. I couldn't have done without your help. I'll be off now."

I started to cry. I wanted to go with my mother, but Father O'Duggan hadn't remembered me. I stood on the front stoop, wondering what I should do. Clancy cocked his head toward me. "What about the little girl, Father?"

"Aye, I nearly forgot. Surely the Mulligan sisters will watch her, don't you think?" Father O'Duggan jogged up the steps past me and knocked on the Mulligans' door. Miss Aileen had gone back inside her apartment.

"I'll be driving Mrs. Bauer to the hospital now," he said when she answered his knock. "Could you and Miss Kate take care of wee Gracie for the night?"

Aileen frowned. "Ordinarily we would, but the doctor said our mother could pass away tonight . . . and then we'll be having the wake here and all. . . ."

"I understand, but it's just for one night. I don't know who else can take the child. Mrs. Bauer has no relatives in the city as far as anyone knows. And she can hardly stay with old Clancy, now, can she?" he added in a low voice.

Miss Aileen's face showed her irritation. "Well, in that case I suppose you'll have to take her to the county orphans' home."

"Surely not! That's a terrible place for a child. I can scarcely stand to visit there."

"Face facts, Father O'Duggan—with no other family, she'll end up in the orphans' home anyway if Mrs. Bauer dies."

"Aileen," he said through clenched teeth. "She can hear, don't you know?"

Yes, I could hear, and her words terrified me. I tried to wipe my tears but they fell faster and faster.

"Please, Miss Mulligan. Can't you find it in your heart to take her?"

"I'm sorry, Father. We have enough to deal with."

Father O'Duggan opened his mouth as if to rage at the heartless old crow, but the rebuke for her lack of charity died on his lips. "Good evening to you, then," he said abruptly. He jammed his hat onto his head and pulled her apartment door closed behind him. He stood perfectly still for a moment, with his fists bunched and his mouth set in a straight line, then he exhaled wearily and crouched beside me. He seemed about to draw me into his arms to soothe away my tears, but his outstretched arms dropped to his sides as he realized he was nearly a stranger to me. He pulled his handkerchief from his breast pocket instead and pressed it into my hands.

"Come, then, button your coat. You can ride with your mother to the hospital."

As we drove through the icy streets to Sisters of Mercy Hospital, the blast of warm air from the car's heater couldn't melt the fear that froze my heart. Was my mother going to die like old Mrs. Mulligan? What would happen to me if she did? Was there no one who wanted me?

As soon as Father O'Duggan carried Mother through the hospital doors, the smell of disinfectant and the hurried squeak of shoes on the spotless tile floors thawed the edges of my dread. I felt hope returning even before the orderly whisked Mother away on a rolling bed.

"There, now. The doctors will take good care of her," Father O'Duggan murmured. "The sisters will restore her to health in no time." I didn't know what he meant because I didn't have any sisters and, as far as I knew, neither did Mother. But his voice was soothing, just the same.

As he filled out a bunch of papers, I took a long close-up look at Father O'Duggan, face-to-face, not through a crack in the door. He was big and sturdy and solid compared to Mother and the Mulligan sisters, like a wall of flesh and bone that I could hide behind. The only other man I knew was Clancy—and he was wrinkled and frail like old Mrs. Mulligan. Clancy smelled bad too, but Father O'Duggan smelled nice, like the spices in Mother's kitchen cupboard. He had tiny golden hairs on his wrists, peeking out from the cuffs of his black jacket, and sparkling golden hairs on his chin and around his mouth. He had removed his hat inside the hospital, and I could see the marks of his comb on his slicked-back hair. It was golden too. I stared at him from head to toe, fascinated. I had never seen shoes as big as his.

When an elderly woman, dressed in a strange black gown and headdress, asked him into her office, he reached for my hand. His hand was huge and warm and strong. It swallowed mine completely.

"Please, sit down, Father O'Duggan," the woman said. I sat beside him. "Dr. Kelly has just seen Mrs. Bauer and . . ."

"What did he say?"

"She's gravely ill, Father. It's pneumonia. You might want to administer the Blessed Sacrament before you leave."

It was a moment before he spoke. "She isn't Catholic," he said quietly.

"One of my parishioners owns the rooming house where she lives."

"She should have been hospitalized days ago."

"I know, but she has no one to take care of her, you see. No family . . ."

The woman made a slight nod toward me. "Where is Mr. Bauer?"

"He's not . . . that is . . . Mrs. Bauer's husband has divorced her." He cleared his throat. "About the child," he said softly. "Could you possibly find a place for her here, near her mother? It's just for tonight."

"We're already full with this influenza epidemic," the woman said, spreading her hands. "Even if we had a spare bed, which we don't, the child would risk infection herself if she stayed here."

"I see. Well, might you suggest another place?"

"There's always the county home."

"Aye. I know all about the county home, Sister Mary Margaret, and so do you." His voice sounded angry and tight. "That place is like a black-and-white photograph. Everything in it is a dreary shade of gray, from the stone walls that surround it to the dingy paint and grubby bed sheets inside it, to the grim despair on the children's faces. I can't leave this child there. They would bleach the very life from her." He stood, as if suddenly impatient to leave. "Please call me at the rectory right away if there's any change in Mrs. Bauer's condition."

He steered me out of the office, then stopped near the door to button my coat and pull my knitted hat over my ears. I was so tired I stumbled when I tried to walk, and Father O'Duggan swept me into his arms to carry me to the car. I leaned against his chest. It wasn't soft and yielding like Mother's, but solid and firm. The ground seemed a long way down.

He glanced at me from time to time as he drove away from the hospital. I tried to stop my tears, but they kept falling and falling just the same. I saw the concern in his eyes by the light of oncoming cars. "Are you warm enough, Gracie?" he asked. I nodded, even though I was shivering.

"Dear God, what to do with you?" he said with a sigh. "I would gladly take you to the rectory for the night if it weren't for the bishop's visit. There must be another answer besides the county home. . . ."

He drove in silence for another minute or two. Houses and trees flew past my window in a blur. Then Booty's tires squealed as Father O'Duggan suddenly jammed on the brakes. He made a U-turn on the highway and headed back into town. Ten minutes later, he stopped in front of a neat brick bungalow with lace curtains at the windows. Smoke curled from the chimney, and lights glowed from the rooms inside like a picture from a storybook.

"Come with me, Grace," Father O'Duggan said. I slid across the seat behind him and climbed out on the driver's side. We followed a sidewalk that led around to the kitchen door. Father O'Duggan knocked softly, then opened the door and stepped inside. "It's me, Mam."

A plump, white-haired woman stood by the stove, waiting for the kettle to boil. As I followed him inside, the warmth of the tiny kitchen engulfed me like bath water.

"For goodness' sake! What's wrong?"

He kissed her cheek. "Nothing, Mam . . . not with me anyway."

"Sit down, take your coat off. I was just fixing m'self some tea . . . or maybe you'd like a wee drop to warm you on such a cold night?" She indicated one of the cupboards with a tilt of her head.

"Just the tea, thanks." He remained standing.

I was half-hidden behind Father O'Duggan's legs, and she didn't appear to notice me. She bustled around the kitchen—retrieving the cups, warming the pot, measuring the tea, lifting the kettle off the stove when it boiled—all in one smooth, practiced movement.

"Listen, I need to ask a favor, Mam. I just drove a woman to Sisters of Mercy Hospital. They think she has pneumonia."

Mam clucked her tongue in sympathy as she pulled the tea cozy over the pot. "I shouldn't wonder if we all caught pneumonia, what with the weather such as it's been lately."

"The thing is, you see . . . she has no family here in the city, and so there's no one to take care of her child."

"Aren't any of the other families from your parish willing?"

"The woman isn't from my parish." He waited until she paused to look at him. "It's Emma Bauer."

Mam froze. Her expression was so cold as she turned away from us that I expected frost to form on the inside of the kitchen window as she stared out. "And why is a divorced woman's child any of your business, might I ask?"

"Will you take her for the night, Mam?"

"I will not. Emma Bauer is a shameful woman who divorced her husband, and if you had half the brains God gave you, you wouldn't be mixing yourself up with the likes of her."

"Mixing up! The doctor said she might die!"

Mam's face turned an alarming shade of scarlet, and her chins quivered with anger. "And if she does die, how are you going to explain to your parish why you're stuck with her child? Not only is the woman divorced, she isn't even Catholic!"

"For the love of mercy, Mam, it's not the child's fault! She's just a babe!"

He scooped me up in his arms so abruptly my hat fell off. He snatched his own hat from his head and threw it to the floor beside mine. "We're all sinners. Every last one of us. Will you look at the child, for the love of God?"

Mam did look at me then, and her eyes suddenly filled with tears. She groped for the kitchen chair with one hand and sank into it. She stared at Father O'Duggan for a long moment, then turned away, pulling a linen hand-kerchief from her sleeve to dab her eyes. He set me on my feet in front of him again, resting his hands on my shoulders.

"Her name is Grace," he said quietly. "Like the grace of God which covers all our sins."

"Aye. I know the word," Mam whispered.

"Will you take her, then?"

Mam reached out and stroked my hair. Electricity from my woolen hat had made it stand on end, and she gently patted it down again. "There, there . . . such a pretty child. Would you like me to take care of you till your mam's feeling better?"

Before I knew how it happened, I was curled up on Mam's lap, enveloped in her soft arms and warm bosom. I closed my eyes and wept, secure in the comfort of her embrace and the familiar, floury smell of her apron.

Father O'Duggan bent to retrieve his hat. "I'll come by in the morning," he said hoarsely.

Mam nodded as she slowly unbuttoned my coat and slid it from my shoulders. "There, now . . . we'll get on fine together, won't we, Gracie?"

I loved Mam from that very first night. She must have heard my stomach growling because as soon as Father O'Duggan left, she set a bowl of bread pudding in front of me. It was thick with raisins and fragrant with cinnamon and cloves. I had never tasted such a wonderful treat before. After I'd washed it down with a glass of milk, Mam took my hand and led me toward her spare bedroom in the back of the house. I got no farther than her sitting room, though. I stopped and gazed around in amazement. If ever a house was made to fit a person, Mam's cottage fit her. The room was small and soft like Mam, the furniture plump with pillows and topped with a white frosting of doilies, like her cap of lacy white curls. The house was as cozy and warm as her embrace, even when you weren't standing near the stove. Framed pictures stood on every flat surface—photos of men, women, and children; all ages, shapes, and sizes.

"Look, that's Father O'Duggan," I said, pointing to one of them. "But he isn't wearing black."

"Aye, the picture was taken five years ago before he became a priest. He's my son, you see. I'm his mam. These are his sisters and brothers. Six children in all, Lord bless them. And this is his daddy, God rest his soul."

I studied each picture, and when I found one of myself, clinging to Mam's skirts with my wild mop of curly hair all in tangles, I knew that I would be safe here, that I belonged in this house because they had a picture of me. I fell asleep in her spare room all by myself without even crying for my mother.

When I awoke the next morning, the first thing I did was go into the front room to look at the pictures again. I found the one of Father O'Duggan in his white shirt, but the one of me was gone.

"Where's my picture?" I asked as Mam shuffled in from the kitchen in her robe and slippers. She lifted me into her arms.

"I don't have any pictures of you, little luv. But I'll get my daughter Agnes to take one when she comes over, and we'll put it here by the lamp with all the others. Would you like that?"

She set me down at the kitchen table in front of a steaming bowl of porridge, sprinkled with raisins. I might have been dreaming about the picture, but at least the food had been real.

As I was finishing my second bowl, Father O'Duggan came through the back door. "Well, aren't you up and about early this morning," Mam said. "Will you eat something?"

"No, thanks. I'm having breakfast with the bishop in half an hour. Then I'll be tied up in meetings all day. That's why I needed an early start . . . to take care of . . ." He glanced at me and cleared his throat. "I'm going to talk to the Murphys this morning and see if they'll take her."

"Maggie Murphy and her clan, do you mean?"

"Maggie's oldest son, Keith, and his family."

Mam scooped me off the chair and into her soft arms as if she needed to protect me from something. I loved being held by her. It was like being surrounded by a mountain of lavender-scented pillows. "Now why would you be wanting to send the poor wee thing to that house?"

"Well, they're the only ones who can afford another mouth to feed."

"Aye, not that they'd willingly spend a cent on a stranger's child!"

"I don't know where else—"

"That Maggie Murphy is a bitter old woman, and such a miser with her money it would give you indigestion just to eat a tea biscuit with her!"

For a long time, neither of them spoke. Mam seemed to be turning something around in her mind.

"Let her stay here with me," she finally said. It was what I had wished for with all my heart. "You'll need to bring me her clothes and things, though."

"There is nothing to bring, Mam." Father O'Duggan's voice was tight, his face angry. I was afraid he was mad at me for some reason, and I burrowed deeper into Mam's bosom. "I went to their apartment this morning," he said, "looking to find some extra clothes, a favorite toy . . . What I found would fit in my pocket."

Mam's arms tightened around me. "Poor little luv. Leave her with me, then."

"It may be several weeks, you understand." His voice was quiet again. "I stopped by the hospital this morning—"

"Never mind about that right now." Mam set me down and began scrubbing the porridge off my face and hands with a wet cloth. "Go on with you then, or you'll be late for your breakfast with His Excellency."

"All right," he said, kissing her cheek. "And thanks, Mam. You've got a grand big heart, you know."

"Aye, go on with you," she said, waving him away with a frown. "Save the blarney for all the Maggie Murphys in your parish!"

———

Even with me underfoot, Mam kept to her daily routine. On Monday she did the washing in her basement tubs, scrubbing linens and dress shirts for the rich people who were her customers. Her cavelike cellar was cold, and the steam from the hot water fogged the air with the scent of starch and blueing. Mam let me turn the crank on the wringer. When everything was clean and wrung, Mam gave me a pair of mittens to wear, and I played in the snow in her tiny backyard while she hung the wash on the line to dry. In the unspoken race against the neighboring housewives, Mam's laundry was unfurled on the clothesline first.

On Tuesday she did the ironing and mending. Mam didn't own a modern electric iron, and watching her juggle three irons on the coal stove as she pressed shirts and pillowcases and bed sheets was like watching a circus act. I loved the smell of freshly ironed linen and quickly learned the words to all the Irish ballads she sang as she worked.

Early Wednesday morning, Mam piled the carefully folded washing in a cart made from an old baby carriage, and we pushed it up the hill to the rich people's house. The huge mansion had tall columns in front and a wrought-iron fence all around it, but I never saw what it looked like inside. We weren't allowed. A housekeeper in a gray-and-white uniform met us at the service entrance in back.

"Is this one of your grandchildren, Mrs. O'Duggan?" she asked.

"Gracie's mam is in the hospital," she explained. "My son Thomas asked me to look after her. He's a priest over in St. Michael's parish, you see."

The woman counted out Mam's wages, and we walked to the grocery store to do the weekly shopping. On the way home she let me push the carriage full of groceries. Again and again, I heard Mam explain who I was to the people we met, and I saw the pride in her eyes when she mentioned her son Thomas, the priest. From everyone's reaction, I learned that having a priest in the family was a truly wonderful thing.

On Thursday Mam turned the cottage upside down, dusting and waxing and scrubbing the floors. The best way to help her, she said, was to keep out from underfoot. But the next day was Friday, the best day of all. Mam did her baking on Friday. Wonderful smells filled the kitchen as cookies and pies and loaf after loaf of Irish soda bread emerged from the oven. Mam tied an apron around me and let me kneel on a chair to lick the spoons and mixing bowls. I ate fistfuls of sweet, gooey dough.

At first I wondered who would eat all these marvelous baked goods, but I soon found out. Every afternoon swarms of Mam's relations filed in and out, staying only long enough for a cup of tea and a bit of gossip. Everyone who came brought her something to eat—a bit of black pudding, a plate of leftover corned beef—and when they left they took something Mam had baked with them. This dizzying exchange of food and serving plates mystified me. I eventually met all six of Mam's children as well as her eighteen grandchildren, who adopted me into their midst like one of their own cousins.

As word spread that I needed clothes, hand-me-downs began to arrive along with the visitors. Every evening Mam sat in her chair in the front room and mended things for me to wear, sewing on buttons, letting seams in and out, darning woolen stockings. Within days I had more clothes than I'd ever owned in my life, including three extra pairs of bloomers and a nightgown to wear to bed. Best of all, Mam made me a rag doll to sleep with so I wouldn't miss my mother so much. I named the doll Nellie.

Once my wardrobe was taken care of, Mam resumed her usual evening task of making vestments for Father O'Duggan. She put such loving care into each stitch that I didn't have the heart to tell her I'd never once seen Father O'Duggan wear any of them. I loved to feel the luxurious fabrics—soft, warm velvet; smooth, cool satin; nubby white brocade. When she saw how much I admired them, Mam gave me the scraps and a needle and thread and taught me to sew.

Toward the end of that first week, I became the object of much discussion as Mam sat at the kitchen table with one of her daughters and sipped tea. "What ever will I do with the poor wee thing while I'm in church?" she wondered.

"She'll have to go to mass with you."

"But her people are Protestant."

"The woman needs our prayers, doesn't she, Mam?"

"Aye, that she does."

"Then I shouldn't think she'd mind who's doing the praying, or where it's being done."

In the end, Mam decided that I would accompany her to church on Sunday, as well as to confession on Saturday afternoon. She pinned a huge white bow to the top of my head for both occasions and covered her own head with a swath of Irish lace.

Confession was a mysterious ritual. Mam waited in a long somber line of people to go inside one of two little booths and talk to the priest. She said he was sitting in the middle booth, but I never saw him. "Is Father O'Duggan in there?" I asked.

"Nay," she whispered. "He hears confession at a different church in a different parish."

Some of the people stayed inside the booth a long time; others were in and out in moments. Some came out smiling, others wiping their tears. And once, everyone in line had to back up a few steps when the priest began to shout. The man who emerged afterward was very red in the face.

Mam's turn in the secret booth turned out to be a short visit. I waited outside the door where I could hear the mumble of voices but not their words. Then we sat quietly in one of the pews for a while as Mam fingered her rosary beads. On the way home I learned that the huge shopping bag she had hauled along with us contained more food, which she delivered along the way.

Sunday Mass the next day made a deep impression on me. The wash of stained-glass color and light, the gentle winking of candles, the chant of the priests echoing through the nave seemed like a glimpse of a heavenly world.

But I stared the longest at the crucifix on the wall above the priest's head and never forgot the patient suffering I saw on Christ's face. The gilded paintings and statues scattered throughout the sanctuary were the most beautiful things I'd ever seen, but none held such magnetic power over me as the man on the wooden cross.

When mass ended, Mam took me into a little alcove on one side of the church where there was a statue of a beautiful woman with her hands outstretched. "It's the Blessed Virgin," Mam said. "You may light a candle and say a prayer for your mother." I put the coin she gave me into a special box, and she showed me how to light one of the small candles in front of the statue. Then I folded my hands like Mam did and touched my chin to my chest and closed my eyes.

Father O'Duggan came to visit us early the next day. Mam abandoned her washing, and we climbed the steep cellar steps to fix him some tea. I stood close beside his chair in the kitchen, inhaling his spicy scent and wishing I could touch him, when he suddenly pulled me onto his lap.

"I just visited your mother in the hospital," he said. "She asked me to give you a big hug. She's much better than she was, but it will still be some time before she can come home again."

"I lit a candle and prayed to the Blessed Virgin for her," I said.

He looked up at his mother and frowned. "Mam, you didn't!"

"Aye, I did." She folded her arms across her chest and stuck out her chin. "What was I supposed to do with her, then? You tell me."

"I guess you're right. . . ." he said with a sigh. "I offered to take Grace up to her grandparents in Bremenville, but Emma wouldn't let me."

That was the first time I ever heard of Bremenville or the fact that I had grandparents there. It was also the last time anyone mentioned them for many years.

TWENTY

Mother was very weak after she came home from Sisters of Mercy Hospital. She looked gray and ghostly, like old Mrs. Mulligan downstairs had looked before she died. "Are you going to die, Mommy?" I asked one night as she tucked me into bed.

"Of course not. Only the good die young," she said, laughing. "That means I'll live a long, long time."

Even if she had been strong enough to work, the Great Depression had begun and she no longer had a job at the diner. A few pieces of coal magically appeared in our box whenever the weather turned cold, and Booty Higgins became a good friend to us, allowing Mother and me to take groceries home from his store on credit. But the day soon arrived when we didn't have enough rent money to pay the Mulligan sisters. The whole neighborhood had witnessed the shame and humiliation of the Sullivan family down the block—their landlord had thrown them and all their possessions out into the street for not paying their rent, then boarded the door closed behind them. Mother didn't want the same thing to happen to us.

On a warm spring day in 1930, Mother got out her prettiest dress from the back of the closet, spruced herself all up with lipstick and rouge, then walked hand in hand with me down the street to Booty's store. The bell jangled as Mother yanked open the sagging screen door. Through the bluish haze of cigarette smoke and drifting dust motes, we saw Booty manning the cash register beneath the Camel cigarette clock. Mother looked around carefully for Mrs. Booty Higgins. I was scared of her, and I think Mother was too. Whenever Mrs. Booty stood at the register, we would just leave again because she didn't allow anyone to charge groceries.

But this day Mother hadn't come for groceries. She waited until the other customers left, then walked up to the counter. "We've known each other a long time, Booty," she said in a low voice. "I need a favor."

"Sure, Emma. Wha . . . what kind of a favor?" I'd noticed that men sometimes acted silly and tongue-tied around my mother, but I didn't understand the reason for it yet. Booty was one of the silliest-acting. He would stand up a little straighter and tuck in his shirttails whenever Mother walked into the store, then comb his dark hair back with his fingers, and gaze at her the way a puppy stares out of a pet store window. I had heard other people say that Booty was too Irish-handsome for his own good, but Mother never seemed to take notice of him or any other man.

"I'm laid off work and all out of money," she said quietly. "I need you to tell me where O'Brien's speakeasy is."

He raked his hands through his hair again and shook his head. "I . . . I can't tell you that, Emma. I promised Father O'Duggan—"

"How's he going to find out, Booty? I don't go to confession. I'm not going to tell him. But I just might decide to have a word with your wife about—"

"No, no! Don't do that!" he said, glancing over his shoulder.

"I need to make some money," Mother said. "I want to ask O'Brien if he'll let me play the piano at his place, that's all. I'm not planning a career as a lady legger or a floozy."

"Aw, c'mon, Emma. I give you and Gracie food—"

"And I appreciate that, but I need to earn my own way. Where's O'Brien's place?"

"What's all the whispering about out there?" Booty's wife suddenly hollered from the room in back where they lived.

"Nothing, Sheila . . . I'm not whispering nothing."

It wasn't until Mother picked me up and set me down on the counter in front of Booty like a pile of groceries to be rung up that he finally gave in and told her what she wanted to know.

"The Regency Room at the hotel downtown on Clark Street is a blind pig for O'Brien's place. Talk to the matron in the ladies' powder room. She lets members through into the speakeasy in back."

"Thanks. I love you, Booty. You're a good friend."

That evening Mother and I took the streetcar downtown to the hotel. I had never seen a place as fancy as the Regency Room before. It looked like Cinderella's ballroom with sparkling chandeliers and crystal and silver and white linen cloths on all the tables. The aroma of food made my mouth water, even though Mother and I had shared a can of tomato soup before leaving home. I gazed around, wide-eyed, until a sour-looking man in a black tuxedo stepped smoothly in front of us.

"May I help you, ma'am?" Judging by the way he glared at us and by the lavish way all the other customers were dressed, I knew he didn't want to help Mother and me at all.

"No, thank you," Mother said, smiling. "My little girl and I would like to use the powder room."

"Sorry, ma'am." He didn't look sorry, either. "Our facilities are for dining customers only."

"Really? I thought that friends of Mr. O'Brien could use them too."

He stepped aside without another word. Mother took my hand and we went into the ladies' powder room, just like Booty told us to. The inside looked like every other rest room I'd seen, with a mirror over the sink, two toilets in metal stalls, and a narrow storage closet. An enormous woman with black skin sat on a stool dispensing paper towels and soap to earn tips.

"I'm a friend of Booty Higgins," Mother told the matron. "Is O'Brien here?"

"Who wants to know?"

"Tell him it's an old friend of his, Emma Bauer."

The matron heaved herself off the stool and opened the storage closet door with a key. She squeezed through it, shutting it behind her. A few minutes later the door opened again and a wiry, redheaded man burst through it, sweeping Mother into his arms.

"Emma darlin'! It really is you!"

"It's great to see you too, O'Brien." I was surprised to see that Mother had tears in her eyes. "And this is my daughter, Gracie."

O'Brien crouched down to smile at me. "Has it really been this long, Emma?" he asked, shaking his head. "She was just a wee babe. . . ."

"I'll be five years old in May," I told him. He patted my head, then stood.

"This is no place for friends to talk. Come on back to my office and we'll toast old times, eh, Emma?"

He led the way, stepping through the closet door, but I hesitated, afraid to follow him. It seemed like something Mother had read to me from *Alice in Wonderland* to walk into a mysterious closet. Mother took my hand and we ducked through together.

On the other side was a darkened room about one-fourth the size of the Regency Room. It was also filled with tables and chairs, but this room fairly rocked with the sound of laughter and clinking glasses. O'Brien signalled to a large, hulking man on the other side of the room, and he headed toward us. I hid behind Mother's skirts, terrified by his size and sinister face, but Mother flew into his arms as she had O'Brien's, and he lifted her clear off the floor.

"I've missed you, Black Jack," she said when he set her down again. He had tears in his eyes too.

"Is this baby Gracie?" he asked, looking down at me. I wondered how he knew my name. "She's as beautiful as you are, Emma."

O'Brien herded us all into his office. The tiny room behind the bar was smaller than the ladies' powder room and smelled like cigars. All it contained was a wooden desk, covered with papers, and a sagging black leather sofa. O'Brien sat behind the desk and pulled a bottle of amber-colored liquid from the bottom drawer.

"How about a drink, Emma?"

"No, thanks. I'm much too young to die."

O'Brien laughed as he sloshed some of it into three tiny glasses. "This won't kill you. It's much better than that coffin varnish Booty used to make. Try it."

"I need work, O'Brien. I can play any kind of piano music you need—fast, slow, dinner music, dancing music . . ." I gazed at my mother in amazement. I'd never heard her play the piano in my life. "Let me play for the dinner customers out in the restaurant."

He drained the contents of his glass in one gulp. "Times are tough, Emma. I can't pay you. . . ."

"I understand. Let me work for tips."

They talked some more, and then we walked back out to the dining room. O'Brien let Mother play that very night. I sat on his lap at one of the tables and listened, fascinated, as lush melodies and toe-tapping tunes flowed from Mother's fingers, one after the other. She seemed to sense the mood of the room and changed songs accordingly—fast, slow, happy, sad. He gave her the job.◆

That night I rode on a streetcar for the first time, but by the time Prohibition ended three years later I knew every stop, driver, and regular passenger on the route. I could have found my way to the Regency Room with my eyes closed. Mother and I went there every night but Sunday. O'Brien put a little bowl on top of the piano for tips, and people must have liked Mother's music too, because we never missed a rent payment. The chef gave us free dinner every night and all the plate scrapings we could carry home. We ate like royalty.

Mother would start the evening with soft dinner music, playing songs like "Embraceable You" and "Stardust." But as the night wore on, she picked up the tempo, playing louder, livelier tunes to drown out all the ruckus the drunks made in the speakeasy behind the powder rooms. I went to work with her every night and fell asleep on the leather sofa in O'Brien's office to the sound of music and laughter and clinking glasses. O'Brien drove us home in his car after the club closed at two A.M., and in the morning I wouldn't even remember walking up the back fire stairs with Mother so that the Mulligan sisters wouldn't know how late we'd come home. It seemed perfectly natural to fall asleep on O'Brien's sofa and wake up in our own apartment.

The people at the club became my family. Now I had three more fathers to watch over me, besides Booty and Father O'Duggan. Booty wore a grubby white apron, and Father O'Duggan always wore black, but O'Brien, Slick Mick, and Black Jack were by far my best-dressed fathers. They wore white dinner jackets with black bow ties and cummerbunds.

O'Brien was no taller than Mother and had a wild mop of tangled hair like mine—only his was red. He had so many freckles that you could hardly see his real skin. Once, when he took off his jacket, I saw that the freckles covered his arms too. When he saw me staring he lifted his pant cuff and I saw them all over his leg. O'Brien loved to tease me. When I got the measles and had to stay home, he came to the apartment to visit me and brought me a jigsaw puzzle.

"You're not sick at all," he said, laughing. "You're just catching my freckles!"

O'Brien was very smart, and though I rarely saw him in the kitchen with the chef, he was always talking on the phone about the deals he was cooking. When I was old enough to go to school, he helped me with my homework every night, especially my arithmetic.

"I'm pretty good at numbers," he bragged. "Good with the ponies too."

"Can I ride one of your ponies sometime?" I asked.

"Not them kind of ponies, Toots," he said, laughing. "Your mother don't want you learning nothing about them kind of ponies." I didn't ask O'Brien for help with my grammar assignments.

Black Jack was the club bouncer. I think he got his nickname because he had black hair and a blue-black shadow on his chin. He used to be a prizefighter in Ireland and had the lumpy nose and knotted arm muscles to prove it. He was a head taller than everyone else and very scary and tough-looking if you didn't know him. He was as gentle as a lamb to me. Black Jack talked kind of slow and took a long time to think things through. "That's because he's been knocked in the head too many times," O'Brien said.

Once, a drunk stopped me when I was on my way from the office to the bathroom, and Black Jack lifted the man right off the floor by his shirtfront. "You ever lay another hand on that baby, and it will be the last thing you ever do!" he told him. Black Jack loved me and I loved him.

My third father down at the Regency Room, and by far the most handsome, was Slick Mick the bartender. Mick's hair was as kinky as the powder room matron's, only his was light brown. He had fair skin and a mournful face that made you want to do something to try and cheer him up. "Poor Slick is unlucky in love," O'Brien told me once.

Mick came into the office to talk to me whenever he took a cigarette break, and he talked so much I couldn't get a word in edgewise. I guess it was because Mick didn't get a chance to talk when he was tending bar—he would have to listen to all the sob stories his customers dished out. When I first met Mick, I couldn't understand a word he said.

"We got another stash of John Barleycorn coming in tonight from some new barrel house one of the whisper sisters put me on to. The rum runner claimed it was brown plaid, but I wouldn't be surprised if it was coffin varnish. The last legger who claimed to have the real McCoy delivered soda pop moon."

Mick had a million descriptions for people who drank too much—words like fried, boiled, canned, and crocked; pickled, pie-eyed, bleary-eyed, blotto; plastered, primed, polluted, paralyzed; stewed, soused, squiffy, and stinko. He never seemed to use the same word twice—and we saw a lot of drunks!

When it was time for me to turn out the office lights and go to sleep, Mick always came into the back and sang an Irish ballad to put me to sleep. Some of the tunes were the same as Mam O'Duggan's ballads, but the words were very different. When I asked Mother what they meant, she said never mind if I couldn't understand them, it was for the best.

One night when Mick got a little corked himself, he sat down on the sofa beside me. "Do you know the reason I love to sing to you, lass?" he said with a tear in his eye. "It's because I have a wee daughter of my own somewhere, just like you. When I'm singing to you, I'm singing to her."

"Do you ever visit your daughter?" I asked.

"She doesn't know I'm her daddy, you see."

I thought about my own father who I'd never seen and gave Mick a big hug. "I'll bet she thinks about you all the time, Mick," I said softly. "I'll bet your little girl misses you too." He kissed my forehead, then went back out to tend bar without another word.

Every other Thursday night O'Brien would hold a "fire drill," and we'd all have to practice what to do if the Feds raided the joint. Mother watched for them out front in the restaurant, and if she saw them coming she was supposed to play "Alexander's Ragtime Band." That was the signal for everyone in the speakeasy to spring into action. Mick would dump all the glasses of hooch down the drain and stash any open bottles under my bed. Black Jack would give all the rummies the bum's rush out the back door, and O'Brien would scurry along with them because he was on parole and wasn't supposed to hang around where there was any juice. My job was to try not to giggle when I was pretending to be asleep, and to go into crying hysterics if the Feds came near my bed where the hooch was hidden. It was all great fun.

I loved Mick and Black Jack and O'Brien, but even so, I would sometimes peer through the windows at the other families in our neighborhood and long for a real family. I gradually realized that not only didn't I have a father, but my mother wasn't like the other mothers either.

For one thing, she slept all day while I was in school instead of washing and cooking and tending babies like the other mothers. I knew she worked until very late at night at the club, but I was still ashamed of the fact that she didn't hang our laundry on the line until late in the afternoon.

She never dressed like all the other mothers either, in housedresses and aprons. Mother sewed her own clothes from things people gave her. Once she made a chemise from a parlor curtain, trimmed with lace from a tablecloth, fringe from a lampshade, and sequins from a worn-out purse. It looked like something out of a fashion magazine. When she came to my first open house at school, she arrived in a turban and long beads and one of the flapper dresses she wore to the nightclub. Her clothing embarrassed me at first, but within minutes Mother made everyone laugh out loud with her crazy stories, even the sour old principal, Mr. Dorsey. The open house became so much fun once Mother arrived that no one seemed to notice that her dress looked like something you'd wear to a dance hall.

We were different in other ways too. One Sunday morning I watched the steady stream of mothers and children coming and going to mass at St. Michael's church around the corner, and I wished we could go with them. Mother and I had our own Sunday morning ritual of reading the funny papers together and cutting out paper dolls from old catalogues, but I still remembered how beautiful the services had been when I'd gone to church with Mam.

"Can't we go to St. Michael's too?" I asked my mother.

"No, dear, we don't belong there."

"Why not?"

"We're not Catholic."

"But I went to Mam's church when you were sick."

"I know, but that was because Mrs. O'Duggan is Catholic. Now, which shall we read first, 'Little Orphan Annie' or 'Tom Mix'?" She waved the comics section to tempt me, but I couldn't concentrate on the funny papers. I had another urgent question that needed to be answered.

"Mama, was I ever baptized?"

"Who wants to know, dear?"

"Bridget Murphy and Mary Katherine Bailey said I'm in a state of mortal sin and I'll surely go to hell if I die because I wasn't baptized in the Catholic church."

"Let them believe what they want," she said with a wave of her hand, "we'll believe what we want."

"But is it true? Will I really go to hell?"

"Don't be silly. Hell is for Catholics. We're not Catholic."

"What are we, then?"

"We're Protestant."

"Then why don't we ever go to a Protestant church?"

"Because we don't belong there."

That's the way Mother always was—cheerfully evasive. I would wear out long before she did and stop asking questions. Why bother when I couldn't get any answers?

My questions changed once I started school. That's when the other girls began hounding me for information about my father. I grew to hate the sound of the dismissal bell at 3:15, knowing they would quickly surround me in the cloakroom and the interrogation would begin.

"Where's your daddy, Grace? How come he doesn't live with you?"

Our teacher praised the girls for walking home with shy little Gracie every afternoon, but I dreaded the ordeal.

"The O'Malleys are the only other family in the entire school who don't have a father," Mary Katherine Bailey informed me, "but their daddy died in a mining accident."

"Is your daddy dead?" Bridget Murphy asked.

It would have been easier to lie and tell everyone that he was than to try to explain something I didn't understand myself. "I don't know anything about my daddy," I said tearfully.

"Liar! Liar! Pants-on-fire! You'll go to hell for lying, Gracie."

The other kids invited huge mobs of aunts and uncles and grandmas to the Christmas program at school that year, along with their mothers and fathers. My mother invited O'Brien and Black Jack and Mick. They were easy to spot in the audience, wearing their white dinner jackets and black bow ties and cummerbunds. Black Jack grinned and clapped his enormous hands so long that Mick had to nudge him to stop. O'Brien put two fingers in his mouth and whistled through his teeth. Mick was so proud of everything I did that he got all teary-eyed, even though I didn't have a speaking part.

"Which one is your daddy?" Bridget Murphy whispered as we pretended to be angels singing to baby Jesus.

"None of them."

"Who are they, then? Why are they sitting with your mother?"

"They're our friends from work."

"Why doesn't your daddy ever come?"

I asked my mother the same question when we got home that night. "Because he doesn't," she said.

"Why not?"

"He doesn't need a reason."

"But where is my daddy?"

"He lives far away from here."

"Why doesn't he ever come to see me?"

"Because he lives far away."

By the time I was eight years old, the harassment had evolved to a different form. Now the other girls talked endlessly about their own fathers, bragging about their strength or their good looks, telling stories about the things they did with their daddies. Their stories created a longing in me that was so fathomless that I began to invent stories in my head of what my father was like and what we did together.

My imaginary father was as tall and strong as Black Jack—much taller and stronger than their fathers. He was smarter and richer too—as smart as O'Brien and even richer than Booty because he owned a store, too, and let me eat all the candy I wanted. My father sang to me every night in a rich tenor voice that brought tears to everyone's eyes, like Mick's singing always did. And my daddy was the most handsome daddy in the world, blond and blue-eyed like Father O'Duggan, and as patient and kind as he was too. I whispered secrets to my imaginary daddy in the darkness of O'Brien's office every night, then cried myself to sleep to the muffled sounds of drunken laughter and my mother's piano music.

The highlight of my school week was Wednesday. That was the day that

Father O'Duggan met the other girls and me in front of St. Michael's rectory and paid us a nickel for each of the books we'd read that week. I loved to read, and I loved to make him laugh with delight as I described all the stories I'd read. Five cents seemed like a lot of money, but his gentle words of praise were worth more to me than the nickel.

One Wednesday, when Father O'Duggan was more than ten minutes late, the girls began to tease me so mercilessly about my missing father that I finally ran away from them in tears, unable to endure their heckling any longer. My tears fell so fast I could barely see, and as I rounded the corner onto King Street, Father O'Duggan hurtled into me, nearly bowling me over.

"Whoa! My fault, I'm sorry!" He gripped my shoulders to keep me from stumbling backward. "Are you all right, Gracie?"

I nodded, keeping my head lowered and my face turned away so he wouldn't see my tears, but he crouched in front of me and brushed my cheek with his thumb.

"You're crying, Gracie! I've hurt you, haven't I, lumbering into you like a great oaf?"

"You didn't hurt me," I said.

"Well, won't you tell me why you're crying, then?"

I shook my head. "It's wrong to tattle."

Half a block away, we heard the squealing laughter of the other girls, skipping rope while they waited in front of the rectory. As another tear rolled down my cheek, Father O'Duggan tilted his head in their direction. "Those girls are jealous of you, you know. You put them to shame each week, earning twice as much money as they do—and you being so much younger than they are." He stood and dug into his pocket for change. "So how much will I be owing you this week?"

"They're not jealous of me," I said softly. "They're making fun of me."

"Making fun? Why? Because you love to read?"

I looked down at the scuffed toes of my shoes. The tip of one sock peeked through the torn stitching. "No . . . because . . . I don't have a daddy."

All the air rushed from Father O'Duggan's chest as if he were blowing out a bunch of candles. "I see," he murmured. "Do they tease you like this very often?"

"Sometimes." When I realized that I had just ratted on the others I was horrified. "I didn't mean to tattle, Father O'Duggan, honest I didn't. You won't tell them what I said, will you?"

"You didn't tattle, Gracie, I made you tell. Besides, they're wrong to make fun of you, especially for something that isn't your fault. And it isn't your fault about your father, don't you see? You shouldn't let their words hurt you." But they did hurt me, and he must have read the truth in my eyes, because he suddenly took my hand. "Come with me," he said. We walked back to where the others were playing.

Maureen O'Flannery jumped breathlessly as the rope sailed over her head, then skimmed the sidewalk beneath her feet. Her sister and Mary Katherine Bailey each turned one end of the rope for her. The three Sullivan girls stood beside Bridget Murphy, chanting the sing-song rhyme to the beat of the rope slapping the pavement.

"First comes love, then comes marriage, then comes Maureen with a baby carriage . . ."

"Stop!" Father O'Duggan shouted. Maureen froze in place, her knees bent slightly as if still poised to jump. The rope whirled over her head and slapped against her ankles, stopping as seven pairs of eyes met the priest's gaze.

"I just bumped into Gracie, here," he said, his hand still clutching mine. "She was crying, and she didn't want to tell me why. Might any of you girls be able to tell me?" All seven of them quickly looked away, staring at the ground or glancing uneasily at one another.

"If you've said or done something to upset her, then I expect you'll be needing to tell me all about it in confession, won't you? Suppose I save you the trouble and hear your confessions right now." He turned to the nearest girl who was gazing steadily at her feet as if she expected to sprout an extra toe. Unlike my shoes, hers were shiny and new. "Mary Katherine? Do you have something to tell me?"

"We were only teasing, Father. We didn't know she would cry."

"What were you teasing her about?"

Silence.

"Won't you tell me then, Maureen?"

"I wasn't the only one, Father. We all . . ."

"I know. Just tell me what you said to her." He waited patiently while they squirmed with guilt. Maureen was the first one to crack under the pressure.

"We thought . . . we thought if we teased her a little . . . about her daddy . . . we could make her tell us who he is."

"What do you mean?" he said sternly.

"Everyone's wondering . . . you know . . . about what happened to him and why he doesn't live with them anymore."

"My daddy says he's probably a gangster and he's rotting in jail," the oldest Sullivan girl said importantly.

Not to be outdone, Mary Katherine suddenly found her voice. "We heard that he was a drunkard who beat them all the time and so they came here to hide."

Bridget Murphy planted her hands on her hips. "You're both wrong. She doesn't have a daddy. Grandma says Grace is a *bastard*." When the other girls gasped in shock, Bridget clapped her hand over her mouth. They stared fearfully at Father O'Duggan's horrified face, waiting for him to deliver the wrath of God on poor Bridget's head for using such a scandalous word. It took him a long time to find his voice.

"I don't ever want you repeating such slander again, Bridget Murphy, do you hear me? Grace's mother was legally married before God as surely as your own mothers were!" He glared at them, squeezing my hand so hard it ached. "And why are you tormenting poor Grace about it? It isn't her fault, you know. Don't you think she would love to have a home with a father like all the rest of you?"

"Do *you* know where her daddy is?" Barbara O'Flannery asked shyly.

Father O'Duggan gazed up at the rectory for a moment, until the glare of the afternoon sun on the windows made him squint his eyes. "It happens that I do, Barbara."

"Where?" they all shouted at once.

"Is he dead, Father O'Duggan?"

"I'll bet he really is a gangster, right?"

"He's neither one. Mr. Bauer's whereabouts are none of your business, and you can tell that to your parents the next time their tongues start wagging about him around the dinner table. Tell them that Father O'Duggan said spreading gossip and rumors is a terrible sin. Would you like me to be sharing everything you tell me in the confessional with the very next person who comes along after you?"

"No, Father."

"All right, then. Leave poor Gracie alone from now on. Try to show her a bit of Christian compassion. The Scriptures say, 'Be ye kind one to another, tenderhearted, forgiving one another, even as God for Christ's sake hath forgiven you.' From now on I want you to remember that. And don't you be teasing Gracie anymore." The girls had grown very still.

"Yes, Father."

"We're sorry, Father O'Duggan."

I had never loved any of my fathers as much as I loved Father O'Duggan at that moment. He had defended me against my tormentors, just as my imaginary daddy did in all my fantasies. He dropped my hand as abruptly as he had taken it and strode up the steps of St. Michael's church. Just as swiftly, all the girls vanished. I stood alone on the sidewalk for a moment, then followed Father O'Duggan into the empty church.

I had never been inside St. Michael's before. It was cold and hushed, the afternoon sunlight barely able to penetrate the shadowy stillness as it slanted through the windows in a rainbow of color. Father O'Duggan didn't hear me come in. He paused to make the sign of the cross, then slowly walked down the aisle, his shoes echoing hollowly on the stone floor. When he reached the front, he ducked into one of the pews and sank to his knees on the rail. He slumped forward and rested his forehead on the pew in front of him.

On the crucifix above the altar, Jesus hung in silent torment, the muscles of His arms stretched taut, His bare feet pinned to the rough wood with a spike. The same look of patient suffering that I'd seen at Mam's church was etched on his face.

I tiptoed down the aisle so silently that I startled Father O'Duggan when I touched his arm and spoke his name. "Father O'Duggan. . . ?"

"Wha—? Gracie!"

"Father O'Duggan, I want to find my daddy. You said he wasn't dead. You said you knew where he was."

"Oh, child . . ." He closed his eyes.

"I know you can't tell the others because it's none of their business, but won't you tell me? Please?"

"Gracie, I . . . I can't," he whispered.

I was so angry and hurt that I whirled around to run out of there, but he grabbed me by my arm and pulled me back. "Grace, listen to me," he said. "The reason I can't tell you is because it's none of my business any more than it is those girls' business—"

"Could you tell me if I was Catholic, like you?"

"What. . . ? No . . . no, that doesn't matter. Listen, you and I are good friends, but it's your mother's job to answer all your questions about your father. It's not my place."

"She won't tell me either. She never answers my questions."

"Then I have to respect that, don't you see? When she wants you to know, she'll tell you."

"But I want a daddy now!" I couldn't stop the tears that washed down my face. "I don't care if he is a gangster or a drunkard, I just want to run to meet him after work like all the other girls do and hug him and sit on his lap, and—"

He pulled me into his arms, holding me so tightly against his chest that he cut off my words. "Don't, Gracie . . . don't. He isn't worth all these tears. Your mother loves you more than twenty fathers ever could. You're better off without him, child."

I clung to him, weeping, until I'd made a dark, wet patch on the front of his shirt with my tears. Finally he set me on the floor in front of him again and took both my hands in his. He was about to speak when I said, "Will you be my daddy, Father O'Duggan?"

"Oh, Grace . . ."

My longing came out in a rush of words. "It can be a secret, and no one else will ever have to know. I'll call you Father O'Duggan like the other girls do when we're with them, but when we're all alone, won't you please let me sit on your lap and pretend you're my daddy?"

I gazed at him hopefully, waiting for him to take me in his arms again and let me call him Daddy for the first time. Instead he dropped my hands.

"I can't let you do that, Grace. I'm so sorry. . . ." His eyes shone with tears, and I saw the muscles of his face working as he tried to hold them back.

"But it could be a secret and . . ."

"It wouldn't be right. I made a vow to God that I would never have a wife or children. That I would serve Him and be a father to all the people He places under my care, not just one. I can't break my promise, Grace."

"Not even one time?" I pleaded. "Can't I call you Daddy, just this once?"

"No," he whispered. He lost the battle with his tears, and they slowly rolled down his face. "No, I'm sorry."

I turned to run up the aisle again, and this time he didn't stop me. When I reached the door I looked back. The sanctuary was still, the sounds from the street outside muffled by its thick stone walls and dark, polished wood. Father O'Duggan knelt at the rail with his face in his hands.

TWENTY-ONE

Father O'Duggan had refused to let me call him Daddy, but he became even more of a father to me after that day. He always walked his daily visitation rounds on foot, and they ended right outside my school, just as classes were dismissed. I met him there nearly every day, and he escorted me through the gauntlet of girls, eliminating their taunts and nosy questions. The Catholic girls were in awe of him, just like the rowdy drunks were in awe of Black Jack. I think it was because Father O'Duggan knew all their sins and could assign their penances. I was in awe of him too, but in a different way—mine was more an amazed sense of wonder that a man as important as Father O'Duggan would take time to be with me. He was my best friend.

He had a slight limp, and I could always see him approaching by the way he walked. I loved the softness of his uneven gait and the vulnerability it revealed in a man who was otherwise so solid and strong and commanding. We talked all the way home from school.

"Did you have a good day?" he asked as we walked to my apartment building around the corner from the rectory. "How was your geography test?"

"Easy. Thank you for loaning me your globe. It helped me study."

He kept close track of the subjects I took and the grades I received, encouraging me when a subject seemed difficult, praising me when I did well. Best of all, he nurtured in me a great love for books.

"What did you think of *Treasure Island*, Gracie?"

"Oh, Father O'Duggan, it was so exciting! I had to stay up late reading it so I could find out what happened!"

"I knew you'd like it. It's one of my favorites too. Remind me to find *Robinson Crusoe* for you next."

I spent most of the book money he paid me on the movies, my second great love. I laughed with the Marx Brothers in *Duck Soup*, gave myself nightmares with Boris Karloff in *The Mummy*, envied Jean Harlow in *Dinner at Eight*, and fell in love with Clark Gable in *It Happened One Night*.

"I hope you won't squander all your time at the movies," he warned. "Books are still a better way to travel and see the world because they make you use your imagination."

"But movies are educational too," I said. "The theaters show newsreels about world events before the feature presentation." He laid his hand on my head like a blessing and laughed his warm, rolling laugh.

"Aye, so they do . . . so they do." He dug into his pocket and pulled out a handful of change. "Do me a favor, Gracie, and buy me some jujubes next time you go, okay?" He patted his middle, then added, "I'm only allowed to have two or three, though, so you go ahead and eat the rest while you're watching the show."

———

When Prohibition ended in 1933, all the fun went out of my nights down at O'Brien's speakeasy. We no longer needed to have "fire drills" now that the bar was legal—though I still got an adrenaline rush whenever Mother played "Alexander's Ragtime Band." The Regency Room closed for a week for renovations, and when we returned I hardly recognized the place. The owner of the hotel had knocked out the back wall of the restaurant, making one huge room, and he installed a dance floor where the speakeasy had been. Mick's bar got a new coat of shellac and brand-new barstools.

"I'll be serving real hootch from now on," Mick told me proudly. "No more rot-gut."

He and Mother adapted well to the changes. She put together a dance band with trumpets and saxophones and trombones and drums, and she even started singing while she played the piano. But O'Brien grew more and more restless and unhappy. He snapped at all the waiters, and his freckled face seemed to take on a permanent frown.

The storm cloud I had seen brewing came to a head one night when Mother and I arrived for work and found O'Brien in his office, cleaning out his desk. "What are you doing?" Mother asked.

"What does it look like I'm doing?" He pulled out the bottle of bootleg gin he kept in his bottom drawer and set it in front of Mother. "Here. A little present to remember me by."

Mother was supposed to be tuning up the band, but she sank down on the tattered sofa as if she'd already played three sets without a break. "You've got to give yourself more time, O'Brien. You can't expect to adjust to earning a respectable living overnight."

"I gotta make more money than this, Emma. Me and Black Jack gotta live in style."

"But . . . but this is the same job you always had, isn't it? Running this place?"

O'Brien scooped up a pile of papers from his desk and shoved them into a cardboard box. "The money was in the booze, Emma, not in managing the club."

Mother sprang to her feet, her hands on her hips. "Is it the money you're addicted to, O'Brien, or the danger? The excitement of breaking the law? Outscoring the cops?"

He looked down at his desk top, clean for the first time that I ever recalled. "Maybe you've got something there. . . ." he mumbled. "But I still can't help it. This isn't the life for me and Black Jack—"

"Go ahead then, open your stupid gambling den!" Mother shouted. She pulled me close as if to protect me from him. "But don't come around me or Gracie anymore if you do! I don't want anything to do with criminals!" She was crying hard—and Mother seldom wept.

"Aw, now, Emma . . . don't cut us off from Gracie. You know how much we love that kid. Black Jack will die of a broken heart."

"Do you love her enough to go straight?"

The answer must have been no because Black Jack and O'Brien kissed me good-bye that night as if their hearts would break, then they both disappeared from my life. Not only had my real father abandoned me, but now these two fathers had left me as well. The loss overwhelmed me.

I poured out my sorrow to Father O'Duggan. When I was little, Mother had soothed away my tears with Great-grandma's crying cup. Now he was my crying cup, able to comfort me in my grief.

"I'm sure they never wanted to hurt you, Gracie," he said as we talked on the crumbling cement steps of my apartment building. "But grown-ups are complex creatures, and the choices they make are seldom black-and-white. Just because they are forced to choose between two things doesn't mean they love one less and the other more."

"But I miss them so much!"

"Aye, poor lass. It's like a death, isn't it? The sad truth is that people are sure to come and go from our life as we grow older—some die, some move away, and some leave us because they change so much that we hardly know them anymore." He handed me his handkerchief to dry my eyes. "You won't always feel this sad, Gracie. The Bible says, 'Weeping may endure for a night, but joy cometh in the morning.' "

"Mother says, 'Joy and sorrow come and go like the ebb and flow.' "

"Aye, she's right, you know."

"Are you going to move away too, Father O'Duggan?"

"No . . ." he said softly. "No, I think the good Lord wants me here in St. Michael's parish for a while longer."

About a year later, Mick got homesick for Ireland and decided to return. "Please don't go!" I begged when he told Mother and me the news. "Who will sing lullabies to me, Mick? And you promised to teach me the meaning of life someday—remember?"

"Aw, Gracie . . . don't make me feel any worse than I already do." His mournful face was filled with sorrow as he hugged me hard. "You'll meet a handsome laddie someday who'll sing sweeter songs to your heart than I ever could. And as for the meaning of life . . . well, that's something we all have to figure out for ourselves."

"I'll never forget you, Mick."

Mother cried even harder than she had when O'Brien and Black Jack left. Mick surprised me when he took her into his arms. O'Brien had hugged her often, but I'd never seen Mick hold her before.

"Come with me to Ireland, Emma . . . you and Gracie both. We'll start all over again."

"You know we don't belong there, Mick. We'd never be happy away from our home."

"Aye. That's why I can never be happy in America, you see. It's not my home."

Mother and I went to the train station to see him off to New York, hoping he'd change his mind. He didn't. We never heard from him again. Not even a postcard.

Now I had only two fathers, Booty and Father O'Duggan. Booty kept us supplied with food during those hard depression years when Mother and I had so little. He always had a smile and a pat on the head for me—provided Mrs. Booty wasn't around. I couldn't understand how he could be so loving at times and so distant at others. I also couldn't understand why his wife didn't like me. As far as I could recall, I had never done anything to cause it.

" 'Tisn't just you, lass . . . 'tis all children," he explained one afternoon.

"Is that why you and Mrs. Higgins never had any children of your own?"

I asked. But Booty was busy lighting another one of the cigarettes he chain-smoked and didn't answer.

I loved going into the store to visit with Booty and looked for an excuse to go every day after school. If I came in with a little money to buy groceries, he would swear that those exact items just happened to be on sale that day. But there were no special sales when Mrs. Booty sat at the register. I loved the creak and slap of the rusty screen door; the cozy, crowded aisles jumbled with dusty cans; the dark, smoky haze that hung over the entire store. I often stole a peek into the mysterious apartment behind the curtain where the Higginses lived, but I never once went inside.

"Say, lass . . . how would you like to earn two bits?" Booty asked me one day when I was twelve years old. "I could use some extra help today."

"Sure! I'd love to! What do you need me to do?" He gave me an ancient feather duster and put me to work cleaning the shelves. In truth, I probably stirred up more dust than I eliminated.

After that I worked in the store nearly every day, stocking shelves for him or making a small delivery if it was close by. In return, he would give me a couple of potatoes or a stick of oleo, saying, "I've got to get rid of this anyway, before it goes bad," and he would make it seem as though I were doing him a big favor.

The day I turned thirteen, I went to the store after school to take Booty a piece of my birthday cake. Mrs. Higgins stood behind the register. I looked all around but there was no sign of Booty. I returned every day that week until the cake was too stale to eat, but he still hadn't returned.

"What? You again?" Mrs. Higgins said when she saw me on the fifth straight day. "What do you want, coming in here all the time?"

"Where is Mr. Higgins?" I asked.

"He's . . . he's sick." Her voice sounded different. When I looked at her closely, I saw that she didn't look angry, she looked worried.

"Tell him I hope he's better soon," I said. To my utter amazement, Mrs. Higgins covered her face and wept. Mrs. Murphy, who had been examining eggs one by one, set her shopping basket down and hurried over to console her. I quietly left, careful not to bang the screen door on the way out. Mrs. Higgins hated that most of all.

The following day, Father O'Duggan wasn't there to meet me after school. I ran all the way home in a panic. As soon as I walked through our door, I knew by Mother's face that something was wrong. She wasn't smiling. Her eyes were red from weeping.

"Gracie, honey . . . something terrible happened. Booty . . . Booty's gone."

"Gone? Gone where? Did he go away like O'Brien and—?"

"No, sweetheart. Booty died this morning."

"No! I don't believe you! It's not true!"

Mother held me close, pouring out the story in a rush of words. "He accidentally stabbed himself on a huge nail from a packing crate, and he didn't see a doctor or even tell anyone he was hurt until he had a high fever and greenish-white streaks down his side. By then it was too late. He died of blood poisoning."

I twisted out of her arms and ran into our bedroom, flinging myself onto my bed. My grief was inconsolable.

Mother took me to Booty's funeral at St. Michael's. It was the first time that I'd ever seen Mother step inside a church. Everyone in the neighborhood came because everyone loved Booty. Father O'Duggan conducted the funeral, wearing a long black robe and one of the vestments Mam had made him. He wept along with all of us.

I had lost all of my "fathers" but one, and I was terrified that Father O'Duggan would leave me too. Then I remembered that I had a real father somewhere. I began to hound my mother for information about him, and when she gave me her usual, maddeningly evasive answers, I decided to go to Bremenville and find him myself. I got the idea from the movie *Dick Tracy Returns*. He solved mysteries and tracked down missing people all the time.

I didn't tell anyone about my plans, not even Father O'Duggan. For the next few weeks I read twice as many books as usual and skipped the Saturday matinees until I had saved enough for a bus ticket. But of course I never made it out of the bus station. Mother hauled me home again and told me the painful truth—my real father didn't want me. He had tried to kill me before I was born. She had run away from him to protect me. Piled on top of all my other losses, the truth devastated me.

That night, after Mother left for the nightclub, Father O'Duggan showed up at our apartment door.

"Hello, Gracie. May I come in?"

"I guess so." I didn't really want him to. I was a mess, my eyes red and swollen from crying. He left the door open and sat down at the kitchen table across from me.

"Your mother asked me to come over and talk to you," he said. "She's very worried about you."

"Did she tell you what happened?"

"Aye, Gracie. She did." I looked up at him for the first time and saw such tender compassion in his blue eyes that I started weeping all over again. He reached across the table for my hand. "It must be very painful for you, knowing what Karl Bauer wanted to do."

"I wasn't even born yet! He didn't even know me! How could he hate me so much?"

"God knows," he said softly, "God only knows . . . But any man who knows you for the lovely young lady you are today would be proud to call you his daughter. I know I would be." He held my hand and let me cry for a while, then handed me his handkerchief.

"Did I ever tell you why I walk with a limp, Gracie?" I looked up at him, puzzled by the change of subject. I shook my head. "Aye . . . well, it was my very own father who crippled me. When I was ten years old, he beat me with a length of iron pipe and broke my leg in three places. It never healed right, and I've limped ever since."

"That's horrible!" I whispered. Then I realized what Father O'Duggan was really telling me—that his father had been as cruel as mine.

"My father was a decent man when he was sober," he continued, "but he couldn't control his drinking. We lived in Ireland, and sometimes Da would stop off for a pint or two after a long shift at the docks. By the time he arrived home, he'd be roaring drunk. He was the meanest man alive when he was drunk, and he'd take out his anger on Mam. My brother and I would try to protect her, and of course he would start beating us."

Father O'Duggan stood, as if the memories he'd stirred made him restless. He paced the floor of our tiny room as he talked, his huge hands stuffed into the pockets of his trousers. "As strange as it sounds, we accepted this as normal for our family. It was just the way Da was. But what I couldn't accept was the fact that he cheated on my mother. Do you understand what I mean by that, Gracie? He was married to my mother, but he went to bed with other women. When I was your age, one woman's husband caught my father with his wife and killed him in a drunken rage. After that, Mam and the six of us left Ireland and came to America to live with our aunt and uncle."

He stopped pacing and leaned against the table, resting his hand on my shoulder. "I've been a priest for fifteen years, Grace. I've been in a good many homes and heard thousands of confessions—and I've seen far too many fathers like mine . . . and like Karl Bauer. You see, gazing through the windows at other families isn't the same as living there day after day and knowing what really goes on behind closed doors. There is a heartache like the one you're feeling right now in a good many homes."

My tears started falling all over again. "I used to dream about what my father was really like," I said. "I used to imagine that he was a hero like Charles Lindbergh and all the other girls would be so jealous when they found out. Now I wish I'd never learned the truth. I wish my real father was dead!"

Father O'Duggan looked stunned, then sorrowful, and I regretted that I had spoken so harshly. "No you don't, Gracie. You must never wish that anyone was dead." He sank down in his chair across from me again. "I'm trying to help you understand that earthly fathers and mothers are human beings—that every last person on this earth is a sinner. Even the most loving parent will disappoint us at times in one way or another. And sometimes the poor example our father sets gets in our way when we try to understand what our heavenly Father is like. One of the tasks God has entrusted to me as a priest is to try to show people who don't have loving fathers what God the Father is like. Again and again I've counseled people whose view of God has been twisted by their experiences. They can't accept that God loves them unconditionally because their own father didn't love them. They don't believe that God will never leave them or forsake them because their own father abandoned them. They don't think God will forgive them because their own father wouldn't forgive them. Or, if they had a father like mine, they fear God and run from Him because they're afraid He's a God of anger and wrath. I understand your longing for a father. I understand why you wanted to find Karl Bauer. But, Grace, he isn't the father you're really looking for."

"He isn't?" I longed to hear that Mother had made up the whole story—that my real father wasn't the monstrous Karl Bauer. "Where is my father, then?"

"Your real Father is God. He's the only Father who will never disappoint you. And from the time He formed you in your mother's womb, He already knew you and loved you more than Karl Bauer or any other man ever could."

Father O'Duggan's words fell on my heart like a welcome rain. I longed to believe that they were true, but I was afraid. "If my real father didn't want me," I said, "how do I know that God will want me?"

He pulled the familiar leather volume he always carried from his breast pocket. "Because God wrote everything He wants us to know about Him in the Bible. And one of the things He wrote was this: 'Can a woman forget her sucking child, that she should not have compassion on the son of her womb?

Yea, they may forget, yet I will not forget thee. Behold, I have graven thee upon the palms of my hands.' "

He laid down the book and held out his broad hands to me. I reached across the table and laid my hands in his. "Remember the statue of Jesus on the cross in front of St. Michael's?" he asked. "God became a man, and He died on that cross to show us His love. The nail prints on the palms of His hands are the imprints of His love for you. Search for *Him*, Gracie, not Karl Bauer. *He's* your real Father."

"Mother says we're not Catholic."

"I know. Don't tell the bishop this," he said with a smile, "but God isn't limited to one church or denomination. He will find you wherever you look for Him. But churches are a good place to start because they're designed to help us meet with God . . . we can set up an appointment with Him every Sunday morning. And a priest or a minister can point you in the right direction as you search."

"How will I know what to do? How do I look for God?"

"Simply sit in His presence and listen . . . and wait. He longs to speak to you, Gracie. Because one thing I know for certain—earthly fathers may reject us and hurt us and disappoint us, but God never will. He'll never leave you or forsake you, Gracie. He already knows you and loves you more than you can possibly imagine. Isn't He the kind of Father you're really looking for?"

———

Mother knew I was still angry with her when I didn't snuggle up to read the comics with her on Sunday morning. Instead, while she lay propped in bed with the newspaper and a mound of pillows, I made my own breakfast, combed my hair, and dressed in the nicest dress I owned.

"Now where are you going?" she asked. "You didn't buy another bus ticket, did you? I thought I already explained that you're not welcome in Bremenville."

"I'm not going to Bremenville. I'm going to church."

"I've told you a hundred times, dear, we're not Catholic." She unfolded the fashion section and tried to pretend that she didn't care, but I could tell by the sharp edge to her voice that she did.

"You said we're Protestant, so I'm going to Peace Memorial Church over on Fountain Avenue."

"You're not a member there, dear. They won't—"

"They'll let me come. Father O'Duggan said so."

She gave a short laugh. "What would a Catholic priest know about Protestant churches, for pete's sake!"

"He said I should tell them that my grandfather is a priest in the same kind of church."

Mother dropped the paper and sank back against the pillows as if she were suddenly very tired. "Not a priest, Gracie . . . they're called ministers."

"That's what Father O'Duggan said, but I forgot the word. He said they're the same thing, except ministers can get married and have children."

"I'm surprised Father O'Duggan didn't try to talk you into going to his church." I detected a note of bitterness in her voice.

"I wanted to go to St. Michael's, but he said you wouldn't approve."

"He's right about that." She picked up the paper again and snapped it open, pretending to read. I walked over to her bed and waited until she looked up at me.

"So is it true, Mother? Did your daddy work in a church like Father O'Duggan does?"

"Oh, it's true all right."

"Why didn't you ever tell me about him?"

"About Papa?" Mother lowered the paper and gazed at me for a long moment, but she had such a faraway look in her eyes that it seemed as though she were looking straight through me. Her eyes glistened with tears. "Church services usually start at eleven," she said softly. "You'd better hurry or you'll be late. Protestant ministers don't like people to be late."

I walked to Peace Memorial Church that Sunday with a longing too deep for words. As soon as I stepped into the vaulted sanctuary, I felt the same tense excitement I'd felt as I'd waited in the bus station to go to meet Karl Bauer. *My Father.* I was about to meet my Father.

The Protestant church was less ornamented than St. Michael's or Mam's church had been, but it was beautiful, just the same. There were no statues, no alcoves with candles to light, and no figure of Jesus on a crucifix—only an empty wooden cross hanging above the altar. I slipped in quietly, while the usher escorted someone else down the aisle, and took a seat in the rear by myself. Stained-glass windows dappled light over me like a sprinkling of jewels.

At first the service seemed alien and confusing to me. The minister talked and read from a book, then everyone sang a song I didn't know. Disappointed, I almost walked out. But when everyone bowed their heads to pray, saying the words in unison, I began to cry.

"Our Father . . . Who art in heaven . . ."

They were talking to God. He was my Father too. I could bow my head and talk to Him just as easily as I talked to O'Brien or Booty or Father O'Duggan.

We sang another hymn, and this time I turned to it in the book and found the words along with everyone else. The room seemed to spin when I realized they had been written just for me:

> *My Father is rich in houses and lands,*
> *He holdeth the wealth of the world in His hands!*
> *Of rubies and diamonds, of silver and gold,*
> *His coffers are full, He has riches untold.*
> *I'm a child of the King, a child of the King!*
> *With Jesus, my Savior, I'm a child of the King.*

I allowed the words to sink deep into my heart. Here, at last, was the Father I had longed for all my life. He was rich—in wealth and wisdom and love. I was His child. He loved *me*.

I don't recall everything else that happened that first Sunday. I'm sure there must have been Scripture readings, a sermon, more prayers. All too soon we were asked to stand for the closing hymn. The tune reminded me of the Irish ballads Mick used to sing to put me to sleep. But oh, the words! Once again, the lyrics echoed the longing of my heart:

> *Be Thou my wisdom, and Thou my true Word*
> *I ever with Thee and Thou with me, Lord.*
> *Thou my great Father, I Thy true son,*
> *Thou in me dwelling, and I with Thee, one.*

It was my prayer, my heart's cry. As I sang, I felt the Lord's presence for the first time in my life. His Spirit washed over me, surrounded me, lifted me. He shone His love in the deepest part of my heart where I'd carefully hidden all of my fears and hurts, and He healed them. I wept with pure joy. I'd found my Father.

As I walked out of the church in a daze, the minister stood at the door, shaking hands. He was tall and thin, with wire-rimmed glasses and silvery hair swept back from his lined face. He looked very kind, smiling at everyone as he greeted them. I thought of the grandfather I'd never met. He was also a minister, like this man.

"Good morning," he said as he gripped my hand in his. "You're not Grace Bauer by any chance, are you?"

I was stunned. "Yes, I am. How did you know?"

"We have a mutual friend—Father Tom O'Duggan. He mentioned that you might be paying us a visit sometime. Welcome to the house of God."

"Thank you."

"Why don't you come an hour earlier next week, and you can join our young people's Sunday school class? We're studying the life of Jesus this year."

"The man on the cross?"

"That's right. God's Son."

"I'll be back," I told him. And I was, though the week seemed ten years long.

———

That Sunday I took the first step in my lifelong journey to get to know my Father. I no longer cared about finding Karl Bauer. Eventually I professed my faith in Christ, was baptized, and became a member of Peace Memorial Church. The pastor, Reverend Hudson, gave me my first Bible.

The pastor led the young people's class himself, held in the musty basement of the church. I loved Sunday school, even though the room smelled of stale coffee and fried chicken from all the church suppers. Our class was next to the furnace room, and every time it kicked on, the pastor had to shout to be heard above the ominous rumbling. It gave his lessons an added touch of drama if we happened to be studying the battle of Jericho or the fall of Jerusalem.

A few weeks after I started attending, I made friends with a girl my age named Frances Weaver. "You go to my school, don't you?" I asked.

"Yes! I didn't know you were Protestant too," she said. Nearly all of the other girls in our school were Catholic. "I thought you were a Papist because you always walk home with that priest."

"Father O'Duggan? He's an old friend. He knows Pastor Hudson too."

"I'll walk home with you from now on . . . if you want me to."

Frances and I became best friends, even though we didn't have much in common. I loved school and worked hard to get good grades. Frances loved movie stars and spent more time reading about their private lives than doing her homework. She was the youngest in her family, with two older sisters and an older brother, and Frances's parents spoiled her. She ate all the sweets she wanted, any time she wanted, and was as plump as a cream puff.

"Want to come to my house after school?" she asked one day. I had never been invited to another girl's house before. "We can do homework together," she said. "You can stay for supper."

For the first time in my life I saw what it was like to live in a real home with a father and a mother, sisters and brothers. The truth shocked me.

"You'll never believe what it's like!" I told Mother when I got home. "Frances and her sisters fight with each other day and night. Her parents yell and scream for them to stop, and threaten all sorts of punishments if they don't, but they keep fighting anyway."

I was suddenly grateful to be an only child, grateful for a mother who made me laugh, even if we were so poor that we ate soup all the time, and bought our clothes at church rummage sales. But I'd never noticed how dreary and run-down our apartment looked until I saw Frances's apartment. The Weavers had three bedrooms and a rug on their living room floor instead of linoleum. They even had a bathroom all to themselves. In spite of all the bickering, life at the Weavers' house fascinated me. I spent a great deal of time there.

One day when I met Frances after school she was fairly dancing with excitement. "What's the matter with you?" I asked, laughing. "Do you need a privy or something?"

"No! Guess what? My two older sisters are going to be away next weekend, and my mother said I could invite you and Dotty and Marian to a pajama party!"

I had heard of pajama parties, but I'd never been invited to one. Now it was my turn to dance with excitement. But as we walked home from school the day before the big event, Frances and the other two girls came up with a new idea. "Wouldn't it be fun," they decided in a fit of giggles, "if we all wore our fathers' pajamas to the party?"

"Oh yes, let's! That's what all the older girls are doing at their pajama parties!"

They must have forgotten that I didn't have a father because they waved good-bye to me at the corner of King Street and went on their way assuming it was all arranged. I had wanted to go to the party so badly, but now all my fun was ruined. I couldn't be the only one who didn't wear her father's pajamas. I sat down on the front stoop of our apartment house and cried. I didn't want to go upstairs because I didn't want my mother to know. She became as crazed as a mama bear if anyone hurt her cub, and I knew she would read the riot act to all three girls *and* their mothers if she heard about it.

I had just decided that the only solution was to pretend I was sick and avoid the party altogether when Father O'Duggan suddenly rounded the corner and came limping up King Street.

"Good afternoon to you, Gracie," he called.

I threw him a halfhearted wave, shielding my reddened eyes. He halted midstride, turned, and came up our short front sidewalk to sit on the stoop beside me. Neither of us spoke for at least two or three minutes. Then he said, "Will you tell me what's troubling you?"

I heaved a heartbroken sigh. "I know that God is my *real* Father, but He doesn't wear pajamas!"

"Excuse me?" His voice sounded strangled. I glanced sideways and saw him fighting a gallant battle not to laugh. He frowned in an effort to look deeply concerned and pressed his fist to his lips to hold back a grin. When I realized how ridiculous my statement must have sounded I started to giggle. Father O'Duggan exploded into laughter like a cork let out of a champagne bottle.

"I'm sorry . . . I'm sorry," he said at last, wiping his eyes. "I'm sure the situation isn't funny at all. But why would God be needing pajamas, if you don't mind telling me?"

"He doesn't need them, Father O'Duggan—I need them. Frances Weaver invited me to her pajama party, and all the other girls are going to wear their fathers' pajamas."

"Ah, I see the problem." He took a moment to ponder my dilemma, stroking his chin thoughtfully as if my dilemma was as important as all the other issues he'd considered that day. "Could you borrow a pair from someone?" he said eventually.

"I don't know anyone. There's Mr. Harper, the traveling salesman, but Mother would never let me ask him because he's sweet on her. And Mr. O'Malley, who lives on the first floor, is too old! His pajamas would give me the heebie-jeebies."

"Well . . . I was thinking you might borrow a pair of mine." I couldn't believe my ears. I wouldn't have dreamed of asking Father O'Duggan for his pajamas, remembering how he had refused to let me call him Daddy years ago. I looked up to see if he was serious.

"Really?"

His blue eyes sparkled with laughter. "Aye . . . unless they would give you the heebie-jeebies as well."

"Are your pajamas black, like all your clothes?"

He laughed and hugged my shoulder. "Nay, I'm allowed to wear other colors besides black at night. Come along, then, and we'll see if my housekeeper can rustle up a clean pair, shall we?" As we walked to the rectory together it was like old times. I realized how much I had missed talking to him since I'd started walking home with Frances Weaver.

"What should I tell the other girls if they ask whose pajamas they are?"

"Hmm. I suppose it isn't nice to tell them it's none of their business, which it isn't. . . ." He held the door of the rectory open for me. "But since I've been 'Father' O'Duggan to you all these years, I don't think it would be a lie if you told them they were your 'Father's' pajamas—with a capital 'F,' of course. But they won't be knowing about the capital letter, will they now?"

The rectory had a lot of dark, polished wood panelling like the inside of the church. It smelled good, like Mam's soda bread, but I was surprised at how chilly the rooms were. As I followed him through the foyer and down a dark hallway to the kitchen, he called out for Mrs. O'Connor, his housekeeper.

"But what should I say if the other girls start asking me all kinds of questions about my father?" I asked when I caught up with him. He stopped short, as if surprised by the question, and turned to me.

"You don't have to answer their questions, Gracie. The girls are wicked to be so nosy. You won't be in the wrong if you use that excellent imagination of yours to avoid answering them."

"You mean like Mother always does when I ask her questions?"

"Exactly. Make a game of it. You can do it without telling a lie, Gracie, I know you can."

That's precisely what I did. By the time we fell asleep at three A.M., I had won everyone's admiration as the girl with the most mysterious father. And Father O'Duggan's blue-and-white-striped pajamas—so huge on me that I looked lost inside them—had won the prize for the ritziest pj's.

———

"What does your father look like?" Frances asked me a few days after the party. We lay sprawled across her bed, doing our homework together.

"My mother has a picture of him in her photo album," I said. "It's their wedding picture. Come up to my apartment sometime and I'll show you."

"Can't you take it out and bring it over here with you?"

Frances's question stunned me. I stared at her in surprise, watching her stretch her bubble gum out of her mouth with her fingers, then stuff it inside again. "What's wrong, Gracie? Why are you looking at me like that?"

"I just realized something! We've been friends for more than a year, and you've never been inside my apartment—even on Saturday afternoons."

Frances jumped up from the bed to get another candy bar out of her dresser drawer, but not before I saw the guilty look on her face.

"Want some?" she said, breaking a Hershey bar in half.

I shook my head. "Tell me why you've never been to my house. Is it because we live in such a run-down building?"

"No . . . I . . . I can't say." She quickly stuffed half of the candy bar into her mouth.

"Then I guess I'm not really your best friend after all, am I?" I gathered my school books together, preparing to leave.

"No, wait! Don't go, Grace!" she said with a full mouth. I waited, hands on my hips, while she chewed and swallowed. "It's because your mother is divorced."

"I don't understand. What does that have to do with coming to my apartment?" Frances didn't want to say, but I forced her to tell me, with the threat that I'd never speak to her again.

"My father says divorced women usually live in sin," she told me, "and your mother . . . well, you know . . . your mother doesn't go to church . . . she works in a nightclub . . . she dresses like a Bohemian. . . ."

"My mother doesn't live in sin!"

"I know, I know . . . just be glad she doesn't have a boyfriend. My father said if she starts entertaining boyfriends or if you get a stepfather, we can't be friends at all."

I went home feeling saddened and confused. The older I got, the wider the gulf seemed to grow between me and all the other girls. That Saturday night as Mother was dressing to go to the nightclub, I pleaded with her to go to church with me the next day so that at least the question of her sinfulness would be laid to rest. She wouldn't budge. I finally lost patience and blurted out, "People think you're immoral because you're divorced and you don't go to church!"

Mother calmly applied a layer of scarlet lipstick, then blotted her lips. "Gracie, I refuse to live my life to please other people. I married Karl to please my parents and it was the worst mistake I ever made in my life. I don't care what other people think of me and neither should you."

"Do you have a boyfriend?" I asked, remembering what Frances's father had said.

"No, dear . . . do you?"

"I'm too lumpy and awkward. Boys will never like me."

She planted her hands on her slender hips, outraged. "Grace Eva Bauer, you are not! You've become a lovely young woman! I'll be beating the boys off with a carpet beater in another year or two."

I didn't reply, but I knew that if the other parents felt the same way the Weavers did, their sons would never be allowed to date me. I also saw that my mother had deftly changed the subject.

"Are you going to get married again someday?" I asked.

"Certainly not! Once is enough! You don't understand that now, but you will after you've been married for a year or two, I guarantee it!" She tried on a cloche hat, appraising the results in our tiny mirror, then pulled it off and tried on a beret. It looked gorgeous on her. Mother turned and took both of my hands in hers. It was one of those rare times when she wanted to have a serious talk.

"When the time comes, Gracie, choose your husband carefully. Don't make a terrible mistake like I did. I married Karl because I was lonely, and he was nice to me while we were courting. And as I said, I wanted to please my parents. I didn't stop to think about what Karl was really like until it was too late. Set a high standard for yourself, look for qualities that really matter in a husband, and don't say yes until you find a man who has all of them." She pulled me into her arms and hugged me hard.

"Mother, can we buy a radio?"

She laughed out loud as she held me at arm's length again, studying my face. "Goodness, you leap from one topic to the next like a frog on a hot sidewalk. What does getting married have to do with buying a radio?"

There was a connection in my mind. My mother wasn't getting remarried, she didn't have boyfriends, and she wasn't immoral. If the Weavers were going to make accusations without getting to know her, then I didn't want to go to their house anymore. But that meant I would miss all my favorite radio programs.

"I'm tired of walking back and forth to Frances's house to hear *Little Orphan Annie*, especially when the weather's cold. If we had a radio, I could listen at home."

"You're right," she said softly, and the depth of her love for me shone in her eyes. "I think we should get a radio."

Mother brought home a used one from the second-hand shop a few days later. When Hitler invaded Poland that September, we followed all the latest reports as we sat at our kitchen table. The radio brought World War II—and our favorite programs—right into our apartment.

We were listening to it on a Sunday afternoon two years later when the announcer interrupted the program with a special bulletin—the Japanese had attacked Pearl Harbor. As we listened in shock to the reports of all the casualties and destruction, Mother began to cry. I didn't understand why. She was usually so optimistic about life.

"This war will change our lives," she said, wiping her tears. "That's what happened during the last war. It changed everyone's life forever."

The next day I asked Father O'Duggan what he thought she meant. He was walking me home from school again now that my friendship with Frances had cooled. "I imagine your mother is remembering the First World War," he said. "So many things did change after that war." His voice sounded soft and faraway.

"Do you think she's worried about all the rationing?"

"I don't know. Rationing is going to change the way a lot of people live, I suppose."

"But it won't change the way Mother and I live. We don't have a car, and we rarely have money for meat and sugar anyway, so we won't have to sacrifice much."

"No one likes change, Gracie," he said when we reached my apartment. "But you don't have to be afraid of it if you trust in God."

The first big change came when Mother's nightclub band broke up. Everyone but her and two ancient saxophone players had gone off to boot camp. Then the Regency Room closed due to lack of business. Mother got a job in a local factory that had retooled for the war effort. She wore huge brown coveralls to work and joked about being "Rosie the Riveter."

Now that Mother worked the day shift, we were home together in the evenings for the first time since she started working in O'Brien's speakeasy. We ate supper together, followed the events of the war on the radio, then listened to all our favorite programs. Mother loved *Fibber McGee and Molly*. She said that our kitchen cupboard, crammed with mismatched dishes and dented pots, was worse than Fibber's closet.

Mother was forty-two and often exhausted after a long shift at the factory. "Think about your future, Gracie," she told me one night as we sat in our gloomy kitchen. "Get a good education so you don't have to work in a factory all day like I do."

"I don't know what I want to do after high school," I said. "I don't suppose we have any money for a college education."

Mother smiled sadly. "I'm sorry, baby."

Then, just as Mother predicted, the war changed my life. Because of the need for nurses, full scholarships were available if I trained to become a registered nurse.

"It's your salvation, Gracie," Mother said. That was the closest she ever came to mentioning religion.

TWENTY-TWO

I graduated from high school in 1943 and started nursing school in Philadelphia the following fall. I would be away from home for the first time since staying with Mam when I was four years old.

"I promise I won't cry buckets when the time comes to say good-bye," Mother said, but she did anyway. So did I.

I dreaded the idea of traveling to Philadelphia alone on the train, but as it turned out, Father O'Duggan had a meeting there with the bishop that same weekend, so we rode down on the train together. We sat side by side in the crowded coach section, watching the grimy view of warehouses and rail yards give way to city neighborhoods, then suburbs, then open countryside. We talked like the old friends that we were, comfortable with each other.

"I imagine you must be very excited about all the changes that are ahead for you," Father O'Duggan said.

"Yes . . . and a little scared too. I've never been away from home before."

"May I ask you, Gracie . . . do you know much about . . . about dating . . . and about men?"

"I've never had a boyfriend or even been on a date. I think it's because I'm not very pretty."

"Nay, you're a lovely girl. I may be a priest, but I'm also a man, and I can still spot a pretty girl when I see one. May I tell you what I see?" He turned in his seat to face me, his blue eyes warm with candor. "You have the dainty quality of a fine porcelain doll with your fair hair and skin, your tiny delicate bones. You have your mother's beauty, Gracie, and I think you've seen the way she has always attracted men's notice."

"You're very kind, Father O'Duggan, but believe me, the boys don't notice me at all."

"Your looks are not the reason you haven't had any dates. The majority of boys in our neighborhood are Irish-Catholic, you see, and their mams drill it into their thick skulls that they may not date a Protestant girl."

"Much less one whose mother is divorced."

"Aye," he said with a weary sigh. "There is that problem, too, I'm afraid. But you see, the boys in Philadelphia aren't going to know your mother is divorced, and a good many of the soldiers roaming around the city aren't going to care if you're a Protestant or a pagan. They'll simply see a lovely, available young woman, and they'll want to ask you out."

I found that difficult to believe, even though I trusted Father O'Duggan not to lie to me. I must have appeared skeptical because he continued to assure me that it was true.

"I'm worried about you, lass," he said, frowning slightly. "You're not only pretty, you're naïve. There are many unscrupulous men out there who will try to take advantage of you. Unless they've taken a vow of celibacy as I have, most young men have only one thing on their minds . . . and I think you know what that is."

"Yes," I said quickly. We had both begun to blush.

"Gracie, they'll tell you all kinds of things . . . they love you, they have 'needs,' they want to marry you someday, 'it isn't wrong if we love each other' . . . but you mustn't give in to them. A respectable man, an honorable man, will know that God considers any physical relationships outside of marriage a sin. Wait for a man who respects you enough to wait for marriage. You deserve it."

"Mother already warned me to choose my husband carefully. She doesn't want me to make a mistake and marry the wrong man like she did." Since he had raised the subject, I hoped I could pump some information from Father O'Duggan about Karl Bauer. "Do you know what kind of a man her husband was?" I asked.

"I've never met Karl Bauer," he said, looking away.

"Oh. For some reason I thought that you had."

He shook his head. "No, like you, I never have."

By the time we reached the train station in Philadelphia, we both felt travel-weary. Father O'Duggan hired a cab, and since we were going in the same direction, we shared it all the way to the nurses' home across the street from the hospital. He helped the driver carry my belongings up the stairs.

"God be with you Gracie," he said as we hugged good-bye. "You'll be in my prayers—as you always are." I couldn't help crying. I looked at his beloved face and saw that he was still a handsome man in middle age, even if his forehead was a little higher now, his golden hair a little thinner. His blushing attempts to warn me about the wiles of men had touched me, but I didn't know how to thank him properly. I thought I saw tears in his eyes, too, as he hurried away. I climbed the steps to the dormitory alone. It was one of the hardest things I'd ever done.

I was painfully shy, probably because I hadn't had many friends growing up and I didn't know how to act around other girls. But I soon discovered that Father O'Duggan had been right—my roommate Lois didn't know or care that my mother was divorced and never asked nosy questions about my father. We were both away from our parents for the first time, and the less we thought about them the better.

My homemade clothes didn't matter anymore either, since all of us cadet nurses wore uniforms, a crisp, white dress with a gray collar, and thin gray stripes. We were issued dress uniforms to wear in public, too, designating us as nurses-in-training, so we could get into movies and dances for free like members of the armed forces. I got on well with my roommate, a popular, outgoing brunette. She helped me experiment with styling my wild hair and using makeup.

"Your hair is such a gorgeous color!" Lois raved. "Are you sure it doesn't come from a bottle? Most girls would pay a lot of money to be a strawberry blonde like you. And it's naturally curly too . . . you don't need a permanent wave."

A few weeks after school started, I went to my first USO dance. The club was very crowded and pulsing with energy. I had never seen so many men together in one place before, and almost all of them in uniform. I would have run back to the nurses' home in a panic if my roommate hadn't forced me to stay.

Ten minutes after we arrived, a dark-haired sailor strode over to our table and asked me to dance. "Me?" I squeaked in surprise.

"Yeah," he said, pulling me onto the dance floor. "I always go for the prettiest girl in the room first." He danced with me the entire night.

We went out quite a few times before he was shipped overseas. He was the first boy who ever kissed me. I had nothing to compare it with, but I thought the sensation was heavenly. I floated all the way up the stairs to my room.

I thought of Father O'Duggan's words often, and I couldn't escape the feeling that he was sitting in the backseat, watching over me every time I went out on a date. I quickly learned that he had been right—the boys did find me attractive. I had no shortage of dates on Friday and Saturday nights. But every

Sunday I walked to church a few blocks from the hospital to talk to my heavenly Father.

During the week I took classes in biology and chemistry and gradually spent more and more time on the hospital wards, taking care of patients. As a first-year cadet nurse, I didn't do much besides take temperatures and plump pillows, but I knew I had found my calling. I loved nursing. Best of all, I lived an entirely new life—far from the poverty and disgrace of my mother's divorce, far from girls who weren't allowed to befriend me and boys who weren't allowed to date me, far from the endless, nagging questions about my father. Every time I looked at the woman in the mirror I barely recognized her. I was a new Grace Bauer, a cadet nurse with pretty hair and a snappy uniform. I had been reborn.

———

"I've felt sick all day," I told my roommate in January of my second year of nursing school. I had arrived home from classes that afternoon with a sore throat and an upset stomach. I flopped onto my bed, too sick to eat. "Go to supper without me."

"Shall I bring something back for you to eat?" Lois asked.

"No thanks."

By the time she returned from dinner, I was burning with fever and talking nonsense. She ran down the hall yelling for Mrs. McClure, the nursing director.

I was delirious throughout the great flurry of activity that followed, but when my fever finally broke a few days later, I lay all alone in the hospital's communicable diseases ward, recovering from a case of scarlet fever. Since I was allowed no visitors, my recovery seemed long and tedious.

"Can you please have Lois send my Bible over?" I asked one of the nurses. I began with Genesis and read it straight through to Revelation.

Aside from my doctor and the occasional nurse bringing me my daily ration of applesauce or rice pudding, the only people I saw were medical students and interns. They paraded through in their gauze masks to peer cautiously at my sandpapery rash—a classic case, Dr. Reynolds informed them—then hurried out again. Most didn't dare return or hang around too long for fear they would catch scarlet fever too, but one intern showed up every morning for five days straight. I recognized his inquisitive hazel eyes above the mask. He wore his light brown hair in a crew cut, and his sharp widow's peak made his face look heart-shaped.

"Are you planning to specialize in communicable diseases by catching all of them?" I asked when he reappeared on the sixth day. Grateful for the company, I didn't want him to leave. He thought my question hilariously funny.

"I'm going to be a pediatrician," he said when he could stop laughing. "I'll probably see scarlet fever in my practice and I wanted to watch how it progressed."

"In that case, I'm happy to have obliged you," I said. "Are there any other diseases you'd like me to catch?" I couldn't see his mouth, but I could tell by his eyes that he was smiling.

"Not this semester. I'll let you know when my rotation changes. Thanks for the offer, though."

I didn't see him again until the day before I was to be released. He came with the others to observe my peeling skin. "I hear you're graduating from solitary confinement tomorrow," he said. "Congratulations."

"Thanks. But I'm not going very far. Dr. Reynolds wants to take out my tonsils so I don't have a relapse."

He winced. "Get all your talking done now, while you have a chance. Your throat's going to be pretty sore for a couple of days. I know. I had my tonsils out when I was four. My mother said it was the only time in my entire life that I ever stopped talking."

I was eating my first dish of ice cream after my tonsillectomy when the hazel-eyed intern strode into my room. It took me a moment to recognize him without the mask. The lower half of his face was as handsome as his eyes, with a magnificent smile and a deep cleft in his chin.

"I was right about the sore throat, wasn't I?" he said.

I nodded and quickly wiped dripping ice cream off my chin. I shuddered to think how I must look after two weeks in the hospital.

"I thought I'd stop by . . . I might see a few tonsillectomies in my practice too." He had an easy, confident manner, seemingly at home in any hospital room, but I got the impression he could quickly take charge in a crisis. If I lived to be a hundred, I could never be as bold and self-assured as he was. He took my chart from the bottom of my bed and studied it for a moment before replacing it.

"Actually, that's a lie. I came to see you." He pulled up a chair beside my bed and sat down. "My name's Stephen Bradford . . . no, don't try to talk. I already know your name is Grace Bauer. And I know you're a second-year nursing student, right?"

I nodded again, then gestured to remind him that I could write if he would hand me paper and a pen.

"No, no, no," he said, laughing. "I'm going to enjoy this one-sided conversation. I've been out on dates with some girls and couldn't get a word in edgewise."

I would have asked if he considered this a date if I could have talked. He leaned toward me, propping one elbow on his knee, resting his chin on his hand.

"I saw you reading the Bible when you were in the other ward. That impressed me. It's usually not the favored reading material of women your age. At first I was afraid that you might be planning to become a nun or something—which would be a tragic waste of a beautiful woman—but then I remembered seeing you at Christ Church. You go there sometimes, right?"

I nodded, feeling more and more like a trained horse.

"See, that intrigues me. Attending church is obviously your choice, since your parents aren't around to drag you there by the hand. I'm a physician not a detective, but unless I'm reading this all wrong, I suspect that there is some spiritual depth to you, Grace Bauer—along with beauty and intelligence. Sorry—I confess that I peeked at your grades too."

By now I was blushing fiercely. I longed to duck beneath the covers to escape his probing eyes, but I knew I would look foolish. I was glad I couldn't talk because I had no idea what to say. Nor could I imagine ever conversing with someone as poised and articulate as Stephen Bradford.

"Am I right? Have you had some sort of . . . spiritual experience?" he asked.

"My faith is very important to me," I whispered. The effort hurt my throat, bringing tears to my eyes. He sprang to his feet and poured a glass of water, then lifted my head so I could drink.

"Hey, you're not supposed to talk. You'll start hemorrhaging. Do you taste blood?"

I shook my head.

"Good. Dr. Reynolds will murder me if he has to pack your throat. Let me do the talking, okay?" He settled back in the chair again. "My parents dragged me by the hand to church when I was small, and I thought it was okay—pretty music, nice people. But nothing much happened inside me, you know? It didn't mean anything. Then I came down with appendicitis when I was twelve. My appendix ruptured and I nearly died of peritonitis."

I had the feeling I was seeing a side of Stephen Bradford he rarely revealed.

"I started talking to God. I told Him I wanted to live, and I pleaded with Him like King Hezekiah did in the Old Testament. When Hezekiah prayed, God gave him fifteen more years to live. Of course, I was secretly hoping for a few more years than fifteen, but I would take what I could get. Obviously, God answered my prayer. I lived. This is my fifteenth year, by the way." He gave a quick, shy smile before continuing.

"But as I lay there recovering, I started to get the feeling that now it was God's turn to talk to *me*. It seemed like He was saying that everything I'd gone through had been for a reason. He had given me a firsthand look at doctors and hospitals and saving lives because He wanted me to serve Him by becoming a doctor—if I was willing. On my first Sunday home from the hospital we sang the song in church, 'Take my life and let it be consecrated, Lord, to Thee.' I told God I was willing."

Stephen stopped suddenly and looked away, as if embarrassed that he'd told me so much. "I don't know why I'm telling you all this—I hope you don't think I'm crazy. I just had the feeling, somehow, that you'd understand."

"I do," I whispered. He stood and put his fingers on my lips.

"Shh. You can tell me all about it in a couple of days." He gazed at me for a long moment, and he was a completely different man than the nonchalant doctor who had first strolled into my room. I liked this man very much.

"So do you think you'll be going to church next Sunday?" he asked. I nodded. "Great. I'll wait for you in front of the building. We can sit together."

I got out of bed early Sunday morning, giving myself plenty of time to fix my hair and put on my makeup. Stephen had seen me at my worst in the hospital. Now I wanted him to see me at my best. I arrived at Christ Church twenty minutes early and saw Stephen already waiting for me, pacing a bit and glancing at his watch.

"Oh good. You came," he said when he saw me. His magnificent smile lit his face and I couldn't utter a sound. Fortunately, we walked up the steps and into the sanctuary, so I didn't have to. After sitting in church alone all my life, it felt like a dream to sit beside Stephen, sharing a hymnbook, hearing him sing in his booming baritone voice. That's when I knew that I could never get seriously involved with any man who didn't share my faith.

"Let's go for lunch," he said afterward.

"Sure." I had progressed from nodding to monosyllables. Great. I would have to do better than that if I ever wanted to see Stephen Bradford again. When we were seated in a diner near the hospital, I said, "What did you think of the pastor's comments on faith versus works?"

"I thought his logic was flawed in some places," Stephen said, "but I agreed with the basic content of his message. The book of James has always been controversial in that respect. In fact, Martin Luther thought it should be thrown out of the Bible—but then, he was reacting to its misuse by the Catholic church."

I could tell by his quick gestures and the excitement in his voice that Stephen enjoyed a vigorous debate. I took a risk, daring to disagree with some of his opinions as we talked, playing the devil's advocate. Father O'Duggan used to do the same thing with me in some of our conversations, and I'd loved the challenge of defending my ideas.

"Were you in debate club in high school?" Stephen finally asked, laughing as we finished eating our pancakes.

"No, but one of my best friends since childhood was Father O'Duggan, the parish priest. You should debate him sometime."

"A Catholic priest? My impression is that they are usually all wrapped up in Catholic doctrine at the expense of faith in Christ."

"Father O'Duggan must be different, then. He truly loves God."

For the next several weeks, Stephen and I met at Christ Church every Sunday. Afterward, we would go out for lunch if he wasn't working, and if the weather was nice, we'd walk the long way home through a nearby park, stopping to sit for a while on our favorite park bench beside a pond. I told him how I'd first sensed God's presence when I was thirteen, and how I'd learned to rely on Him as my heavenly Father ever since.

"It's so refreshing to be with a woman I can converse with," Stephen said. "Someone whose mind isn't on shallow things."

Stephen and I became good friends, but that was all. To my great disappointment, he didn't hold my hand or try to kiss me.

Then my rotation changed and we ended up on the pediatrics ward at the same time. I saw him as Dr. Stephen Bradford, and it was painfully obvious why he didn't ask me out. He was so completely unattainable—suave, good-looking, self-assured. He strode through the corridors like he owned the hospital, not at all like a lowly intern. He was slightly under six feet tall, with the compact muscles of a man who'd been the star quarterback on his high school football squad and rowed for the winning crew team at his Ivy League college. All the nurses that worked for him fell in love with him.

"Isn't he dreamy?" they sighed when he walked onto the floor. "Wouldn't you love to lip wrestle with him?" Stephen seemed to take their adulation for granted.

At work he treated me no differently than any of the other student nurses, as if I had dreamt all our Sunday mornings together. With so many women competing for him, I knew I didn't stand a chance. That's why when he finally did ask me out I was speechless.

"Do you like to dance, Grace?" he asked one Sunday as we walked home through the park. "I'm supposed to have Friday night off. I thought we could go to a dance."

"Y-yes . . . I'd love to go."

Instead of going to the club near the hospital where all the nurses and interns went, we took a bus to the USO club where I'd first danced with the sailor more than a year earlier. For the first time, Stephen took my hand in his as we walked. When we danced, he pulled me snugly to himself like a prized possession. As with everything else he did, Stephen was excellent at dancing. We seemed to float above the floor, our feet barely touching the ground, like Ginger Rogers and Fred Astaire. He held our clasped hands against his chest and pressed his cheek to my face. I hated for the slow songs to end, revelling in the nearness of him and the musky scent of his after-shave.

"Mmm, you feel so good in my arms," he murmured as we danced to "I'll Be Seeing You." "It feels as though you belong here. I don't want to let you go, Grace."

I remembered Father O'Duggan's warnings. Stephen might have been spinning me a line. But the attraction I felt for him was as strong and as irresistible as gravity.

After the dance we sat outside on the bench, waiting for the bus. Stephen had grown very quiet and still, his hazel eyes locking with mine. Then he closed his eyes and slowly bent his head until our lips met. The night seemed to come to a halt, like a child's game of freeze-tag—except that I was far from cold. I'd kissed a few men by then, but I'd been in the hands of amateurs. By the time the bus came, I could barely stumble up the stairs.

For the next four months I turned down dates with every man but Stephen—and since his schedule as an intern was so demanding, I spent a lot of weekends alone. We would steal time together whenever we could though, and sometimes our date was a short walk to the park or a quick cup of coffee in a nearby café. I didn't mind. As an intern, he probably didn't have much money to spare for dates.

"You're so easy to talk to, Grace," he told me in the coffee shop one day. He had been telling me about the patients he had treated that week—the ones he had helped and the one or two he hadn't been able to help.

"I enjoy listening to you share your triumphs and frustrations," I said.

"Yeah? Well, today I'm frustrated."

"Tell me."

"I signed on to be an army doctor, but now it looks like the war will be over before I finish my internship, and I'll miss everything! All my old friends from college are in Europe or the South Pacific . . . and here I am. I thought about enlisting as a regular soldier, then finishing medical school after the war, but the need for doctors was too great. Now that I'm almost done, so is the war."

"You've been cheated, Stephen! I think you should write to the president and ask him to prolong the war a little longer, just for you."

He laughed, then reached across the table for my hand. "You know what else I like about you, Grace? You never let me get too full of myself."

I knew exactly what he meant. There were two sides to Stephen—the self-assured doctor that most people saw, and the gentle, vulnerable man he often was with me. That warmhearted man was the one I longed to be with every spare moment I had.

"How about a movie this Saturday?" he said suddenly. "I'll pick you up around seven."

"I'd love to."

———

That Saturday night, I eagerly waited in the lounge of the nurses' home for Stephen to pick me up. I stood at the front window, watching through the blinds for him, ready to run outside and meet him on the front steps as soon as I saw him. The web that was slowly being woven between us seemed like such a delicate, magical thing that I didn't want anyone to know how I felt about him. I was afraid that if I acknowledged it, the spell would be broken and our relationship would end as abruptly as it had started. Romances between medical students and nurses were notoriously fickle and short-lived. I had decided to simply enjoy my time with Stephen for as long as it lasted, promising myself that I wouldn't be foolish enough to fall in love with him.

In the lounge behind me, four senior nurses sat around a wobbly card table playing gin rummy and loudly discussing all the unmarried residents and interns. As they laughed and joked their way through several categories such as "nicest physique" and "dream date," I wasn't surprised to hear Stephen's name mentioned several times. I glanced at my watch. It wasn't like him to be this late.

Suddenly a fourth-year medical student dressed in hospital scrubs stuck his head in the door. "Which one of you gorgeous dames is Grace Bauer?"

"I am."

"Steve Bradford asked me to run across the street and tell you, sorry—he can't make it tonight after all." He covered his head in a gesture of self-defense, as if I might throw something at him. "Please, don't shoot!" he said, grinning. "I'm just the messenger!" The other nurses laughed at his antics.

"How about you, pretty boy?" one of them asked. "Are you free tonight?"

He lounged against the doorframe. "That depends. I usually ask Steve's girls out after he's broken their hearts. He has great taste in women. How about it, Grace Bauer? I'm crazy about blondes."

"No, thank you." I tried to duck upstairs, anxious to hide my flaming cheeks, but one of the senior nurses stopped me.

"Hey, Gracie, I didn't know you were dating Dr. Bradford or I would have warned you sooner."

"Warned me about what?"

"To be careful. Bradford has quite a reputation around here."

I felt my stomach turn over. I tried to sound nonchalant. "What kind of a reputation?"

"We call him Candy Man. He loves pretty young nurses in their striped uniforms. He gobbles them up like candy, then breaks their hearts when he moves on to the next one. He's already left a trail of tears a mile long."

"Besides, everyone knows he isn't going to marry a lowly nurse," one of the others added. "His parents are very high society, you know. One of the wealthiest families in Pennsylvania."

Their warning came too late. I already cared about Stephen Bradford. I cared too much. My sleepless night and sopping pillowcase told me that.

Had he been feeding me a line when he'd said how refreshing I was? How comfortable I felt in his arms? Would he grow tired of me as he had all the others? And why hadn't he told me that his parents were rich? During all the months we'd been together, we'd never talked about our families. I had been grateful, afraid I'd lose him for sure if he knew about my background. But it was even worse than I'd feared. The son of high society parents would never marry a poor divorced woman's daughter. If only I had known how hopeless our future was, I never would have fallen in love with Stephen.

Fallen in love. I faced the truth for the first time. I had fallen in love.

How had it happened? And how did a person fall out of love again? I wished Father O'Duggan were here to confide in. He had always helped me sort through my problems in the past. But what would a priest know about falling in love?

After my long, sleepless night I felt groggy the next day, my eyes puffy and red. I stayed home from church. On Monday, I couldn't seem to concentrate on anything except my own misery, and the head nurse had to reprimand me three times for making sloppy mistakes. I was relieved when I didn't run into Stephen at the hospital, then I found him waiting for me outside after my shift. My heart began to race the moment I saw him leaning against the hospital zone sign.

"Hi. Have time for a walk?" It wasn't really a question. He seemed confident that I would agree.

I felt torn. The nurses' warnings made me afraid to trust him. But I also wanted to know why he had pretended to be a starving intern, riding city buses and eating in greasy cafés if his parents were wealthy people.

"Sure," I finally said. He held my hand as we walked to the park.

"I wanted to apologize for standing you up the other night. We had an emergency come in about an hour before my shift ended, and I wanted to see it through until the patient was stabilized." He pulled me down beside him on our favorite bench and draped his arm around my shoulder. "Doug told me how gorgeous you looked. I'm glad you didn't take him up on his offer to replace me."

"You can't be replaced, Stephen. You're one of a kind." I felt relieved that my voice sounded neutral. He could interpret my words any way he liked.

"So are you, Grace." He sounded so sincere. "You're very different from all the other girls. You're never demanding of my time and attention, and you would never give me a hard time about a broken date." As we sat on the bench watching the geese, I decided I'd better tell him just how different I really was.

"You've never asked me about my parents, Stephen, but I think I should tell you about them anyway. They're divorced. I've never even met my father because my mother left him before I was born. He took her to a back-alley quack and tried to make her abort me." He shifted on the bench to face me, and I could tell by the stunned look on his face that he was shocked. I hurried on, spilling everything.

"I've lived my entire life in a tiny two-room apartment with my mother. We were poor . . . I mean, barely-enough-to-eat poor. In fact, we still are poor. My mother is an out-of-work dance band musician who is currently making tank parts in a factory."

Stephen suddenly pulled me into his arms. I had the unsettling feeling as he crushed me to his chest that it was because he wanted to silence my words. He didn't want to know anything about me. It would be easier to dump a girl he had never gotten close to. I pushed him away after a moment. He would probably break up with me anyhow now that he knew about my past, but if what the other nurses said was true, why postpone the inevitable?

"I'm not telling you this so you'll feel sorry for me, Stephen. I don't want pity. I wouldn't trade my childhood for anyone else's. My mother is such a dynamic, free-spirited soul that she made it an adventure to be poor. She's a marvelous person . . . and thoroughly unconventional. I spent three years of my childhood in a speakeasy being raised by a bunch of bootleggers, because the only job my mother could find was playing the piano for them."

He tightened his grip on my arms. "Grace, stop it. Why are you trying to shock me?" His face was puzzled and angry.

"I just thought you should know the truth," I said quietly. "You've been hiding the truth about your family from me, for some reason, but I wanted you to know that we're from two entirely different worlds."

He dropped his hands, sagging back against the bench. "Who told you?" he said.

"Told me what?"

"About the 'world' I come from?"

"The senior nurses."

"Curse them all!" He pounded the back of the bench with his fist. A moment later he sprang to his feet, as if needing an outlet for his rage, and strode down to the edge of the lake, his shoulders hunched, his hands jammed into his pockets.

I didn't know what to do. I was hopelessly ignorant when it came to men, much less their moods. But Father O'Duggan had always waited patiently for me when I was upset, giving me time until I was ready to talk. I decided to do the same.

Eventually, Stephen returned and sank down beside me again. Anger still etched his features. "I'm sorry, Grace," he said, and the fury in his voice brought tears to my eyes. I was in love with him. He was about to break up with me, and in spite of all the warnings, my heart felt like shattered glass.

"Once! Just once!" he continued, "I wanted a woman to like me for myself, not because my parents have a few bucks! I deliberately avoided talking about my background or yours because it shouldn't matter! All my life I've had to wonder, 'Is this girl dating me because she likes me or because she likes my money?' I'm fed up with debutantes and their rich daddies, looking to make a socially prestigious match! I'm fed up with gold diggers trying to strike it rich. And I'm fed up with senior nurses who can't mind their own business!"

I waited for the stillness of the afternoon to descend again, for the geese to settle on the water after Stephen's shouts had disturbed them. "I understand why you might feel that way," I eventually said. "One of the things I loved about coming to school here in Philadelphia was the anonymity. No one knew I was poor, no one knew my mother was divorced. But I've always had the opposite problem you do—men don't want to date me because I'm *not* a socially prestigious match."

He looked at me as if that was a totally foreign idea to him. "Not date you? But if they only knew you . . ."

"It's true," I assured him. "In fact, I wonder what your parents would say if they knew you were dating me?"

I saw his jaw muscles tighten. "I don't care what they'd say! I don't care if the woman I date is rich or poor!"

"Well, believe it or not, Stephen, it doesn't matter to me if the man I date is rich or poor either. I'm not a gold digger. I had no idea your parents had money until last night, but by then it was too late—I had fallen in love with you anyway." I stood and hurried up the path out of the park, afraid to look at him, unwilling to see how he had reacted to my words. I had foolishly revealed my heart, and now I didn't know how I would ever be able to work beside him again. We had another full year of studies in the same hospital.

I wasn't surprised when Stephen didn't follow me. I walked faster and faster. My only thought was to get to my room, to get through the night of sorrow that awaited me, then to get through tomorrow. I thought I finally understood why my mother avoided men. She must have had her heart shattered as well. I would be like her from now on. No medical students. No interns. No men, period. Maybe I'd become a missionary after the war. In the meantime, I would chalk up this experience as my first broken heart. Someday in the future I would vaguely remember Stephen Bradford the way I remembered the sailor who had given me my first kiss.

As I neared the nurses' home, I realized that I wasn't ready to face anyone yet, knowing that my pain was probably visible for all to see. The senior nurses who hung around the lounge would take one look at me and know that Dr. Bradford, the Candy Man, had added another broken heart to his collection. When a city bus pulled up to the curb beside me, I boarded it without bothering to read its destination.

Evening fell as I rode through the unfamiliar streets, gazing at office buildings and storefronts, my tears still close to the surface. The bus passed houses and apartment buildings where warm lights glowed behind curtained windows, then street after street of row houses in neighborhoods I had never seen before. Many of the homes had stars posted in their windows, a sign that a son or a daughter served in the armed forces. Occasionally I saw a gold star and knew that a loved one had been killed in action. I recalled Father O'Duggan's words from so long ago: *"Gazing through the windows at other families isn't the same as living there day after day and knowing what really goes on behind closed doors. There is a heartache like the one you're feeling right now in a good many homes."*

As I rode on, too numb to move from my seat, a steady stream of strangers got on and off the bus. Few people spoke, each passenger an island in the crowd. The bus filled with the evening rush until it was jammed, then it emptied again as evening turned to night.

"End of the line, ma'am," the bus driver said. I looked around as we pulled into the bus station. I was the only passenger. I climbed down from the bus and wandered into a nearby diner. It smelled of fried foods and stale coffee. All the booths were filled, many people straddling suitcases and duffle bags as they waited for bus connections out of the city. I found an empty chrome stool at the counter and ordered a cheese sandwich, watching people as I ate, wondering what stories they had to tell.

When I finished eating I went outside into a starless night. A raw, damp wind had begun to blow, turning the city cold. I thought of returning to the nurses' home and shuddered.

Suddenly a bell began to toll. I looked toward the sound and saw a large stone church at the end of the block, outlined against the dark sky. Jeweled windows glowed with light from within, and a graceful steeple pointed toward heaven, the direction I should have been looking all along. I crossed the street and ran to the church like an injured child running to her father for consolation.

The doors were unlocked. A scattering of people sat or knelt in prayer as a robed clergyman moved silently around the altar. I sank into an empty pew in the rear of the church and closed my eyes, allowing my Father to comfort me in the echoing silence.

"He was despised and rejected of men; a man of sorrows, and acquainted with grief . . . Surely he hath borne our griefs, and carried our sorrows. . . .

"Come unto me, all ye that labor and are heavy laden, and I will give you rest . . . I am with you always . . . I will never leave you or forsake you . . ."

God knew what was best for my life—whether that was marrying Stephen or not. As painful as it would be to let Stephen go, I had to trust Him. *"All things work together for good to them that love God."* I curled up on the pew and wept without making a sound.

———

A car horn woke me from a deep sleep. I sat up, disoriented, my heart pounding as I gazed around the shadowy, unfamiliar church. Then I remembered where I was, and the pain that had caused me to flee here. The sanctuary was deserted and dark; pale light filtered through the stained-glass windows from the early morning sun.

I scrambled off the pew. I had slept all night! No one from the nurses' home knew where I was! I ran from the church, my muscles stiff with cold and cramped from spending the night on the hard bench. I boarded a bus that would take me back to the hospital. The ride seemed interminable as I imagined the consequences of what I had done.

I was in a great deal of trouble. I hadn't signed out overnight or phoned my roommate to tell her when I would return. I could be expelled. My empty stomach was a knot of worry on the long ride across town.

As soon as I staggered into the lobby of the nurses' home, I saw Mrs. McClure, the director of nurses, talking to a policeman. My roommate stood beside her, weeping. Then I saw Stephen. He wore a haggard look, and the same clothes he'd worn yesterday. When he saw me he bounded across the lobby and crushed me in his arms.

"Grace! Oh, thank God . . . thank God!" I felt his tears on my neck. I began to cry, too, as fear and exhaustion settled over me. Finally Stephen pulled away, holding my arms tightly as he searched my face. "Are you all right, Grace? I've been worried sick! I was trying to catch up with you yesterday when you just vanished and—"

"Why didn't you call when you knew you'd be gone overnight?" Mrs. McClure demanded. "You had this place in an uproar!"

"I'm very, very sorry for worrying everyone. I jumped on a bus and I got lost and then I went into a church to pray and . . . and I didn't mean to be gone all night—I fell asleep! I'm so sorry!" I burst into tears.

Stephen pulled me into his arms again to comfort me. "It's all my fault. You thought I was angry with you, Grace, but I wasn't. I never meant to hurt you. My words came out all wrong."

After thinking that I'd lost him, his embrace seemed like a miracle. Then another thought struck me. "I hope you didn't call my mother and get her all worried!"

"You're not considered a missing person until twenty-four hours have passed," the cop said, closing his notebook. "Like yourself, most 'missing' people aren't missing at all."

After he left, my roommate told her story, admonishing me for all the worry I'd caused her. Then Mrs. McClure gave me a stern lecture, making very sure I understood the seriousness of my offense and the punishment that would inevitably follow. Through it all, Stephen never stopped clinging to me.

As I was about to be banished to my room for a very long time, he turned to Mrs. McClure. "May I please speak to Grace in private first?"

"Certainly, Dr. Bradford." Only Stephen's wealth and social status could explain her deference to a lowly intern.

He led me into the empty lounge and sat beside me on the sofa. He caressed my hair, my face, my shoulders, as if to reassure himself that I was all in one piece. Tears glistened in his hazel eyes.

"I've been out of my mind the past few hours, worrying about you. If anything had happened to you . . ." He paused until he could go on. "So I started asking myself why I was so upset. It took me a long time to come up with the answer because I've never been in love before. I had no idea it would feel like this. My life is bound up with yours, Grace. I can't explain it . . . but you matter to me. I don't want you out of my sight or out of my arms or out of my life for more than ten seconds. I love you . . . I . . . I love you." He clung to me as if he'd never let go. I wondered if I was dreaming.

"I love you too," I whispered.

"I know. You told me you loved me yesterday and I was so surprised I . . . I was speechless. I thought, this can't be true! This amazing, incredible woman really loves an arrogant, opinionated, selfish chump like me?"

Two first-year nurses strolled into the lounge, saw us, then backed out again. "Oops . . . sorry."

Stephen crushed me to himself and kissed me. "Will you marry me, Grace?" he asked when he could breathe again. "I want to take care of you and protect you. I want to give you all the things you've never had growing up. I want . . . I want to share my life with you. I know you have one more year of school, but when you graduate and the war finally ends . . . will you marry me?"

"Yes!" I could barely speak through my tears, so I said it again to make sure he heard me. "Yes, Stephen. Yes!"

TWENTY-THREE

As Suzanne pulled the car into the driveway, Grace sighed. She was thankful to be home again, thankful—as her mother must have been—to be far away from Bremenville. But she didn't move to get out of the car right away. Glancing at Suzanne, she saw that there was unfinished business, unanswered questions between them.

"So that's all there is to tell of my story," Grace said. "Germany surrendered that same month, and Japan surrendered four months later. I graduated from nursing school in June of 1946, and your father and I were married in August. Your brother was born in 1948, and you know the rest of my life story because you joined us two years later."

"I guess I never realized before that Daddy felt bad about not serving in World War II. Is that why he was so hostile to Jeff when they first met? Because Jeff protested Vietnam instead of doing his duty?"

"Maybe so." In spite of all the personal turmoil their trip had caused her, Grace was grateful for the insight it seemed to have given her daughter. She felt closer to Suzanne than she had in a long time. "Sue, I know you've always criticized what you call my 'perfect *Father Knows Best* life.' You think your father is some sort of monster because he likes things orderly and organized. But you have to understand that I was raised in an upside down home that was an embarrassment to me. All I ever wanted was to be like everyone else. I wanted the security that your father offered. I was attracted to his self-confidence and the fact that he had everything under control. He had the best qualities of all my fathers: he was as generous as Booty Higgins, as smart as O'Brien, as protective as Black Jack, as sentimental as Mick, and he loved God as much as Father O'Duggan did. Stephen wanted a house and two children and a wife who wore sensible dresses with aprons and kept to a weekly routine like Mam, and I was happy to give it to him. With your father, I finally had the kind of life I'd dreamed of ever since I was a child. We had a boy and a girl and a house in the suburbs—we were the perfect family."

"But you could have had all that and a nursing career too," Suzanne said.

"I didn't care about a career. I grew up in an era when women were supposed to be helpless and frail. We needed a husband, not a career, if we wanted to be powerful. Besides, I had a full-time job learning to be a wife and mother because I didn't have a clue what real wives and mothers were supposed to do. My mother had never cooked a meal that included all the basic food groups in my entire life. Our two-room apartment above the Mulligan sisters was practically bare."

"So you just let Daddy's decorator design everything for you." Suzanne raked her dark hair from her eyes with an impatient flip of her hand.

"Yes, because I didn't have a clue where to begin with a real home. I used to study homemaking books when I was first married, and believe it or not, they told me I should comb my hair and put on makeup before my husband came home at night. I was supposed to have the house in order, dinner on the table, and a smile on my face. I shouldn't hit him with all my domestic problems when he walked through the door, the experts said, or present him with two naughty kids that needed to be spanked."

Suzanne looked unconvinced. "So you can honestly tell me you never wished you could return to nursing?"

"I'll admit it was hard after you and Robert went away to college. I felt useless and unneeded for a while. But my volunteer work is just as fulfilling as any nine-to-five job—with the added bonus that I can arrange my hours around your father's schedule. I'm available when he needs me."

"Are you going to tell Daddy what we found out in Bremenville?"

"Of course. I tell him everything. And I'm going to ask his medical opinion about how the mumps might have affected my father."

Suzanne seemed deep in thought. She reminded Grace of Stephen when he had a difficult medical diagnosis to make. Like her father's, Suzanne's analytical mind had to process all the information in an orderly way until she was satisfied she had reached the correct solution.

"I have a question," she said suddenly. "Which of your five 'fathers' do you think helped Grandma the most?"

Grace reminded herself to be patient, even though she didn't like where this line of questioning was headed. "Well, I'd have to say either Booty or O'Brien. Mick, Black Jack, and Father O'Duggan were more my friends than hers."

"That makes sense. . . ." Suzanne mused to herself. "Booty was married . . . Mrs. Higgins didn't like you . . ."

Grace climbed from the car and retrieved her suitcase from the trunk. Then she walked around to the driver's side to talk to Suzanne again. "Thanks for an interesting weekend. Will I see you soon?"

"How about next Saturday night? Can you and Daddy come for dinner? Bring Grandma too."

"I hope you're not inviting us so you can interrogate Grandma."

Suzanne made a face. "No, I'm inviting you to keep me company. Jeff's taking the girls out somewhere that night."

"Sure. We'd love to come. I'm sorry for questioning your motives, but it's just that I have a very bad feeling that this trip is only the beginning, as far as you're concerned, and not the end. Am I right?"

"There are too many unanswered questions, Mom."

"Like what?"

"Is Karl Bauer your real father or not?"

"It doesn't matter to me if he is or he isn't. I have a heavenly Father who loves me."

Grace reached through the open window and rested her hand on Suzanne's shoulder. "Sue . . . is there anything I can say that will convince you to drop all this nonsense about my father?"

"No, I'm sorry, Mom. I have to know the truth."

———

The facade of Suzanne's home, a two-story brick Colonial, was tastefully lit with floodlights, the yard immaculately groomed and landscaped, but Emma couldn't help thinking it looked vacant and cold as she and Grace pulled into the driveway. "It doesn't look as though anyone is home," she said to Grace. "Are you sure we have the right night?"

"I'm sure. Sue is home alone. Jeff took the girls somewhere for the weekend. I think she invited us to dinner to help chase away the blues."

Suzanne had the door open before they reached the front step. "Where's Daddy? Didn't he know he was invited?"

"He was called to the hospital just as we were leaving. He promised to come over as soon as he's finished."

"That's typical. I might have known he wouldn't come." Suzanne's voice had a bitter edge to it.

"You feel so thin, Suzy!" Emma said as she hugged her. "Have you lost weight?"

"I don't know. Jeff took the bathroom scale."

At first Emma didn't realize what she meant, then she walked into Suzanne's living room and saw the gaping holes, like extracted teeth, where Jeff's belongings had once been. Faded rectangles on the walls marked the places where his paintings had hung, dusty shelves stood empty where stereo components and books were missing. Twin scars of crushed carpeting revealed the absence of Jeff's favorite recliner.

Emma's eyes filled with tears. Two lives, joined together as one flesh, had been cruelly ripped apart. "Where did it all go?" she murmured, meaning the love that had once flamed between Suzanne and Jeff.

"He boxed everything up and stored it in the garage until he finds an apartment in Chicago," Suzanne replied. "And that was just the stuff we agreed on. There are a bunch of other things, like the antique rolltop desk in the den, that we're still battling over."

"I hope you don't argue in front of the girls," Grace said.

"Sometimes it can't be helped. When the girls and I came home the other day, he had a real estate agent here appraising the house. Needless to say, I lost my temper. This house is joint property, in both of our names. He can't sell it unless I agree—and I don't!"

"Can you afford a house this big on what you make at the magazine?" Grace asked.

"Of course not, but Jeff can. He's going to pay big time too! I refuse to live the typical, substandard life of a single mother." Suzanne bent to pick up a few scattered toys, as if she needed an outlet for her restlessness.

"This bitterness and greed is so unlike you," Emma said.

"Well, you and Mom should know firsthand that the majority of single mothers live well below the poverty line. Would you rather the girls and I subsisted like you did during the depression?"

"Divorce is such an ugly word," Emma said with a sigh.

"Supper is all ready, so we may as well eat," Suzanne said, gesturing to the dining room. "We would have starved to death years ago if we had always waited for Daddy."

Emma followed Suzanne into the dining room, where the table was beautifully set for dinner. Nothing seemed to be missing from that room, but when they took their seats around the table and Suzanne served the food, Stephen's empty place setting was an unwelcome reminder that they were three women on their own, without husbands. The sadness that enshrouded the house began to descend on Emma.

"You know, Suzanne, Karl Bauer was a prosperous man," Emma said. "I was very well-to-do when I was married to him. But it isn't the loss of material things or the poverty that makes divorce so difficult. It's the loneliness. In my case, I was lonely before I left Karl. We'd never had a loving relationship to begin with. But from the very first time I ever laid eyes on Jeff, the two of you were twined together like a vine and a trellis. You loved each other."

"That was ages ago, Grandma," Suzanne said briskly. "We've been busy raising a family and building careers since then."

"Maybe you and Jeff should have worked as hard on your marriage as you did on your careers," Grace said.

"Mom, please. I didn't invite you here to give me a lecture."

"I know. You need our company and our support. Believe me, honey, Grandma and I do support you—but not in the way that you think. We're not going to take your side against Jeff—"

Suzanne slammed down the bread basket. "Oh, that's a switch! You and Daddy should be happy we're getting a divorce, since you didn't want me to marry him in the first place."

"I was wrong about that." Grace's voice remained gentle in spite of Suzanne's bitterness. "I've grown to love Jeff. He's the father of my grandchildren. God joined the two of you together, and I'm not giving up until your marriage is restored."

Suzanne shook her head. "Well, that isn't going to happen. Jeff's gone."

A sorrow-filled silence descended over the table. Emma ate the casserole Suzanne had prepared without tasting it. Grace didn't even pretend to eat. Emma saw tears in her eyes.

"Sue, what do your girls think about their father leaving them?" Grace asked. "What will they think about God because of it? Will they think that He'll leave them and move far away too? Remember what Father O'Duggan once told me about how our fathers shape our attitudes toward God? How will Amy's and Melissa's attitude toward God be affected if you get a divorce?"

"It was Jeff's choice to leave home, not mine."

"But it was your decision not to move to Chicago and make a new home with him there."

Suzanne pushed back her chair and sprang to her feet. "Did you ever stop to consider what I learned about God from Daddy? That I have to constantly work to win his approval, that I'm always begging for the smallest scraps of his love, that he's always too busy for me!" She picked up Stephen's unused dinner plate and threw it to the floor, shattering it.

Emma quickly rose and drew Suzanne into her arms. She had never been fooled, like most people, by Suzanne's tough exterior and fiery independence—inside, she was a wounded child. In spite of Suzanne's seeming indifference, the breakup of her marriage was hurting her deeply. Emma remembered well the painful years after her own divorce, and how—even as she'd made everyone around her laugh—she'd wept within.

Grace sat across the table from them in stunned disbelief. "Suzanne. . . ? Is that really the way you see your father?"

Suzanne was weeping too hard to answer. Emma answered for her. "You're much too close to Stephen to see it, Gracie, but Sue has tried all of her life to win his approval—even at the cost of her own happiness. But she could never be the kind of daughter Stephen expected. She could never be you, Gracie. Sue is too independent, too spirited . . . too much like me! I did the same thing when I was young. I tried so hard to fit into my mother's mold, to be the kind of daughter Papa wanted. That's why I married Karl. But I didn't fit Mama's mold, I wasn't like her at all, and the effort to be someone I wasn't cost me dearly."

Grace looked shocked. "So you're saying Suzanne should do the same thing you did? Divorce her husband?"

"Not at all! I think Jeff and Sue were perfectly suited for each other—free-spirited, creative, life-embracing. That's why they fell in love, and that's why I encouraged them to get married against your wishes. But Jeff is not in the least like Stephen, and Sue is nothing like you . . . and I think they both tried to fit your molds to win your approval. It didn't work. And I think that's why they fell out of love. Am I right, Suzanne?"

"It's such a mess, Grandma." Suzanne's hands still covered her face. "We started out so happy . . . and now everything is in such a mess."

Emma bent to pick up the pieces of the shattered plate, laying them one by one on the tablecloth in front of Suzanne. "Your mother is right. It isn't too late to put the pieces of your marriage back together. But it won't be the same marriage it was before. It shouldn't be. That pattern was flawed, which is why it broke apart to begin with."

She gently pulled Suzanne's hands from her face and held them in her own. "I'm taking a pottery course at Birch Grove," Emma said. "It's great fun, you know, getting splattered with mud up to my eyeballs! But one thing I learned is that before you can create a good pot, you have to get the clay perfectly centered on the wheel. Otherwise, as you try to shape it, the pot gets more and more deformed as the wheel spins faster, until the whole mess flies off and crashes into the wall. How did your marriage get off-center, Sue? How did it come to this?" Emma gestured to the shattered plate. "How did you get here from where you started?"

Suzanne scrubbed impatiently at her tears. "I don't know . . . I suppose there's a lot of truth in what you said about wanting to please Daddy and not fitting into Mom's mold. . . ."

PART FOUR

Suzanne's Story
1950 - 1980

TWENTY-FOUR

From the time I was a little girl, I knew I wasn't cut to fit Mom's mold. I think I first realized it one day while playing hospital with my brother, Bobby. I was five years old and he was seven. He had gotten a toy doctor's kit for Christmas, and I, of course, got a nurse's kit. We used my Betsy Wetsy doll and some stuffed animals for the patients and set up an operating room on the coffee table in the den.

"Scalpel!" Bobby demanded, his hand outstretched. His voice was crisp and bossy like Daddy's. He always tried to be exactly like Daddy, from his crew cut to his arrogant swagger. "Nurse! Scissors!"

It didn't take long for me to grow tired of doing the boring jobs, like handing Bobby all his surgical instruments. I looked at his outstretched hand and rebelled.

"No. It's my turn to operate now. It's my doll." I folded my arms across my chest.

"You can't operate, you're only the nurse."

"I don't want to be a nurse anymore. I want to be a doctor. I want to operate too."

"You can't be a doctor. You're a girl. Girls are nurses, like Mommy. Boys are doctors, like Daddy."

I whacked Bobby on the head with his doctor's kit. The blow quickly wiped the smirk of superiority off Bobby's face. When he ran crying to Mom, I collected all the patients and opened my own hospital in my bedroom. I promoted myself to chief surgeon. I didn't want to be like Mom with her pearls and lipstick and high heels. I could never be as sweet and soft-spoken as she was.

Once at a backyard cookout with my parents' friends, Mom was circulating through the crowd in pink pedal pushers and a peasant blouse, serving hors d'oeuvres while Daddy grilled everyone's T-bone steaks to perfection on perfectly heated charcoal briquettes. Bobby and his friends had climbed up in his "boys only" tree house to devise pranks against the girls. And I was supposed to be twirling my Hula-Hoop with those girls, but I had grown bored with swivelling my hips. I decided to hang around the adults, instead.

"What line of work are you in?" Daddy's golf partner asked our next-door neighbor.

"I'm an attorney . . . And you?"

"Obstetrician." Ritual handshakes and nods of respect followed this exchange of identities.

Daddy introduced a late arrival to the group by saying, "This is my friend John Moore. He's my stockbroker."

I wandered over to where the women lounged beneath a flowered patio umbrella. "This is our neighbor, Gloria Clark," I heard Mom say. "Her husband is an attorney."

"What does your husband do?" Gloria asked the other woman.

"He's an architect. His firm designed the new Crawford building downtown." Judging by the admiring *oohs* and *ahhs*, the woman might have selected every brick and support beam in the building herself, instead of merely ironing the architect's shirts and cooking his hard-boiled eggs.

I was a tomboy, confronting snakes and spiders and starting fires as fearlessly as my brother, Bobby. Mom despaired of ever making a young lady out of me. "Don't sit like that, Suzanne, it isn't ladylike. Please use a hanky, Suzanne, not your sleeve. . . . Young ladies walk, Suzanne, they don't gallop."

My brother could sit, sneeze, or gallop any way he wanted to. When he crawled around under the pews after church one Sunday morning, Daddy said, "He's all boy." I tried it the following Sunday—ripping my crinoline and scuffing my patent-leather shoes in the process—and was declared a disgrace. Bobby never had to wear hats to church that looked like straw saucers with glued-on flowers, or suffer in hot white gloves that made his hands sweat. Daddy served on the board of elders—Mom served chicken a la king at potluck suppers. Daddy passed the collection plate and shook hands with people after church—Mom stood a few demure steps behind him, smiling and looking pretty.

The older I got, the more I rebelled against my Sunday school teachers for reinforcing this stereotype of submissive women. "Why did God give me talents and brains and curiosity if I wasn't supposed to use any of them?" I asked the pastor once during catechism class. "Why can't women pass the blasted collection plate too?" My behavior outraged Daddy. I quickly learned that if I wanted his approval and affection, I had to be quiet and ladylike. Impossible.

My brother didn't have to do anything to earn Daddy's approval except brag about how he was going to be a doctor someday. At first I was determined to go into medicine too, just to prove that I was as smart as Bobby. But my straight As in biology and advanced algebra didn't impress Daddy the way I had hoped they would.

He called Bobby and me into his den, one at a time, on report card day to discuss our grades. Bobby had already emerged from the dark-panelled room smiling. But Daddy was very quiet as he read over mine. I hopped from one foot to the other in front of his desk, reading all his diplomas and awards hanging on the walls and waiting for the words of praise that were sure to come.

"So do you think my grades are good enough to get me into a pre-med program?" I blurted when he finally looked up.

"Pre-med?" he repeated. He made the word sound shocking. "Is that what your guidance counselor at school recommended?"

"Of course not. My guidance counselor is a jerk!"

"Suzanne . . ."

"Well, he is. He told me I was 'college material,' but he advised me to choose a profession that would work well with a family, such as teaching or nursing." I did a nasty impression of the counselor's prissy voice.

"He has a point."

"No! The last thing in the world I want is a June Cleaver life like Mom's. She's nothing more than your glorified maidservant!"

Daddy held up a warning finger. "You be careful how you talk about your mother. Don't you dare be disrespectful."

"I respect her as a person, I just don't want her life."

"What do you want, then?"

"I'm just as smart as Bobby. I could go to medical school too."

Daddy frowned and leaned back in his leather chair, toying with the stethoscope on his desk. "There is always a handful of intelligent girls who try medical school," he said, "but it's a very difficult field for women to break into. They're not readily accepted. And in the end, it seems like a waste of time and money because they'll eventually give up medicine to get married and have children anyway."

There were those dreaded words again—*married* and *children*. "How come every time my future is discussed, those two words always surface? Why is my future so narrowly defined when the whole world is open to Bobby?"

Daddy shook his head. "I never know what to say to you, Suzanne. I don't understand you at all."

Say you are proud of me, I thought. *Say I'm just as smart, just as important to you as Bobby*. But I said nothing to my father.

Throughout high school, I wavered between trying to prove I was as good as my brother by going into medicine, and doing what I loved the most, which was editing the school newspaper and expressing my opinions in scathing editorials. I loved books, loved manipulating words and ideas, loved telling stories much more than I liked dissecting worms and bisecting angles. I decided I would be a career woman on my own terms; I would win a Pulitzer prize in journalism, then advance to editor in chief of *The New Yorker* magazine, and eventually retire as CEO of a publishing empire. I would *not* be a housewife.

Bobby enrolled in the pre-med program at the Ivy League college where Daddy had done his undergraduate work. Tired of living in my brother's shadow, I chose a college that was renowned for its literature department. The pastor of the church I attended near campus was the first minister I'd ever met who didn't seem to consider women an inferior species under man's dominion.

"God has a unique plan for your life, Suzanne," he told me. "He expects you to use the gifts He has given you, not wrap them up in society's expectations." I was on good speaking terms with the pastor's God.

Being away from home suited me. By my junior year I had joined the best sorority, found a steady boyfriend, and earned the kind of outstanding grades that put me on the dean's list. I steered clear of the campus radicals and avoided all the turmoil of the '60s, like pot parties and love-ins and campus take-overs. I preferred to attend classes rather than protest the Vietnam War. My life hummed along nicely. Daddy approved.

Then, the first semester of my junior year, I took Introduction to Art.

———

The art building seemed like a foreign country to me, a messy, disorganized, third-world country with bizarre people in exotic costumes. The halls smelled like turpentine and plaster dust and wet clay. I hadn't wanted to take art, but my schedule gave me few choices, so I dragged myself to class three times a week, not daring to miss a lecture and ruin my grade point average. As if studying art history wasn't challenging enough, the professor made us learn the fundamentals of drawing too. Once a week, he would set up a bowl of fruit or a vase of flowers and we'd have to practice sketching it so we could learn about perspective and proportion and shading.

One day he brought in a live model to pose for us—a guy I'd seen around campus, hanging out with the "peaceniks." The hippie sat sprawled on a wooden chair wearing only his bell-bottoms and sandals, and I saw right away why the teacher had chosen him to pose. His shoulders and torso were as beautifully muscled as the Italian statues we'd studied.

I pulled out my sketch pad and began to draw, my eyes traveling from the paper to the model and down again. While I sketched, I analyzed him as if he were a biology specimen—strong biceps, solid pectorals, tight abdominals. The next time I glanced up, the hippie was staring back at me. His simmering gaze totally unnerved me. I didn't want to admit it, but I found him extraordinarily attractive. I usually preferred the clean-cut fraternity-type like my steady boyfriend, Bradley Wallace. This guy wore his dark hair tied in a ponytail, and the bottom half of his face was obscured by a thick brown beard and mustache. A peace necklace on a leather thong hung around his neck, dangling against his bare chest. Every time I glanced up to sketch him he was looking straight at me, staring intently with a dangerous Jimmy Dean look in his eyes. I decided to concentrate on his foot.

When the professor came around to comment on my efforts he said, "You'll have to work a little faster, Miss Bradford, if you hope to sketch more than his big toe before the semester ends." I was so relieved when the bell rang that I slammed my sketch book shut and raced out.

As I hurried across the campus toward my dormitory, the guy I'd just been sketching suddenly appeared beside me. He had shrugged into his shirt but hadn't bothered to button it. "What's your hurry, *Irish*?" he said.

"Are you talking to me?"

He spread his arms to encompass the empty sidewalk and pivoted in a slow, hip-swaying turn. "Do you see anyone else? A leprechaun, perhaps?"

"Why were you staring at me like that in art class?"

He gave a lazy, lopsided smile. "It seemed only fair. You were staring at me."

"I was drawing you! But you were very rude, in case you don't know."

"Wow! You've got an Irish temper too! Far out!"

"I don't know what you're talking about." I turned to leave, but he stepped smoothly in front of me.

"Have coffee with me." He smiled broadly this time, and I thought my heart would go into cardiac arrest. He slowly fastened the buttons on his shirt while his magnetic blue eyes held mine. I'd never had such a heart-stopping reaction before. I was both fascinated and terrified.

"No, thank you," I managed to say.

"Why not?"

"Well, in the first place, I don't even know you."

"Jeff Pulaski. Art major. Born and raised in Pittsburgh." He extended his hand.

I shook it briefly, then said, "And in the second place, I'm pinned."

He laughed uproariously.

"I'm glad you find that amusing, Mr. Pulaski."

"I do! Ever see those butterflies in the museums, all stretched out on a piece of velvet with pins holding down their wings? Here's this beautiful creature, meant to fly, but it's just lying there, trapped, held down by pins. That's what I think of whenever some chick says, 'I'm pinned.'" He fingered my boyfriend's fraternity pin, fastened just above my breast, and laughed again. "He's got you all stretched out under glass like his prize specimen, and no one else can touch you."

"How dare you!" I said, slapping his hand away. "I'm nobody's possession!"

"Then prove it by having a cup of coffee with me." There was that smile again.

I didn't have to prove anything to him, but something compelled me to accept his challenge. Part of it was stubbornness, part was curiosity, but mostly it was the sheer excitement of being with such a dangerous person. How much longer could my heart continue its wild stampede before they had to rush me to the emergency room?

The campus coffee shop pulsed with life, the crowded room ringing with the noisy bustle of students trying to be heard above The Rolling Stones. I couldn't tell if the dull, throbbing sound was my heart or the bass rhythm. I laid claim to a table and two chairs while Jeff ordered our coffee at the counter. I watched him saunter smoothly through the crowd without spilling a drop.

"Here you go, Irish." He set down the cups and lolled in the chair opposite mine, his legs outstretched.

"Why do you keep calling me that?"

"An artist is trained to pay attention to details. I could tell right away by your dark hair and fair skin and that freckled nose of yours that your ancestors are Irish." He traced his finger down the bridge of my nose.

"You couldn't be more wrong," I said, pushing his hand away. "I'm one hundred percent German on my mother's side, and Daddy is pure WASP—Bradford and Biddle."

"Sounds like a law firm," he said with a grin. " 'Bradford & Biddle, Attorneys at Law.' "

"Not even close," I said, laughing. "Daddy is a pediatrician, and he's definitely not Irish. His ancestors date back to before the Revolutionary War. I could join the DAR if I were so inclined—which I'm not."

He shook his head. "Someone must have switched babies at birth. You're pure Irish."

"Well, don't tell that to Daddy, or he'll throw me into the river like a litter of kittens. He thinks the Irish aren't quite human. Trust me, there's no Irish blood in these veins. What nationality are you?"

Jeff sat up straight. "Pure Polack and proud of it. We're one generation off the sausage boat. You ought to see me do the polka." He lifted his coffee cup in a mocking toast as if it were a beer stein, then swallowed a gulp. "My dad was a steelworker until he injured his back—now he's a laid-off steelworker collecting disability pay." He took another swallow and set the cup down. "Hey, got a pen I could borrow?"

I dug around in my purse and produced a pen. He proceeded to sketch a picture of me on his paper place mat. I sipped my coffee and watched him draw, fascinated. He was very good. In a few simple strokes he had my likeness.

"Well, you did say you were an art major."

"Yep, me and Michelangelo. What about you?"

"I'm a lit major who ended up in art class by accident."

He stopped drawing and gazed at me with interest. "Oh? How's that?"

"Well, you know how we have to take either music or art as part of the curriculum? I wanted Introduction to Music, since Daddy always buys season tickets to the symphony and I know a little more about music than art. But by the time I registered, the music courses were all filled."

He leaned so close I could smell the coffee on his breath. "Would you like some private tutoring?" He made the word sound as dangerous as skydiving without a parachute.

"Um . . . no thanks. I'm doing okay, so far."

He flipped the place mat over and reached for my hand.

"What are you doing?"

"Relax, I'm not going to hurt you." His palm was warm and dry and as rough as sandpaper. White paint speckled the backs of his hands. He held my hand in his as if appraising a diamond, then he began to sketch it on the back of the place mat. "You have Irish hands," he told me as he worked.

"Are you deaf, stubborn, or just plain dumb? I already told you, there's not an Irish bone in my body."

He laid down the pen and gripped my hand in both of his, gently massaging all the tiny bones in the back of my hand with his thumbs. "I think I feel a few. . . ." His touch was so sensual that I pulled my hand away in self-defense. I had to get this conversation back to firmer ground.

"So . . . how do you plan to make a living with your art major after you graduate? Accost women on the street and charge them for drawing their portraits on place mats?"

"Who cares about making a living?" he said with a lazy shrug. "I'm not going to get sucked into that middle-class rat race."

"Spoken like a true hippie!" I said, laughing. "Haven't I seen you burning draft cards and protesting the war in Vietnam?"

"Darn right! It's a fictitious, immoral conflict, created by the capitalistic Pentagon establishment to increase the corporate profits of the arms industry. If they try to draft me, I'm moving to Canada. I've already got friends up there."

"Wow! You're the kind of guy who really raises my dad's blood pressure. It would be very entertaining to bring the two of you together for a little chat." I smiled at the thought.

"Geez, you're beautiful!" he said suddenly. He leaned across the table and held my eyes with his smoldering gaze. "Will you let me paint your portrait sometime?"

"Um . . . I guess so. . . ." I don't know how I ever managed to get the words out, since my heart was in my throat and beating like a hummingbird's wings. Something was happening to me that I didn't understand. I remembered watching an experiment in physics class as iron filings blindly paraded to the beat of a magnet, and I felt as powerless as those filings, pulled toward this magnetic man against my will. I didn't understand how or why any more than I had understood the force of magnetism in physics class, but I knew I had to escape from his power while I still could.

"Look at the time!" I said with a gasp. "I'll be late for class!"

"I'll walk with you," Jeff said.

I followed him out of the coffee shop on shaking legs. He didn't see me shove the place mat with his drawings into my sketchbook.

When I checked my campus mailbox the next day, I found an index card with a delicate painting of a monarch butterfly, rendered in pen-and-ink and watercolor. Wicked-looking steel pins held down its wings. Scrawled across the bottom was a note: *Thanks for the coffee.*

———

Two days later, I was eating lunch in the cafeteria with my boyfriend when Jeff plopped down across the table from us with his tray of food. "Hi, guys. What's happening?" He sounded as casual as a lifelong friend. My heart immediately began another idiotic tap dance.

"Um, not much," I said. "Just having lunch with my boyfriend, Bradley Wallace. Brad, this is—"

"Jeff Pulaski. Art major. Born and raised in Pittsburgh." Jeff extended his hand. Today it was speckled with blue paint. He smelled vaguely of mineral spirits and another scent I recognized from the art studio. Brad wrinkled his nose in distaste. He didn't offer his hand in return.

"Don't all you hippie types usually hang out in front of the ROTC building to eat your veggie burgers?"

"Yeah, Brad, but I just found out that I don't need a fraternity jacket to eat in this cafeteria, after all . . . so here I am! Pass the salt, will you, Irish?"

"Do you know this person?" Brad said, turning to me. He sounded as stuffy as my father.

Before I could answer him, Jeff did. "Yeah, we're old friends. She's going to pose for me. We've made all the arrangements."

The subtle lift of Jeff's eyebrows and the sultry tone of his voice had Brad scrambling to his feet, fists clenched. "You want to step outside and say that?" Brad was an honor student, not an athlete. I had seen what Jeff looked like beneath his tattered tie-dyed T-shirt. I knew who would win this contest.

"Lighten up, Brad," I said. "Jeff's just joking around. You know me better than that." I pulled Brad down beside me again and kissed his cheek. "But it's sweet of you to want to defend my honor."

Jeff made a face. "Gag! I'm getting cavities over here!"

"Listen, freak. I don't recall inviting you to join us." Brad's voice was low and menacing.

"Aw . . . having memory problems again, huh, Bradley?" Jeff tilted his head, feigning sympathy. "You haven't been yourself since they put in that steel plate." It took every ounce of willpower I possessed to keep from laughing. I knew Brad would never forgive me if I did.

"Come on, guys, let's all lighten up, okay?" I said, biting my lip.

"Peace, brother!" Jeff made the sign with his fingers. Brad ignored him, concentrating on his lunch. "So what's your major, Bradley? No, wait! . . . Let me guess. You want to be a proctologist, right?"

Thank heaven Brad didn't know what a proctologist was or he would have been on his feet again. "Bradley is going to be a clinical psychologist," I said quickly. Jeff made a face.

"Ouch! You have to wear a suit and tie for that, don't you? You'll never catch me in a suit and tie!"

"Surprise, surprise," Brad said dryly.

"A suit is just an overpriced straitjacket. A tie is a silk noose—"

"Spoken like a true Neanderthal."

Brad used one of Daddy's favorite epithets—Neanderthal. I glanced at Brad in his button-down oxford shirt, khaki slacks, and penny loafers and saw a younger version of my father. The image scared me. Daddy approved of Brad. They understood each other. Daddy wouldn't let someone like Jeff wash his Cadillac. Grandma Emma, on the other hand, would adore Jeff. They were two generations apart but cut from the same mold.

"Bradley, Bradley . . . do I sense some latent hostility here?" Jeff stroked his beard in a mocking imitation of Sigmund Freud. "Do you always color between the lines, Bradley?"

"Do you deliberately avoid the lines?"

"Yes, I find it makes a very striking effect."

Brad pushed his chair back and picked up his tray. "Let's go, Suze."

"Sooze? Oh, Irish! Tell me you're not going to spend the rest of your gorgeous life with a man who calls you Sooze!" I gave Jeff a weak smile and followed Brad out of the cafeteria. Why had I never noticed before how irritating the nickname "Suze" was?

When I opened my mailbox the next morning, I found a picture of a clown that had been torn from a children's coloring book. Jeff had colored it with crayons, completely outside the lines, creating a beautiful, delicately shaded effect that was almost three dimensional. The note read: *Marry me! I promise I will never call you "Sooze" like that other clown.*

My heart not only thumped when I was with Jeff, but now it did its bongodrum imitation whenever I looked at one of his drawings.

I had a date that night with Bradley—a dance at his fraternity house. In his navy blue blazer and frat tie, Brad looked exactly like the other sixty clean-cut, crew-cut guys in his fraternity. They probably all colored between the lines too. The thought depressed me.

Later, when Brad kissed me in his Mustang, I remembered the sensual hand massage Jeff had given me and wondered what it would be like to kiss him. Would his beard feel soft against my cheek or coarse and bristly? I had never noticed it before, but it seemed to me that Bradley kissed like a fish. When he finally broke away, I felt relieved.

"Hello? Anybody home?" he said. "Why do I get the feeling you're a million miles away, Suze?"

"I don't know . . . I have a lot of things on my mind."

"And I don't think I'm one of those things, am I?" He pouted just like my brother, Bobby, did when he didn't get his own way.

I thought of Jeff's butterfly painting, and I felt "pinned." I didn't know what to do. "I'm really sorry . . . but can you take me home, Brad?"

"We have another forty minutes left until curfew!"

"I know. I'll be my old self tomorrow, I promise."

Brad did a slow burn all the way back to the dorm. He didn't get out to open my car door or walk me to the lobby. He didn't even kiss me good-night. The first thing I did when I got to my room was to pull all three of Jeff's drawings off my bulletin board and stash them in my desk drawer. Maybe now I could keep my mind on Brad.

I liked Brad. He was a really cool guy, a member of the coolest fraternity. We'd been dating for almost a year and had even talked about getting married someday. We had a lot of things in common—among them, the desire to pursue careers and join what Jeff called "the middle-class rat race." But my pulse had always stayed normal around Bradley Wallace. Maybe it was because he was as bland and as good for me as oatmeal.

When I came out of art class on Monday afternoon, I found Jeff Pulaski waiting in the hallway for me. "How's it going? Need any tutoring yet?" That dangerous word again.

"Um, no thanks. I'm content with a B."

"Are you sure? I could help you get an A. . . ."

"I'm sure you could," I said, swallowing. What on earth were we talking about? It certainly wasn't art because I couldn't seem to breathe properly. Jeff stood very close, blocking my path.

"Hey, I've got tickets to a Simon and Garfunkel concert next weekend. Come with me."

"Is Bradley invited too?" I asked weakly.

"Who's Bradley?"

"Um, my steady boyfriend . . . I'm pinned, remember?"

"Oh, *that* Bradley. The guy who doesn't own you. The guy who calls you 'Sooze.' "

"Yeah. That's the guy. Thanks for asking though, Jeff. I've got to go."

"Hey, be careful with his fraternity pin, Irish," he called after me. "It can draw blood."

The following weekend, Brad came to the dorm to pick me up for our date. We were going to a reshowing of the movie classic *Dr. Zhivago*. But as I bounded down the stairs from my room to the lobby, the first person I saw was Jeff Pulaski. He had his dark hair untied, and it hung down to his wide shoulders in waves. He casually raked it out of his eyes with one hand, and he looked so good I froze in place, staring open-mouthed.

"Thanks, *Irish*. You look great too," he said with a grin.

"Sorry. Was I that obvious?" I wanted to crawl under the stairs and hide.

"Yeah. But you look far out when you blush like that. That's one thing I really like about Irish girls. They blush very easily."

Before I could reply, a voice behind me said, "Excuse me . . . you're blocking the stairs." I moved aside, and a pretty blonde with hip-huggers and long ironed hair sashayed past me into Jeff's arms. "Ooo, I can hardly wait to hear Simon and Garfunkel!" she purred. I watched them stroll from the building together, Jeff's arm casually draped over her shoulder, her arm circling his waist. I was astonished to discover that I was jealous.

I went to the movies with Brad, and as I watched Dr. Zhivago's dilemma— married to the respectable Tanya but in love with the beautiful Lara—I wasn't sure if my tears were for the Russian doctor or for myself.

———

In the weeks that followed, I grew increasingly discontented with Bradley Wallace. He reminded me more of Daddy every day. Why had I never noticed how arrogant Brad was? Or how easily he assumed that I would always be at his beck and call? I hadn't seen Jeff Pulaski since that night in the dorm, but I couldn't get him out of my mind. As I sat in the library, daydreaming about being tutored by Jeff, Bradley plunked two university catalogues down on the table in front of me.

"I've narrowed my graduate school choices down to these two schools," he said. "What do you think, Suze?"

"You're way ahead of me," I said, leafing through them. "I haven't even ordered any catalogues yet."

"What are you talking about?" From his tone, he might have been addressing a child.

"You know . . . catalogues for graduate schools that have a Masters' program in journalism."

He rolled his eyes. "You're not still serious about grad school, are you, Suze? I thought we talked about getting married after we graduate."

My temper flared like a supernova. "We did. But what does one have to do with the other?"

"Well, if you marry me, what do you need a Masters' degree for?"

I was so outraged, it took a moment before I could speak. "Oh, I get it! You're going to be the daddy and go to graduate school and have a career, and I get to be the mommy and put you through school. Then I get to stay home with the kids! Is that it?"

Brad glanced around the library as if I was embarrassing him. "Shh . . . Why are you getting all riled up, Suze? Don't you want children?"

"This isn't the Dark Ages, where women stay home pregnant and barefoot while the men bring home the bacon. Wake up, Brad! Women have careers too, nowadays."

"I know that. My mother resumed her teaching career after all of us kids were grown."

"Fine! Then why don't you lay aside your career and stay home until all of our children are grown? And if you say 'because I'm the man,' I swear I'll deck you!"

A library aide tiptoed over to our table. "Please lower your voices or I'll have to ask you to leave." I gathered up my books and left, gladly. Brad caught up with me outside.

"I didn't realize you felt this way, Suze."

I whirled to face him. "What way? I feel the same way you do! I'm studying my brains out so I can get into the best graduate school—just like you! I want a career—just like you! Why is that so strange? Because you're a man and I'm a woman?"

"I don't know. I always assumed you were more . . . traditional. That we shared the same conservative values. I didn't know you were some crazy feminist. Next thing I know you'll be running around burning your bras and all that other feminist stuff."

"Well, I'm not 'traditional' according to your definition. I don't plan to be just like our mothers. I have a brain in my head, and I plan to use it. I don't happen to think children and a career are two mutually exclusive options like you do—pick one, you forfeit the other. I want both someday, and I also want a marriage between equals. If that's not what you want, Bradley, then you'd better speak up right now."

That was the end of my relationship with Bradley Wallace. Any tears I shed were tears of profound relief at my narrow escape.

TWENTY-FIVE

There are few secrets on a small college campus. A week after Bradley and I broke up, I found another note from Jeff in my mailbox. This time it was a photograph, torn from a *National Geographic* magazine, of a field filled with hundreds of monarch butterflies. On a patch of blue sky at the top, he had painted another butterfly, soaring freely. The note read, *Congratulations! Meet me on the front steps of the art building at 9:12 tonight. We'll celebrate. Jeff.*

It took me all day to decide whether or not I should meet him. Getting involved with this wild, unpredictable hippie couldn't possibly be good for my cardiovascular system. And if Daddy ever found out I was seeing Jeff, it wouldn't be good for his blood pressure either. In the end, I went. Curiosity compelled me. I sat down on the steps at exactly 9:10, my pulse racing. Two minutes later, I was about to bolt back to my dormitory when I heard the door open behind me.

"Hey, Irish, you're here. Come on, I want to show you something." I followed Jeff through the door and into the art building, certain that I was making a huge mistake. I barely knew this guy. The building was dark and nearly deserted. The last class had ended at nine o'clock.

"Elevator or stairs?" Jeff asked when we reached the lobby. His face betrayed no clue to what he had in mind.

"Um, elevator." My knees were too shaky for stairs. We stepped inside and the elevator doors slid closed. We were alone. My stomach gave a small lurch as we began to ascend.

"So . . . too bad about old Bradley the proctologist," Jeff said with a grin.

"That's *psychologist*," I said, "and I'm not sorry in the least. Do you mind telling me where we're going?"

"You'll see. What time is it?" He reached for my arm, peered at my wristwatch, then dropped my arm again. "Oh, good. There's time." He might have been a human generator, for the amount of electric current that raced through my body at his touch. I wondered if my hair was standing on end.

We got out of the elevator on the top floor, and he led the way to a closed steel door. It took him a moment to wiggle a key out of the pocket of his jeans and unlock it. It opened to a flight of stairs.

"After you," he said with a small bow. I didn't move.

"Where are you taking me?"

"Up to the roof."

"Are you crazy?"

He furrowed his brow, pondering the question for a moment in mock seriousness. "I don't think so. Why, are you?"

"I must be." I sighed and climbed the inky stairwell to a trapdoor that opened onto the flat roof.

Jeff climbed up behind me, then closed the door. Above our heads was an unhindered view of a trillion stars.

"Wow! That's incredible!" I breathed.

"Oh, that's not the best part. The show hasn't even begun yet." He led me around to the other side of the building, where the view looked out over the rolling Pennsylvania countryside instead of the college town. We sat side by side, our backs against an air conditioning unit, and gazed at a row of hills in the distance. He made no move to touch me. Only our shoulders brushed slightly.

Slowly, magnificently, a full moon began to rise above the hills. It looked enormous near the horizon, and nearly as luminous as the sun. I could scarcely breathe from the sheer beauty of it, and the exquisite intimacy of sharing the experience in silence with Jeff Pulaski. I turned to face him, waiting for his kiss. He looked into my eyes and smiled. We were close enough to kiss, but he didn't move.

"Thanks for the show," I whispered.

"You're welcome."

When I couldn't stand waiting a moment longer I asked, "Aren't you going to kiss me?"

He shook his head. "No."

"Why not?"

His lips were just inches from mine and I could feel his breath on my face when he spoke. "When I was a little kid," he said slowly, "whenever someone gave me a piece of cake, I would always peel off all the icing first . . . very carefully . . . so it all came off in one layer." He held an imaginary slice of cake in one hand and peeled imaginary icing off of it with the other hand. "Then I would eat just the cake . . . saving the sweetest part, the best part,

for last. Tonight I'm still eating my cake. . . . I want to save the icing for last."
He brushed my cheek with his fingers, then licked them. I shivered.

"That's the most romantic thing anyone has ever said to me. And from a
hippie, no less." I barely restrained myself from kissing him.

When the moon was high above the horizon and ordinary-looking once
again, Jeff walked me back to my dormitory. I saw other couples in the shadows in front of the building kissing good-night. But Jeff reached for the door,
not for me, and held it open.

"See you around, okay?" I watched through the window as he sauntered
away, hands in his pockets.

Another drawing appeared in my mailbox the next day, this time done in
pastel chalk on a piece of lined notebook paper. It was a slice of yellow cake
with a single bite out of it—the thick pink icing was still intact.

"Why me, Jeff?" I asked when I found him waiting for me outside my art
class that afternoon.

"Why you what?"

"Why are you standing here waiting for *me* instead of one of the hundreds
of other girls on this campus?" He fell into step beside me as I walked to my
next class.

"You mean aside from your classic Irish beauty?" I waved the comment
away with a shake of my head. Jeff suddenly turned serious. "I don't know
. . . but ever since that first time we had coffee together, there has been a weird,
metaphysical, chemical sort of thing going on between us . . . have you noticed?"

"Yes, I have," I said, recalling his electrifying touch.

"Did you ever feel anything like it before?"

"No. Have you?"

"No. I've dated a lot of women, but this is new. This is . . . this is terrifying!" He grinned when he said the word and his eyes held mine. "It makes
being with you so much fun."

"Feeling terrified is *fun*?"

"Yeah, haven't you noticed?"

We walked down the steps of the art building, and as I recalled the fear
and the excitement I'd felt last night waiting for him, I knew exactly what he
meant. I wondered why I'd been content to play it safe all my life.

"And I also have to say that I find you very wholesome," Jeff continued.

"Thanks a lot."

"That was a compliment. See, this campus is like a huge Hostess Baking

Company." He gestured to all the buildings and scurrying students as we walked down the sidewalk. "Some girls are Twinkies. You know, pretty on the outside, fluff on the inside. Ten minutes later you're hungry again. You're a Wonder Bread woman. Wonder Bread looks good on the outside, too, all white and fluffy, but it's fortified with essential vitamins and nutrients. Wholesome. 'Wonder helps build strong bodies twelve ways.' You've got a brain and a mind that you put to good use."

"How do you know?"

"I saw your name on the dean's list. What do you want to be when you grow up?"

I laughed. "I'm a literature major. I want to get my Masters' in journalism."

"Go for it! But can I ask you a question? I notice you always wear a cross around your neck. Does it mean something or is it just a decoration?"

I pondered it for a moment, sensing that Jeff wouldn't be content with a careless answer. "It means something. I've discovered that the things that happen in my life make a lot more sense when I include God in the picture. It's like trying to work a jigsaw puzzle without the picture on the front of the box. You can do it, but the task of putting thousands of tiny pieces together will sure go easier and make a lot more sense if you can take a peek at the bigger picture now and then."

I stopped walking and pulled Jeff to a stop beside me as a thought suddenly occurred to me. "Is there a reason why you asked—or is it because you're an artist, trained to notice the details?"

"I'm a Christian too," he said quietly. "I wasn't raised in the church, so I'm a brand-new believer. I have a lot of catching up to do."

"So how did you end up deciding to be a Christian?"

"When I started studying art, I saw the whole story of Christ spelled out for me in the great masterworks. They were paintings of incredible passion and beauty and devotion. I was curious. I wanted to know what all these great artists knew that I didn't know. What inspired them to paint like they did? Who inspired them? I guess you could say I came to faith in Christ through the art museum door. You would probably find my beliefs very unorthodox."

"I'd love to hear about them."

He stared down at his tattered sandals, suddenly shy. "Well, I'm much better with visual explanations than with words."

"So I noticed." When he gave me a questioning look I said, "All the pictures you've sent me. They speak volumes."

"Yeah? Well, listen, why don't you come to New York with me this weekend? I'll take you to the Met and the Guggenheim . . . I'll show you what I believe."

"New York is awfully far away. Can we make it back to the dorm by curfew?"

"Probably not. Just sign out overnight. I have a friend in the Village we can stay with."

My heart began racing out of control at the suggestion. I felt the warring conflict of attraction and fear that Jeff had mentioned. "I'll have to pass," I finally said. "It sounds much too dangerous."

"Come on, Goody-Two-Shoes. What are you worried about? Afraid I might take advantage of you?"

"No, of course not."

I was afraid I might let him.

———

We went to New York two weeks later in Jeff's yellow Volkswagen Beetle. The car had no heater, but it did have rust spots that resembled terminal leprosy and a peace symbol spray-painted on the hood with black paint. I had never spent an entire day in an art museum before, but with Jeff as my guide, the day flew. He took my hand for the first time as we climbed the stairs to the Metropolitan Museum of Art, and like the opposite poles of two powerful magnets, we didn't come unstuck for the rest of the day. He draped his arm around my shoulder as we sat on a bench to study a painting by Rembrandt. He circled my waist as we strolled through the corridors to the Impressionist gallery. And once, when a Van Gogh moved him to silent awe, he clenched my hand tightly between both of his.

As he led me from room to room, explaining the paintings, comparing one to another, I saw Christ portrayed as clearly as in any sermon. Jeff showed me how he had come to faith. Using masterpieces instead of the Bible, he showed me what he believed. His spiritual insight staggered me.

"That's what I want to do," he said. "Show Christ to the world, whether it's a picture of Jesus or not."

"How can you do that?"

"Come here, I'll show you." He pulled me back to the gallery we had just left and pointed to a canvas. "See this picture? It's not a religious theme, but can you tell what the artist's world view is? Life makes sense; there's order and beauty. God is in control." He dragged me by the hand to a gallery across the corridor. "Now compare it to this painting. See? There's no hope. Only death and darkness and destruction."

"I get it! Now I understand!"

"Yeah, I can almost see the little light bulb switching on above your head."

"I want to do that too, Jeff. I want to proclaim Christ in my writing, even if it's not about religion. I want to say, 'God is in heaven, the world is under His sovereign control.' "

" 'I will sing your praises among the nations,' " Jeff quoted, " 'Your kindness and love are as vast as the heavens. Your faithfulness is higher than the skies.' "

By the end of the day, I had fallen hopelessly in love with Jeff Pulaski.

———

"This is the rattiest hole-in-the-wall I've ever seen in my life," I whispered to Jeff when I saw his friend's apartment in Greenwich Village. "If Daddy could see this place, he would call in the Board of Health to light a match to it—right after he recovered from his massive coronary, that is."

"I've seen worse."

"Are you bragging or complaining, Mr. Pulaski?"

"Just stating the facts, ma'am."

The door to the apartment had been unlocked. Jeff led me inside without bothering to knock. The only furnishings in the barren living room were a sofa with the stuffing falling out, a coffee table with surgical tape around one broken leg, a shadeless floor lamp, and a giant hookah with four smoking pipes. There were no curtains over the windows, no rug on the plank floor, no pictures on the gouged plaster walls. Two hippies sat on a bare mattress on the bedroom floor smoking pot. I couldn't tell through the bluish haze if they were male or female. The music of Jefferson Airplane blasted from an undisclosed source.

"Jeff, I don't think—"

"Don't worry. I don't do drugs. And I assume that you don't either." He closed the bedroom door to contain the smoke and muffle the sound.

"If you don't, then why do you hang out with friends who do?"

He grinned. "Gee, do you think Bradley and all his frat brothers would let me hang out with them?"

"Hardly. Which one is your friend who rents this place?"

"He won't be here tonight." Jeff opened a scarred door off the kitchen and gestured inside. "Here's the bathroom. It's free at the moment if you want to wash up or brush your teeth or something."

We had stopped to eat a pizza after the museum closed, then walked around Greenwich Village for a few hours, people-watching. Now it was nearly midnight, and we were both tired. I dug my toothbrush out of my cosmetic bag and went inside. The bathroom made me gag. The toilet had no seat and the sink dribbled a continuous stream of rusty water. I saw a cockroach slither into the shower drain and retreated to the living room.

"Jeff, I can afford a hotel, you know."

"I can't."

"Are you too stubborn and old-fashioned to let a woman pay for your room?"

"Not at all," he said with a shrug. "I'll drive you to a hotel if you want, but don't waste money on a room for me. This place is fine. I've stayed here before and lived to tell about it." He began hopping from one foot to the other and scratching himself as if he'd contracted a bad case of fleas or scabies. I laughed.

"Do you think I'm being spoiled and squeamish?" I asked.

He rested his hand on my shoulder. "Don't ever apologize for who you are or the way you were raised. Your father is a doctor—that's great. I don't think any less of you because you haven't experienced poverty before. Everyone's different. That's what makes life so much fun." We looked at each other for a long moment. I loved looking at him. I didn't want him out of my sight. And I still wondered what his beard would feel like when we finally kissed.

"So where do I sleep?" I asked with a sigh of resignation.

"You staying?"

"Why not."

"Good. You get the couch, I get the floor." He had brought two sleeping bags with him from the car. I watched him unroll one on the sofa, then spread the other one on the floor right below it. The thought of sleeping so close to Jeff made my heart hammer.

"Okay?" he asked when he was finished.

I gave him two thumbs up. "First-class."

Jeff switched off the living room lamp. The sparkling lights of the city shone through the bare windows like stars. I kicked off my shoes and bent to unzip the bag.

"Wait. Don't get in yet," he said.

I turned and Jeff pulled me toward him, all the way into his arms. He held me tightly against his chest for the first time. I pressed my face against the hard muscles of his shoulder. He had to be able to feel my heart pounding against his ribs. I couldn't seem to catch my breath, but Jeff gave a slow, contented sigh.

Then we separated and he held my face in his hands, drinking me in with his eyes. At last he slowly bent to kiss me. He was tender at first, but his kiss slowly built in passion until I couldn't seem to think straight. When our lips parted again we were both breathless. He rested his cheek against mine, and I felt the brush of his beard—soft and silky, not wiry.

"See?" he whispered. "The icing always tastes sweeter when you wait for it."

With that, he flopped down on the floor and crawled into his sleeping bag. I was left standing beside the couch, wobbly kneed, stunned.

I heard his voice below me a few moments later. "Wow! That's really far out! I never knew that Irish girls sleep standing up like horses."

I collapsed onto the sofa, laughing. "You crazy hippie! I've told you a thousand times I'm not Irish!"

"Sorry, I keep forgetting. Good night, Irish."

———

By the time the school year ended eight months later, Jeff and I were deeply in love. "I don't know how I can live all summer without your kisses," he said, "I'm addicted to them." We sat on the roof of the art building beneath a pale quarter moon, saying good-bye for the next three months. Jeff was covering my face with kisses as if trying to kiss each individual freckle. Tomorrow I would go home, and he would return to his usual summer job in Pittsburgh, framing houses for his uncle's construction company.

"That explains where your Greek-god muscles came from," I said when he told me about his job.

"Let me drive you home, and we can be together one day longer," he pleaded.

"Trust me, you don't want to meet my father."

Jeff stopped kissing to gaze at me. I saw the hurt in his eyes as he asked, "Are you ashamed of me?"

"No! Oh no, Jeff, not in the least! I'm trying to spare you! Daddy will skewer you alive. He hates hippies. Bradley Wallace was his idea of a perfect boyfriend . . . get the picture?" I twined my fingers in his long wavy hair and pulled him close for another kiss.

"I don't care what your father thinks of me," Jeff said when we came up for air. "But if I'm going to spend the rest of my life with you, I need to meet him someday."

For a moment, my heart felt as though it had stopped beating. "What did you say?"

"I said, if I'm going to spend—"

"Jeff Pulaski! Are you proposing to me?"

"It's not a proposal, it's a matter of life and death. I can't live without you. I never felt this way about anyone before, and I pray to God that I never do again. It hurts. I love you so much it hurts."

"You wonderful, crazy hippie! Why do you always say things that make me cry?" I clung to him, my tears soaking his T-shirt.

"I don't have a fraternity pin, and I can't afford an engagement ring, but I'll give you my peace necklace, if you want it . . . to seal our engagement."

"I love you, Jeff Pulaski." I kissed him. "I don't need an engagement ring." I kissed him again. "Fraternity pins draw blood . . ." I kissed him a third time. ". . . and your necklace looks much better on you than it would on me."

"So does that mean you'll let me drive you home and meet your family?"

"You'll be sorry!" I said, laughing. "And you'll also see that there's not an Irishman in the bunch!"

I tried to warn my parents as well as Jeff on what to expect, but after that, all I could do was sit back and wait. It was like watching a storm cloud approach, knowing there would be thunder and lightning and hail, but I was helpless to do anything about it except hunker down and wait.

My father's first words when he opened the front door and saw Jeff were, "Oh, good grief!" Daddy turned and strode into the house, but the expression on his face had said it all—disgust, disapproval, disdain.

"Daddy! How can you be so rude!" I said, storming into the house behind him.

"I'm not rude, he's rude. If a young man is going to meet a girl's parents for the first time, he should have the decency to dress up a little, out of respect for her, if not for her parents."

"Actually, I did dress up," Jeff said cheerfully. He had followed Daddy and me through the entrance hall and into the living room. "This is the nicest set of clothes I own, Dr. Bradford. The cleanest too. You see, my parents can't afford to outfit me at Saks Fifth Avenue like you folks, but lucky for me, the hippie look is in style."

"I suppose you can't afford a haircut, either?" Daddy said scornfully.

"No, sir. I can't."

Daddy pulled his wallet out of his pocket. "If I give you twenty bucks, would you go get a shave and a haircut?"

"Sure!" Jeff plucked the twenty-dollar bill out of Daddy's hand, folding it neatly. "Thanks. But I should warn you, sir . . . my hair will only grow back again."

I pulled the money away from him and stuffed it into the pocket of my father's blazer. "Don't listen to him, Jeff. I like your hair the way it is."

"So do I!" Grandma Emma strolled in from the kitchen. "I think he's a very handsome young fellow. Sort of a psychedelic Samson, wouldn't you say?" Jeff took her hand and bent to kiss it.

"Thank you, ma'am. I can see where Suzanne gets her beauty from—and her good taste."

Grandma was still laughing when my mother joined us. Mom was polite throughout the introductions, but I caught the look of dismay that crossed her face when she first saw Jeff. Unlike Daddy, who would try to intimidate Jeff into breaking up with me, Mom's solution to every crisis was to pray. I could already imagine her fervent, silent pleas to the Almighty that I would come to my senses quickly.

Jeff's final ordeal was meeting my brother, Bobby, who was home for the summer from his first year of medical school. Bobby and Jeff got along about as well as Jeff and my old boyfriend Bradley Wallace had—Jeff was mocking, Bobby scornful.

When Daddy announced that he was taking us all to dinner at the country club that evening, I was furious. "You're deliberately trying to embarrass Jeff! You know he's not allowed to eat there without a jacket!"

Jeff rested his hand on my shoulder to soothe me. "It's okay. I have a jacket in the car." He wore such a mischievous grin on his face that I knew he was up to something. I watched helplessly as the storm clouds built in strength.

When Jeff finally emerged from my brother's room, dressed for dinner, he looked like one of the Beatles on the cover of *Sgt. Pepper's Lonely Hearts Club Band*. Grandma applauded.

"Well done, young man!" she said. "You remind me of the bandleader at the Chautauqua when I was a little girl. He wore a white jacket with gold braid and epaulets, just like that one."

"It probably is his jacket," Jeff said, laughing. "I bought it at a second-hand store."

Mom said nothing, but her smile was tense and strained. Daddy shook his head and muttered, "Good grief!"

"If you're embarrassed, Daddy, you get what you deserve for trying to embarrass Jeff," I said. I saw his angry, tight-lipped frown and added to myself that it would also serve him right if his blood pressure soared right off the Richter scale.

Robert looked around at all of us and said, "If you don't mind, I think I'll skip the family circus and go out with my own friends tonight."

"We'll follow you in Jeff's car," I said as everyone else slid into Daddy's Cadillac. I wanted a few moments alone with him. "I'm so sorry for putting you through this, Jeff," I said as I huddled beside him in the Volkswagen. "This is even worse than I imagined it would be. I never knew my family could be so . . . so rude!"

"It's because they love you very much," he said patiently, "and they're doing their best to get you to see me the way they see me. I'm a rebel, a good-for-nothing hippie, and a dangerous threat to their way of life. They didn't raise you to marry someone like me."

"You know what terrifies me, Jeff? That you'll start seeing me as a reflection of them and you'll bolt for home like a greyhound."

He shook his head, smiling. "That won't happen. I know the real you. I know your heart. The woman I love grew up with them, but she isn't them."

"I apologize for my father—"

"Don't. He can't help who he is. If you had grown up in his shoes, you might be him too. By the way, I love your grandmother."

"Arrgh! I feel like I'm walking a tightrope! Is it going to be this horrible when I meet your parents?"

"Oh no. Of course not. It will be much worse."

"I hope you're kidding."

His grin faded. "I wish I were. You want to know what will happen with my family? Before they ever meet you, they'll build a wall a mile high that you'll never get past. They'll think you're putting on airs because you have a big vocabulary, and they'll think you're snobbish because you have manners, and they'll think that *you* think you're better than them because you're a rich doctor's daughter and they're uneducated Polacks. They'll never let you get close to them. They'll never consider you part of the family, because no matter how hard you try, you won't ever be like them. That's not your fault or theirs. It's just the way it is." He wrestled with the Volkswagen's stubborn stick shift as we pulled into the parking lot behind Daddy.

"I wish we could go back to college and forget we have families," I said.

"No, this is good for us. If we can survive this, we can survive anything."

I looked up at the glittering country club. It seemed symbolic of Daddy's life—and everything that Jeff and his fellow hippies renounced. "I'm really sorry about this country club ordeal, Jeff. I never imagined . . ."

"Sorry? Are you kidding? I'm having the time of my life! I've never been inside a country club before—much less dined in one with a beautiful, rich woman. I hope your father brought his wallet because I'm going to order prime rib. Maybe lobster too. This is going to be fun."

I walked into the country club on Jeff's arm and watched heads turn. If he hadn't been with my parents, the manager probably would have tossed Jeff out. When the menus came, I watched him order the most expensive item in each category, from shrimp cocktail and French onion soup to baked Alaska. He was right, it was fun—until Daddy mentioned Vietnam, that is.

"I suppose you're one of those radicals who go around protesting the Vietnam conflict?" he said as he cut into his medium-rare T-bone steak.

"Yes, sir. In fact, I took part in the demonstration at the Pentagon last year."

"You young people have had everything handed to you all your life, and now you want your rights as Americans without any of the responsibilities," Daddy said, waving his steak knife. "When your country asks you to do your duty in Vietnam you say, 'Make Love, Not War.' I never heard that attitude during World War II. I lost friends in that war, but my generation cared enough about democracy to fight for it."

"There are dozens of differences between Vietnam and the Second World War, Dr. Bradford." Jeff's tone was serious, yet polite. I held my breath as if watching him skate across thin ice. "For one thing, the average age of our fighting men in the Second World War was twenty-six; the boys dying in 'Nam are nineteen—too young to vote, but old enough to die in a rice paddy. There are no clear combat zones in Vietnam, no objectives, no fronts. Your generation knew what you were fighting for—or against. This war is none of America's business."

"You probably would have thought it was none of America's business to stop Hitler because he was across the ocean invading Poland and Czechoslovakia!" When Daddy raised his voice a notch, Jeff raised his to match it.

"The United States voted to declare war after Japan invaded us. That was clear aggression on Japan's part. America is the aggressor in this case. Besides, Congress never voted to declare war in Vietnam, and that makes it unconstitutional. Your ancestors during the American Revolution protested taxation without representation—boys are being drafted to fight an immoral war without representation!"

Daddy scooped his napkin off his lap and threw it onto the table like a gauntlet. "Congress voted to pass the Gulf of Tonkin Resolution—"

"Yes, because a U.S. ship was attacked. But what was an American warship doing in Vietnamese waters to begin with? I'll tell you, sir! It was sent there by our imperialistic government. It's another chapter in our long, sordid history of exploiting poor countries for America's economic benefit. There is no other goal—"

"There are very clear goals," Daddy interrupted, waving his forefinger. Our waiter scurried over in response, then quickly fled again when he heard Daddy's angry words, fired like missiles at Jeff. "The Communists are the ones who expanded the Cold War into that part of the world, not us. If we lose Vietnam to the Communists, we'll lose all the other nations in southeast Asia to them."

"The so-called Domino Theory is a bunch of baloney. The Vietnamese people should be allowed to decide for themselves which form of government they want, not be dictated to by the U.S. military." I had my hand on Jeff's arm, trying to hold him back, while Mom tried in vain to restrain Daddy. They ignored both of us.

"You realize, of course, that your protests are actually helping the enemy. North Vietnam would have surrendered by now if all you radicals weren't giving them hope that America will pull out. And by helping the Hanoi government, you're fighting against our own American soldiers."

"I'm trying to end the war so more soldiers won't have to die! What about all those American kids who have already died—for what! We have nothing to show for it!"

"It's your protests that are prolonging it. You're the reason men are dying." Mom eyed Daddy's scarlet face with concern. If she'd had a blood pressure cuff in her purse, she would have pulled it out and clamped it to his arm. "You and your radical groups like the SDS are taking over college campuses, disrupting education—you want to tear the government down, but you don't have a clue what you're going to replace it with."

"I'm not trying to overthrow the government. I'm protesting to end the draft and end the Vietnam war!"

"And what if you don't get your way, young man? What then? What if they draft you?"

"I have no quarrel with the Vietnamese people," Jeff said, suddenly quiet.

"They aren't threatening me or my country. I could never aim a gun at them and kill them. If the government drafts me to fight in this immoral war, I'll move to Canada."

"A draft dodger? How can you be so cowardly and irresponsible?" People at the other tables had begun glancing our way. Mom and I watched, paralyzed, not knowing how to stop the argument. In the end, it was Grandma Emma who quietly ended the melee.

"You know, Stephen, my father was a draft dodger." Daddy and Jeff both turned to stare at her. "It's true," she said, laughing. "Don't look so shocked. That's how my family came to America. The German government changed the draft laws in the 1890s, making Papa eligible for conscription. War was against his religious principles, so when he got his draft notice, he felt he had no other choice but to defy the government and leave the country. He crossed the border into Switzerland illegally, just like these young men who flock to Canada are doing. Papa wasn't cowardly or irresponsible. What he did was no different from what young Jeffrey plans to do. And in the end, everything worked out for the best. I was born in America because of Papa's decision, and so was your wife, Stephen. Isn't it funny how history repeats itself?" She smiled sweetly, then patted Daddy's hand, now resting limply on the white linen tablecloth. "Do you suppose, Stephen dear, that you could find our waiter? I'd love to order some dessert."

Early the next morning, Jeff left for Pittsburgh. We said a somber goodbye, not only because we would miss each other, but because the morning news had reported the assassination of Bobby Kennedy. With so much turmoil going on in the world around us, I wondered if Jeff and I would ever get a chance to live "happily ever after."

My parents now had all summer to convince me that Jeff was a loser. They didn't waste any time. The first assault began at breakfast.

"You can do better, Suzanne," Daddy said. "Why shortchange yourself? How is he ever going to earn a living as an artist? Or is he planning to let you support him?"

"Mom *lets* you support her," I said. "What's the difference? I love Jeff. I'd be glad to support him."

"What is Jeff's religious upbringing?" Mom asked. "I don't recall him mentioning which denomination he belongs to."

"If he's Polish, his people are probably Roman Catholic," Daddy said.

I knew there was no way to explain Jeff's beliefs. It had required a trip to New York and a full day at the art museum before I understood them myself. "Jeff is a Christian," I said. "But he isn't into denominational labels, and neither am I."

Mom winced as if I'd pinched a painful nerve. "Suzanne, try to understand why your father and I are concerned about you. Your young man seems to have had a very strong influence on you already, and—"

"And we don't want to see you throw your life away!" Daddy gathered up his keys and wallet, preparing to leave for his hospital rounds. "It would be a terrible waste for you to leave your home and your family to follow some vagabond hippie to Canada."

Once again, Grandma jumped into the fray, this time saving me from losing my temper. "You know, it's interesting that you would feel that way, Stephen. My mother's parents told her she *had* to leave Germany and follow Papa to America. They said her place was with her husband."

"Jeff isn't her husband." Daddy may as well have added, *and that's final!*

"He will be my husband someday," I said. "Jeff asked me to marry him and I said yes." That earned a big hug from Grandma, looks of stunned shock from my parents.

Daddy's parting words as he stormed out of the door were, "If you marry Michelangelo Pulaski, you can forget about receiving any financial support from me for graduate school!"

When it was time for Grandma to return to her apartment in the city, she asked me to drive her home. "I don't get to see Suzanne very often now that she's away at college," she told Mom. "This will give us some time together."

When we were alone in the car, I thanked her. "At least I can escape the anti-Jeff campaign for a little while."

"You two are very much in love, aren't you?" she said.

"Is it that obvious?"

"Oh yes. Every time he looks at you, it's like he's memorizing you, like it may be the last time he'll ever see you. Whenever he's near you he just has to touch your hand, your shoulder, your face . . ."

"Daddy says he's always pawing me."

Grandma laughed. "I think it's more like he's grounding himself. Otherwise, the electric current that arcs between the two of you might kill somebody. And you look as though you want to eat him for dessert! Have you slept together yet?"

"Grandma!" I nearly steered the car off the road.

"Sorry, I say outrageous things sometimes. You don't have to answer."

"It's okay," I said when I could speak. "We haven't slept together. Jeff feels very strongly about waiting, and so do I."

"I'm proud of you both, dear. You won't be sorry you waited."

"The funny thing is, Bradley Wallace—whom Daddy adored—was always trying to get me to give in."

"Was Bradley that last fellow you brought home?"

"Yes, the guy with the crew cut like Daddy's."

"Ugh! Good riddance to him! He reminded me of my husband, Karl." She shuddered. I thought of how close I had come to spending my life with Brad and I shuddered too.

"Mom and Dad don't have a clue what Jeff is really like," I said after we'd driven in silence for a while. "They just see the outside, how different he is from them. They see a hippie, and they've already made up their minds to hate him. I never dreamed they would be so bigoted. But I'm in love with him, Grandma. I've never really loved anyone before. Jeff is so . . . he's so *alive*! I'm different when I'm with him. I'm more real, more *me*. He's made me see life from a totally different perspective and think about things I've never thought about before. I'm more creative when I'm with him. Even my professors have noticed the difference. Every story or poem I've written since meeting Jeff has been better than anything I've ever done before. I love him, Grandma. Mom and Dad just can't accept that."

"Don't let them break you apart, Suzy!" I had never heard my grandmother speak so vehemently. When I took my eyes off the highway to glance at her, I saw tears in her eyes. "Whatever you do, don't let them break you apart!"

"Grandma—?"

"I never told your mother what I'm about to tell you, Suzanne, but I went through the same thing you're experiencing. Before I married Karl Bauer, I fell in love with a man my father disapproved of. Patrick's family was against me as well. If we had married, both sides would have disowned us. In the end, we decided to part. It was a horrible choice to have to make. Patrick was the only man I've ever loved. Don't make the same mistake we did, Suzy. If you love Jeff, then marry him."

I gazed at my grandmother in amazement. "I can't believe you're telling me to defy my parents."

"I am. Because they're wrong. I'll do everything in my power to help you and Jeff. I don't have much money, but you're welcome to all that I have. I'll co-sign a loan for your schooling if you need one, but get married, Suzanne.

Move to Canada with Jeff if he goes. The rest of your family might disown you, but you'll always have me."

"You would really do all that for us, Grandma?"

"Absolutely!" I saw the determined set of her jaw and knew she meant it. Then her face suddenly softened. "You know, Jeff reminds me so much of Patrick. Your love for each other is like ours was. Promise me you won't allow anyone to break you apart." Her voice broke, and I saw her swipe at a tear.

"I promise."

"Because if I can just convince you and Jeff not to make the same mistake we did," she wiped another tear, "then it's almost as though Patrick and I will have a second chance."

"I'm going to the Democratic National Convention in Chicago," Jeff told me in August when we talked on the phone. "We're going to demonstrate against the Vietnam War."

I tried in vain to talk him out of it. "Jeff, Mayor Daley is not only putting the entire police force on alert, he's even calling in five thousand National Guard troops!"

"That's all those bureaucrats know—intimidation and force!" I held the receiver away from my ear as he shouted into the phone.

"Jeff, please don't go. I don't want anything to happen to you. I love you."

"I love you too, but the war is wrong."

"Jeff, listen. . . ."

"I'm sorry, but I have to go there and let my voice be heard."

When riots broke out in Chicago, I watched the violence on TV, horrified, knowing that Jeff was somewhere in the middle of it all. As the number of arrests and injuries soared, I could only pray that Jeff wasn't among them. When he finally called to tell me he was okay, that he wasn't in the hospital or jail, I wept.

"I can't even begin to describe what happened there . . . what I saw . . ." Jeff's voice was subdued, but I sensed his anger boiling beneath the surface, waiting to explode. I knew he had to release it somehow, but I dreaded the thought of him attending another protest. Instead, Jeff poured all the passion and horror of his experience in Chicago into a painting he entitled *Protest*.

I sat behind him in a corner of the art studio that fall and watched him create. Sweat poured off him, mingling with the paint that spattered him from head to toe. Music blasted in the background as he worked. When the time came for me to return to my dormitory, Jeff continued working late into the night.

I saw the genius of his creation and stood in awe of his talent. No one who saw *Protest* was surprised when it won first place in a national art contest to depict the turmoil of the times. Art galleries all across America displayed Jeff's painting as it traveled on a nationwide tour. When Daddy read an article about it in *Time* magazine, his attitude toward Jeff softened—slightly.

"I really hadn't thought much about Vietnam until I met you," I told Jeff as we ate lunch together in the cafeteria.

"You didn't?"

"No, I was much too preoccupied with my own selfish concerns and ambitions. But now I'd like my voice to be heard too."

"You're a writer—write something!"

" 'The pen is mightier than the sword' and all that?"

"Maybe so. Try it."

As we talked, one of Jeff's hippie friends, a shaggy fellow named Moon-dog, came over to our table. "Hey, Jeff. You're going to the Vietnam Moratorium next week, right? Think I can bum a ride?" Jeff glanced at me guiltily. Moon-dog caught the tension he'd suddenly created between us and backed away. "Right. Talk to you later, Jeff."

"What was he talking about?" I asked as he hurried off.

"The Vietnam Moratorium? It's a national day of protest. They're calling for demonstrations and work stoppages. . . ."

"I'm going with you," I said.

"I know what happened in Chicago," Jeff said. "It's too dangerous. You're not going with me!"

"Don't you dare tell me what to do, Jeff Pulaski! If it's too dangerous for me, then it's too dangerous for you. You're not going either."

He scrambled to his feet to glare down at me. "Like blazes I'm not! I've already made plans!"

I stood too. We faced each other eye to eye in spite of the fact that he was six inches taller than me. "Then you'd better include me in those plans because I'm going—with or without you!"

In the end, Jeff and I went to the demonstration together. October 15, 1969, turned out to be a gorgeous fall day, the leaves at their peak of color. "If it weren't for this rotten war, I'd be painting a whole different scene," Jeff said as we rode in his Volkswagen to the nearby state university campus for the moratorium.

"True, but there isn't much drama in a bunch of dead leaves," I said. He gave me a wry grin.

We arrived with swarms of other students and followed the crowd to the mall in front of the administration building. The students had erected thousands of white wooden crosses all over campus to represent the American casualties. When I saw them, the war struck home for me with full force.

"Jeff, those soldiers were our age. They'll never have a chance to fall in love and get married and have careers like we will."

"I know. That's why I have to fight to end this war—before any more of them die." He squeezed my hand, and I knew he felt the same impotent rage that I did.

The anti-war rally began peacefully as, one after another, various speakers ascended the platform to address the crowd. Jeff and I pushed our way toward the front. "I have a little surprise for you," he said when we reached the platform. "As the prizewinning artist of *Protest*, I've been invited to say a few words."

"Jeff! I'm so proud of you."

"Wait right here until I'm done, okay?"

I beamed like a searchlight out in the audience while Jeff spoke. He briefly described the experiences in Chicago that had produced his painting, then spoke eloquently about recognizing the God-given dignity in our fellow man. "All men are made in God's image," he said. "That includes policemen and the Vietcong, as well as our own American soldiers. Only after we lay down our weapons and end this war will we truly obey Christ's command to love our enemies." The cheers were deafening.

"Were you nervous?" I asked after congratulating him with a kiss. He had climbed down from the platform again.

"I was petrified."

"You didn't seem to be." In fact, while he should have been limp with relief, Jeff seemed more tense now than before he'd spoken. "What's wrong?"

"Listen, Suzanne, we have to get out of here. Now." His voice was an urgent whisper, but the fact that he called me by my given name conveyed even more than his tone. "There's going to be trouble."

"Jeff, wait . . . how. . . ?"

"There isn't time to indulge your Irish temper. Do you trust me?"

"Of course."

"Then hang on to my arm and follow me. Don't let go, no matter what." He towed me through the mob, heading back across the mall the way we'd come a few hours ago. During that time, the crowd had swelled from thousands to tens of thousands, and now they were all tightly packed into the open area between the buildings, unable to move. There was nowhere for Jeff and me to go, and people didn't like us pushing against the flow to force our way through. I felt deliberate, painful elbow blows to my ribs and knew that Jeff was suffering even more in front of me. I fought a wave of claustrophobia as I tried not to panic.

"Jeff, wait—this is crazy. We'll never get through."

He turned around to face me, panting from exertion. He pulled me into his arms and whispered in my ear. "Suzanne, listen. When I was on the platform waiting for my turn, I overheard the student leaders talking. They have an agenda, and it isn't Vietnam. They're going to use the momentum of the crowd to storm the administration building and take over the university."

"Oh, Jeff."

"The campus police have called for outside help. I saw the state troopers arrive while I was speaking. They're wearing riot gear and gas masks. That means tear gas. But that isn't all—there's another mob of students in the parking lot behind the police lines. They're arming themselves with stones."

"Go ahead and say it, Jeff."

"Say what?"

" 'I told you so.' "

He smiled in spite of himself and shook his head. "Stubborn, pigheaded Irishwoman! Come on."

He plowed forward again like a ship through a turbulent sea. There seemed no end to the people. Jeff edged toward the safety of the buildings on one side, away from the center of the mob. Behind us the Students for a Democratic Society leader, who controlled the microphone, spewed out a tirade of recrimination against the college administration. The answering cries of the crowd deafened me.

Suddenly Jeff stumbled backward, slamming into me. The mob had stampeded forward. It was too late to escape. We were trapped in the riot.

"Turn around!" Jeff cried. "Turn around!"

In my panic, I didn't understand what he meant. Jeff grabbed my shoulders and whirled me around. If I hadn't turned, the momentum of the crowd would have bowled me over backward and I would have been trampled. But now I couldn't see him.

"Jeff!" I screamed. "Jeff, where are you?"

"I'm right here. I've got you! I won't let go!" I felt his arm lock through mine. We stumbled forward, bobbing like corks in a flood. It was a horrible, helpless feeling.

I heard shouts and screams behind us and remembered the riot police. The noise grew louder. Then a series of dull thuds sounded, the concussions echoing off the buildings in front of us. "They're firing at us!" someone screamed. "The pigs are firing at us!" The forward movement turned into pandemonium.

"It's not bullets, it's tear gas!" Jeff shouted. "Don't panic, they're just firing tear gas!" But judging by the terrified screams and the frantic elbowing all around us, no one was listening to him. I was being kicked and pummelled as people tried to escape in every direction.

There was a gap between two buildings on our left, and as the panicked mob turned to surge through it, Jeff and I were pulled apart like taffy. His hand reached out for me, and I felt him grip my jacket in his fist, then we were torn apart again, the force ripping my sleeve as he tried in vain to hang on. As the crowd poured between us, I struggled to keep him in sight. "Jeff! Where are you?"

Suddenly everyone ducked, raising their arms above their heads as a barrage of stones rained down on us. I caught sight of Jeff for a brief second and saw blood pouring down his face from a gash on his forehead. Pain and shock filled his eyes. He held his hands to his head and tried to stop the bleeding, but it poured through his fingers. He staggered, as if he might faint.

I had to reach him. I had to help him. Frantic, I started toward him again, using my elbows to push people out of my way. It was like swimming upstream against a powerful current. All the while, rocks continued to fall out of the sky like hailstones. I had Jeff in sight. I had almost reached him. Then he disappeared again as a stinging cloud of tear gas blinded my eyes.

The acrid, rubbery smell filled my lungs and I began to cough. As I stumbled blindly forward, a woman in front of me tripped and fell. Before I could help her up, someone pushed me from behind and I fell over on top of her. Immediately, hundreds of people trampled us as if we were rag dolls. Their weight crushed me to the ground. I cried out in agony as pain hammered me all over. I tried to stand and was knocked down again. Someone kicked my head like a soccer ball.

"Help me!" I screamed. "Somebody help me, please!" I couldn't hear my own voice above the din of cries and screams.

Then a strong pair of arms gripped me, lifted me. Through my tears, I recognized Jeff's bloody face. "I've got you," he said. "It's all right, I've got you."

I lost consciousness.

———

When I awoke, my father hovered over me. I couldn't imagine what he was doing at a Vietnam demonstration. "Daddy. . . ?" A look of immense relief filled his face.

"Yes, Sue. It's me."

I heard my mother's tearful voice. "Suzanne? Is she waking up, Stephen? Oh, thank God! Thank God!" She hurried to my side and took my limp hand in hers. Mine was connected to an IV line.

I looked around and saw that I was in a hospital room. My head throbbed with pain. I tried to concentrate, to understand what Daddy was saying to me, then realized he was asking me a bunch of stupid questions. "How many fingers am I holding up? What month is it?"

"Where's Jeff?" I mumbled. "Is he okay?" It hurt every time I drew a breath, making it difficult to talk. My father's face flushed with anger.

"Jeff's gone! I sent him out of here!"

"No . . . go get him . . . I want to see him. . . . He saved my life."

"Saved your life! He almost got you killed!"

"He's probably back at the college by now," Mom said. She smoothed my hair off my face. "You've been here since yesterday, Suzanne."

"And you're going to be here a while longer too," Daddy added. "You needed surgery to stop the internal bleeding, thanks to that miserable hippie, and you also have two broken ribs, a broken collarbone, and a moderate concussion!"

He was much too irate to listen to me, so I pleaded with Mom. "Jeff wouldn't leave me . . . please go look for his car . . . is his car still here?"

She reluctantly released my hand to peer through the blinds. "Stephen, it is out there," she said. Daddy muttered something, but when I saw the look on his face I was glad I hadn't heard it. "I'll go look for him," Mom finally said. Daddy sank into the visitor's chair, arms folded across his chest, as we waited.

Mom found Jeff in the chapel. When he walked into my room with her, he was such a ghostly shade of white she might have found him in the morgue. His left eye was swollen nearly shut, and I saw a row of ugly black stitches where they had closed the gash in his forehead. He wore the same clothes as yesterday, crusted with dried blood. Jeff didn't say a word, but he bent to kiss me as if I were made of glass.

My father stood to confront him, so furious his words rushed out in an angry flood of pent-up worry and rage. "My daughter seems to love you, Mr. Pulaski, and you claim to love her. How in the blazes could you let her get involved in something like this? How could you put her in such danger?"

Before Jeff could answer I said, "It's not his fault. I made him take me. He didn't want to."

"You see? That's what I don't understand," Daddy said, spreading his hands. "The men in my generation take care of their women. We put them on a pedestal, we shelter them, protect them. If you love a woman as much as I love my wife, you work hard so she doesn't have to. You want to give her the best of everything. There is no way in the world I would take Grace to something like that riot you dragged Suzanne into yesterday."

"It was supposed to be peaceful, Daddy."

"Oh yeah? Why don't you explain that to all the doctors down in the ER and in all the other area trauma centers? They had to treat thousands of injuries just like yours."

"It was the police. . . ."

"No, Suzanne. You weren't trampled by the police. You were trampled by the mob." Daddy turned to Jeff, their faces inches apart. Jeff hadn't said a word to defend himself against Daddy's tirade. The guilt and shame I saw on his face as my father chastised him brought tears to my eyes.

"You want to marry my daughter? You want my blessing? Then start acting responsibly! If you care for her as much as you claim, then make up your mind which is more important—your infantile protests or my daughter's safety. Grow up, Mr. Pulaski! Get a responsible job!" Daddy gripped Jeff's arm. "Take care of her properly or—"

Jeff cried out in pain. I didn't think it was possible for his face to turn any whiter, but it did. He nearly fainted. Daddy pushed him into a chair and forced his head between his knees.

"What's the matter, son? Are you all right? Where are you hurt?" All the anger had drained from Daddy's voice, replaced by concern.

"My arm . . ." Jeff moaned.

Daddy palpated it gently. "Does that hurt? Can you bend it? Any numbness or tingling?" Instantly he was a concerned doctor, not an irate father. I saw Daddy in his God-given role of physician, saw his genuine concern for people and for their pain, and I was stunned to see a compassionate heart beneath his arrogant facade. I thought about all the times he had left in the middle of my recitals and birthday parties to be with one of his patients, and I finally understood him.

"Didn't those fools in the ER examine you properly?" he asked Jeff.

"I . . . no, I wanted them to take care of Suzanne first."

He helped Jeff from the chair. "I'm taking you down to radiology for an X-ray."

They walked out of the door together with Daddy supporting Jeff. I knew he was in good hands. Even though it wasn't his hospital, Daddy would use his powerful personality to cut through the red tape and get Jeff the help he needed. I closed my eyes and rested.

When they returned a while later, Daddy wore a borrowed lab coat and Jeff wore a cast on his right arm. I never did learn what had transpired between them down in the X-ray lab, but I saw that at last they had reached an uneasy truce.

TWENTY-SIX

Jeff never participated in another demonstration after the Vietnam Moratorium. Moon-dog and all of Jeff's other hippie friends were furious with him. They surrounded us one afternoon as Jeff and I walked across the campus together.

"How can you sit back and do nothing, man?" Moon-dog demanded. "Don't you listen to the news anymore? Don't you care that the government's gonna take away our college deferments? We're all gonna be drafted, man, and you're copping out on us!"

"I'm not copping out," Jeff said.

"So you'll be at the rally then?"

Jeff was quiet for a moment, then he shook his head. "No. The rally isn't going to change the draft laws. It's only going to get a bunch of us beat up by the cops and arrested."

"Serve you right if you get drafted, man!" Moon-dog cried as he strode away. "Serve you right if you end up in 'Nam!"

"I'll move to Canada first!" Jeff shouted back at him.

On December 1, 1969, Jeff and I crowded into the lounge of my dormitory to watch the Selective Service lottery on TV. It would determine his fate. And mine. Blue plastic capsules, containing all 366 possible birth dates, would be drawn one by one from a large glass jar to establish the order in which men would be drafted into military service in the coming year. Jeff's birthday was June 8.

"It's the helplessness that bugs me the most," Jeff said as he grabbed the last empty chair in the lounge. He pulled me down onto his lap. I could feel the anger and tension in his body as we waited for the lottery to begin. "We may as well live in Russia if we're going to have the government controlling our futures."

"It's so unfair," I said. "It's like a scene from pagan mythology, where the gods meet once a year in a celestial council to determine the fate of all the people on earth. The mortals are helpless."

"Gee, thanks. I feel better already," he said, squeezing my hand.

"Sorry. This is hard for me too. We're in this together, you know—Canada or bust." I glanced around to see if the housemother was watching, then gave him a quick kiss. "What is the cutoff number again?" I asked.

"The magic number is 195. If they assign me a number lower than that, I'll have to leave for Canada before I'm drafted. If my number is higher than 195, chances are I won't be drafted and we can go to graduate school next year like we planned."

I saw my roommate and her boyfriend enter the lounge, and I waved them over to sit on the floor near Jeff and me. We listened as all the other couples who had gathered around the television set discussed their options.

"I heard that we'd be better off enlisting if we get a low number," someone said, "rather than waiting to be drafted. At least you can pick your own service branch."

"I think I'll audition for one of the military bands," my roommate's boyfriend said. "If I practice my horn day and night, I could probably get in."

"Do you suppose going to jail is worse than going to 'Nam?" someone else asked.

"Not too many people die in jail," came the grim answer. "Thousands are dying in 'Nam."

"Listen, you'd all be better off in Canada," Jeff said. "I have friends up there already. They say it's not too bad."

"Hey, shut up, everybody! It's starting!"

The laughing and joking turned to eerie silence as we watched Congressman Alexander Pirine of the House Armed Services Committee reach into the jar to draw the first birthday—September 14.

"No!" my roommate's boyfriend cried out. "Not the very first one!" He sprang to his feet and stumbled blindly out of the lounge, heedless of the people he stepped on. My roommate followed him, weeping.

"This is worse than torture," Jeff mumbled. I clung to him, my stomach churning.

When they drew number 20 and said "June—" my heart stopped beating until they said "—four." June fourth, not eighth. Jeff and I held our breath and each other as the numbers slowly climbed toward 195. Sweat poured off of him, soaking the back of his T-shirt, while I sat in the same room and shivered. From time to time, one of the other students watching with us would groan or cry out as his birthday was called. The lounge slowly cleared, the lucky ones, like us, left behind to wait.

A long time later, the lottery finally reached number 194. They still hadn't drawn Jeff's birthday.

"What a cruel twist of fate it would be if you're called now after making it this far," I said. "I can't watch." I closed my eyes and buried my face in his chest, waiting for number 195.

"September 24," I heard the announcer say. I went limp. Jeff was probably out of danger.

"Well, maybe we won't have to move to Canada after all," he said shakily. I lifted my face and kissed him, more relieved than he would ever know. With each successive number after that, I felt Jeff's body relax a little more. By the time they called number 300—March 12—he was actually smiling.

Jeff's birthday—June 8—was the very last one called. In the order of induction for the year 1970, he would be number 366.

"I guess we won't need those down parkas and snowshoes after all," he said, grinning.

———

Now that the fear of going to Vietnam or Canada had been removed, Jeff and I applied to the same state university for graduate studies. It had excellent programs in both journalism and art. We were both accepted. We would have to wait two more years before we could be married, but at least we would be together during that time.

I was in my room studying one afternoon when I heard the roar of Jeff's Volkswagen below my window. He couldn't afford a new exhaust system, so the sound was unmistakable. I abandoned my Shakespeare notes and ran downstairs to greet him.

"You're not going to believe this!" he said, waving a sheet of paper. "I was one of only two students, nationwide, selected to study at the American Art Institute under the world-renowned artist Jacob Krantz."

"The Art Institute? In New York City?"

"The *world famous* Art Institute!" he said, laughing. He lifted me off the ground and swung me around in a circle, the way the handsome hero always did in the movies.

"You have to accept it, Jeff," I said when I could stop laughing. "It's the opportunity of a lifetime!"

We were creating a scene in the lounge. Jeff took my hand and led me outside. We climbed into the front seat of his car so we would have a small measure of privacy. "I know it's an incredible opportunity," Jeff said, "but you'll be in graduate school hundreds of miles away. You're my inspiration, Irish. I can't paint without you. I can't even eat or breathe without you." He leaned across the gearshift and nuzzled my neck, not caring who walked by and saw him.

I stared out at the bustle of students hurrying to and from classes and felt empty inside at the thought of going through the grueling routine of graduate school without Jeff. I needed him too.

"Let's get married this summer. I want to go to New York with you. I want to wake up beside you every morning."

He rolled back to his own side of the car and stared at me, his face somber. "I can't ask you to give up graduate school."

"You're not asking me, I'm volunteering. I can wait two more years for school. I can't wait two more years for you."

"What about your parents? Your father doesn't want you to marry me."

I smiled. "I have a secret weapon—Grandma. She'll fight Daddy for us. She already told me she would."

"But your father won't pay for your Master's degree if we're married and—"

"Jeff, I don't care! Aren't you listening to me, you crazy hippie? You're more important to me than graduate school!" Jeff looked at me as though I had just offered to die for him. I began to laugh. "Oh, wow! I can't believe what I'm saying! This is the reason I broke up with Bradley Wallace!"

"You're really serious, aren't you?" Jeff wasn't laughing. "You'd really lay aside your education and your career to support me?"

I kissed the palm of his hand. "Yeah. I really would."

"I love you, Irish! I can't believe how much I love you!" He pulled me into his arms and hugged me so hard I yelped. "I'll make it up to you, I promise," he said. "I'll make sure you get your journalism degree if I have to rob a bank to do it!"

"I believe you would, but let's try applying for a student loan first."

With that hurdle crossed, my next challenge was confronting my parents. Having Grandma on my side gave me the courage I needed. I waited until graduation day later that spring. Then with Jeff beside me, still wearing our caps and gowns and clutching our brand-new diplomas, I blurted the news.

"Mom, Daddy, Grandma . . . Jeff and I are going to be married this summer."

"But . . . but what about graduate school?" Mom asked.

"I meant what I said about not paying," Daddy said. "The day you marry him or anyone else, you become your husband's responsibility, not mine. That's why you'd better think twice about this. Finish your schooling first."

"We're not waiting," I said. "Jeff has the chance of a lifetime to study at the Art Institute under Jacob Krantz. I'm going to New York with him."

"Are you pregnant?" Daddy asked with his customary tact.

"No, Daddy, I'm not pregnant. You can give me the rabbit test yourself if you don't believe me."

"Well, don't just stand there, Gracie," Grandma Emma said, "give them your blessing!" She gave me a big hug first, then kissed Jeff on both cheeks. "What a handsome groom you'll make!" My parents didn't move. They might have been carved from wax.

"Listen," I told them, sounding braver than I felt, "you can either celebrate with us or disown us. But either way, we *are* getting married this summer."

"I can't say that I'm pleased," Daddy finally said, "but I can see that it's useless to argue with you. You've been stubborn all your life, Suzanne."

The economic and cultural gaps between our two families turned our wedding into a balancing act. The reception had to be classy enough for my parents and their wealthy friends without overwhelming Jeff's family, who could barely afford to travel from Pittsburgh, much less rent tuxedos. Once again, Grandma Emma saved the day. Whenever Mom started to get carried away with plans for an elaborate reception, I called Grandma on the telephone and cried, "Help!"

"Have you forgotten how poor we once were, Gracie?" she told Mom. "You've got to keep things in perspective, dear. Do you want that sweet young man's parents to think you're a snob?"

"You're right, Mother," she finally agreed. "I suppose the Pulaskis would be more comfortable with an afternoon reception on the country club lawn than with a candlelight dinner and a string quartet."

Grandma arrived the weekend before the wedding to attend my bridal shower. From the moment she walked through the door until the big day finally arrived, she lectured Daddy relentlessly about social prejudice and young love—at the dinner table, in his study, when he tried to watch a golf tournament on TV—until even I began to feel sorry for him. "All right, Emma, all right," he said, waving his white handkerchief in surrender. "I admit I was once young and in love with a pauper too. I promise I'll be on my best behavior."

At the rehearsal dinner, Grandma sat at the Pulaskis' table, singing songs in German and Polish. Jeff's father swore his undying adoration for her. "That settles it, Emma," he said when the evening finally came to a close. "You're coming back to Pittsburgh with us!"

But Grandma's *coup d'etat* came at the reception when she somehow got steelworkers and surgeons to mingle on the country club lawn. She punched holes in all the socialites' pretensions, entertaining them with racy stories about rum-running during Prohibition. The hospital administrator's wife wanted to sign Grandma up to entertain guests at her next dinner party. "I'm having some people over next week, Mrs. Bauer. I wonder if you would be free to come?"

After Grandma taught the country club's band to play the "Beer Barrel Polka," none of the guests wanted to go home. "We're playing for another wedding next weekend," the bandleader said. "Come back and join us, Emma."

As Jeff and I prepared to leave on our honeymoon in the Poconos, we didn't know how to thank her. "You did it, Suzy! You defied them all and got married!" Grandma's eyes brimmed with tears. "Seeing you two together is all the thanks I need. I only wish . . . I wish that Patrick and I had been as courageous as you two. We could have made it work."

Jeff and I climbed into his Volkswagen and drove away, trailing a string of tin cans. I was Mrs. Jeffrey Pulaski at last, the happiest woman in the world.

Jeff may have won a full scholarship to art school, but the cost of living in New York City was outrageously high. I couldn't even consider going to school part time because we needed my full-time income to live. I took a job as a receptionist at the Art Institute so we could commute from our apartment together and meet for lunch once in a while. We were poor—starving-artist poor—but so deeply in love with each other that we didn't care. The only piece of furniture we needed in our two-room apartment was a bed.

I loved watching Jeff create. I joined him in his studio after I finished work each day, bringing him deli sandwiches or Chinese food or sometimes a pizza. He made a glorious mess while he worked, flinging paint on the canvas with wild abandon. When he finished a piece, he would be both exhausted and elated. I would fill our ancient, claw-footed bathtub with water and scrub him clean, tenderly wiping the paint splatters from his face and beard with paint thinner.

Jeff excelled in his studies. Several of his pieces won awards. But when I saw price tags on his paintings at his gallery showing, I wept. "You can't sell these, Jeff! They're your children! How can you sell your children?"

"In the first place," he said, wiping my tears with his shirttail, "those price tags are wishful thinking. I probably won't sell any of them. And in the second place, we could use the money. If by some miracle they do sell, I can always paint more, you know."

"I'll bet you a week of kitchen duty that they all sell," I said, pouting.

"And I'll bet you two weeks of kitchen duty that they don't!"

We never decided who had won the bet because, much to our astonishment, all but one of Jeff's paintings sold—and that one hadn't been for sale. It was a picture of me, asleep in the chair in the art studio. He had worked on it all night in secret, then surprised me with it for our anniversary. "I'll never sell this painting," he said. "It reminds me of how you waited for me, how much you gave up for me." He entitled it *The Sacrifice*.

Jeff's paintings earned good reviews from the critics as "an artist to watch." I was proud to be Mrs. Jeff Pulaski. His two years of study flew by quickly.

One month before Jeff graduated, I was home alone on a Saturday morning when someone knocked on our door. When I answered it, I barely recognized the man who stood there. Jeff had cut his long wavy hair well above his shoulders and combed it off of his forehead. He had trimmed his beard short too.

"Oh, Jeff!"

"You don't like it?"

"You look so . . . so different. Is it really you?"

"Come here and kiss me, and find out." He pulled me to him. It was definitely Jeff.

"Where did you get the sport coat?" I asked when I had a chance to look him over. "The only other time I've seen you in a coat and tie was at our wedding."

"I borrowed it from a friend."

"Was his name Bradley Wallace?"

"Ouch! That hurts! I did this for you, you know."

"For me? But I loved your hair the way it was." I tried to grab on to it like I used to, but there was barely enough to grip.

"Yes, for you." He turned in a circle, like a fashion model on a runway. "Recruiters for all the big-name advertising agencies will be on campus Monday. I'm just trying to look respectable for my job interviews . . . Why on earth are you crying?"

"You're giving up part of yourself . . . for me!"

"It seems only fair. You gave up graduate school and all your father's money for me." He let me cry on his shoulder for a minute, then said, "Careful, don't get the tie wet. It's borrowed too." I laughed and cried at the same time.

"It's going to take me a while to get used to this, Jeff," I finally said. "What did Jacob Krantz say when you told him you were job hunting?"

"I can't repeat it in polite company."

"I can well imagine! You said yourself that commercial artists were nothing more than prostitutes, painting for hire. But advertising! That involves greed and manipulation and entering the middle-class rat race—everything you hate!"

"If you're trying to talk me out of this, you're doing a great job."

"Isn't there any other way? I'm just afraid that you're losing so much more than I'll be gaining with my journalism degree."

"It's only for two years. Besides, it won't be a total loss. If I join corporate America, I'll be earning something more than a paycheck."

I looked at him, puzzled. "What else will you earn?"

"Your father's respect."

———

"Guess what!" Jeff said when he came home a week later. "I have my pick of advertising jobs!" His starting salary was twice my receptionist's pay. We felt rich. We moved back to Pennsylvania to begin a new phase in our married life. Now it was my turn to go to school while Jeff rose early every morning to commute to work.

Each time Jeff got a haircut, the barber trimmed it a little shorter. "Congratulations on your new set of ears," Daddy said when he saw him. By the time I finished my first year of graduate school, Jeff owned two suits.

"Hurry up! I'm going to be late for class," I hollered at Jeff through the bathroom door one morning. "What's taking you so long?" When he finally came out, I burst into tears. He had shaved off his beard.

"Jeff, no! What did you do that for? Why didn't you warn me?"

"I shaved it because I have to make design presentations to corporate clients. My boss suggested I lose the hippie look. And I didn't tell you because you would have tried to talk me out of it."

"You look so different!" I wept.

"Yeah, the beard hid my ugly mug, didn't it? Now you see the real me."

I took his smooth face in my hands and kissed him. "Hippie or not, you're still a mighty good-looking man, Jeff Pulaski."

We both enjoyed spending all the bonuses he earned, and we started buying stuff—a decent stereo system, a better car, real bookshelves instead of bricks and boards. Jeff's creativity made him a huge success in advertising. Then, three months before I graduated with a master's degree, Jeff came to the university library after work to find me.

"I'm taking you to dinner," he said. "We have to talk." I needed a break from writing my thesis, but the somber expression on his face had me worried.

"What is this all about?" I asked when we were seated in a trendy restaurant.

"I got a job offer today from a larger, more prestigious ad agency," he said. "They offered to double my salary."

"There must be a catch," I said. "You're not smiling."

"I would have to sign a two-year contract."

"Don't do it," I begged. "Two more years sounds like a life sentence. I'm so close to graduating now. I'll be able to look for a job in a few more months, and you can go back to painting."

"I don't want to quit working until we're out of debt," Jeff said. "If I accept this offer, we can pay off your tuition loan faster. I never liked the idea that Grandma Emma had to co-sign for us. And we're going to need a second car soon."

Jeff signed the contract. He was away on his first business trip for the new company when I received two pieces of news—one astounding and one devastating. I waited until he returned home to tell him, unwilling to share either piece of news over the telephone.

"Which do you want first, the good news or the bad?" I asked when he staggered into our apartment. Jeff looked exhausted. I slipped his suit coat from his sagging shoulders and helped him loosen his tie. He could afford tailored shirts and suits now.

"I don't care, Suzanne," he said, rubbing his eyes, "I'm too tired to—"

"I'm the new assistant editor at *New Woman* magazine."

"Really? Isn't that the job you wanted so badly? That's fantastic! When do you start?" I burst into tears. "Hey, what's the matter? Did I say something wrong?"

"I'm pregnant."

Jeff went limp. "Oh boy," he mumbled. "Oh boy, oh boy, oh boy." They were not cries of joy.

"I don't know how it could have happened," I said, sobbing.

"Oh, I do. Remember that night we . . ." His mouth held a hint of a smile.

"Jeff, what are we going to do?"

His arms came around me. He held me tightly. "My corporate health plan will cover all the hospital costs," he said quietly. "And your new magazine is very hip when it comes to women's rights, isn't it? I'm sure they've thought of everything, from maternity leave to day-care centers. We're going to celebrate, that's what we're going to do."

"But we're not ready to start a family . . . are we?"

"Ready or not, here it comes!"

"You'll never be able to quit your job and go back to painting now."

"I like my job. I don't want to quit."

"But we can't squeeze a baby into this apartment, and your car—"

"Those are hardly insurmountable problems," he said, laughing, "and certainly not worth crying over. People move to larger apartments every day. We're having a baby, Suzanne. Think of it! He'll have your Irish good looks and my enormous talent."

"No, *she'll* be the first Pulitzer-prizewinning Polack!"

"Either way, our kid can't lose."

We started searching for a bigger apartment and discovered that monthly mortgage payments were not much more than a month's rent. Daddy offered to lend us the down payment. Buying a house seemed like the logical thing to do. Of course, that meant buying more furniture. When Jeff went to my father for investment advice, Daddy taught him to play golf. They discussed stocks out on the fairway. Without even realizing it, we had joined the middle-class rat race—and before long, the rats pulled into the lead.

Hurry up and end this dreary sermon, I silently begged. The preacher had been droning for nearly twenty-five minutes, but I couldn't have said what any one of his three points were. I caught Jeff nodding off. We sat in the very last row of the church, an invisible block of ice resting on the pew between us. We had started the morning with a screaming baby and a screaming match— we'd run out of coffee and we each blamed the other for it. Given the mood we were in, it had been a waste of time to get dressed.

The church we attended near our new home had never satisfied either one of us, but by Sunday morning we were much too tired to shop for a new one. We hadn't made any friends there because juggling the responsibilities of marriage, a new baby, new jobs, and a new house left us much too weary to get involved in church activities. Even when we made the effort to come, God seemed very far away.

At last the service ended. "I'll get Amy from the nursery," I said in a monotone. "I don't want to stay and socialize."

"I'll get the car," Jeff said in a growl.

I hurried downstairs to the nursery, hoping to make a quick escape. I always felt out of place among the other new mothers. They were all stay-at-home moms who breast-fed their babies and baked bread from scratch. I nearly groaned aloud when I saw Marlene Rogers bouncing Amy on her shoulder. Marlene was a "Super Mom"—the type who loved staying home with her five children, baking cookies, growing all her own vegetables, sewing frilly curtains.

"Amy was a perfect lamb today," Marlene cooed. "Is she always this sweet and good-natured?"

"She wasn't sweet this morning when we were trying to get ready for church."

"Babies get tired of being hauled around sometimes," she said as she handed Amy over to me. I hoped I had imagined the rebuke I heard in her voice, but I hadn't. "You still work full time, don't you, Suzanne?"

"Yes, I do." I shoved Amy's arms into the sleeves of her snowsuit.

"Have you considered taking some time off to spend with your daughter?"

"No, I haven't."

"Maybe you should."

"Look, Marlene. I worked very hard to get a good education, and my husband and I both sacrificed a lot to get where we are. It would be a terrible waste to throw all that hard work away. Besides, I believe God gave me brains and talent for a reason." I zipped up the snowsuit and tied on Amy's hat. She struggled, hating the confinement and my none-too-gentle handling.

Marlene decided it was her duty to exhort me regarding God's divine will for mothers. "You'll be very sorry that you missed the most precious years in your daughter's life, Suzanne. You can always work again, five years from now, but you can never retrieve your daughter's first steps or her first words once those moments are gone."

There was more, but I strapped Amy into her infant seat and fled. The following Sunday we stopped going to church altogether.

Jeff had worked until after midnight Saturday night on a huge advertising campaign for an important client. "I'm part of the team that will make the presentation Monday morning," he explained. "Winning this account could be a tremendous boost to my career."

I had been up with Amy three times during the night, so when the alarm went off Sunday morning, we both rolled over and went back to sleep. I felt guilty the first few Sundays we missed, but having an extra day to catch up with laundry, shopping, and housework soon overshadowed my guilt. It also gave me more time with Amy. After working fifty or sixty hours a week, Jeff needed the extra day to unwind too. We never discussed our decision, we just stopped attending.

———

Two years later, Melissa was born. Not long after that, *New Woman* magazine promoted me to associate editor. It meant more work, more responsibility, but it also meant climbing the next rung on the ladder. I could be editor in chief one day. It was what I was working toward. I was so excited when I learned of the promotion that I called Jeff's office from work. Maybe we could meet downtown to celebrate.

"I'm sorry, Mrs. Pulaski," his secretary told me, "but he's in a meeting right now, and then he has a conference call scheduled for seven o'clock tonight with a client on the west coast. He probably won't be free until at least nine."

"Oh well. I guess it can wait until the weekend."

"This weekend? Mr. Pulaski will be attending a conference in New York, remember?"

No, I hadn't remembered. "Never mind," I said, hanging up.

My victory felt hollow without Jeff to share it with me. I took Amy and Melissa to McDonald's to celebrate, but the noise gave me a headache. Later, I cried myself to sleep long before Jeff arrived, thinking about how little time we had for each other.

For the next few years, the hurts and slights and missed occasions piled up like snowdrifts. Buried beneath their weight, our relationship cooled. Jeff's scheduled vacations came during the summer when my magazine was busy preparing the holiday issue. My vacation came during the winter when Jeff had new advertising campaigns to plan for the new year. When my magazine won an important press association award, Jeff wasn't free to attend the dinner with me. When one of his corporate clients offered him a trip to California, I couldn't arrange time off or child care to go with him. Jeff flew out of town once or twice a month to attend conferences and meetings. I flew out of town on alternate weeks to interview influential career women for the magazine's main feature. We felt like the proverbial ships passing in the night, and after a while neither one of us made the effort to meet halfway.

We were supposed to share the household duties, but Jeff did his share by hiring a maid and lawn service because he was rarely home. Too tired to cook, I threw fast food in the microwave or ordered takeout. When it came to shared parenting, he missed most of the girls' school programs and teacher conferences, then tried to compensate by being overly lenient with them. I resented the fact that the job of disciplinarian usually fell on my shoulders.

Six years of mounting pressures came to their inevitable conclusion a couple of months ago. I arrived home late from an out-of-town trip, long after the girls' bedtime, and found them eating pizza in the den with Jeff. I exploded.

"It's not fair that I have to enforce the laws around here, and you get to be Mr. Nice Guy, having fun and bending all the rules!"

"Leave it to you to spoil a festive occasion," Jeff grumbled as he stuffed pizza boxes, paper plates, crusts, and pop cans into the garbage. The girls scampered upstairs to bed.

"And what occasion would that be? International Slob Day?"

"No. My promotion. I'm the new vice president in charge of the design team in our Chicago office."

"*What?* We can't move to Chicago!"

"Thank you, Suzanne. I'm very happy for me too." He stormed upstairs into our bedroom and slammed the door. I stormed upstairs right behind him.

"Don't you dare drop your little bombshell, then walk away from me, Jeff Pulaski! We need to discuss this."

"Discuss what?"

"This decision! When does the company need to know your answer?"

He planted his hands on his hips. "I already gave them my answer. There was never any question in my mind. I accepted their offer."

"You *what?*"

"I accepted it! If you had bothered to ask me what my goals and dreams were lately, you would have known that this is the career opportunity I've been waiting for. I'll be the boss for once. No more jumping through other people's hoops. It will also mean a very hefty pay increase. With stock options, I'll be making almost as much money as your almighty father does."

"You *accepted* the job? Without even *asking* me?" He stared at me as if he didn't understand the question. "What about *my* job, Jeff? What am I supposed to do?"

"They know how to read in Chicago. There are plenty of magazines there."

"You expect me to give up my retirement plan, my seniority, and everything else I've slaved for at that magazine and start all over again at the bottom of the ladder somewhere else?"

"No, you could stay home with your children for once. You don't have to work, you know. I make more than enough money."

I yanked off my wedding band and threw it at him. "There are plenty of women in Chicago too. Why don't you find yourself a new wife to go with your fancy new job! I'm not moving!"

1980

"That's the whole ugly story," Suzanne said. "Our marriage did a long, slow, ten-year slide into the garbage can." Emma watched Suzanne shove the last plate into the dishwasher, pour in detergent, and turn on the machine. They carried their coffee mugs out to the screened-in porch and made themselves comfortable on her white wicker furniture. Outside, the yard and shrubbery looked as if it had been immaculately groomed by a team of professionals a few hours earlier. The underground sprinkler system switched on automatically.

Emma closed her eyes, inhaling the scent of mown grass and damp earth. She heard a distant sound, like rushing water, and imagined for a moment that it was the Squaw River—that ever-present stream that had flowed through all her girlhood days. When a siren wailed, she opened her eyes. It wasn't the river after all, but the ebb and flow of traffic on the busy interstate nearby.

"How have we allowed our lives to become so complicated?" Emma murmured aloud.

Suzanne gestured broadly to encompass the porch, the house, the yard. "Jeff would probably say, 'I thought this is what you wanted,' and he'd be partially right. I loved being able to buy nice things, and I loved having Daddy's approval. But we grew further and further apart. We were trying to prove that Jeff wasn't a loser, and we lost each other instead." She took a sip of coffee, then said, "I'm sorry we disappointed you, Grandma."

"Oh, honey . . . I'm just so sorry for the two of you."

"You never told me that story about your first boyfriend, Mother," Grace said. "The one your father didn't approve of." She had been unusually quiet since Suzanne finished telling her story. "What did you say his name was?"

"Patrick," Emma said softly. "His name was Patrick."

"And you fell in love with him before you married my father?"

Emma nodded. She didn't trust herself to speak.

"Grandma, we found a love poem by Yeats in the back of your photo album. It was addressed to you. Was it from Patrick?"

" 'How many loved . . . your beauty with love false or true,' " Emma recited, " 'But one man loved the pilgrim soul in you. . . . ' Yes, it was from him. Jeff wooed you with drawings; Patrick wooed me with poetry. You and he would have gotten along well, Suzy. You both loved the graceful sound of words."

"Whatever happened to him after you broke up?" Suzanne asked.

A warning sounded in Emma's mind. She knew she had to be careful what she said. "Patrick wasn't from Bremenville. He came there to work during the war. When we decided . . . when we knew we couldn't be together . . . he left town. It was easier that way, for both of us."

"Did you ever see him again?" Suzanne asked, sitting on the edge of her seat. "Did he ever get married? Do you know where he is?"

Emma wondered if talking about herself would help Suzanne forget her own pain. "Yes, I know where he is," she said slowly. "Patrick is dead." Tears pressed against Emma's eyes, even after all these years.

"How? When? What did he die from?"

"What difference does it make, Suzy? He was the only man I ever loved . . . and now he's gone. We'll never get a second chance."

Grace set down her coffee mug and leaned forward. "You mean you *never* loved my father? Not even a little bit?"

Emma saw the wounded look in Grace's eyes and was reminded again of how her own mistakes had hurt the people she loved. "I tried to love Karl, for Mama's and Papa's sakes," she said. "I thought our love would grow over time. But Karl never offered me enough of himself to love. And even if he had, it never could have measured up to what Patrick and I once had. You'll never love another man, Suzanne, the way you once loved Jeff. You might meet someone else, you might even marry again someday, but you'll never have what you had with him. Love like that comes only once in a lifetime."

The lights of the neighboring houses blurred through Emma's tears as she gazed into the past. She could almost see Patrick's face, almost picture him the way he looked back in 1918—his smile, the laughter in his eyes. Almost. How could she make Suzanne understand what she and Jeff were throwing away?

"It has been more than sixty years," Emma said. "Yet I would give anything to have Patrick beside me again . . . to be able to grow old with him."

"Please tell us about him, Grandma. How did you meet? Why didn't your father like him?"

Emma sighed. "When I think of the reasons why we didn't marry . . . We were both children of immigrants, but I was German-Protestant, you see. And Patrick was Irish-Catholic. . . ."

PART FIVE

Patrick's Story
1917 - 1918

TWENTY-SEVEN

Papa's Protestant church and St. Brigit's Catholic Church sat on opposite shores of the Squaw River, facing off like two boxers. We celebrated Reformation Day on October 31; they celebrated All Saints' Day on November 1. We rang our church bell before Sunday services; they rang theirs before Mass. The German community never forgot how their fellow countryman, Martin Luther, had fought to reform the errors of the Catholic church. The Irish community never forgot how a Protestant, Oliver Cromwell, had fought to annihilate their people and their religion. There was no love lost between the two faiths.

Growing up on the mostly Protestant side of the river, I viewed all Catholics as pagans. After all, didn't they fill their churches with idols, like God's enemies in the Bible did? Their priests wore flowing robes and spoke their strange incantations in Latin. They weren't allowed to marry like Protestant ministers. Catholic women covered their heads when they went to church and had litters of Catholic children. Catholics ate fish on Fridays and stood in line for confession on Saturday. In our house, the very word *Catholic* was whispered.

Patrick didn't grow up in Bremenville but came there to work in 1917. He was twenty years old, and I was seventeen. I met him for the first time the day the three Irish factory workers attacked my father. Patrick was the man who rescued Papa and me. One minute the bullies were holding me captive and I was scared out of my mind, and the next minute Patrick was pushing his way through the crowd, shouting at them to let us go.

Quick-tempered and quick-fisted, Patrick wasn't afraid to brawl with any man—even if the odds were three against one—and he proved it that day. I'll never forget how he nearly lifted one of the bullies off the ground by his shirt-front, saying, "You want to fight someone, Kevin, fight me, not a harmless man of the cloth!" Fearing his wrath, they eventually spat out their apologies and helped Papa to his feet. "Paddy," as they called him, inspired fear when aroused to anger. You'd have never guessed it to look at Patrick, but he had a poet's heart. Just as swiftly as it came, his anger could dissolve into gentleness. That day, he overflowed with concern for Papa.

"You ought to see a doctor, Reverend. Let me help you."

"Thank you, but I'll be fine." Papa insisted that we forget the matter and go home.

But the following afternoon, I answered a knock on the front door of the parsonage and found Patrick standing outside. He bowed slightly and removed his hat. "Good afternoon to you, miss. I've come to apologize again for what happened yesterday and to ask how the reverend is feeling."

"He feels terrible. Good day." I had made up my mind never to speak to an Irishman again. I would never forgive them for hurting my papa. I tried to close the door, but Patrick wedged his shoulder in the crack.

"Pardon me, miss, but you're doing the same thing Liam and Kevin did. You don't even know me, but you're judging me because of my nationality. Surely you don't want to be like those narrow-minded bullies now, do you?" He said it kindly, and I heard laughter in his voice. I couldn't resist his charm.

"You're right, I'm sorry. Come in. Papa is in his study."

They talked alone with the door closed for twenty minutes. I hovered nearby but couldn't hear their words. When Patrick came out again he said, "Well, I'll be going now. Good day to you, miss."

"Would you like something cold to drink before you leave?"

His smile lit up his face. "Thanks, I believe I will." We sat on the porch while he drank his lemonade, enjoying the weather and the nice view of the river.

When Eva and I emerged from the Red Cross canteen the next day, we found Patrick leaning against a lamppost out in front, cleaning his fingernails with a pocketknife. He straightened up and slipped the knife into his pocket when he saw us, then fell into step beside me. "Good afternoon, ladies. May I walk with you?"

"Why would you want to do that?"

"Well, for one thing, the factory will be letting out soon, and I don't quite trust the lads to—"

"We don't need a bodyguard," I said stiffly.

"Don't I know that!" he said, chuckling. "Didn't I see you standing up to them the other day? But I'm thinking the two populations of this town could do with a bit of understanding, you see. Since you're such a brave lass, Miss Schroder—"

"My name is Emma," I said, warming to him. He had that effect on me. "And this is my sister Eva."

"Well, then, Emma, perhaps you'd be willing to help me set an example for the others to follow. If they see us walking together and talking in a civilized manner, maybe they'll see that Protestants won't bite their heads off, after all."

Patrick radiated zeal like a coiled spring waiting to be released. I got the impression that he yearned for fun or mischief—or both. He seemed familiar to me, as if I'd known him all my life. Then I realized that I did know him— his boundless curiosity and eagerness for adventure were just like my own. In spite of my misgivings about Irish-Catholics, I liked him. We started walking through town toward the bridge.

"I know why there is animosity between our two faiths in Ireland," he said. "But why do the German-Protestants feel the way they do about us?"

"Well, I guess because Germany is where the Protestant Reformation began. The country has been bitterly divided ever since. Papa says there was even a Catholic political party."

"Your father is a very intriguing man."

"He isn't on Germany's side at all, you know, even though he was born there. He isn't on either side. Papa hates war. He hates any kind of fighting, in fact. That's why he wouldn't defend himself against those men. He believes that Jesus would want him to turn the other cheek."

We talked easily, freely, all the way to the bridge, bouncing questions and ideas off each other, hardly pausing for breath. Eva told me later that it was like watching a lively tennis match with a dozen balls in play. From that day on, Patrick and I could say anything and everything to each other and never be misunderstood or misjudged. We parted as friends, each of us hating to go our separate way.

The friendship continued like this for several months, seeing each other once or twice a week, walking together, talking nonstop. I found myself thinking of Patrick in between times, saying to myself, *I must remember to ask Patrick about that*, or *Wait until I tell Patrick about this*. I had never been in love—I had no intention of falling in love. I only knew that the time we spent apart passed much too slowly, and the time we spent together had wings.

———

"Hey, Eva, let's borrow the Metzgers' boat and row out to Squaw Island," I said one warm spring Saturday in 1918. I had recently celebrated my eighteenth birthday. "We'll see if the mushrooms are out and pick a mess of them for dinner."

Eva had her nose in a book, as usual. "Not now, Emma. I raced through my morning chores just so I could finish this book. It's all about—"

"Never mind. I'll go by myself."

Squaw Island was private property, but since the owner lived in the city and rarely used the log cabin he'd built on the island, I felt free to visit as often as I liked. That day, when I saw another boat already tied to the island's dock, I almost turned back. Then I recognized the man sitting on the end of the pier, dangling his bare feet in the water. It was Patrick.

"Ahoy, Matey!" I called out. "Catch any fish?"

Patrick laughed and turned up empty palms. "Nary a one has jumped into my lap!" He stood and reached for my oar as I drew close, pulling my boat to the dock.

"What are you doing here?" we said simultaneously, then laughed.

"I'm trespassing," I said. "I came to hunt morels."

His eyes widened. "You mean . . . with a gun?"

I thought he was joking, then realized he wasn't. His puzzled expression made me laugh.

"Morels are mushrooms, city boy. Want to hunt some with me?"

"Sure. What do I have to do?"

"Follow me. I've been coming out to this island since I was small. I know all the best places to look. Why are you here, by the way?"

"The owner is an old family friend from the city. He said I could use his cabin anytime. I'm spending the weekend."

"Uh, oh. You won't have me arrested for poaching mushrooms, will you?"

"Not if you let me taste some of them. That would make me an accomplice."

We spent a glorious afternoon together, tramping through the woods collecting a large basketful of mushrooms. Once I showed Patrick what they looked like, he was quicker at spotting them among the dead leaves than I was. He had a key to the cabin, and when we'd picked our fill, we went inside to stand side by side at the cabin's sink. With our sleeves rolled, Patrick worked the rusty pump while I carefully rinsed the morels. After sautéing them in a cast-iron frying pan, using a little bacon Patrick had brought, we sat outside on the porch steps and ate every last one.

"Delicious!" he declared, licking his fingers. "And definitely worth going to jail for."

"They're much better if you use butter," I said, laughing with my partner in crime.

It never once occurred to us that it was improper for two young people to be alone on an island, unchaperoned. If it had, neither of us would have cared. I only knew that when we finally said good-bye and I rowed back to shore, I left part of myself on the island. That night in bed, I cried.

"What's wrong, Emma?" Eva whispered.

"I don't know," I said. And I didn't. If I could have put what I felt into words, they would have been that I wanted to spend every day of my life as I had that day—with Patrick.

———

We met on the island the following weekend, not by prearrangement, but because we thought so much alike we both ended up there. We walked beneath the canopy of budding trees, inhaling the rich fragrance of woods and the earth. We sat on the stony beach and listened to the restless sound of the rushing river, allowing our surroundings to feed our souls. We tramped all over the island again, no longer searching for mushrooms but for music and poetry to share with each other.

When we came upon a pair of white birds in a marsh, Patrick pulled me down beside him in a clump of weeds to watch. "Look, Emma, look how they walk, how they fly! They're God's poetry."

"I think they must be herons or egrets," I whispered. "And they're building a nest. Geese mate for life—I wonder if these birds do too?" As we watched in silent awe, Patrick reached for my hand and clasped it in his own as if it was the most natural thing in the world.

"Your hands are cold, Emma . . . do you want my jacket?"

"I'm not cold, just my hands." He cupped them in his and lifted them to his face, breathing on them to warm them. From that first time he took my hand in his, we knew that we were part of each other. We had become lost somehow, but now that we'd found each other again, we would stay together. Always. We were the same person, really—two halves of the same apple. Nature abhorred the fact that we had to row to opposite shores of the river at the end of the day.

"I'm going to the dance at the Red Cross canteen tonight," I said as I climbed into the boat to row home. "Why don't you meet me there."

"All right," he promised. "I'll meet you there."

Patrick held me in his arms for the first time as we danced together that night. "I should have warned you, I can't dance," he said.

"It doesn't matter." I enjoyed the warmth of his arms around me. "Just hold me close and pretend that you do."

"Is that all there is to it?" he grinned. "That's easy."

For the remainder of the night, I turned all the other boys away. None of them could compare with Patrick. He was like a shining beacon that blotted out all the lesser suns around him. I needed his warmth, his light, to live. He also made me laugh. He may have been an Irish poet, but he was as full of fun and as restless for adventure as I was. The music and the laughter that rocked the canteen dissolved into the background as we danced together or sat at a table talking. We were causing a minor scandal—Protestant and Catholic holding hands—but we might have been alone in the woods for all we cared.

Late in the evening, while Eva danced with a boy from Papa's church, Patrick and I slipped outside. The music grew fainter, the night sounds louder, as he led me to a shadowy lane behind the building. Then, holding me very close, Patrick kissed me for the first time. When our lips had to part again, I cried.

He didn't need to ask the reason for my tears. He looked into my eyes and wiped my tears with his thumb and said, "I know, Emma . . . I know."

The next day the sky fell. Papa summoned me into his study after the Sunday services. All morning I had wandered around in a fog of joy, thinking of Patrick as I sat in church, recalling his kiss as I helped Mama prepare chicken and dumplings for Sunday dinner. But the sight of Papa in his clerical collar, seated stiffly behind his desk, gesturing for me to sit in the chair facing him jolted me like a bucket of cold water. I perched nervously on the very edge of the seat, waiting.

"Emma, I've been told by several concerned people from our congregation that at the dance last night . . . that your behavior . . . that you behaved indecently."

My heart pounded faster. "I'm surprised that you, of all people, would listen to gossip, Papa."

"People tell me all sorts of things, Liebchen." His voice was gentle but firm. "It's my policy not to believe any of it unless I have proof that it is true. I'm asking you for the truth."

I lifted my chin, trying to sound braver than I felt. "I don't think I acted indecently." The peaceful tranquility of Papa's study did nothing to quiet my growing uneasiness. My eyes darted restlessly around the room, taking in all of Papa's neatly stacked books and papers. He waited until I met his gaze.

"Then, it isn't true that you spent the entire evening dancing with a young man from St. Brigit's Parish? That you turned away all the young men from our own church?"

"How is that indecent? Don't I have a right to dance with whomever I want to?" I was skirting dangerously close to disrespect. Papa's mouth formed a grim line.

"I was told that you openly held hands with this fellow all evening. And that you were seen together . . . kissing . . . behind the building."

"The only thing that's indecent is the fact that someone would spy on us!"

"Emma," he said quietly, "I'm asking you if it's true."

My fear of God outweighed my fear of Papa. I couldn't lie. "Yes, Papa. It's true."

He was quiet for a long time. I knew that he was praying for wisdom, carefully choosing his words. When he finally spoke, his voice was hushed. "You've abused my trust, Emma. You must have known, from all that I've taught you, that it was wrong to allow a young man to . . . to take liberties. And that it was also wrong to become involved with an unbeliever."

"Patrick isn't an unbeliever!"

"I was told that the young man you were seen with was Irish-Catholic."

"You've met him, Papa. He helped us the day you were attacked. He came here to see how you were the next day. You've talked to Patrick, Papa. You know he isn't a heathen."

"I'm grateful for what he did that day. I'm appalled, however, by what the two of you did last night. Your behavior would be shameful even if it was with one of our own people."

"*Our* people?"

"Yes. Our fellow German-Protestants."

"These aren't my people! I'm not German, I'm American! You and Mama have recreated the old country right here. You live in your own little world on this side of the river and you're comfortable in it. But it's not my world, Papa. I'm American. And the man I marry will also be American!"

Papa's face went very white. "It is God's will that you honor your parents by asking for their blessing on your marriage. It is never God's will that you become unequally yoked with a man of a different faith, whether he is German, Irish, or American. I only hope that the shame of what you did won't ruin your chances of marrying a respectable Christian man."

"All we did was kiss!"

"That's *all*? A kiss is something holy and God-given, Emma. A symbol of union. It should be reserved for a serious relationship, where there is a commitment that will eventually lead to marriage. It's shameful when it's done in dark alleyways and squandered on mere physical attraction."

I stopped arguing with Papa, not because I agreed with him but because I saw that it was useless. He proceeded to spell out my punishment like the voice of God, inscribing the law on tablets of stone. "From now on you are forbidden to work at the canteen, forbidden to attend dances, forbidden to go into town unchaperoned, and forbidden to date any young man unless he attends our church and comes to the house first to escort you."

I would be a prisoner, cut off from happiness and fun—and Patrick. "What *may* I do?" I muttered miserably.

"When you graduate from school in a few weeks, you may choose either courtship and marriage, or a job as a domestic helper with a respectable German family. Under no circumstances are you to be seen with Patrick. Do you understand, Emma?"

"Yes, Papa. I understand."

He hadn't forbidden me to go to Squaw Island.

The following Saturday I went—hoping, knowing, that I would meet Patrick. Papa had said I wasn't to be seen with him, but no one would see us there.

Patrick was waiting for me on the dock. We both knew by the bottomless joy we felt that we were in love. I fell into his arms, hugging him with all my strength. He gasped in pain. It wasn't until I stepped back and held his face in my hands that I noticed all the cuts and bruises. "Patrick, what happened?"

"Some Irish blokes saw us together at the dance. They tried to convince me not to see you anymore, so we had a bit of a scuffle."

"A scuffle! You look as though you've been through the war! Are you all right?"

"I am now. Come on, let's sit on the cabin steps, where we can't be spied upon."

"I thought only Papa and his congregation were that narrow-minded," I said as I gently kissed Patrick's bruised knuckles.

"No, we'll have to fight centuries of Protestant hatred on my side of the river. There were about six of them who sat me down to spell things out. 'How can you be forgetting what her people did to ours all those years?' they asked. 'Emma isn't an Irish-Protestant landlord,' I told them. 'What about all the martyrs who died for our faith, Paddy? When it was illegal to hold Mass

. . . when priests hid in caves? And now you want to marry one of them?' "

I froze, my lips still pressed to his hand. "You said what?"

"I told them I wanted to marry you. It's true, I do . . . that is, if you'll have me. Careful!" he cried when my arms flew around him again. "That's how I got my ribs all smashed up—when I told them I was in love with you and nothing anyone said or did could keep us apart."

My father had called it a physical attraction—and it was that. Patrick and I were like two sides of a wound trying to knit themselves together again to heal and be whole. But it was so much more than a physical attraction. We talked without ever saying a word. We both saw life so much more clearly when we were together, as if each was the spectacles the other needed to correct his vision. We could have lived happily on our island ignoring the rest of the world if we both hadn't yearned to see it so badly. Patrick's passion for life burned as brightly as mine, and he was as dissatisfied with the thought of living an ordinary life as I was.

Hand in hand, we walked down to the marsh to see the white birds we had watched all spring. We found them guarding their nest. As we sank down into our thicket to watch, Patrick drew me into his arms.

"We can be married as soon as I turn twenty-one in October," he said. "If people can't accept us here, we'll become vagabonds, roaming from city to city until we've seen every city in the world."

"I'll play the piano when we run out of money," I said, laughing.

"And I'll work at odd jobs until we can earn train fare to the next town. We'll live like outlaws."

"I'd rob a bank for the chance to spend my life with you."

"Where shall we go first, Emma? I've always wanted to see the Pacific Ocean."

"Do they have orange trees out there? I've always wanted to see oranges growing on trees."

"When fall comes," Patrick said, "and the white birds fly away, we'll fly away with them."

———

Two days after I finished school I started work. Papa had found a job for me with a German farm family with seven children. They lived up the river near the Metzgers. I agreed to work there, provided that I didn't have to live there. Patrick and I continued to meet on the island that summer, falling ever more deeply in love. He recited volumes of beautiful poetry to me as we sat beneath the trees—some by Irish poets, some that he had written himself. We counted the days until his twenty-first birthday on October ninth.

One scorching day near the end of August, I was surprised to find Papa waiting outside with the carriage to take me home when I finished work. "I'm so glad to see you, Papa," I said as I climbed up beside him. "I wasn't looking forward to the long walk home in this heat. I spent all morning in a steaming kitchen and all afternoon manhandling sweaty children. I feel like a wilted flower." I leaned against the carriage seat and peeled my dress away from my sticky skin, longing for a bath. The horses trotted down the road.

Papa didn't slow the wagon when we got to the parsonage. We rode past it. "Where are you going, Papa?"

"Be quiet, Emma." The ice in his voice sent a chill down my spine, in spite of the heat. When we crossed the river, I almost asked him to stop the wagon, afraid that I might be sick. Papa was never this cold, this still, unless he was very angry. And if he was angry with me, then it could only be because of Patrick.

He drove to where Patrick worked and stopped the wagon. We waited in agonized silence beneath a relentless sun until Patrick emerged through the doors. Papa climbed down from the wagon seat and slowly walked toward him. "May I have a word with you, please . . . about my daughter?"

Patrick looked startled, then wary. By the time they walked back to where Papa had parked the wagon, I saw by the fire in Patrick's eyes and on his flushed cheeks that he was angry too. I could barely climb down beside them on my quivering legs.

"I've been told that you've been meeting my daughter on Squaw Island, unchaperoned. Is this true?"

Patrick held his chin high, unashamed. "Yes, sir. It's true."

I saw Papa's chest heave. "Then I'm going to ask you straight out—have you dishonored her? Whether or not you think Emma was willing, have you . . . have you had your way with her?"

"No, sir. Our relationship has been chaste. I will swear to that on a Bible, if you would like me to. I love Emma. I want to marry her."

"You want to *marry* her? How is that possible? According to your religion, a marriage isn't recognized in the sight of God unless it takes place in a Catholic church, before a Catholic priest—am I right?"

Patrick flushed. "Yes, Reverend, that's right."

Papa whirled to face me, catching me off guard. "Emma, can you honestly embrace all the theological differences that exist between our two faiths? Can you pray to Catholic saints or to Mary, instead of to our Lord and Savior? Can you confess to a priest each week, knowing that only God can forgive our sins?"

I was afraid to answer. I felt as though I wasn't arguing with Papa, but with God. And He was on Papa's side. "The fact that I love Patrick doesn't change what I believe."

"No? Will you stand in a Catholic church then and lie, saying that you believe what they teach, just so they'll let you get married there?" He turned to Patrick again. "Or maybe you're willing to give up your religion rather than make Emma give up hers?"

"Papa, we worship the same God," I said when Patrick didn't answer. "We'll find a way to make our two faiths work."

"How? What makes you think you will succeed where thousands of mixed marriages before yours have failed? And what will happen when you have children? The Catholic church will not recognize your marriage, Emma, unless you sign a paper agreeing to raise your children as Catholics—isn't that correct?" he asked Patrick.

He looked flustered, trapped. "Yes . . . that's true, but—"

"Will you agree to that, Emma? Will you let my grandchildren be raised as Roman Catholics?" He made it sound as though I'd be raising them to be pagans.

"We haven't talked about that yet . . ." I began, but Papa continued his tirade, relentlessly piling up the obstacles as if measuring them on a scale, showing us that they outweighed our love.

"The Bible says that in a marriage, two people become one flesh. You want to begin a marriage with a breach already existing between you? A breach that will only get wider when you have children? Unless one of you sacrifices his faith, how will you bridge that gap? Patrick, are you willing to walk away from your family and your faith for Emma? Or what about you, Emma? You know that our faith is our family's most precious possession. Your mother and I gave up our work, our families, and our homeland because of our beliefs. Can you throw all that away so carelessly?"

"I'm not throwing it away, Papa. I still believe. . . ."

"Do you believe the Bible is God's Word? Do you believe we should live our lives and base our decisions by that Word?"

"Yes, sir. We both do," Patrick said.

Papa shrewdly added the final weight to tip the balance in his favor. "The Bible says, 'Honor thy father and thy mother that thy days may be long upon the land which the Lord thy God giveth thee.' Will you explain to me, please, how you can honor your parents and please God if you get married?"

Patrick and I were both speechless. Papa looked from one of us to the other, then said to Patrick, "I must ask you to stop seeing my daughter."

"I can't do that, sir. I love her. We want to be married."

"The only way I will ever bestow my blessing on your marriage is if you convert to Emma's faith. Do not come near my daughter again unless you are willing to do that."

I loved Patrick, but I also loved Papa. The thought of choosing between the two of them made me physically ill. Days passed, as summer changed to fall, when I could barely haul myself out of bed. Papa wouldn't allow me out of his sight when I wasn't working. I didn't see or hear from Patrick.

What was he thinking? Had Papa convinced him to forget me? Or was he saying good-bye to his family so he could convert to my faith and marry me? As September turned into October, I realized that Patrick's birthday on the ninth would provide the answer. That was the day we had planned to be married. If I hadn't heard from him by then, I would probably never hear from him again.

Either way, I had known for a long time now that I could never marry Markus Bauer. I answered Markus's next letter with a short note, telling him not to write to me anymore, telling him that I had fallen in love with someone else.

The day before Patrick's birthday, the cold, dismal weather matched my mood. I walked home from work in a downpour, the road muddy beneath my feet. Sodden brown leaves drooped from the tree branches, dripping more rain. When I passed the Metzgers' farm and saw their boat tossing on the waves, I paused for a moment to gaze out at Squaw Island. If I'd had any tears left, I would have wept.

I started down the road again and saw a small boy walking toward me. He didn't belong to any of the families that lived on this side of the river. He halted in the middle of the road and waited until I reached him.

"Is your name Emma?" he asked.

My heart leaped. "Yes."

"This is for you." He handed me a piece of paper, then turned and took off at a trot, going back the way he had come. The note was from Patrick. He wanted me to meet him inside the movie theater that night.

I knocked on the door of Papa's study after dinner, then sat in the chair facing him when he asked me inside. "I've obeyed you all these months, Papa. I haven't seen Patrick. Could you find it in your heart to lift my punishment a bit? I'd like to go into town tonight. I'd like to visit with Sophie and her new baby."

The grim look on his face as he studied me brought tears to my eyes. Papa no longer trusted me. And with good reason. Even now I was trying to deceive him. "I will permit you to go under two conditions," he said. I waited, hoping that one of them wasn't that he would drive me there. "The first is that Eva must go with you. And the second is that you stay away from any public places until this Spanish influenza epidemic runs its course."

"Yes, Papa."

We visited my sister Sophie for about an hour, then I dragged Eva to the movies with me against her will. I left her watching the main feature, saying that I was going to buy popcorn. Patrick was waiting for me in the lobby. He was tense, like a clock that had been wound too tightly. I wanted to hold him in my arms and feel his arms around me, but we didn't dare embrace in such a public place. Patrick led me into a dim hallway outside the restrooms and kissed me for all the weeks we had been apart.

"I haven't changed my mind, Emma," he breathed. "I love you more than ever, and I still want to marry you. Have you changed yours?"

"No," I whispered. "Never!"

"When we're apart I feel like I'm dying. I don't know how I'll ever leave you in the morning to go to work after we're married."

"I know! I love you so much!"

"Then let's be married by a justice of the peace. Maybe if both of our families see that we're willing to sacrifice for each other, they will accept us in time. That's my hope. But even if they don't, I want to be with you. Do you agree?"

I hesitated for a moment as I faced the terrifying thought of being disowned by my parents. Papa had talked about the breach between our two faiths, but Patrick was willing to step into that abyss for me. I knew how much his faith meant to him, how very much he would be sacrificing when he married outside his church. I drew a deep breath and stepped over the edge with him.

"Yes, I agree. When?"

Joy and relief paralyzed him. It was a moment before he could speak. "I'll leave for the city tomorrow. I'll find a job and a place for us to live and come back for you next Friday. Will that give you enough time to get ready?"

"Yes."

"I'll walk out to your farm a week from tonight. I'll be waiting in the backyard for you. I love you, Emma."

"I love you too," I whispered.

Three days later, Eva fell critically ill with the influenza virus. She had caught it at the movie theater. I begged God to punish me, not Eva. I was the one who had disobeyed my parents. I was the one who deserved to die. I pleaded with God, promising to obey Papa, to give up Patrick, even vowing to marry Markus Bauer. I would do anything, if only Eva lived.

But Eva died.

Then I learned that Markus had also died. After Mama and Papa left with Uncle Gus to grieve with the Bauers, I sat alone on the front porch in the dark, numb with despair and guilt. Like a fatal crack in the dam, one lie had led to this devastating flood of sorrow. My life, my parents' lives, would never be the same.

As I gazed out at the swath of darkness that was the Squaw River, I saw a man walking up the road toward our house. I recognized him by the slant of his shoulders and by his determined stride as he headed into the wind.

Patrick.

I rose from the porch and walked across the yard to meet him like a woman in a dream. He took one look at my face and said, "Emma, what's wrong?"

"I can't go with you. I can't leave Mama and Papa. Eva is dead."

"What? How—"

"It was my fault. I made her go to the movie so I could meet you, and she caught the flu and died. We buried her today."

"No . . . Emma, no!" He tried to draw me into his arms, but I pulled away.

"There's more. I wrote to Markus Bauer and told him I was in love with you, and now he's dead, too, over in France. We just heard the news a little while ago." Patrick sagged as if I'd punched him in the stomach. I spoke the words that I knew we were both thinking. "It's God's punishment on us, Patrick."

"No!" It was a cry of horror, not denial.

"It's true, you know it is. God knew that it would take something as drastic as Eva's death to prevent us from going away together, and now she's dead."

"Please . . . no . . ."

"Remember Papa's words about honoring our parents? We've hurt too many people already. Both of our families. I can't hurt my parents anymore. I can't . . . I can't go away with you."

"Emma, I love you!"

"And I love you. But how can we start a new life together under such a weight of guilt? Eva is dead because of us."

Patrick groaned and covered his eyes. "Ah, God . . . why? Why?"

"He won't answer, Patrick. He didn't answer any of my prayers for Eva. This pain we feel is His punishment. I only wish those two graves were ours. We're the ones who sinned."

"Let me hold you, Emma . . . please. Once more . . ."

We clung to each other in the darkness alongside the road while the wind swirled dead leaves around our feet. I don't remember any moon that night, or any stars. I think the leaden sky must have wept along with us. I longed to find comfort in his embrace, but I didn't.

Our lips met for the last time, a final kiss that would have to sustain me for the rest of my life. Then we turned from each other to walk separate paths.

Leaving Patrick was the hardest thing I'd ever done. I loved him. The longing never went away. I've heard of limbs that have been amputated that still ache with pain years later. That's the way it was when God ripped Patrick from me. Such terrible pain . . . I feel it still.

The day after Patrick left me, I met the little Irish boy along the road as I walked home from work. Patrick had sent him to me with a book of our favorite poetry. Tucked inside, in Patrick's handwriting, was a final poem:

To my beloved Emma,

> *When you are old and gray and full of sleep,*
> *And nodding by the fire, take down this book,*
> *And slowly read, and dream of the soft look*
> *Your eyes had once, and of their shadows deep;*
>
> *How many loved your moments of glad grace,*
> *And loved your beauty with love false or true,*
> *But one man loved the pilgrim soul in you,*
> *And loved the sorrows of your changing face;*
>
> *And bending down beside the glowing bars,*
> *Murmur, a little sadly, how Love fled*
> *And paced upon the mountains overhead*
> *And hid his face amid a crowd of stars.*

1980

Emma's story brought tears to Suzanne's eyes. The mysterious Patrick had sprung to life for a little while, and when the story was finished, she felt Emma's loss. Suzanne busied herself with refilling their empty coffee cups in an attempt to disguise her tears, wondering which was the greater tragedy—a love that had never had a chance to flower, or a love that had blossomed for a while in a glorious burst of color, then died.

Patrick was the key to the entire mystery, she suddenly realized. If Karl Bauer wasn't Grace's real father, and if Emma had never loved any man except Patrick, then Patrick must be Grace's real father. If she could find him, she would find the man who had loved Grace "more than life itself." But how could she go about finding him?

"You haven't heard a word I've said, have you?" Grace said, interrupting Suzanne's thoughts.

"Me? No, I'm sorry, Mom. I was a million miles away. What was your question?"

"I said that I didn't want any more coffee unless it's decaffeinated, but you went ahead and refilled my cup anyway."

"It's decaf," Sue said. "I was just thinking about something else."

Why *was* she so obsessed with the past? Was she using it as a diversion, the way women use soap operas to distract themselves from their own problems? No, she simply couldn't escape the conviction that if she solved the mysteries of the past, it would help her unscramble the mess that she and Jeff had created. Like the wooden nesting dolls Emma had once mentioned, if Suzanne could make sense of the lives of the women before her, her own life might fit into its proper place.

"Mom," she said suddenly, "I'd like to go along with you tomorrow afternoon when you take Grandma to her friend's funeral, all right?"

Grace's carefully groomed eyebrows lifted in surprise. "Sure. But why on earth would you want to do that?"

"The funeral is in your old Irish neighborhood, right? I'd like to see what it looks like."

Before Grace or Emma had a chance to respond, the doorbell rang.

"That's probably your father," Grace said. She and Emma followed Suzanne into the living room to greet him. A few hours ago Suzanne had been angry with her father and would have greeted him coldly, but after retelling her own story and listening to Emma's, all of her anger had drained away.

"I'm sorry I'm so late," he said. "It's been a grueling night." He seemed strangely subdued, his usual bluster and self-assurance gone. Grace noticed it immediately.

"What's wrong, Stephen?" She eased his sport coat from his drooping shoulders and helped him loosen his tie. He exhaled wearily.

"I've been a pediatrician for thirty years, but I still can't get used to losing a child." He ran his hand over his short, bristly hair and sighed again. "In the end, when I've done everything I can, when death is inevitable, I often wish I'd become a minister instead of a physician."

"I'm so sorry," Grace murmured. She seemed to know exactly what he needed, the right touch, the right amount of sympathy, the right words. Suzanne watched as her mother waited on her father, reheating his dinner, choosing the kind of salad dressing he liked, rubbing his tired shoulders after he was seated at the dining room table. Suzanne had always disparaged her mother for giving him such lavish attention, but tonight she felt differently. Tonight she couldn't forget her grandmother's words—"*I would give anything to have Patrick beside me again . . . to grow old together.*" Suzanne wiped another tear.

"Thanks for saving me some supper," her father said. But as he pushed it around on his plate, she saw that his appetite was no better than the rest of theirs had been. He looked up at their somber faces, glanced at the broken dinner plate, and said, "I'm really sorry, Sue. What did I miss?"

"Suzanne was telling us about her career, among other things," Emma said. She sat down at the table across from him and smiled. "Stephen, tell us what you think of your daughter and what she has accomplished."

Suzanne was suddenly afraid. "Don't put Daddy on the spot, Grandma. He probably doesn't feel much like talking."

Stephen looked from one woman to the other again, then leaned back in his chair. "I've never been very good at saying what I feel. You understand that, don't you, Grace? I'm a scientist. I've been taught to analyze data, to seek solutions—not to pick apart my emotions. But tonight you've caught me at a vulnerable time. I had no solution for that child's cancer, and that's a very hard thing for me to accept. I was thinking about my own kids as I drove here—how I didn't tell them often enough that I loved them. It didn't matter so much with Bobby—he and I are a lot alike, he understood. But you've always been different, Suzanne, not like your mother or me."

Her father looked at her, and she saw the sorrow in his eyes. "The truth is, I've always envied Jeff," he said. "He was so spontaneous about expressing what he felt—I'll never forget that piece he painted about the Vietnam protests.

He was comfortable with his feelings, and he understood you in a way that I never did. I also think that Jeff has changed a lot in the past few years. Maybe he and I understand each other better now—but you and he have lost something in the process. Watching what's happened between the two of you these past few months has been like watching a slow death—like the death I witnessed tonight—and both losses are especially tragic because like that child, your marriage was so young and fresh and alive just a short time ago. As I said, it's very hard to accept. I want to do something, solve something, change things . . . and I can't."

Suzanne's tears rolled down her face as her father spoke. He rarely shared so much of himself, and she accepted his words and his willing vulnerability as a precious gift. He paused for a moment and looked up at Emma. "I haven't answered your question, have I? You asked me what I thought about Sue's career. . . ." He turned to face Suzanne again, and she saw his love for her shining in his hazel eyes. "I don't know much about your work, I'm sorry . . . but I do know that I'm very, very proud of you."

Suzanne rose from her chair, and for the first time in many years, she embraced her father.

TWENTY-EIGHT

Grace pulled her car beneath the canopy of the funeral home the next day and waited while Emma climbed from the car. "Are you sure you don't want us to come inside with you, Mother?" she asked.

Emma waved her away impatiently. "I'm not a helpless old lady yet! And why would you want to sit through Katie Hogan's memorial service? You didn't even know her. I'll get a ride with someone to the cemetery. You can pick me up in front of St. Michael's in . . . let's say two hours." She strode off, carrying the two bird-of-paradise flowers she had bought at a florist's shop near Birch Grove. The bright orange flowers created a vivid splash of color against Emma's gray suit.

"All right, we've got two hours," Suzanne said.

"To do what?" Grace asked. "I still don't understand why you wanted to come along to take Grandma to a funeral, for heaven's sake. How interesting can that be to warrant an afternoon off work?"

"Hearing your story made me curious to see your old neighborhood. That's why I asked you to bring Grandma's old photograph album along. I thought it would be fun to compare how it looked then and now. I've never seen the old apartment where you lived with the Mulligan sisters. As far back as I can recall, Grandma always lived in the apartment house she just moved from."

"That's because she moved there right after your father and I were married. Stephen insisted. The Mulligans' place was too run-down. He bought the other apartment building and moved Mother into it."

"Daddy *bought* the building?"

"Please don't tell her. He knew she wouldn't take charity, so it was the only way he could get her into a decent, affordable apartment."

"Did he buy Birch Grove too?" Suzanne's voice dripped sarcasm. Grace ignored it.

"Not exactly. But he did make a substantial donation. Where do you want to go first?"

Suzanne raked her dark hair from her eyes. "Start with your old street. I want to see Booty's store and the cemetery near the church. We have two hours to find Patrick. He's the key to this mystery."

"Oh, Suzanne. I hope you're joking. Why has the past become such an obsession with you lately? First you wanted to find my 'real' father, now you want to find Patrick?"

"They are one and the same," she said matter-of-factly. "I'm convinced that Patrick *is* your real father."

"But that's ridiculous! Their relationship ended in 1918. I was born in 1925. There is no reason to believe that he's my father."

"If they loved each other as much as Grandma said, it's inevitable that they would meet again."

"Have you been reading Victorian romance novels, Suzanne? You're usually so pragmatic."

"Humor me. The key here is the fact that when Grandma left Bremenville she moved to the Irish-Catholic section of the city."

"She was hiding from Karl Bauer."

"No, Mom. He found her, remember? Aunt Vera said it was Karl who gave them Grandma's address in the city. That means he must have known where to look for her. He must have known she would go straight to Patrick. And since she came to *this* neighborhood, Patrick must have lived here."

"Oh, brother!" Grace muttered as she steered her car out of the funeral home's parking lot. She was starting to regret letting her daughter come along. "Your analysis sounds very logical, Sue, but life itself seldom is."

"Someone had to have been helping Grandma. Someone who also filled your coal box and paid for your groceries. Remember, it was 1924 and Grandma had no job skills. How would a pregnant woman find work? Doesn't it make sense that she would seek out Patrick's help after leaving Karl? He would help her, even if he was married to someone else. He loved her."

"This is all wild speculation," Grace said as she waited for a traffic light. "Besides, I asked your father about Karl Bauer having the mumps, and he said only fifteen to thirty-five percent of mumps cases affect the reproductive system. Even then, he said there might be impaired fertility but that true sterility is very rare. Karl *could* have been my father, regardless of what his adopted son said."

"Then why didn't his second wife ever get pregnant? Why did they adopt two sons?"

"And another thing—Mother was pregnant with me when she left Karl, right? How did the mysterious Patrick get her pregnant if he was living here in the city and she lived in Bremenville? It doesn't follow logically at all."

"I'll bet it will make sense once we figure out who Patrick is. Maybe he traveled to Bremenville regularly on business, or maybe he had relatives there. I'm guessing that Patrick was one of your five 'fathers.' They each helped you and Grandma in one way or another."

Grace drove around a corner and slowed as she pointed to a shabby stone building in need of a new roof. A sign out front read *Neighborhood Health Clinic.*

"That used to be Peace Memorial Church," she told Suzanne. "That's where I became a Christian years ago. My girlfriend, Frances Weaver, lived about two blocks up the street from the church." Grace felt a wave of sorrow as she gazed at the boarded storefronts, aging tenements, and crumbling sidewalks. The neat Irish-Catholic bungalows of her childhood, with their lace curtains and flowers in the windows, had sadly disappeared. "I can't believe how run-down everything is," she said, "and I thought it was pretty bad during the depression. Maybe we'd better not linger too long. I would hate to get mugged." She maneuvered the car through the alien, yet familiar streets.

"St. Michael's Catholic Church," Suzanne said, reading the sign. "Was that Father O'Duggan's church?"

Grace braked, catching her breath at the sight of the old gray stone church. Her emotional reaction surprised her. Seeing Father O'Duggan's church was almost like seeing him again.

"Yes, that was his church. It hasn't changed very much at all. And that used to be the rectory, next door—oh my, it's a women's shelter now? Well, that's what he wanted. He always said the house was much too big for one priest. Around this corner on King Street is where—oh, the Mulligans' house is gone . . . that bar is new . . . Booty's store is gone too. It used to be right where that vacant lot is." Grace pulled the car over to the curb and surveyed a row of shabby storefronts and post-war brick bungalows that had been built after her mother had moved away. Even these "new" houses looked sadly in need of repair. She felt an odd sense of loss. "Well, that's all there is to see of the old neighborhood," she said. "Where to now?"

"Go back to St. Michael's church. We're going to take a walk through the cemetery."

"Do I dare ask why?"

"I want to find Booty Higgins' grave. He must have had a very strong connection with you and Grandma if he fed you during the depression. Booty is obviously a nickname, so it's not going to say 'Booty' on the tombstone."

"And you think maybe his name was Patrick?"

"Grandma said Patrick was dead, remember? And Booty died when you were thirteen."

"I can't imagine Booty Higgins reading poetry!" Grace laughed to disguise how nervous she really felt. Suzanne's probing was starting to get to her, upsetting her equilibrium. "Booty wore a grungy apron and stood behind a counter all day in a dingy, smoke-filled store. If there was a poetic side to him, I never saw it. But who knows, I was only a child."

She found a parking space across the street from the church and they climbed out, locking the car. Suzanne fed quarters into the meter. Grace felt the years rolling backward, the past returning to life as they crossed the street and entered the cemetery.

"Do you know where he was buried," Suzanne asked, "or do we need to look it up in the office?"

"I think I can find it. I remember it was along the fence on this side, not too far back. Mother and I used to walk through here on Sunday afternoons, and we usually visited Booty's grave."

"See? That must mean something!"

"It means that the cemetery was the closest thing we had to a park. Booty's grave is this way. I remember there was another huge marker with a stone bench nearby that just read, 'Higgins.' "

Trees that had been saplings in her youth were full-grown now, but Grace surprised herself and Suzanne by walking almost directly to Booty's grave on the first try. The large tombstone that read "Higgins" was easy to find. Near it lay Booty and his wife, Sheila.

"*Ian*," Grace said, reading his name aloud. "That's right, his name was Ian Higgins."

Suzanne's disappointment was almost as great as Grace's relief. "Are you sure this is his grave?"

"Yes, he died shortly after my thirteenth birthday. And look—the marker says May 29, 1938. And I know his wife's name was Sheila."

"One down, four to go," Suzanne said with a sigh. Her steps were much slower as they began walking back to the car. "But I'm not giving up. What about O'Brien? He sounds the most like Patrick, with his zest for adventure. Grandma said Patrick didn't want to live an ordinary life, remember? That certainly fits with an outlaw like O'Brien. What was his first name?"

Grace pursed her lips in thought. "He was just O'Brien. I can't recall ever hearing him called by a first name. I think that was how he wanted it. I'm sorry."

"You said that the first time Grandma went to ask O'Brien for a job, he and Black Jack seemed to know her . . . they greeted her like long-lost friends."

"That's true. I remember a lot of hugs and tears. And they made a huge fuss over me."

"What about Slick Mick? You said he was sentimental, that he sang ballads. Can you picture him reading poetry?"

"Well, yes. He's the most likely candidate in that respect."

"And Mick said he had a daughter your age. Was Mick his real name or did they call him that because he was Irish—you know, the way they call all Irishmen 'Mick'?"

"Sue, I'm sorry, but I just don't know the answers to your questions."

"What about Black Jack? He was a fighter, like Patrick."

"Those were the only names I ever heard any of them called."

"If we went downtown to the Regency Room, do you think someone might remember O'Brien?"

"The hotel is long gone. There's a parking garage there now."

"Well, that leaves Father O'Duggan. He played the biggest role in your life."

"Yes, but his name was Thomas. I know that for a fact. Besides, he was a father to everyone in his parish, not just to me. He was a very godly, caring man—and not at all the type to engage in affairs with married women!"

As they neared the front gates. Grace saw a hearse slowly enter the cemetery, followed by a line of cars. It was probably the funeral Emma was attending. Good. They would be going home soon and the probing would stop. It would be better for everyone if the past remained buried.

When the last car had passed, Suzanne said, "I'm convinced that one of the men in your life was Patrick, and that Patrick is your real father. Why else would Grandma live here in Little Ireland?"

"I admit it would make a great story, Suzanne, but it would have to be fiction. In spite of all your brilliant speculation, we may never know the truth." They had reached the car once again. Grace looked at her wristwatch. "We still have forty-five minutes. What do you want to do now? Since we're meeting Mother here at the church, I hate to give up my parking space, but I'm not sure it's safe to wander too far."

"There has to be a way to find out what O'Brien's first name was!"

Grace threw up her arms in a gesture of defeat. "Give it up, Suzanne. We're never going to know."

"I can't! It's driving me crazy!"

As Grace stared at the facade of St. Michael's, she suddenly thought of a way she could distract Suzanne from her obsession. She glanced at the meter and saw that they still had time remaining on it. "You know what? While we're waiting for Mother, I'd like to see Father O'Duggan's grave. He must be buried in this cemetery somewhere, since he worked here all his life. Do you think we could find out where?"

"Sure, we can easily get that information in the cemetery office. Come on."

"You go ahead. I want to buy some flowers from that vendor down the street. Find out where his grave is, and I'll meet you outside the office."

While Suzanne went to consult the register, Grace bought a huge bouquet of daffodils and tulips. She met Suzanne coming out of the office a few minutes later.

"That was easy," Sue said, waving a piece of paper. "The section for all the priests and nuns is along one side. I wrote down directions."

They walked through the peaceful grounds again. Unlike the frantic pace in the city streets outside the gate, the cemetery was quiet and serene. Restful. Grace glimpsed the line of dark cars parked near the back of the graveyard. Sue led the way as they strolled up and down the rows.

The clergy graves were very plain, marked with small identical markers that lay flat on the grass. Grace silently read the names of long-forgotten priests and nuns: *Sister Angelica . . . Sister Benedict . . . Father Hogan . . . Father O'Sullivan.*

Suzanne counted out loud, searching for the right row. "It's the fourth one in from the road—one, two, three . . . here it is, Mom. 'Father Thomas—' " She inhaled sharply.

Grace looked down at the grave and the bouquet of flowers she carried slipped from her grasp. The tombstone read, *Father Thomas Patrick O'Duggan.*

Two bright orange bird-of-paradise flowers, just like the ones Emma had brought from home, lay on his grave.

"No . . ." Grace whispered. "Oh, please . . . no!"

Somehow, Grace made it back to the car on wobbly knees. Too shaken to drive, she let Suzanne get behind the steering wheel.

"It could simply be a coincidence, you know," she told Suzanne. "Patrick is probably the most popular name there is for Irish boys. He's the patron saint of Ireland, for goodness' sake. We could probably find a hundred markers in that cemetery that say Patrick."

"Are the flowers a coincidence too? It has to be him, Mom. Grandma said she met Patrick during World War I, right? Why didn't he serve in the armed forces if he was twenty years old? Father O'Duggan wouldn't have been able to serve because he limped. And another thing, why did Grandma have his prayer book?"

Grace felt sick all over again. "I don't know."

"Father O'Duggan *must* be Patrick. It all fits together. He was probably so in love with Grandma that he became a priest after they broke up."

"Look, even if all this is true, even if he is the mysterious Patrick, it still doesn't mean he's my father. Their relationship ended in the fall of 1918. I was born almost *seven years* later. Father O'Duggan worked at St. Michael's all his life. He would have no reason to return to Bremenville. Maybe Mother did go to him for help after she left Karl, but that doesn't make him my father."

Suzanne reached over the seat and retrieved the photograph album from the back. "I want to look at his picture again."

Grace gazed across the street at the unchanged facade of St. Michael's church. Once again, she was transported into the past. She saw Father O'Duggan striding toward her after school with his gentle, rolling gait. She pictured his smile and the way his face lit with joy when he saw her. As she did, it was as if Grace's eyes were opened and she saw what she had never seen before—his face. His familiar face. In an instant, Grace's life exploded with the force of a bombshell. All the lies she had once believed rained down painfully like shrapnel.

"No, Suzanne!" she moaned. "Don't look! Please don't look!"

It was too late. She had already found his picture.

"Mom, look at the man! The answer has been staring us in the face!"

Grace closed her eyes. "I don't need to look." Grace knew what she would see, even in a black-and-white photo—the same oval-shaped face as hers, the same bright blue eyes, the same pale brows. His hair was the identical shade of blond as hers, and would have been just as unruly if Father O'Duggan hadn't slicked it down with hair tonic every morning.

"Let's go home, Suzanne," she begged. "Please . . . let's go home."

"We have to wait for Grandma. And you have to confront her."

"No, I can't. It's too awful . . . I don't want to believe that this is true. Father O'Duggan wouldn't . . . I can't believe it. Not him. And I don't want to upset Mother by accusing her. . . ." She felt as though she was babbling.

"Upset *her*? Mom, you're the one who's upset. She owes you an explanation. Besides, maybe she'll be glad to get it off her chest after all these years."

"No, she's near the end of her life now. It's much too late to start unearthing all her secrets. She must have kept them buried for a reason."

"Listen, Mom. When Grandma comes back, I think we should show her what we found, show her his tombstone. We'll just ask her if Father O'Duggan was Patrick. That's all we'll ask, I promise. If she doesn't want to tell us more, we'll leave it at that."

It can't be true . . . it simply can't be true, Grace told herself over and over as they waited in front of the church for her mother. *Not Father O'Duggan.* Twenty minutes later, Emma strode through the cemetery gate, smiling in spite of the somber occasion. She hugged all her old friends good-bye, then crossed the street and got into the car. She seemed like a stranger to Grace as she sank into the backseat with a weary sigh.

"Oh, that was dreadful!" Emma said. "Poor Katie, stuck with such a tiresome priest for her funeral. I think he was in league with the undertaker, and they were both trying to drum up more business by boring us all to death. Grace, promise me you'll shoot off fireworks or bottle rockets or something when I die. Anything to liven things up! . . . Where are you going, Suzanne?"

Without a word of explanation, Suzanne had driven across the street and through the cemetery gates. She parked the car near Father O'Duggan's grave.

"Where on earth are you taking me?"

"Can we show you something, Grandma?" Suzanne helped Emma from the car. Grace trembled from head to toe as she stood between her mother and her daughter, gazing down at Thomas Patrick O'Duggan's grave. The bouquet of flowers that Grace had dropped lay strewn beside Emma's birds-of-paradise.

"Oh my," Emma breathed.

"Father O'Duggan was Patrick, wasn't he, Grandma," Suzanne said.

Emma was silent for a long moment before answering. When she spoke, her voice sounded very old. "I guess . . . I guess it's obvious, isn't it? With the flowers . . ." She exhaled wearily. "He was named Thomas, after his father, and he didn't want to be. His father was not a very nice man. So Patrick was always known by his middle name—at least when I knew him."

"Was Father O'Duggan a priest when you met him?" Suzanne asked.

"No, but he had attended seminary for a year before the war. He came to Bremenville to help out in the church in 1918. He was having doubts, and it was supposed to be a time of reflection for him, to decide if God had really called him to become a priest or not. We fell in love, as I've told you. He wanted to marry me."

Grace waited in anguished suspense for her mother to reveal more, but Emma grew silent. Grace wanted to know the truth, yet she didn't want to know. Suzanne kept her promise not to ask.

It can't be true. It can't be, Grace repeated to herself. Yet in her heart, she knew that it was.

"Mother, I need to know the truth," she finally said in a shaking voice. "He was my real father, not Karl Bauer, wasn't he?"

Emma stared at Grace, open-mouthed, her face a mixture of surprise and alarm. Then she quickly turned away to stare down at the grave again. Grace longed for her mother to deny it. She wanted to continue believing what she always had—that Karl Bauer was her father, that Father O'Duggan was a devout man of God.

Emma finally looked up. Their eyes met. "Yes, Gracie. Patrick O'Duggan was your father."

Grace felt the bomb explode a second time, more painfully than the first. She covered her face. "No! Mother, no . . . how could you? How could *he?*"

"It wasn't something we planned, Gracie. Neither one of us ever meant for it to happen."

"But how could you lie to me all these years!" Grace wept.

"I'm sorry. . . . I hope that you'll forgive me, but I wouldn't blame you if you didn't. I never forgave myself."

Suzanne pulled Grace into her arms and held her tightly. Grace knew that if her daughter let go, she would shatter into a thousand pieces. She wanted to run, wanted to crawl into a hole somewhere, to weep and mourn. She didn't want to face the awful truth that she was illegitimate, that her parents had committed adultery. When her tears were under control again, she pulled away from Suzanne.

"Did Father O'Duggan know I was his daughter?"

Emma stared at the ground. She hadn't moved, as if frozen in place. "You were the image of him, Gracie. The first time he saw you at the Mulligans' when you were about four years old, you gave him a shock. He saw the same eyes looking back at him that greeted him in the mirror each morning, and he knew without asking that you were his daughter. In fact, you noticed the resemblance yourself. His mother had to hide his childhood picture because you thought it was yourself."

Grace remembered the night Father O'Duggan took her to Mam's house—how he had thrown down his hat and scooped her up into his arms, their faces side by side. *"Will you look at the child, for the love of God?"*

"Mam knew I was her granddaughter!"

"She refused to believe Patrick at first when he told her I was pregnant with his child. She said I was trying to ruin him and make him quit the priesthood. But when she saw you . . . well, there was no longer any doubt in her mind. To her credit, she loved you as one of her own."

Grace recalled the comfort of Mam's arms, the lilt of her Irish brogue, the security and love Mam had lavished on her during those months. Then she had vanished from Grace's life once again.

"Why did you lie to me all these years?" she asked again.

"I had to lie. I had to protect the two people I loved—you and your father."

Her father. The shadowy image of Karl Bauer had been violently ripped away like a page torn from a book, replaced by a tall golden man in a clerical collar, a man she had once revered and admired. As Grace's shock began to subside, a stronger emotion replaced it—anger.

"My *father*! He was my *father*! Why didn't he tell me? He knew how much I wanted a father. I begged him to let me call him Daddy, just *once*. He refused me!"

Emma gripped Grace's arms as if to steady her. "That was my fault, not his. I made him swear that he'd never tell you the truth or I would disappear and he'd never see you again. He kept that promise, even though it broke his heart to do it. He had to, don't you see? We both had to lie to protect you from scandal. I had to make you and everyone else believe that you were Karl's daughter. I dragged out the divorce proceedings for as long as I could so that I would be legally married when you were born. I didn't care if the stigma of divorce fell on me. But the stigma of illegitimacy, to be branded the child of an adulterous Catholic priest—that shame would have fallen on you and on Patrick. I couldn't allow that to happen. You were the two people I loved most in all the world. Patrick said he didn't care about his reputation, but he agreed to keep the secret for your sake. He loved you, Gracie. Your father loved you more than life itself."

PART SIX

Patrick and Emma
1918 ~ 1948

TWENTY-NINE

"I want to serve God," Patrick told me as we sat on the beach on Squaw Island, "but I can't accept His terms. God is asking too much of me. He's demanding that I give up . . . life! Living! Going places and seeing things!"

"I feel exactly the same way!" I said.

"The dean of the seminary says that I haven't surrendered all of myself to Him. That I won't make a good priest until I do. He suggested that I take a year off from school and work here."

My father had recognized God's call on Patrick's life the day they had talked in his study after Papa's beating. In spite of his disagreement with many of the tenets of the Catholic faith, he said that Patrick was "God's workman in another vineyard." He warned me not to oppose God's will. I wouldn't listen.

When Patrick decided we would elope and be married by a justice of the peace, he was not only abandoning his church, but his calling to the priesthood. The pressure on his side of the family was even worse than on mine. They were so proud to have a future priest in the family, someone who could redeem the name of Thomas O'Duggan. But that would all be lost if he gave up his calling, especially to marry a Protestant girl. But God had the final say over all our plans. God wielded a weapon more powerful than love—He held the power of life and death. Eva died. Our disobedience killed her. Patrick belonged to God, and He wanted him back.

We held each other that night after Eva's funeral, standing beside the desolate road, our eyes finally opened to our sin.

"When Jonah ran from God, he plunged everyone on board the ship into the hurricane," Patrick said. "Now I've done the same thing. I've brought all this misery on you and your family by my disobedience. I don't know how you can ever forgive me, Emma. I won't even ask you to. But I know I will never stop loving you. When I take the vow of celibacy, it will be because I can never marry you."

I lost my two best friends, Eva and Patrick. When I started dating Karl Bauer in the spring of 1919, I still hadn't touched the bottom of my grief. It was so fathomless that I accepted Karl as part of my punishment. I would serve out my life sentence with him in Bremenville.

Karl knew all about Patrick and me. The entire town knew. In his jealousy, he never quite believed that we had been chaste. "Is that the way you greeted your Catholic lover?" Karl said when I didn't rush to the door to meet him every day. "Would your holy man have bought you all these nice things?" he said as he fastened a diamond necklace around my throat. For five years Karl poked at the wound, keeping it bloody and raw, never allowing me to forget Patrick.

Then in August of 1924, Karl went away for three days. The morning he left was a beautiful sunny day, and since Karl had taken the car, I decided to walk across the river to the parsonage to visit my mother and my sister Vera. But when I got to the church I kept walking, for some reason. I found the Metzgers' boat tied where it had always been and got in and rowed across the river to Squaw Island.

The river, like my soul, was at the lowest ebb of my lifetime. There had been no rain all that summer and the woods were so dry there were warnings about the danger of forest fires. I remember thinking how appropriate it was to return to the place where Patrick and I had fallen in love and find it as dry and desolate as my soul.

My boat ran aground on the beach a long way from the dock. I hauled it out of the water and set out to explore the now-alien landscape. The marshlands, once teeming with wildlife, lay barren and exposed. Rotting fish and dead reeds littered the cracked, sun-baked clay. I looked for our white birds but found only their abandoned nest. The island, like my life, had changed. Nothing looked the same. I sat on the rock where Patrick had once read poetry to me and recited our favorite verse aloud.

> "I am haunted by numberless islands,
> and many a Danaan shore,
> Where Time would surely forget us,
> and Sorrow come near us no more;
> Soon far from the rose and the lily
> and fret of the flames would we be,
> Were we only white birds, my beloved,
> buoyed out on the foam of the sea!"

Later, I wandered across the island to the cabin. I remembered standing beside Patrick at the cabin's sink, pumping water together, frying mushrooms on the potbellied stove. But as I peered through the dingy window at cobwebs and dust, I saw a house devoid of life. At last, I lay down in the sun on the porch swing and cried myself to sleep.

I opened my eyes to find Patrick standing over me. I thought I was still dreaming. He was much too handsome to be real, a golden-haired Apollo with eyes as blue as the sky. Then his eyes clouded with tears.

"Emma? Is it really you?"

"Shh. Don't talk," I whispered. "I don't ever want to wake up."

He sank down on the porch steps as if too weak to stand. "You're not dreaming . . . I'm real. . . ." I watched his chest rise and fall with each breath and saw a vein in his temple throb with his pulse. I sat up, never taking my eyes off of him.

"Then I must have conjured you with a magic poem," I said. "I wished . . . oh, how I wished that you would appear. And now you have! Our birds have flown, Patrick, but you're here. You're here, so everything is all right again."

I wiped my tears as fast as they fell, afraid to take my eyes off him, afraid he would disappear. But even in our joy we didn't embrace, as if we instinctively knew that a single touch would spark a conflagration. Instead we sat on the cabin porch, talking quietly.

"I thought I would be alone here," Patrick said. "I didn't know you still came back to our island."

"I'll leave. . . ."

"No. Please don't. I came back to Bremenville because I wanted to see you, but I promised myself that I would just watch you from a distance—just drive past your house and see if you were happy. I needed to find out if your husband takes you to all those places we talked about, if he's shown you the ocean and oranges growing on trees." A mixture of emotions played across Patrick's face—joy, longing, apprehension. "I drove past your home and your husband's drugstore, but I didn't see you. I was never going to let you know I was here."

"Because you're a priest now?"

"Yes. Because you're married and because I'm a priest now. I was ordained a year ago, on June fifth. I asked for a parish in the same city where I was raised, and they assigned me to St. Michael's—a mostly Irish parish, much like the one I grew up in."

"I'm glad it has all worked out for you."

He shook his head, looking away for the first time. "I'm not a very good priest, Emma. I'm frustrated. And I'm angry. All the time. I see my congregation yawning and whispering through my homilies, as if salvation wasn't really a matter of life and death, and it makes me furious. I listen to their confessions—the same sins week after week—and I think of my father. I remember his sins, and how he didn't even try to change because the kindly old priest assigned him a few Hail Marys and told him he was forgiven."

Patrick plucked a blade of grass from beside the steps and tore it into pieces as he talked. "It's my job to dispense God's grace to those who confess, but I can't bring myself to do it. They're abusing the grace of God, abusing His forgiveness. And that grace was purchased at such a staggering price! I'm angry with people, angry with their weaknesses and their sin. I administer the sacrament, the body and blood of Christ that restores them to communion with God, knowing their sins will crucify Him all over again."

I watched him swat at a mosquito that had landed on his neck, longing for the warmth of his broad, golden hands. He was quiet for a moment, then said, "The bishop suggested I make a spiritual retreat. He said I'm still carrying a huge weight of unforgiveness from my past. I'm supposed to be a father to the people God has given me. But I don't know how to be a father, you see, because my own father—" He stopped again, waiting until he could trust himself to speak. "Maybe if I'd had a father like yours . . ."

"Like mine. . . ?" I forced my gaze away from him and stared across the river. I could barely see the steeple of Papa's church through the treetops. "When I was a little girl, I thought my papa was the wisest, most wonderful man in the world. I remember telling him once how I planned to travel all over the world, playing the piano, and he spoke as though he understood exactly how I felt. But he couldn't have known. He couldn't have understood me at all. He let me give up my dream. He let me marry a man who has wounded me and broken me until there is nothing left of *me* inside. I can't play the piano anymore. Not at home, not even at church." I heard the bitterness in my voice when I spoke the word. I wondered if Patrick did.

"Karl Bauer doesn't love me. I was only his prize. He won't let me have children because he knows that I'll love them more than him. You talk about the 'cheap grace' of your church, but in my church there is no grace. We pay the consequences of our sins for the rest of our lives. Karl is my penance for causing Eva's death. All the Hail Marys in the world wouldn't free me from the vows I made to him."

"I'm sorry," Patrick said softly. "When I'd heard that you'd married, I prayed that you would love him, that you would be happy with him."

"And I hoped that you would be happy in the life God called you to."

We gazed at each other, and the longing to hold and comfort each other pulled at both of us. Patrick had the spiritual strength to resist. I drew strength from him.

"Are you hungry?" he asked suddenly. "I brought some lunch." He pointed to the box of groceries he had abandoned on the cabin steps. Coming from any other man besides Patrick, it would have been a ridiculous question to ask when our hearts were so full of pain, but I understood him perfectly. We had only a few hours together, and so, by unspoken agreement, we would live in the present, finding joy in each moment before we returned to our empty lives.

We cooked bacon and eggs in the cabin, then washed the dishes together, just as we had the time we'd hunted mushrooms. Sometimes we talked without words—one in heart and thought—always careful not to touch, not to so much as brush against each other.

Later we strolled around the island, reading poetry in the trees as they bent in the wind, delighting in a carpet of dainty wild flowers that had miraculously survived the drought. We sat on the beach, listening to the music of lapping water and the melody of bird song. The island didn't seem nearly as dry and desolate with Patrick beside me.

Too soon, the day drew to a close. As we stood together on the porch of the cabin, we both grew quiet, sensing the end. When we said good-bye this time, it would probably be forever. We would both return to honor the vows we had made before God. We stood looking out at the woods and the water beyond, not at each other.

"It's so unfair," I murmured. "We should have spent a lifetime together, not one day. . . ."

"Hush, Emma. Don't."

"I'm sorry."

"I believe in a God of design, and I know you do too. He's teaching us through our present circumstances, but we have to listen closely to understand what He's saying, just as we listened to the wind and to the bird song today. I'll pray for your marriage, that you'll find happiness in it. Will you pray that He'll make me a better priest?"

I nodded, but somehow Patrick knew that I was lying. The woods seemed to grow still.

"Tell me what's wrong, Emma."

"I can't pray. I haven't prayed since the day Eva died."

"I see. . . ." He drew a breath, as if about to speak, then exhaled with a weary sigh. "If I were a better priest I would know what to say to you, but I don't. I'm sorry."

"It doesn't matter. There is really nothing you can say." The moment I had dreaded all day had finally come. "I should go now," I said. "Good-bye, Patrick."

"Good-bye," he whispered. We turned to each other at the same time.

I remember thinking, *If only I could feel the strength of his arms around me and the warmth of his embrace once more. If only I could inhale the scent of him, just once . . . just one more time . . . to remember . . .*

We hesitated for the same moment. Then he took my face in his hands. And from the moment our lips touched, we were swept away.

I remember the force of the flood when I was a child, and how I'd felt the bridge tremble and sway beneath us the moment before the deluge washed it away. Mama backed the carriage away in time, and we escaped. But Patrick and I made a mistake. We didn't step back in time. We lost our footing, and we were swept away. After that, nothing could have restrained the flood of stored-up love and longing that was unleashed with that single kiss. Nothing.

———

I spent the night with him. What happened between Patrick and me in that cabin was as different from Karl and me as a spring shower is from a hurricane. The aftermath would prove just as destructive. We lost ourselves in each other's embrace, never thinking about the consequences.

As I lay in his arms the next morning after dawn, we heard a man's shout outside. "Hello? Anyone home?" Patrick froze.

"Answer him," I whispered. "He knows someone is here. The windows are open . . . our boats are on the beach. . . ."

Patrick scrambled out of bed to pull on his trousers. "Who's there?" he called.

"It's Alan Metzger."

"We can't let Alan see me!" I whispered frantically. "He goes to Papa's church!"

Patrick stumbled to the door and opened it a crack. "Uh . . . good morning. What can I do for you?"

"My father's boat disappeared from his dock across the river yesterday. I was out fishing this morning and happened to see it on your beach."

"Yes, it was there when I arrived," Patrick said truthfully. "That's the boat I used alongside it."

I slipped into my clothes as they talked, then crawled across the floor on my hands and knees to the woodpile in an alcove behind the potbellied stove. We had been using the older, seasoned wood from the back of the stack, leaving a narrow space behind the pile of newer logs. I crawled into the space and hid.

"That's strange," Alan said. "I guess it must have come unmoored and drifted over here. What did you say your name was?"

"Um . . . Thomas O'Duggan. I'm up from the city for the week."

"Nice to meet you. What kind of work do you do there?"

"I . . . I'm a priest . . . a Catholic priest." Patrick's answer was barely audible.

"You're here on vacation, then? The fishing sure is great in this river, isn't it?"

"I . . . uh . . . I haven't caught any fish yet," he said with a nervous laugh.

"I'll give you a couple of mine if you want. I caught my limit already. My wife doesn't even like fish." He rambled on and on about nothing and never seemed to notice that Patrick's answers were short and clipped. "Well, I guess I'll be going," Alan said at last. "Come on down to my boat and help yourself to some fish."

"Sure . . . thanks."

"And if you don't mind, I'll just tie Dad's boat behind mine and take it home."

"That's fine." I heard them tromp down the stairs, then a few minutes later I heard the door creak open again as Patrick returned. I didn't come out of the wood pile until Patrick said, "He's gone."

I limped from my hiding place, brushing sawdust and bark from my clothes, my leg numb and tingling. Patrick stood in the open doorway with his back to me. When he finally turned around his face was white, his eyes wild with horror. I knew before he even said a word that he would never hold me in his arms again.

"What have I done?" he whispered. "Dear God . . . Emma . . . *what have I done!*" It was a cry of utter anguish.

"It's all right, Patrick. We—"

"No! It's not all right! It will never be all right! Oh, God . . . Oh, God . . . what have I *done*!" He staggered out the door toward the privy, but he didn't make it. He dropped to his knees along the path and was sick.

I watched him through the window for a long time as he knelt there, retching. At last he struggled to his feet and came back inside. He couldn't look at me, as if he no longer saw my face but his own sin and guilt and shame.

"Emma, I'm sorry . . . I'm so sorry. . . ."

"I'm not."

"Will you ever forgive me for this?"

"I don't need to forgive you. That was the happiest night—"

"No . . . stop!" he moaned. "Don't say it! I'm a priest! I broke all of my vows to God! How can I ever face Him? How can I ever partake of the body and blood of Christ again?"

"Patrick, listen. . . ."

"And if that wasn't bad enough, I . . . I slept with a married woman! God help me, I took another man's wife!"

"Were you lying to me when you said you loved me?"

"No . . . the Lord knows it's the truth."

"I went to you willingly, Patrick. You never promised me—"

"Oh, God have mercy on both of us! Don't you realize what we've done? We've committed adultery! *Adultery!* All my life I've hated that word, and I've hated my father for committing it, and now I've done the very same thing! I even used my father's name to cover my guilt. I told Metzger I was Thomas O'Duggan." He hid his face in his hands.

I knew there was nothing more I could say. We stood in the silent cabin, and the sounds that drifted through the open door were no longer gentle, but harsh and mocking—the raucous cry of a crow, the grating of locust wings, the scrape of a tree branch against the roof.

"You'll have to row me back to shore," I said quietly. "Alan took the boat."

"I'll never forgive myself for this," he murmured. "Never."

"Will you forgive me for wanting you?"

He stumbled from the cabin without answering. I let him go. A long time passed as I sat on the bed, unmoving. I could understand Patrick's guilt, but I didn't feel any of it, not even when I thought of Karl. Patrick hadn't stolen a thing from Karl, because Karl had never allowed me into his heart. Nor had he given me any part of himself. Patrick knew my heart more intimately in one day than Karl had in almost five years.

When Patrick finally returned, I was surprised to see that it was evening. I felt empty inside but not hungry, even though I had eaten nothing all day.

"I'll row you to shore now," he said. His red-rimmed eyes were hollow against his pale face. He still wouldn't look at me, nor did he lift his gaze from the floor of the boat as he rowed away from the island. We sat facing each other, but neither of us said a word.

The oars swished in rhythm as he pulled them through the dark water. They seemed to ask, *Why? ... Why? ... Why?* There was no answer. He rowed faster and faster, as if I would burn a hole through the bottom of the boat if he didn't put me on shore quickly. As soon as I felt the hull scrape the gravel of the riverbank, I stepped out and waded onto dry land.

"Emma . . ."

I heard Patrick calling me, but I didn't reply. I kept walking.

"Emma . . . I'm sorry. . . ."

I didn't look back.

THIRTY

When Karl returned home from his trip, I could scarcely tolerate his embrace. I didn't want his nearness to erase the memory of Patrick's. My skin crawled every time Karl touched me or pressed his lips to mine. The next few nights I lied, saying I was indisposed, so that he would stay away from my bedroom.

I hated my life. The only escape from an eternity with Karl, an eternity without Patrick, was death. When the September rains ended the drought, I comforted myself with the thought that once the river rose to its normal level, I would leap from the railroad bridge and die. But before I had a chance to carry out my plan, I discovered that I was pregnant.

I knew the child was Patrick's. And I knew I would protect that new life with every ounce of strength I had. I could tolerate a lifetime with Karl if I could hold Patrick's baby in my arms. But I had failed to consider Karl's need for control. A child wasn't in his plans.

The morning after his abortion attempt failed, Karl drove me home from my sister Sophie's house in icy silence. I wouldn't look at him. I didn't want him to see that I was terrified of him and would run from him again the first chance I got. I had to make him believe that I had forgiven him.

Karl grasped my elbow in his iron grip as he walked me from the car to our front parlor. "Sit down, Emma," he said as he led me to the sofa. He hovered over me, his dark eyes alive with rage like two smoldering coals.

"I know that the child you're carrying isn't mine."

"Wh . . . what are you talking about? Of course the baby is yours."

"*Liar!*" He struck me across the face so hard that my head hit the back of the couch.

In my terror, the only thing I could think to do was to pacify him. "Please, Karl . . . you have to believe me. The baby—"

"*Don't* lie to me again!" He poised his clenched fist in front of my face. His entire body quivered with restrained rage. "I haven't been preventing conception, Emma. I am *unable* to father a child. Now, you *will* tell me who the father is."

I believe he might have tried to beat the truth from me if he hadn't heard a knock at our back door. We both knew that it was our Irish housekeeper, Katie. As quickly as he'd lost it, Karl regained control. "You're a mess!" he said. "Go upstairs and clean yourself up before she sees you."

I staggered up the steps to my bedroom and locked both doors. I wanted to curl up in a corner of my closet and weep in terror, but there was no time. Karl would probably go downtown to open the pharmacy at nine o'clock and let his employees inside, then return home to finish with me. The next train to the city left at 9:10 this morning. I had to be on it. I dumped my knitting out of a carpetbag and began stuffing it with clothes and toiletries. There was no time to change into another dress. I peeled off my ruined hose and pulled on ankle socks and an old pair of shoes. I quickly counted the money in my purse, then added the few dollars I'd hidden in my jewelry box. If I had pawned all the necklaces and rings Karl had given me, they would have been worth a tidy sum, but I slammed the lid shut again, refusing the temptation to steal from him.

My bedroom overlooked the street in front of the house. I watched through the curtain until I saw Karl drive away. I was about to unlock my door when Katie knocked on it, startling me.

"I brought you some tea, Miss Emma," she called from the other side. "Mr. Bauer said you weren't feeling well. . . ." I jerked open the door. Katie saw my wild eyes and disheveled hair and backed up a step. "Oh, Miss Emma!"

"Please help me, Katie. Karl is coming back in a few minutes, isn't he?"

"Y . . . yes, he said he was going to open the store and fetch some medicine for you. He asked me to watch over you until he got back."

"There's no time to explain, but I need to get out of Bremenville before he comes back."

"Where will you go?"

"I don't know. I'll disappear in the city somewhere."

"My brother Ian lives there. You can tell him I sent you and that you need a job and a place to stay." She set down the tea tray and scribbled his address on a scrap of paper. I saw the words *St. Michael's Parish*—Patrick's parish— and felt rescued already. I grabbed an old coat from the closet and hugged Katie good-bye. I didn't feel safe until the train had chugged out of town and was steaming away from Bremenville at full speed.

On the long train ride to the city I made plans. I would find Patrick and tell him about our baby. I needed his help. I had no place to live, no money, no job skills, and a baby coming in seven months. Patrick was unhappy with the priesthood and had probably resigned already by now. I remembered how he'd said he would never be able to partake of the body and blood of Christ again. We would run away together as we'd planned to do a long time ago. When my divorce from Karl was final, Patrick and I would be married.

My biggest fear was that Karl would outrace the train in his car and would be waiting on the platform for me when I arrived. I tied a kerchief over my hair and offered to help a harried mother in the third-class coach with her brood of children. Clutching one child by the hand and another one in my arms, I hid in the crush of passengers as we disembarked. I saw no sign of Karl. When I was sure the coast was clear, I hired a cab to take me to St. Michael's church. The new priest could probably tell me where Patrick had gone after he had resigned.

The taxi dropped me off in front of the gray stone building. I gave the driver the last of my dollar bills. I had only a handful of coins left to my name. I climbed the church steps on shaking legs, tying the kerchief over my head again, as I'd seen Catholic women do. I had never walked through the doors of a Catholic church before.

Inside, the sanctuary was shadowy and serene. I slipped into a pew and allowed the peaceful atmosphere to calm me. There was a mass in progress, and the sound of somber chanting echoed off the wood-panelled walls like a voice from heaven. The priest wore a long black robe with purple vestments and stood with his back to the church, reciting the mass in Latin. Even though I sat in the last row, I knew by the broad sweep of his back and shoulders and the way his golden hair glinted in the candlelight that it was Patrick.

When he turned, holding a chalice in his hands, I saw a look of quiet reverence on his face. I heard the brokenness and humility in his voice, even though I couldn't understand his words. Papa's voice had sounded the same way after the war, after Eva's death, after he had finally accepted all that the hand of God had dealt him. Patrick lifted the bread, the body of Christ, as an offering to God. He had told me he would never be able to partake of it again, but I watched him do it. Somehow, Patrick had made peace with God.

I had heard Papa recite the communion service hundreds of times, and I knew by heart the words Patrick was chanting in Latin: *Take, eat; this is my body, broken for you . . . This is my blood, which is shed for the complete forgiveness of all your sins. . . .*

I remembered the look of shame and horror on Patrick's face when he'd realized his sin, and I knew I couldn't take his peace away from him a second time. I loved him too much. As the handful of congregants filed forward to receive the symbol of Christ's sacrifice from Patrick's hand, I quietly left the church. Patrick would never know that he'd fathered a child.

I stood outside on the steps of St. Michael's, wondering what to do next. If I was going to begin my life over again without him, I would have to find a way to support our baby on my own. As people began to emerge through the church's doors after mass, I remembered the scrap of paper Katie had given me. I pulled her brother's name and address from my pocket and showed it to an old woman. "Excuse me, can you tell me how to get to King Street?"

"Why, that's King Street right there, at that intersection." I found the store around the corner, about a half a block down.

That's how I met Booty Higgins, Katie's brother. I walked into his dusty, jumbled store for the first time that day, and he greeted me with a warm smile. "Afternoon, ma'am. May I help you?" All of a sudden the shock of seeing Patrick as a priest for the first time hit me like a tidal wave. I broke down in tears. "Hey, now . . . it surely can't be as bad as all that, can it?" Booty laid his cigarette in an overflowing ashtray and patted my back awkwardly. I struggled to pull myself together.

"I'm sorry. . . ."

"That's okay, ma'am. I'm sure there's a good reason for . . ."

I thrust the piece of paper Katie had given me into his hands. "I'm looking for Ian Higgins," I said.

"You've found him. That's me."

"I'm a friend of your sister Katie. She said you could help me." He stared from the paper to me and back again, blinking in confusion. "I came down on the train from Bremenville this morning. I need a place to stay."

"Well, I . . . I don't know what to say. . . ."

"Please, Mr. Higgins."

He smiled kindly. "Call me Booty. Everybody does. And your name is. . . ?"

"Emma. Emma Bauer."

I saw by the change in his expression that he recognized the name of his sister's employer. "Well, Mrs. Bauer, it so happens that I do know of a little place where you can stay. Why don't you . . . uh . . . go on out front there and wait for me while I get my wife to mind the store for a while. I'll be with you in a minute." He led me toward the door as he spoke and held it open for me. I watched through the dusty window as he disappeared into his apartment behind the store. A moment later he hurried outside to join me, lighting another cigarette.

"About time for a little break, anyhow," he said as we walked to the corner. "Can I carry your bag for you?"

"No thanks. I'm fine."

"I . . . uh . . . I need to tell you about the room," he explained as we walked. "Maybe you'll want to stay, maybe you won't." He drew a long final drag from his cigarette and threw it onto the ground. "I'm operating a still over there, you see. My wife doesn't even know."

That explained the source of his nickname—Booty. He was a bootlegger, making bathtub gin during Prohibition. He led me to a cramped basement room he'd rented in a tenement several blocks away. It was smaller than Papa's tool shed and not half as clean, but it was comfortably warm, thanks to the stove that needed to run nonstop to power the still. "I'll be happy to let you live here, rent-free," he said as he poured coal into the belly of the stove. "My . . . uh . . . my activities will be less suspicious if the cops see a respectable woman such as yourself coming in and out. You can help me keep the stove going too." I wanted to hug him in gratitude.

"How can I ever thank you?"

"No need," he said shyly. "No need."

I scrubbed the room until my hands were raw, then furnished it with a bed, a hot plate to cook my meals, a washbasin, and a dresser with one drawer missing that I'd salvaged from the trash. Booty gave me some dishes and pots, and a mirror that was so wavy I felt like I'd been sipping his moonshine every time I combed my hair. The stove that powered his gin mill kept the room tropical, even in winter.

Booty came once or twice a day to check on the still; his friends Black Jack and O'Brien, who lived in one of the apartments upstairs, picked up the hooch and delivered it to their customers. Eventually Booty helped me find a job as a waitress in a nearby diner. Both the apartment and the diner were far enough away from Patrick's church and the rectory that I didn't need to worry about accidentally bumping into him.

I worked in that greasy-spoon café as many hours as they were willing to give me, then came home to my tiny room and collapsed. I knew that I could be arrested and thrown into jail if the police raided the apartment, but I felt safe from Karl and that was all that mattered. I'd found refuge on my tiny island, surrounded by a sea of Irish-Catholics.

My sense of security was short-lived. I had just returned to my apartment after working the breakfast and lunch shift one bitterly cold afternoon in November when there was a knock on the door. Always wary of a police raid, I took a minute to hide the still behind the screen Booty had made from an old packing crate. Then I stood on the bed and peered through the basement window.

Karl Bauer stood in the stairwell outside. Papa was with him.

The combination of shock and exhaustion from the long working day turned my knees to water. I collapsed onto the bed, weeping uncontrollably.

"Emma?" Papa called. "Emma, please open the door."

I didn't answer. I didn't know what to do. There was no other way out of the apartment.

"We know you are in there," Karl said. "We saw you come home."

"Go away, Karl! I never want to see you again!" I was terrified of him. I hugged my body to protect the tiny new life it sheltered.

I heard the low mumble of voices as they talked, then Papa said, "May I come in alone, Liebchen?" The sound of Papa's gentle voice addressing me as his beloved child tore my heart in two. I was ashamed to face him. But he had traveled so far to see me.

"Send Karl away first," I finally said.

I stood on the bed again and watched until Karl climbed from the stairwell. I heard an engine start, then a spurt of gravel as the heavy car drove away. I opened the door to let my father in.

Papa wrapped me in his arms and held me tightly. "Liebchen . . ." he said in a hoarse voice. "Thank God we found you." I felt sheltered, safe—a little child in her beloved papa's arms. I savored the familiar scent of his after shave, the damp wool of his overcoat. *My papa.* But in my heart I knew that after today, he would never love me again as he did at that moment.

"How are you, Liebchen? Are you all right?" He held me away from himself and studied my face. His own face was creased with worry, his shoulders bent with weariness.

"Yes, Papa. I'm fine. Here, have a seat on the bed. Let me take your coat." He glanced briefly around the tiny room, then sagged onto the bed, still wearing his overcoat. He never asked about the sound of the dripping still or the sweet smell of Booty's moonshine that wafted from the corner. I sat beside him, numb with dread, and waited for him to speak first.

"Emma . . ." He cleared his throat and tried again. "Emma, I will come straight to the point. Karl says you are expecting a child—and that the child is not his. Is this true?"

"Yes. It's true," I whispered.

"Oh, Liebchen . . ." He closed his eyes. Causing Papa so much pain was one of the worst moments of my life. How could I have hurt this gentle man whom I loved so much? When he lifted his head again he said, "I've come to bring you home. Karl is a good Christian man. He's willing to forgive you for the sake of your marriage vows."

I shuddered at Karl's deception. How could Papa believe he was a good Christian man? "Did he tell you that he tried to force me to abort the baby?"

"Karl said nothing about an abortion."

"No, of course he wouldn't tell you. But that's what he tried to do. That's why I ran away. And that's why I won't let him near me." Sorrow and confusion clouded Papa's gentle blue eyes. And I saw something else there—doubt. "You don't believe me, Papa?"

"I don't know who to believe," he said quietly. He spread his hands in a gesture of bewilderment. "How can I know the truth?"

"Because I'm your daughter! I wouldn't lie to you!" Papa didn't reply. "See? I knew you and Mama would take Karl's side. That's why I left Bremenville." I started to rise, but he seized my hand and pulled me down beside him again. His hand was as cold as stone.

"Emma, I didn't come here to talk about what has already happened. I'm trying to find a way for you to be reconciled. Karl wants you to come home. He's willing to forgive you."

"Under what conditions?" I knew Karl. I knew there would be a price to pay.

Papa sighed. "He'll arrange for you to have the child in secret, then put it up for adoption."

"But it's my child too, Papa! My flesh and blood! How can I give it away to strangers?"

"We can find a good Christian family who will—"

"Papa, no! I can't believe you would agree to this! We're talking about your own grandchild!"

"My grandchild deserves to grow up with parents who love him. Karl may never love your baby as a father should. Can you understand why it might be difficult for him to raise another man's child?"

"Yes. But can you understand why it's impossible for me to give away my baby?"

"Karl is meeting you more than halfway, Emma. He is willing to forgive you if . . ."

"What about you, Papa? Are you willing to forgive me—even if I don't go back to Karl?"

"Repentance precedes forgiveness, Liebchen. It means being sorry for what you've done. I pray that you have confessed your sin to God and have asked His forgiveness. Then of course I will forgive—"

"But I'm not sorry!"

"Oh, Emma." My words stabbed Papa so painfully, I might have shoved a knife into his heart.

"It's the truth, Papa. I love Patrick. I've never loved Karl."

"So," he said, swallowing. "So Patrick O'Duggan is the child's father?"

"Yes. And I'm not sorry we spent that night together. I only wish it could have been a lifetime."

"You're not sorry for the sin of adultery?" Papa asked in a horrified whisper. My words had twisted the knife deeper.

"The only regret I have is that I didn't marry Patrick to begin with. I'm sorry I married Karl. My marriage vows were a sin because I vowed to love Karl and it was a lie. I couldn't love him because I still loved Patrick."

"Emma, your child has been conceived in adultery and—"

"This child I'm carrying is innocent of any wrongdoing. I won't treat it like a dirty little secret that must be hidden under the rug. I won't give Patrick's baby away. It's all I have left of him!"

"If you love your child, then I beg you to repent . . . for the child's sake. The Scriptures say that the sins of the fathers are visited on the children to the third and fourth generation. Is that what you want? Do you want your children and grandchildren to be separated from God as well?"

"How can I say I'm sorry for what I did, when I'm not?"

"Emma, God can't forgive you unless you confess and repent!"

I let the awful truth sink into my heart, then said, "I guess I'll never be forgiven for what I've done."

Papa lowered his head and covered his eyes with one hand. He was silent for a long time. We sat mere inches away from each other, but I knew that the rift that had widened between us was unbridgeable. "That's your choice, not God's," he said at last. "And not mine. Do you remember the story of the Prodigal Son from Sunday school? God will always be waiting for you to return to Him. Waiting to forgive you."

He rose from the bed as if every joint in his body ached and walked to the door. After he opened it, he turned and said, "And I'll be waiting for you too, Emma. With open arms. Every day of my life."

———

Sunday, the Lord's Day, was the hardest day of the week for me, reminding me painfully of both Patrick and Papa. I wouldn't go to church. The diner where I worked was closed, so I often spent the day exploring the city—though I was always careful to avoid the area around St. Michael's. Booty's store was also closed, and he sometimes spent the afternoon in my apartment while I was out tinkering with his still.

One Sunday in December I decided that the weather was too cold for my usual walk. It had begun to sleet. I lay on my bed resting, while Booty lay on the floor beneath the still, trying to unclog a hose. We had been talking quietly, when I suddenly felt the baby stir inside me for the first time. "Oh!" I gasped and sat up.

I startled Booty, who must have thought the cops had arrived. He tried to sit up, too, and banged his head on the leg of the stove. "Ow! Wha . . . what's going on?"

"Oh, that's so . . . incredible! I just felt my baby move, I felt it! It was like . . . like a butterfly's wing or . . . or the fingers of a tiny little hand brushing against me!" Booty wiped his hands on a rag and came over to sit on the other end of my bed. He was dewey-eyed, his voice soft.

"Ah, so that's why you've been hiding out here . . . it's a wee baby, is it?"

I nodded. "Karl . . . my husband, didn't want the child. He tried to make me get rid of it."

"Poor lass . . ."

A furious pounding on the outside door interrupted us. This time we both thought the cops had arrived. Booty froze, too panicked to move, but I quickly climbed onto the bed and peered outside. "It's a woman, Booty. She—"

The next thing we knew, the door flew open and she set upon Booty like a whirlwind. "Aye! So this is what you've been up to behind me back? Mary and Joseph and all the saints! Ye've taken a mistress!"

"No! Sheila, no! It's not what you think at all!"

"I might have known, you lousy, no-good—" She had a huge brown purse in her hand the size of a small suitcase, and she swung it at Booty, clubbing him in the head. The blow stunned him, and before he could react she hit him two more times. When he collapsed to the floor, shielding his head, she began kicking and clubbing him at the same time.

"Stop it! You'll kill him!" I screamed. "Stop!"

She whirled to face me. "You're next, pretty lady! We'll see how many married men will want you after I'm done with you!" I slowly backed away from her.

"No, listen!" I stammered. "I'm not his mistress! I'll swear to you on . . . on a Bible that your husband and I never—"

"Oh, you'll get your chance at confession, girlie, and don't you think that you won't! I'll send for Father O'Duggan, and we'll see what he has to say about this little setup."

"No, please . . ."

Booty had struggled to his feet again. He crept up behind his wife, pinning her arms and her colossal purse to her sides. "Sheila, darlin', listen to me. Mrs. Bauer isn't my mistress. She's a friend of Katie's, and she needed a place to stay. We never—"

Mrs. Higgins wasn't listening. As she wrestled to free herself from Booty, she uttered a stream of Irish curses at the top of her voice that would have left poor Booty deformed and gelded for all eternity if the saints had heeded her. I slipped into my shoes, preparing to run.

"What are you doing here all alone with her, then?" Sheila cried.

"I'm here to fix the still."

"The what?"

"It's a still, Sheila, for making gin," Booty told her. "That's what I've been doing over here all the time."

"You're a *bootlegger*? Breaking the law on top of everything else?"

"Me and O'Brien are just trying to earn a few extra bucks while we can. Lots of people are doing it, Sheila. There's probably a hidden gin mill or two on every block."

Sheila freed herself from his grip and stormed out. Booty followed right behind her. I closed the door behind them and sank onto the bed. But it was a long time before I could stop shaking.

THIRTY-ONE

A week before Christmas, I returned home from a long morning at the diner to find Mama and my sister Vera shivering in my stairwell. I was so ashamed to have them see how I was living and to find out that I was expecting a baby that I almost ran in the opposite direction. But it was too late. They had already spotted me walking toward them. Mama set down the parcels she was carrying and ran to me. She pulled me into her arms, weeping.

"Let's all go inside," I said a few minutes later, "before our eyes freeze shut." I dried my own tears and unlocked the door.

As Mama and Vera glanced around the tiny room, noting my sagging bed, the gray cement walls, and the bubbling still that I'd left uncovered, I knew they were picturing the beautiful home I'd left behind in Bremenville, the home Karl had built for me. I didn't want to ask why they had come, so I busied myself with their coats, then heated a pot of water for tea on the hot plate. Mama would tell me what she had come to say when she was ready.

While my back was turned, Vera wandered over to the still. "What's this thing, Emma?"

"It . . . um . . . it isn't mine. It sort of came with the apartment."

"But what's it for?"

"I'm going to find a better apartment the first chance I get," I explained, "but the landlords all want a month's rent in advance, so I have to save up some money."

"Emma, you don't need another apartment," Mama said quietly. "We've come to bring you home." I looked away.

"Did Papa send you?"

"No, he thinks we're Christmas shopping. Karl paid our train fare."

How clever of Karl, I thought as I turned to finish making the tea. He knew I'd be ashamed to tell my mother the truth or to discuss my reasons for leaving him in front of Vera. I cut a piece of pie I had brought home from the diner into two tiny slices. It was the only food I had in the house to serve them.

"Vera, come sit down and have some pie," I said. She was still walking around the strange contraption, eyeing it curiously.

"Aren't you having any?" she asked as I handed her and Mama each a cup and a plate.

"I only have two cups," I said, trying to smile. "I suppose you could sip from one side and I could sip from the other, but I just ate at work. I'm full." I patted my stomach for emphasis, then felt my cheeks flame when I saw Mama avert her eyes. Papa must have told her about my condition beforehand, but Vera hadn't known. Her mouth went slack with surprise. The silence in the room was deafening.

I wanted to hide from them in shame, but there was no place to go in my tiny cell. I sank down on the floor across from my mother and leaned my back against the wall. "I'm sorry, Mama . . . And I'm sorry you had to come so far for nothing, but I can't go back home with you."

"Please, Emma," Vera begged. "Karl is so lost without you. He—"

"He's lying. It's only his pride that's hurt. He doesn't love me, Vera. Karl and I have been unhappy from the beginning. I know he's Aunt Magda's son and that you think the world of him, but . . . but you've never lived with him. Karl is a different man at home than he is in the store or in church."

"What do you mean? How could he be any different?" Vera was clearly on Karl's side and had come to plead his case. I felt weary with hopelessness.

"See? I knew no one would believe me. That's why I left. But I can't live with him anymore. He's angry and violent and . . . I won't ever go back." I wrapped my arms around my knees and lowered my head in despair. I felt utterly alone.

"I believe you," Mama whispered. If the room hadn't been so small I might not have heard her at all. I looked up and saw her staring with vacant eyes at a scene only she could see. "I believe you, Emma," she said again.

"You do?"

She nodded sorrowfully. "No one knew what Karl's father was really like, either, inside the four walls of their home. I was the only outsider who saw Magda's bruises. And I once saw the welts he'd made on Karl's back with his belt. Magda made me swear to keep it all a secret. She wouldn't leave Gus. She loved him."

"I never loved Karl, Mama. I tried to, but—"

"I know, Emma. I know how hard you tried. You married him to please Papa and me, didn't you."

"I'm sorry. . . ."

"No, I'm the one who should apologize. I made a grave mistake. I thought that you were like me, that you would be perfectly happy living in Bremenville with a husband and children because I was happy with that. I thought Karl would be the kind of husband Friedrich was. But you're not me, Emma. You couldn't walk in my shoes, and I was wrong to expect you to. And Karl isn't like your father. Karl thought he could buy your love with jewelry and servants and a beautiful house, just like he bought the respect of the community with his fancy drugstore. Your father won my love by sacrificing himself for me—that's the purest demonstration of love. You demonstrated it yourself when you set the man you loved free to become a priest. . . . I'm sorry, Emma. I was wrong to encourage you to marry Karl. Now my mistake will cost me my daughter."

I was so relieved and so astounded to discover that she understood that I buried my face in my hands and wept. Mama set her plate and cup on the floor and knelt beside me, gathering me in her arms.

"The truth is, I want you to come home for my own sake. Because I love you, Emma. Because I can't bear the thought of being separated from one of my daughters. But if that means going back to Karl, I won't ask you to do that."

"I could force myself to stay with Karl, Mama, but he doesn't want the baby. He wants me to give it up. I'd sooner live in this hole for the rest of my life than to do that."

"I know. I lost two of my children—Eva and now you. I understand why you can't give away the child you're carrying."

Mama let me weep in her arms for a long time. Vera didn't say a word. She seemed stunned as she struggled with the knowledge that Karl wasn't what he seemed to be. At last, Mama pulled out her handkerchief and helped me dry my tears.

"Come, sit on the bed beside me. I brought you something, Emma—an early Christmas present."

She opened one of her bags and handed me an envelope. Inside were photographs—my three sisters and me in white dresses and high button shoes; Mama and Papa posing in front of the church; Eva in her Red Cross uniform; Karl and me on our wedding day. I wanted to tear the last photo into pieces, but something told me I might want it someday to prove that I really had been married.

"Keep them so you'll always remember us," Mama said. "And I want you to have this too." She unwrapped a wad of tissue paper and laid the gift in my hands—her grandmother's crying cup. "Oma gave this to me to ease my sorrow so I would always remember my home and the family who loved me when I was far away. I don't need it anymore, Emma, but you do. Let it remind you that you have a family who will always love you."

I held the delicate cup to my breast, and when I closed my eyes I was a child again—sipping milk from it in Mama's kitchen to comfort my tears. I smelled her chicken and dumplings cooking on the stove, heard Papa's warm laughter, and Eva's voice begging, *"Come play with me, Emma."* But when I opened my eyes, I was in my squalid basement apartment again. Papa was gone, Eva was gone, and my mother and sister were about to leave me too. Like all the other people I loved, I might never see them again.

"Right now your measure of sorrow is full," Mama said as we kissed good-bye. "But always remember . . . 'Joy and sorrow come and go like the ebb and flow.' "

———

I worked in the diner until my condition became so awkward and obvious, the owner fired me. In those days, expectant mothers went into confinement in their later months. They didn't flaunt their condition in public, and they certainly didn't wait on tables.

I had saved enough money to move, but I discovered that many landlords wouldn't rent rooms to a single woman, much less one who was obviously pregnant. I came home in tears from another unsuccessful day of apartment hunting and found O'Brien, Black Jack, and Booty in my room, huddled around the malfunctioning still.

"Hey, now, what's the matter, Emma?" O'Brien asked when he saw my tears.

"I need to move out of here before the baby is born, and I can't find a decent place to live. No one will rent to me."

O'Brien hurried to my side, draping his arm around my shoulder. "Why didn't you say something sooner? I'll be glad to move in with you and pretend I'm your bloke. I'd much rather wake up in the morning to your pretty face than Black Jack's ugly mug."

"Thanks for the offer, but I'm a married woman." I gently shrugged his arm away.

"Aw, Emma, I ain't gonna try nothing. I'll just come along to help you find a place. I can sleep on the floor for a couple of months, then I'll be a no-good rotten so-and-so and desert you after the baby is born." His offer touched me.

"You'd really do that for me?" I saw him and Black Jack exchange amused glances.

"It wouldn't be the first time that he deserted—" Black Jack began, but O'Brien shushed him.

"Never mind, she don't want to hear about all that. Now then, Emma, is that the only thing that's troubling you, or can we help you with something else?"

"Yeah, we'd be glad to take care of that husband of yours if he's being a problem," Black Jack offered.

"No, no. He's not a problem," I said quickly. I imagined Karl lying at the bottom of the Squaw River with rocks tied to his ankles. "I could use another job now that the diner sacked me . . . but I don't suppose you know of any place besides the circus that will hire a fat lady, do you?"

O'Brien raked his fingers through his mop of wild red hair as he pondered my problem. Before he could reply, there was a knock on the door. Black Jack sprang to his feet. O'Brien tensed, as if ready to bolt. "Who is it?" he asked.

"Sheila Higgins."

Everyone looked at Booty, who was sitting on the floor beside the still. He nodded for O'Brien to open the door. When he did, Sheila rushed inside and grabbed me roughly by the arm.

"Hold it right there, Miss Floozy!" she said. "You're not going anywhere." She turned and called to someone outside the apartment. "You can come in now, Father. They're all in here, including that kept woman I told you about." A tall, black-clothed figure stepped through the door. I found myself standing face-to-face with Patrick.

Instantly, all the color drained from his face. "*Emma?*" he breathed.

Sheila's jaw dropped. "How did you know her name, Father?"

Patrick was incapable of uttering another sound. He stared at me, clearly horrified to see my face when he'd expected to see Booty's mistress. Then he turned whiter still as his eyes traveled to my bulging stomach. I was afraid I was going to be sick. I wanted the earth to open up and swallow me.

Booty scrambled to his feet. "Sheila! You went and called Father O'Duggan? What did you think you were doing?"

"You wouldn't give up your woman or your gin mill, so I had to do something!"

"I told you, she's not my mistress!" He and Sheila began to argue. O'Brien and Black Jack joined, everyone yelling at the same time. I felt faint.

"All right, everybody shut up and listen to me!" Patrick suddenly shouted. He waited until the room was quiet. "Now then, who owns this contraption?"

"The three of us do, Father," Booty said softly. He gestured toward O'Brien and Black Jack.

Patrick took a step toward Booty. "I won't even ask how you got mixed up with the likes of these two, Ian, but I know you're a God-fearing man. Surely you know that what you're doing is illegal. Is it worth going to prison, losing your wife and your store—not to mention your soul—just to make a few extra bucks?"

"I . . . I thought . . . I mean, it seemed like . . ." Booty stammered, staring at his feet. "No, Father. I'm sorry."

"If you're truly sorry, then you can prove it by taking that thing apart and throwing it into the trash."

"Hold on, now—" O'Brien began, but Patrick cut him off.

"Enough! Get started now, Ian—tonight! Or I'll report all three of you to the police myself!" He swung around to face Sheila, managing to avoid looking at me. "Why don't you go on home now, Mrs. Higgins," he said gently. He rested his hand on her shoulder and guided her to the door.

"What about *her*?" Sheila asked, tilting her head toward me.

"I'll take care of everything," he promised. "I'll come by the store tomorrow, and we'll talk."

When she was gone, Patrick stood with his arms folded across his chest, watching Booty and the others dismantle the still. He finally turned to me, but he looked at the floor, not my face. "Let's go outside where we can talk in private," he said.

My heart pounded as I struggled into my coat and followed Patrick outside. He pointed to a deserted bench on the corner at the streetcar stop. "Let's sit over there."

I sank down on it wearily. Patrick sat a moment later. His hands looked pale under the glow of the streetlamp as they rested on his thighs. We were far enough apart that we might have been two strangers waiting for the streetcar to come. An enormous weight of silence sat between us.

I wondered what he was thinking. Did he really believe that I was Booty's mistress? I remembered the look of horror on his face when he saw that I was the accused woman. Now neither one of us knew how to begin. I decided to speak first and get it over with.

"Patrick, I'm not Booty's mistress. His sister is a friend of mine. I needed a place to stay, and Booty was kind enough to take me in and—"

"Hush, Emma. You don't need to explain. I believe you."

I fought back tears of relief. He looked up at me, and our eyes met for the first time since that horrible moment when he first walked through my door. "What are you doing here in the city, Emma?"

"I've left Karl."

"Why? . . . Because of me?" When I didn't answer, he grew angry. "The Bible says, 'What God therefore has joined together, let no man put asunder'! I need to know if I've destroyed a marriage!"

"No. Our marriage was destroyed long before you came back to Bremenville."

"Then why—?" He stopped when we heard footsteps approaching. I turned and saw O'Brien hurrying toward us. Black Jack stood framed in my apartment doorway.

"Hey, Emma, you don't need to be taking any heat from a priest," O'Brien said. "Come on back inside."

Patrick sprang to his feet. "She's not stepping foot in there until that still is gone. Do you have any idea what would have happened to her if the cops had found her living there, guarding your still? She would have gone to prison! For *your* crime!"

"We were looking out for her. The still was safe."

"Yeah? Then why wasn't it in *your* apartment?"

"That's none of your business!" O'Brien's hands curled into fists and he stuck out his chin, challenging Patrick.

Before either of us could blink, Patrick swung his fist into O'Brien's jaw, then followed it with double left-right punches to his gut. O'Brien crumbled to the ground, holding his stomach.

"Get up!" Patrick said, waiting to hit him again.

"Patrick, look out!" I cried. Black Jack was hurrying up behind him to defend his friend. When Patrick whirled to face him, Black Jack halted.

"I don't want to hit a priest, Father, but you gotta leave O'Brien alone."

Patrick grabbed the front of his clerical collar and ripped it off his neck. "Go ahead and have at me, man!" He threw the collar onto the ground. "I could kill both of you for involving Emma in your schemes!" He rushed at Black Jack, swinging another of his deadly punches. They locked in combat. I saw a blur of bloody faces and fists as they pummelled each other, and heard the sickening thud of blows and grunts. Patrick was getting the worst of it, but his anger wouldn't let him quit.

"Stop it! Both of you, stop it!" I screamed.

"Emma, stay back!" O'Brien shouted from where he lay on the ground. But I couldn't stand to watch Patrick's beloved face get beaten to pulp. I rushed forward to stop the carnage. O'Brien scrambled to his feet to restrain Black Jack.

"You've got to get out of here, O'Brien!" I shouted when we'd managed to separate them. "Just go! . . . Get out of here!" They dodged across the street and hopped aboard a streetcar as it pulled to the curb. A moment later it drove away.

Patrick groaned and sank down on the bench again. Blood streamed from his nose and from a cut above his eye. I pulled my scarf out of my pocket and began mopping his face.

"Careful!" he gasped when I touched his nose. "I think he broke it." I shoved the cloth into his hand so he could wipe it himself.

"Why did you pick a fight with Black Jack? He was a champion prizefighter in Ireland. Are you out of your mind?"

"Are you out of *yours*, Emma? What are you doing mixed up with bootleggers?"

I drew a shaky breath and let it out. "I needed help. I can't work anymore . . . and my baby will be born in a few weeks."

Patrick slowly lowered the cloth from where he'd been pressing it against his cut eye. "Is the baby mine?" he whispered.

I hesitated. I was about to lie, but Patrick read my heart. "Oh, God, forgive me!" he cried. He covered his face.

"Karl knew the baby wasn't his," I said quietly. "He tried to make me have an abortion. I left him to protect our child."

I watched a bright bead of blood well up in the cut above his eye, then run between his fingers. A few minutes later, he scrubbed his eyes with the heels of his hands and lowered them again. "We'll be married, of course, as soon as your divorce is official. You don't need to resort to bootlegging, Emma. I'll support you and our child."

I waited for him to pull me into his arms, waited for his comforting embrace. It never came. He slumped forward with his arms on his thighs, his head lowered, his hands dangling between his knees. Blood dripped onto the pavement like tears.

"No, Patrick."

He lifted his head. "What?"

"I won't marry you. I already messed up my own life. I won't mess up yours."

"Emma, it takes two people to make a baby! I'm as guilty as you are! We both messed up, and now I need to take responsibility for what I've done."

"I won't marry you, Patrick."

"Emma, don't be absurd! Of course we'll be married. I've fathered a child!"

"You haven't said that you love me or that you can't live without me. You can barely look at me. Don't give up the priesthood for me, Patrick, because I won't change my mind. I won't marry you!"

I saw another streetcar coming on our side of the street and hurried toward my apartment. I knew that a priest couldn't be seen chasing a pregnant woman, especially a priest with a bloodied face and torn collar. I hurried inside and locked the door, grateful that Patrick didn't follow me.

THIRTY-TWO

I couldn't sleep that night. Whenever I closed my eyes, I saw images of Patrick fighting with Black Jack, and my eyes flew open again. From time to time, the muscles of my womb tightened until my abdomen was as hard as a rock, and I was terrified that I was starting early labor. Meanwhile, the baby thrashed and churned as restlessly as I did.

As the sun rose, I was still staring at the stains and cracks on the ceiling and wondering where I could go. I couldn't stay here, but without O'Brien's help, I would never be able to find another apartment. I didn't know what to do. I certainly couldn't go home to Bremenville. Part of me wanted to lie on the bed until I died, but a wiser part knew I had to live for my baby's sake.

When I heard the sound of footsteps descending my stairwell and a soft rapping on the door, I was too weary to rise and look out the window.

"Who is it?" I called, not moving.

"It's me."

I pulled myself to my feet and opened the door to let Patrick in. His eye was purplish-black, and his swollen, bruised face looked even worse than it had last night. Someone had attempted to doctor the worst of his cuts with iodine and taped the gash above his eye. It should have had stitches. He closed the door and leaned against it. He wasn't wearing his black clerical suit and collar.

"I haven't stopped loving you for one second of my life, Emma. I'll never stop. I'm sorry I worded it so poorly last night. Please, I want to marry you and raise our child together."

I turned and put a pot of water on the hot plate to make tea, fighting the urge to run into his arms.

"Emma, why didn't you come to me right away?"

I opened the door to the potbellied stove and dumped in a shovelful of coal before answering. "I did. I came to your church, thinking you had probably quit. I was going to ask the new priest where you'd gone. But then I saw you serving communion. I could tell that you had asked God for forgiveness. And that He had accepted you back."

Patrick sighed. "You're right, I did quit. The bishop wouldn't accept my resignation. He made me read the story of how David sinned with Bathsheba, and how he'd found God's forgiveness. He told me to pray David's prayer of repentance." Patrick's voice trembled as he softly recited the words. " 'Have mercy upon me, O God, according to thy lovingkindness: according unto the multitude of thy tender mercies blot out my transgressions. . . . Against thee, thee only, have I sinned, and done this evil in thy sight. . . . Create in me a clean heart, O God; and renew a right spirit within me. Cast me not away from thy presence; and take not thy holy spirit from me. . . . Then will I teach transgressors thy ways; and sinners shall be converted unto thee.' The bishop said that experiencing repentance and forgiveness would make me a better priest. So I renewed my vows."

"Has it, Patrick? Has it made you a better priest?"

"I don't know. I was so ashamed of what I did at first that even after I confessed, it seemed like no amount of penance could ever ease my guilt. I knew Christ offered forgiveness, but I couldn't feel it. Then one day I read the words, 'while we were yet sinners, Christ died for us'—and I knew it was true. That was the whole point of His sacrifice, Emma. I couldn't be sinless on my own, I couldn't do it—so He became sin for me." Patrick shook his head at the wonder of it.

"Sometimes I sit in the confessional now and weep with people, because I know I'm just as guilty, just as capable of sin as they are. I look up at the crucifix and see His love for me in spite of what I've done, in spite of the kind of man I am, and it brings me to my knees. I want to fall on my face every time I stand before His cross. So in the end, I stayed in the priesthood out of gratitude. Offering my life to Him seemed like the very least I could do. Every sermon I preach is on grace—and people listen, Emma. The grace of God changes their lives, just as it changed mine."

Tears ran down my face as I gazed at the beautiful golden-haired man that I loved. But Patrick didn't belong to me. He belonged to God and to his parish.

"You aren't free to marry me, Patrick. You're married to God."

"No, Emma. Listen to me. . . ."

"How will people learn about God's grace if you don't tell them? I won't let you break your vows a second time. Someday you would hate me for taking you away from God's work."

"It's too late. I talked to my mother last night, and she agreed to let me live with her after I move out of the rectory. I made an appointment to talk with the bishop later today. I'll find a job—"

"I won't do it. Even if you quit the priesthood, I won't marry you. Help me find a place to live. That's all I need from you."

"No, it isn't right. You're my responsibility." He moved toward me, his arms outstretched to enfold me. I held up my hands to keep him back.

"Don't, Patrick. Don't! I won't change my mind." His arms fell to his sides, but his eyes pleaded silently with me. I turned away. "Please go. And please don't ask me to marry you again."

Patrick slammed out of the apartment and ran up the steps to the street.

Late that afternoon he returned. He was wearing his clerical suit and collar once again. I was grateful for the distance it created between us.

"I found you a place to live," he said as he stood in the doorway. "I have a borrowed car outside, if you'd like to come and see the apartment."

"I really don't care what it looks like," I said. "It can't be worse than this place."

"I know, but the landladies want to meet you first."

"That will be the end of it," I said, resting my hand on my stomach. "They'll take one look at me and turn me down. I've been through this before."

"Let's give it a try anyway, shall we?" He removed my coat from the nail near the door and held it for me while I put it on.

We drove the few blocks to the Mulligan sisters' house on King Street and parked in front of the ramshackle, three-story building. I made no move to get out of the car. "I don't think this is such a good idea, Patrick. It's too close to Booty's store, too close to . . ."

"To me?"

"I think it will be much too difficult. For both of us."

He turned in his seat to face me. "Emma, I have no money. I took a vow of poverty when I became a priest. Unless I quit the priesthood and get a job, I have no means to support you and the baby. And whether you like it or not, it's my responsibility to do that. If you live nearby, I can make sure you're taken care of here in the community. These are good people. They help each other out, especially if their parish priest asks them for a favor. I promised the bishop that once I found you a place to live I would have no further contact with you—and I won't. Will you at least try it this way, Emma?"

I felt the muscles of my womb contract again, in preparation for labor in a few short weeks. I couldn't afford to argue with him. "All right." I opened the car door and walked up the steps to meet the Mulligan sisters for the first time. Aileen Mulligan opened her apartment door before Patrick had a chance to knock.

"Is this the boarder you told me about, Father?"

"Mrs. Bauer, I'd like to you meet Aileen Mulligan and her sister, Kate—"

"You didn't tell me she was expecting!" Aileen said before anyone could reply.

"Oh? Didn't I?" Patrick said with a bemused grin. "It must have slipped my mind."

"We don't want any children living here, Father. They run up and down the stairs and—"

"Aye, they do. But you have my solemn promise that Mrs. Bauer's child will not be doing any running for a while . . . and stairs will be entirely out of the question for at least a year or two."

"What kind of a woman is she, with no husband?" It was humiliating to be talked about as if I wasn't standing right there. Patrick was doing his level best to be charming, but I could tell by the bright spots of color on his cheeks that he was battling his temper.

"She needs a place to live, Aileen. Mrs. Bauer has left her husband for reasons I'm not at liberty to discuss, but they concern the safety of her child. She will pay half of the rent each month, and the child's father has agreed to pay the other half through me."

"She can't be a very good Catholic if she's getting divorced."

"She isn't Catholic. But she was raised in the church, if that makes you feel any better. In fact, her father is a minister of the Protestant faith."

"Kate and I will not have sinners living under our roof," she said sternly.

Patrick heaved an enormous sigh. "Well, then, Miss Aileen, it will be a terrible shame having this grand big house sitting empty, won't it?"

"What do you mean, 'empty'?"

"The Scriptures tell us that 'all have sinned and come short of the glory of God.' If a person has to be sinless to live here, then only our Lord and Savior Jesus Christ will be renting a room."

Aileen made a face. "You know what I mean, Father. We'll not have anyone who is immoral living under our roof."

Patrick removed his prayer book from his pocket and laid his hand on it.

His eyes were very bright. "You have my word of honor as a priest that Mrs. Bauer is no more immoral than I am."

"That's a relief to know, Father." She gave a grudging wave toward the steps. "She can go on upstairs, then, and have a look at the place."

———

Three weeks after I moved in I sent Crazy Clancy, my elderly next-door neighbor, for the doctor. The long hours of labor that followed were the loneliest hours of my life. I cried for Mama and Papa; for my sisters Sophie, Eva, and Vera; and I silently cried for Patrick. Old Dr. Bailey patted my hand from time to time and made soothing noises, telling me I was making progress. But I struggled on, alone.

Then, after a final burst of pain, I held my baby in my arms for the first time, and I knew I would never be alone again. I saw Patrick in the curl of her lip, the cleft of her chin, and in the downy tuft of golden hair on her head. I couldn't look at her without weeping.

I awoke the next morning to find Patrick standing over me. His eyes shone with tears as he gazed down at our daughter, asleep in my arms. "Emma, you have to marry me. Please. I can't walk away from you and from our child. She's so tiny . . . so helpless. . . ."

"You've seen the way people like Sheila Higgins and the Mulligan sisters treat me. You've seen the stigma I bear every day of my life because my husband is divorcing me. Imagine how your daughter will be ridiculed and ostracized—the illegitimate child of a fallen priest. If you love her, Patrick, you won't do this to her. You won't damage her life. As far as she and the rest of the world are concerned, Karl Bauer is her father."

"No! She's mine! *I'm* her father!"

I struggled to sit up and the baby stirred in my arms. "If you so much as breathe those words aloud again, Patrick, I swear I'll leave and you'll never see your daughter as long as you live!"

"When she's older we can tell her. . . ."

"No! We can *never* tell her. She won't understand. One slip of the tongue and the scandal will ruin her. You'll be ruined too."

"I don't care about my reputation. My daughter is more important—"

"No, Patrick. She'll be labeled a bastard. You can't let anyone know!"

He sank down on the edge of the bed, pleading with me. "We can move away from here to another city, another state. Emma, please marry me. If not for my sake, for our daughter's sake." Everything in me longed to be his wife and to have him be a father to our child. But I loved Patrick too much. I couldn't take him away from his ministry, his life, his God.

"No," I whispered. "Don't ask me again. Now swear that you'll never tell our daughter the truth. Swear it on your Bible!" I wrung the promise from him, but I may as well have asked him to tear out his own heart. Afterward he pulled himself to his feet and walked from the room. I thought he was gone for good, but a moment later he returned and stood over us again, gazing down at his daughter.

"Have you named her?" he asked.

"I'm going to name her Eva, after my sister."

Patrick shook his head. "No. Her name is Grace . . . like the gift of God that brings forgiveness from all our sins. I can't imagine a more beautiful word or a more beautiful name."

He lifted the baby out of my arms and walked across the room with her. I saw him pull a small vial of holy water from his pocket.

"What are you doing?"

"It's important to me that she be baptized. The sacrament is part of my faith."

"No! I don't want her—"

His Irish temper flared. "You're having your own way by not marrying me, Emma. But I will have my way in this!"

His angry voice woke the baby. She stirred and gazed up at her father, blinking in the sunlight. Patrick smoothed her downy hair with his huge hand. "Shh . . . shh . . . It's all right. I love you, my little one . . . and so does God."

He opened the bottle of water with one hand. "Grace Eva . . . Ba—" He couldn't force Karl's name from his mouth. He wiped his eyes and started again. "Grace Eva . . . O'Duggan . . . I baptize you in the name of the Father . . . and of the Son . . . and of the Holy Spirit . . . Amen."

He didn't need the holy water. He baptized his daughter with his own tears.

———

When Grace was three days old, I answered a knock on my door and found Booty standing there, his arms loaded down with a box of groceries.

"I thought you might be able to use a few things," he said. I helped him set the groceries on the floor. I had no other place to put them. I saw canned goods, eggs, packets of flour, tea, and sugar. Booty pulled out a bar of castile baby soap and a tin of talcum powder from his pockets. "Sheila sent these special for you. She wants you to know how sorry she is about what she said. Father O'Duggan explained about your husband—"

"It's all right, Booty. Will you tell her I said thanks?"

He nodded. "You, um . . . you look real good, Emma."

"A lot thinner, right?" I said, laughing. "Would you like to see the baby?"

"Sure." He followed me like a timid schoolboy over to where Grace lay sleeping. I had fashioned a crib for her out of an empty dresser drawer. "She's lovely," he whispered. "I can't begin to imagine why her father wouldn't want her."

I thought of Patrick's tears and pleas, then realized that Booty was talking about Karl Bauer. If that was the lie I had to perpetuate, I'd better get used to repeating it from the very beginning. "My husband came from a very large, very poor family. That's why he didn't want any children."

"Doesn't seem fair, does it?" Booty murmured. "The ones that don't want children have dozens of them . . . and the ones that would love a wee babe like this one can't have any." I looked at him in surprise.

"Are you talking about yourself, Booty? You and Sheila?"

"She miscarried four times, and two other babies died soon after birth. We don't dare try for any more." I felt my heart soften toward Sheila Higgins.

"I'm so sorry."

"Aye. So am I."

A few hours after Booty left, O'Brien and Black Jack showed up at my door. "Congratulations, Emma! Booty told us you'd had a baby girl."

"Would you like to come in and see her?"

O'Brien looked around warily. "That punching priest isn't lurking about, is he? He packs a wallop like a kangaroo!"

"I don't want to hit him again," Black Jack added. "I feel awful about the last time. I never laid a hand on a priest before, and I surely wouldn't want to do it again . . . but he just came at me!"

"I know. It wasn't your fault. Come on in." I led them over to see Gracie.

"Wow! I never seen a person that small!" O'Brien said. "She have a sunburn or something?"

"All babies are red at first," I said, laughing. "Do you want to hold her?"

O'Brien appeared horrified by the idea, but Black Jack's sinister face softened into a smile. "Could I?" he asked.

The sight of that huge, powerful man holding little Gracie in hands the size of cinder blocks brought tears to my eyes. "What's her name?" he asked.

"It's Gracie . . . Grace Eva." I couldn't force myself to say Bauer any more than Patrick could.

"We've come to find out if you need anything," O'Brien said. "We feel real bad about the still and all."

"I knew the risks."

O'Brien smoothed back his thatch of red hair. "We want to do something for you. We was wondering how things stood with the kid's father."

Again, I caught myself picturing Patrick. I forced myself to change the image to Karl. "My husband has filed for divorce. He didn't want a baby in the first place—which is why I left him—so I don't think he'll cause any problems. But thanks for the offer."

He grinned and draped his arm around my shoulder. "I'm available whenever your divorce is final."

I laughed and gave him a quick hug before freeing myself. "I plan to live here very quietly with my daughter. Your life-style is a bit too exciting for me, I'm afraid."

"We're gonna give up rum-running for a while till the heat cools. We're operating a blind pig downtown now."

"A what?"

"A speakeasy . . . you know, a rum joint that operates behind a legit place."

"It still sounds illegal to me."

He laughed. "Yeah, well . . . you know what they say about leopards changing their spots. If you ever need work, Emma, look us up. We'd trust you with our lives, right, Black Jack?"

Black Jack hadn't heard a word we had said. He held Gracie in his arms, his eyes fastened on her tiny face as if hypnotized. I rested my hand on his shoulder. "You'd make a marvelous father, Black Jack."

"You think so?" he whispered.

"I know so."

After they left, I found two brand-new twenty dollar bills stuffed inside Gracie's diaper. I couldn't help wondering if they were counterfeit.

THIRTY-THREE

I didn't talk to Patrick again for four years. He kept his promise to the bishop not to contact Grace or me. He anonymously paid half our rent, but we rarely saw each other—and even then it was at a distance.

Grace was such a quiet, timid child that the Mulligan sisters allowed us to stay in the apartment. They even watched her for a few hours every day when I went to work part time at the diner again. I was working there one afternoon when Dora the cashier pulled me aside.

"Did you ever see a bigger waste than that?" she asked, nodding toward one of the tables. I looked and saw Patrick sitting alone in a booth by the window. "A man as handsome as Father O'Duggan wasted on the priesthood!" Dora shook her head. "But I suppose if he wasn't a priest he'd be breaking women's hearts, right?"

"Yes . . . I suppose so," I stammered.

"Well, don't just stand there, girl . . . take the man some coffee. He's sitting in your booth."

My hands shook as I retrieved the coffeepot. I would probably spill it all over him. Patrick looked up as I approached. "Coffee?" I asked.

"Thanks."

Sure enough, I slopped it all over the saucer as I poured. I had to pull napkins from the chrome holder on his table to wipe it up. "Anything else? Do you want a menu?"

"I need to talk to you, Emma," he said softly. "Do you have a minute?"

I glanced around. My other customers didn't need anything, and the cashier was momentarily hidden behind a man who was paying his check. "I guess so. For a minute."

Patrick exhaled. "I had to pay a call on old Mrs. Mulligan today. I saw Grace. The Mulligan sisters didn't introduce her to me, in fact they quickly shooed her off to the kitchen, but I knew right away who she was."

I glanced around again to see who was watching. "She has your eyes, Patrick. The color of the sky."

"Aye . . . and my hair. I had to resist the urge to caress her curls and feel the wrinkled texture of them. Her hair is so much like my own that if I bent my head to hers, no one could ever tell where mine ended and hers began."

"That's why you have to promise me you won't go near her," I whispered urgently, "that you'll stay away from her."

"I came to ask you if I could see her once in a while, talk to her—"

"No! You have to stay out of her life!" I looked over my shoulder and saw the cashier watching us. When I turned back, Patrick was staring into his coffee cup. His broad shoulders sagged.

"I suppose this is the punishment for my sin, the penance I'll be forced to pay every day of my life. To see my daughter, to ache with love for her, but to be unable to hold her in my arms." He looked up at me and I saw the sorrow in his eyes. "Like Cain in the Old Testament, 'My punishment is greater than I can bear.' "

"I'm sorry. I have to go. Dora is watching us."

"Emma, wait. Is she okay? Does she need anything? Is she . . . is she happy?"

I thought of Grace's rippling laughter, the sound of her feet clattering up the stairs to bring me a bouquet of dandelions. I was luckier than Patrick; I had Gracie. I could snuggle beside her to read bedtime stories and feel the warmth of her arms around my neck as she kissed me good-night.

"I wish you could know her," I said. "She's a beautiful child—contented, curious, loving. She's the joy of my life."

"Are you okay?" he whispered.

"Yes. I'm okay too."

A customer at the counter signalled for more coffee.

"I have to go. Please stay away from Grace."

I carried the coffeepot to the man and refilled his cup. When I glanced at the booth again, Patrick was gone, his cup of coffee untouched.

———

That winter I became ill with pneumonia. I had felt the illness trying to overpower me for several days, but I thought I could fight it off. Who would take care of Gracie if anything happened to me? I couldn't get sick. I couldn't. Then the fever gripped me with blazing fists and I nearly died.

When I first awoke and realized that I was in the hospital, I became hysterical. "Where's Gracie? Where's my baby? I have to go home to my baby!" I would have run out into the snow to find her, barefoot and in my nightgown, if one of the nursing sisters hadn't hurried into the room to calm me.

"Shh . . . it's all right Mrs. Bauer. I'm sure your daughter is being cared for."

"Where is she? Please tell me where my Gracie is!" My chest ached with every breath I drew. I felt as though I were drowning.

"I don't know where your little girl is, but she was with your priest the night he brought you in."

"With my priest? Was it Father O'Duggan?"

"Yes. He's been coming to the hospital every day to see how you're doing. I'll tell him to look in on you when he comes today. He'll ease your mind about the child. Try to rest until then."

But I couldn't rest until I found out where my Gracie was. It felt as though hours had passed before I finally heard his voice in the corridor outside my ward. He walked through the door behind the nursing sister, and our eyes met. I warned myself to be careful what I said to him with a room full of other patients and the nun hovering beside us.

"Here he is, Mrs. Bauer," the sister said cheerfully. "She's been so worried about her little girl, Father O'Duggan. I told her you could ease her mind."

"Gracie's just fine," he said. "She's in very loving, capable hands. How . . . how are you feeling?" I knew by the stilted way he spoke and by the way his hands clutched the brim of his hat that Patrick was struggling with his emotions. I willed the nun to go away and give us some privacy before he broke down, but she stayed close to his side.

"Father O'Duggan, could I . . . I mean . . . I would like to make a confession." I hoped it was the right thing to say. I saw by the relief on Patrick's face that it was.

"Of course," he said. "Would you excuse us please, Sister Mary Margaret?" The nun smiled sweetly and drew the curtain closed around my bed. Patrick's tall body slumped with emotion as soon as we were alone. "Thank God! . . . Emma, I was so afraid you were going to die!" He groped for my hand.

"Don't, Patrick. Please don't."

He closed his eyes for a moment, then backed up a step. "I'm sorry."

"Where's Gracie? Is she all right?"

"Yes . . . she's fine. I took her to my mother's house."

"What?" I stared at him, horrified at the thought of our secret being exposed. "Why did you take her there? Does your mother know?"

"Hush, Emma. She knows, but no one else does. I only asked her to keep

Grace the one night because there was no other place for her to go except the orphans' home. But from the very first moment they met, Gracie stole Mam's heart. Mam won't even consider letting me take her someplace else. And Gracie is happy there. I wish you could see them together, baking cookies—"

"Stop!" I covered my face, weeping. "Please stop . . ." I couldn't bear the image of Gracie nestled in her grandmother's arms. I knew she would never see Mam again once I got well.

"Is there some other place you'd rather I take her?" he asked quietly. "Do you want me to contact your parents in Bremenville?"

"No! You can never take her there! If Karl sees her he might make trouble!" I was so upset I began to cough uncontrollably.

"I'll get help . . . a nurse . . ." Patrick cried in alarm. I shook my head. At last I got my coughing under control again. I lay back against the pillow, exhausted and wheezing.

"Emma, the doctors say you're going to be here for a few more weeks. You're still very ill with pneumonia. Even if you went home, you couldn't take care of Grace."

"Why did you make her part of your life? She knows you now, and after I'm well . . ."

"I want to continue to be part of her life. I told the bishop that I will either take proper care of my daughter from now on, or I'll quit. I can't have my child starving, her mother freezing. I can't believe that would be God's will. My priestly vows don't change the fact that I have responsibilities as her father."

"But I don't want anyone to know."

"They won't know. I've asked for an increase in my coal allowance at the rectory. It will make its way into your coal bin, anonymously. And I've arranged for a line of credit for you at Booty's store. No one but the three of us will know who's paying your bills. But you have to tell me what you need from now on . . . what Gracie needs. You have to let me help you."

"You swore you'd never tell Gracie the truth. You swore on your Bible."

"And I'll keep my promise. But I want to be part of her life. I want to talk to her, be her friend. I've held her in my arms, Emma. You can't ask me to go back to the way things were before. You can't ask me to pretend to be a stranger again. It isn't fair to Grace . . . or to me."

"No, Patrick! You can't! I appreciate all your help, but things *have* to go back to the way they were! There's no other way to disguise the truth!"

"Emma, listen. . . ."

"No. Please leave now."

He drew a deep breath and lifted his chin, composing himself. Then he shoved the curtains aside and strode from the room.

When the doctors finally discharged me a month later, Patrick borrowed Booty's car to drive me home from the hospital. He brought Gracie with him. I was so happy to see her again, I didn't want to let her out of my sight or out of my arms.

"What on earth are all those bags for?" I asked when I saw the backseat full of parcels.

"Those are all my new clothes, Mama. Wait until you see. I have warm stockings and a nightgown, and Mam knit me a new pair of mittens—and she even made me a dolly."

"I can't wait to see everything, sweetie." I glanced at Patrick and saw him staring very intently down the road. We might have been an ordinary family, returning from a trip to Grandma's house—but we weren't. Gracie chattered away happily. I had never heard her so talkative before.

"Mam sent home some food to eat too. I helped bake the soda bread. It's my job to put the raisins in. She says no one else can do it as good as me. Can we have some for a treat when we get home, Mama? Can Father O'Duggan stay and have some too?"

"He's probably too busy," I said quickly. But Gracie turned to look up at him, her eyes full of longing.

"Are you too busy?" she asked. I sensed Patrick's struggle. He didn't want to hurt Gracie by refusing, but he knew I didn't want him to stay.

"Your mother will need to rest when she gets home," he finally said.

"Oh." Gracie managed to convey the full measure of her disappointment in a single word. I looked at their faces, so hauntingly alike, and knew that Patrick was right. I was being unfair to both of them by keeping them apart. I lifted Gracie's chin and smoothed the hair from her forehead.

"I'm not too tired for a tea party, sweetie. And Father O'Duggan is welcome to stay." She and Patrick smiled simultaneously, like images in a mirror, and my heart nearly shattered.

Before I could recover, Gracie started chattering again. "Mam said you might be in farm for a while. What does that mean, Mama? Are you in farm?"

I looked to Patrick for help. "I think she means 'infirm,' " he said, grinning. "Gracie, infirm means that even though your mother can leave the hospital, she might not be completely well and strong for a while."

"I'll take care of you, Mama. I promise I will."

When we arrived at the apartment, I discovered that someone had been there before us, tidying up, filling the shelf with canned goods, building a fire in the stove. The coal scuttle was full.

"Oh, it's so good to be home!" I said, sighing. Patrick had to make two trips up the stairs with Gracie's things and all the food his mother had sent. As he paused for breath after the second trip I said, "Would you stay and have tea with us?"

"Only if you'll sit down and let Gracie and me fix it."

I watched them work side by side, heating the water, arranging three mismatched cups on the tray, slicing the soda bread. Patrick's hand swallowed Grace's completely as he helped her guide the knife. He looked so solid and protective beside her, yet he was so gentle and patient with her. I thought of my own papa.

We ate our little meal companionably, as if we belonged together. I'd rarely seen Gracie so happy. But my heart was breaking, and I knew that Patrick's was too. All too soon it would have to end.

"Gracie, why don't you take this last piece of soda bread next door and see if Clancy would like it," I said when we'd eaten our fill. "Let him know that we're home again, okay?" After she had skipped off on her errand, I turned to Patrick. He was jiggling the grate in the stove to remove the ashes before adding more coal. "You were right," I said softly. "It would be much too cruel to expect you to walk out of Grace's life again. I can't do that to either one of you." He stopped with a shovelful halfway to the door. His eyes shone with hope.

"You mean. . . ?"

"Yes. You're already part of her life now. You have to continue . . . but promise me you'll only be Father O'Duggan, the priest, to her . . . not her father. You can't play favorites with her, Patrick. No one can ever know she's your daughter."

"I'll figure out a way to include her with all the girls in my parish. I'll make it work, Emma, I swear."

"I know you will."

He closed the stove, then peered out the front door to see if Gracie was coming back. When he saw no sign of her, he walked over to where I was sitting and pressed something into my hand.

"What's this, Patrick . . . coal?"

He shook his head. "It's a diamond-in-the-making. God will use pressure and stress to turn it into something beautiful, something precious. He'll do that in your life too, if you'll let Him, Emma. He's in the business of re-demption. We sinned, but He gave us Grace. We—"

He stopped when Grace skipped back into the room. "Mr. Clancy said thank you very much and welcome home," she said.

Patrick quickly shoved his arms into his overcoat, then bent to caress Grace's head. "Take good care of your mother, all right? And thanks for the tea."

I said good-bye and watched Patrick walk away, as I had so many times before.

———

That was the last time we spoke until Patrick showed up at the Regency Room one night, four years later, wearing a suit and tie. I nearly fell off the piano stool when I saw him from across the room. My love, my longing for him, hadn't diminished in the least. He asked O'Brien for a table near my piano, then sent a message that he wanted to talk to me when the set was over. My fingers could barely find the right keys.

"Emma, why are you still hanging around with that gangster?" Patrick asked as soon as I was seated across the table from him.

"Is that what you came here to talk to me about?"

"No. . . ."

"Then drop it, all right?"

He stared down at the table, toying with a book of matches. I remembered the warmth of his hands, the touch of his strong, gentle fingers. I wanted to lift his palm to my cheek and feel his warmth again, then kiss the knuckles of his hand. But Patrick didn't belong to me.

"Emma, the other girls are making fun of Grace," he said eventually. "They're taunting her, badgering her. When I bumped into her today after school she was crying. It seems there is a great deal of speculation and gossip among my parishioners about her father. . . ."

My hands flew to my face. "Grace and I should move away! You can't be seen with her! They'll know!"

"Emma, they don't suspect me, they . . . they think she's a bastard. That's what Bridget Murphy called her, but she's only repeating what she's heard at home."

I saw him struggling for words, a rare thing for Patrick, and I sat back to let him empty his heart without interruption.

"The word shocked me, but only because I realized that she had spoken the truth. And for the first time, I really saw what my sin has done to my daughter."

He dropped the matchbook and leaned back in his chair, his hands dropping into his lap. We both waited until he could go on. "I lectured all the girls about kindness and Christian compassion—not that it'll do any good with that heartless lot—but I didn't know what else to do. I felt so helpless, so . . . so angry, mostly with myself. Those schoolgirls hadn't caused Gracie's tears—I had. How had I ever imagined that by spending ten minutes with her every week, tossing her a smile and a couple of nickels, I could somehow fill the role of a father in her life?"

He stopped again, this time biting his lip so hard I feared it would bleed. I started to speak but he held up his hand. "No, let me finish. I went inside St. Michael's to pray. The first thing I saw was the crucifix above the altar and Christ hanging there in silent torment. How had Father God ever endured it? To watch His beloved Son suffer unjustly? To see Him scorned and mocked? I had just a taste of what He endured when I saw my own child mocked, and I wanted to murder every last one of those girls. I can't understand how God could ever forgive me. I don't understand why He hasn't turned His face away from me, why He hasn't destroyed me for what I've done to His Son—and to you and Gracie."

Patrick rested his elbow on the table and propped his forehead on his hand. I didn't want to think about his words and the long-suffering of God. I couldn't. I deserved His wrath too. I stared at Patrick's thick golden hair instead, remembering the texture of it beneath my fingers. Finally he looked up.

"Gracie interrupted my prayer, Emma. She followed me into St. Michael's to ask . . . to ask if I knew where her real father was and why he didn't live with her. I didn't know what to say. I told her she had to talk to you about him. Then . . ." Patrick swallowed hard. "Then she asked if I would be her father. She begged me to let her call me Daddy . . . just once . . . in secret."

"You didn't let her!" I was horrified.

"No." Patrick's jaw trembled. "But I longed to hear her call me Daddy every bit as much as she longed to say it. It nearly broke my heart to tell her no. I'm a priest—it's my job to comfort and console people who are in pain. But I couldn't give my own daughter what she needed the most in all the world—someone to call Daddy."

Patrick closed his eyes and lowered his head. "Forgive me, Father," he whispered, "for I have sinned." When he lifted his head again, his eyes pierced mine. "This is why God hates sin, Emma. Why He forbids adultery . . . because He loves us. Sin hurts *us*. But it hurts the innocent people we love the most."

I didn't know what to say. The image of Gracie being taunted and crying for her daddy made me see my sin afresh as well. It was as though Patrick and I had tossed a pebble down a slope eight years ago, and now we watched in helpless horror as it turned into an avalanche. Our daughter stood in that avalanche's path.

"I think Gracie and I had better move away," I said again. "I knew this wouldn't work—living so close to you."

"You're missing the point, Emma! She needs a father! She longs for one, like all the other girls have. She doesn't understand why her father abandoned her, why he doesn't love her. And he's *me*! *I'm* the one who abandoned her, not Karl Bauer! Moving someplace else isn't going to change how Gracie feels or make her stop wanting her father. And if you do move, I'll find you. I won't let you take my daughter away from me. I came here tonight to tell you that I'm going to do much more than throw her a couple of nickels from now on. I'm going to walk her home from school every day, protect her from the other girls, listen to her fears and her dreams. I'm going to be a father to her!"

"You can't! People will see the resemblance!"

"Emma, I don't care!"

"Please! For Gracie's sake . . ."

"They're calling her names now. How can it get any worse? At least this way she'll have a father—not a priest, a father. Someone who loves her and cares for her. Someone she can run to and confide in when she's upset."

"You promised you would never tell her!"

"I'll keep my promise. I won't tell her the truth."

"I can't let you do this, Patrick!" I was desperate to stop him, but he wouldn't listen to me.

"I didn't come for your permission, Emma. I came to tell you the way it's going to be. I told the bishop the same thing this afternoon. I'm Grace's father. And I will be a father to her, no matter what it costs me."

"But anyone with eyes to see will know! Your hair . . ."

Patrick shoved his chair back and stood. "I'll keep my hat on."

———

Over the next few years, I watched from a distance as Patrick became Grace's confidante, her ally, her friend. He's the reason she started going to church every week. He even let her borrow his pajamas. When she left home for nursing school, he maneuvered a way to take her there himself, all the way to Philadelphia.

I thought he might move on to another parish once she was away in school, but he didn't. I met him on the sidewalk in front of Booty's store one day as I was going in and he was coming out. His right eye was blackened with an enormous shiner.

"Hello, Emma."

"Patrick! What on earth happened to your eye? Did you run into a door?"

"Just a bit of a scrap with Denny O'Hara. He'd had too much to drink, you see."

"So he attacked a priest?"

"Nay, Emma," he said quietly. "He attacked his wife and little ones." His words chilled me when I remembered Patrick's own past.

"The O'Haras are lucky to have you nearby. And they're lucky their priest isn't afraid of a brawl . . . though perhaps he should be, at his age."

He smiled, but when the corners of his eyes wrinkled he winced. "Ouch! It hurts when I laugh," he said, tenderly touching his face.

"Why do you stay here, Patrick . . . struggling with these people? Now that Gracie's on her own, couldn't you move up the ranks, go to a bigger church, become a cardinal or something?"

"The bishop asked me the same thing just a few days ago. But I can't leave. These people are my children, my family. Thanks to Gracie, I'm finally learning what it means to be a father to them. Will the next priest be willing to brawl with a drunken fool like Denny O'Hara? I can't be sitting in comfort in a bishop's residence somewhere, wondering if the little O'Hara boy will be getting his leg broken in three places like I did."

"You can't save the whole world, Patrick."

"No, but I can save one child." He gazed into the distance, his eyes shining as blue as the sky. "If I can ever pry some money from the church after the war, I'd like to convert all those grand rooms that are going to waste in the rectory into a place where women and children can go to be safe. I remember how desperate you were when you came here, running from Karl Bauer, expecting a baby. You had no one to turn to, no place to go. Lord knows I don't need all those rooms."

Tears came to my eyes. I loved him more with the passing of time, not less. "God answered your prayer, Patrick."

He looked back at me again. "Which prayer is that?"

"You're a wonderful priest."

About a year after Grace and Stephen were married, I heard the news about Patrick—from Sheila Higgins, of all people. I said hello to her in the bank, and her eyes filled with tears.

"'Tisn't it awful about poor Father O'Duggan? Such a young man, barely past fifty . . ."

A huge fist squeezed my heart. "What happened to him?"

"You haven't heard? The whole parish is reeling. He's in Sisters of Mercy Hospital and not expected to live the week."

"How . . . what—?"

"Acute leukemia. It was very sudden. And the doctors say it's very deadly. There's nothing they can do."

I ran straight out of the bank and hailed a taxi. Patrick couldn't be dying. He had always been so strong, so capable. Grace and I and everyone else in his parish knew we could run to him whenever we needed him. If I could have prayed, this is the one time in my life when I would have. But I had no right to ask God for anything, especially where Patrick was concerned.

I rushed into the hospital like a crazy woman. The head nursing sister wouldn't let me past the front desk. "You aren't the only person in the parish who loves Father O'Duggan, God bless him. There's been a line of people a mile long asking about him, wanting to see him. Why, there wouldn't be room to let them all into the lobby, let alone his room! But the doctors are only allowing his immediate family and fellow priests to see him. I'm very sorry."

"No, listen. You have to let me in. I . . . I am family."

The nun frowned. "Oh? And how might you be related to Father O'Duggan?"

"Tell him it's Emma . . . Mrs. Emma Bauer. Please! Ask him! You have to ask him if he'll see me!"

"Just a minute." She looked annoyed as she dialed a number on her telephone. "Hello, Sister Angelica? There's a woman down here asking to see Father O'Duggan and claiming to be a relation. Yes, her name is Mrs. Emma Bauer." She nodded knowingly as the nun on the other end talked. "Yes, that's what I thought. All his relations have already been heard from. . . ."

"Tell Father O'Duggan my name!" I shouted desperately. "Let him decide if he'll see me!"

She frowned again, then spoke into the phone. "She wants you to give Father O'Duggan her name and let him decide."

I nearly wept. "Thank you!"

"It will take a few minutes for Sister Angelica to check with him, Mrs. Bauer. If you'd like to have a seat . . ." She propped the phone receiver against her shoulder and spoke to three other people while I paced the lobby floor, waiting.

When she finally received the answer, her frown softened. "He wants to see you. He's on the third floor, Mrs. Bauer, room 315."

Sister Angelica was waiting for me when I stepped off the elevator. "Please remember that Father O'Duggan tires very easily."

"Is he really going to die?" I asked, still struggling to absorb Sheila's words.

"I'm afraid so," the nun said. Her eyes filled with tears, but she said in a brisk voice, "Visits are limited to five minutes."

I walked down the hall in a daze of shock and grief. How could I say everything I wanted to say in five minutes?

Tears sprang to my eyes when I first walked into his room and saw him lying against the cold white sheets. His skin was gray, his golden hair as dim as tarnished bronze. Then he looked up at me and smiled—his glorious, radiant smile—and he was Patrick again. I sat on the edge of the bed and took his hand in mine.

"Your hands were always so cold, Emma. They still are."

"And yours are still warm." We gazed at each other without speaking. We didn't need to.

"I'm so glad you came," he finally said. "The doctors say my life is just about over."

"Is that all right with you?"

"Aye, it's all right with me. My life belongs to God. Let Him do what He wants with it." He smiled, and the skin at the corners of his warm blue eyes crinkled. I wanted to lay my face beside his and weep. "No, don't cry for me, Emma. I'm ready."

"I know you are."

"What about you? Are you still angry with God?" When I didn't answer, he said softly, "You haven't found God's forgiveness, have you?"

"I don't deserve it."

"None of us do. But when the Pharisees brought a woman to Jesus who'd been caught in the act of adultery, He said, 'Neither do I condemn thee.' That's grace. It's our daughter's name. What we did years ago was a sin, but God will forgive us if we ask."

"That's what Papa said too."

"Then why won't you ask, Emma?" I looked away. Patrick had his prayer book in the bed beside him. He pressed it into my hands. "Take this with you. Read the passage where the marker is. It's my favorite one. David and Bathsheba committed the same sin we did. But God can redeem sin and turn it into a blessing. The son of David and Bathsheba became the ancestor of our Lord Jesus Christ. Accept His forgiveness, Emma. He wants to give it. It cost Him His Son."

I couldn't speak. I knew that our five minutes were nearly over. The nurse would be back any moment. I longed to hold him one last time. As if he'd read my mind, Patrick said, "I'm reminded of the last stanza of Yeats' poem, *Politics:*

"'. . . And maybe what they say is true
Of war and war's alarms,
But O that I were young again
And held her in my arms!' "

I bent down and gathered him in my embrace. His arms came around me, but with only a shadow of their former strength. I pressed my cheek to his. Patrick's skin smelled the same as I remembered, and I inhaled him for the last time. Our tears joined and flowed, a single stream.

"If you ever tell Gracie the truth," he whispered, "make sure you tell her how very much I loved her."

"I will. I love you, Patrick."

"I know. And I . . . 'love thee with the breath, smiles, tears, of all my life! And, if God choose, I shall but love thee better after death.' "

———

1980

"I never stopped loving Patrick," Emma said. "Not when I married Karl, not when he became a priest, not even when he died. That's why I didn't remarry after my divorce. I lived in an era where marriage was a lifelong commitment, like the one Louise and Friedrich had made—till death us do part. I broke those vows with Karl. I never should have vowed to love him in the first place because I couldn't keep it. My heart was wedded to Patrick. So after the divorce I took a lifelong vow of celibacy, as Patrick had."

Emma finished her story as Suzanne pulled the car into the parking lot at Birch Grove. She was home again. She felt an enormous sense of relief to have finally told the truth about Patrick, as if a heavy burden had been lifted from her, but she couldn't help wondering about the consequences.

Suzanne sat behind the wheel of the parked car, her eyes brimming with emotion. Emma rested her hand on her granddaughter's shoulder. "You know, when you chose your major in college, I thought of Patrick. I could never tell you this before, but you inherited your love of literature, your love of words, from your grandfather."

"I'm part Irish. . . ." she murmured. "Jeff always insisted that I was."

"Yes, you are. I only wish you could have known him. He was an extraordinary man." Had she done the right thing, telling Grace and Suzanne the truth after all these years? But she could hardly have denied it. Somehow they had unearthed the truth by themselves and had merely asked her to confirm it. Maybe it would help Suzanne and Jeff. Maybe it wasn't too late for their marriage. But Grace . . . what would happen to Grace? All the way home she had sat in a daze. So silent. So stricken.

Emma opened the car door and climbed out. She longed to hold her daughter, to ask for forgiveness, but she didn't dare. Grace wouldn't even look at her.

"Thanks again for the ride," Emma said and hurried away into the building.

Once she was in her suite, the tears came. What if Grace never forgave her? That would be the worst punishment she could possibly suffer for her sin. She had already lost her parents and her home, and she'd forfeited a lifetime with Patrick to pay for what she'd done, but she couldn't lose Gracie too. How could she live without her daughter?

Emma wandered through her rooms as if searching for something. She hadn't felt so alone since the day she had given birth to Gracie. Did Mama and Papa feel this same empty, aching loss when they were separated from the daughter they loved? Did God?

The enormity of Emma's sin stung her anew. She remembered telling Papa that she wasn't sorry for what she and Patrick had done, but every time she thought of Gracie's cold, stricken face she was more ashamed of her sin than she'd ever been before. For the first time, she admitted that if she could go back in time and erase what happened on Squaw Island that day, she would gladly do it. Better never to have given birth to Grace than to be alienated from her like this.

Emma gazed around at her rooms, as if surprised to find herself here in this new place. It was the move that had started her down this long road to the truth. Moving had raised questions about the past and caused her to tell Louise's story—and her own. As in the flood of her childhood, it wasn't until she had picked through the rubble of destroyed homes and lives that she fully realized the impact of the storm of passion that had swept her and Patrick away. And only in examining her own life—and Gracie's and Suzanne's lives—had Emma finally seen the terrible aftermath of her sin.

She closed her bedroom door and sat on the edge of her bed. She took Patrick's prayer book from the drawer of her nightstand. God punished the children for the sin of the mothers to the third and fourth generation, Papa had said. But he'd also said that God would forgive her if she repented. Patrick had said the same thing—God not only forgave sin but brought redemption. Emma opened the prayer book to the place Patrick had marked for her thirty years ago and read the words aloud:

> " 'Have mercy upon me, O God, according to thy lovingkindness:
> according unto the multitude of thy tender mercies blot out my
>   transgressions.
> Wash me thoroughly from mine iniquity, and cleanse me from my sin.
> For I acknowledge my transgressions: and my sin is ever before
>   me. . . .' "

THIRTY-FOUR

Suzanne stood on her mother's porch the next day and pressed the doorbell a second time. Grace's car was in the driveway, so she had to be home. Where else would she be in the middle of the afternoon? Why didn't she answer the door?

Sue rifled through her key ring, trying three of them in the lock before the door finally opened. "Mom. . . ?" she called from the foyer. "Mom, are you home?"

"Up here, Sue."

She padded up the carpeted stairs and into her mother's bedroom. Grace was lying on the bed with a wet cloth over her eyes. "What's wrong, Mom?"

"I'm battling a migraine."

"Can I get you something for it? Do you want me to call Daddy?"

"I already took a pill. It's starting to work, but I still don't feel like facing the world just yet."

Suzanne sank into the chair beside the bed. "It's because of what you found out about your father yesterday, isn't it." Grace didn't reply. "Talk to me, Mom. I feel so bad for forcing you to dig up the past when you didn't want to. I'm so sorry. . . ."

"It's not your fault." Grace removed the cloth and slowly sat up, leaning against the mound of pillows at the headboard. "It's just that Father O'Duggan was such a godly man. I respected him so much for that . . . and I loved him for it. Now I feel as though his memory has been tarnished."

"He was also human," Suzanne said softly. "He made a mistake. You have to forgive him for being human."

Even as she spoke them, the words seemed to stick in Suzanne's mouth. She needed to do the same with Jeff. He was human too. He had yielded to the natural human desire to accept a job for the money, prestige, and power it offered. And although he was wrong to agree to move without discussing it with her, she would be just as guilty of wrongdoing if she refused to forgive him. Unforgiveness was causing her mother's illness—and if Suzanne didn't make peace with Jeff before he moved to Chicago, it would cause an even larger mess in her life, in the girls' lives. She had to forgive him for being human. She and Jeff should at least part as friends.

"I wish I had never learned the truth," Grace murmured. Suzanne turned her attention back to her mother. She looked pale against the pillows, her eyes swollen. "I don't know if I can forgive them or not."

"Mom, it's obvious from what I know about Father O'Duggan that God forgave him for his sin—otherwise, how could he have been used by God all those years?"

"I don't care about his parish, and I don't care about all the good he did for other people," Grace said angrily. "I wanted a father so badly when I was growing up! Why didn't he tell me he was my father and let me know him as one?"

"It seems to me from all the stories you told me that that's exactly what Father O'Duggan was to you. That was the role he played in your life. He taught you right from wrong, he guided you and helped you make decisions, he kept you from making mistakes. . . . He led you to faith in God too. Isn't that what you said? You may not have known he was your father, but that's the role he played in your life. A lesser man would have wanted nothing to do with you for reminding him every day of his sin."

"I'm so angry with my mother for not telling me!"

"Mom, I think she made a very difficult but very wise decision. How could you have faced Father O'Duggan every day if you'd known the truth? You wouldn't have accepted a word he said to you because all you would have seen is that he cared more about being a priest than being your father. And that wasn't true. You wouldn't have believed that Grandma refused to marry him. I think you would have been even angrier with both of them if you'd known the truth." She pulled a tissue from the box on the nightstand and handed it to Grace.

"I think Grandma did the most unselfish thing she could possibly do—for you and for Father O'Duggan," Suzanne continued. "Imagine how hard it must have been for her to be so close to the man she loved, yet never be able to hold him or even talk to him beyond simple pleasantries. Grandma could have taken the support money he gave her and lived somewhere else, started all over again, and made a new life for herself, but she gave you and your father the gift of each other, no matter how painful it must have been for her. She gave Father O'Duggan back to God, and she gave you to your father, in the only way she could under the circumstances."

Against her will, Suzanne found herself thinking about her own daughters and their father. "Mom, if nothing else good comes out of all this, I want you to know that I finally understand what you've been trying to tell me about Amy and Melissa needing a father. I don't ever want to hurt them like you were hurt. Will you pray that I'll find a solution like Grandma did?"

"I've been praying for that, Sue. And yes, I'll continue to pray." Grace wiped her eyes and blew her nose, then took Suzanne's hands in hers. "Thanks for coming and helping me put things in perspective. If you can stand another trip into the past, I'd like to tell you one more story about Father O'Duggan that I don't think I've ever shared with you. . . ."

1946

The summer after I graduated from nursing school I was all in a tizzy, planning my wedding. I had never imagined that I'd have such an elaborate affair, but Stephen's parents had dozens of high-society friends that had to be entertained, and they wanted a big to-do with an expensive reception. They paid for everything, of course, and even talked me into getting married in Stephen's home church. My roommate from school had agreed to be my maid of honor, but I had no one to walk down the aisle with me. It was such a long, beautiful aisle too. I wanted my mother to give me away, but she refused.

"It just isn't done, Grace," she said. "That's a man's role. It's going to be hard enough for me to spend the day with all those wealthy, well-educated people. But I'd only be drawing attention to the fact that I'm divorced if I walked down the aisle with you. Maybe if it was a small, quiet wedding . . . but you're planning a three-ring circus." I was hurt, but for once in her life my mother wanted to do the conventional thing, so I was also relieved. "Isn't there someone else you could ask?" she said.

"If I could have my wish . . . please don't laugh . . . but I would like it to be Father O'Duggan." My mother turned away abruptly. She hadn't laughed at the idea, but one minute she was standing beside the kitchen table where I sat with all my wedding lists spread out, and the next minute she was banging pots on the stove.

"See? I knew you wouldn't understand. But Father O'Duggan is the closest thing I had to a real father when I was growing up."

"I do understand," she said with her back to me. "And I think it's a lovely idea. I think you should ask him." She surprised me.

"Could he do it, legally? I mean, would the Catholic church allow him to go into a Protestant church and be part of the ceremony?"

"I don't know. Ask him. The worst he can do is say no, and then you'll be back where you are now. Father O'Duggan will be honored that you asked though, and if he can't do it, he'll have the grace to refuse without hurting your feelings."

I loved the man, but it took me three days to work up the nerve to ask him. I remembered how he had refused to let me call him Daddy years earlier, and asking him to give me away at my wedding seemed like the same thing. I hadn't talked to him in several months because I'd been away at school. He was easy to find, though. I waited until he came out of St. Michael's after the evening mass, and I walked with him back to the rectory.

"Come in, come in," he said. "Though I must warn you things are in a bit of a mess at the moment."

The hallway and two rooms off the kitchen were stripped to the joists and cluttered with lumber and construction equipment. We stepped over two-by-fours and rolls of electrical wiring.

"What on earth are you building over here?" I asked.

"I'm having these two back rooms converted into a small apartment for myself. The rest of the rectory is going to be a place where people can come for refuge."

"What a wonderful idea."

Father O'Duggan's housekeeper made us a pot of tea, and we sat at his kitchen table, sipping it.

"You've become a lovely woman, Grace. And you're a nurse now, so I hear?"

"Yes, I graduated this spring as an RN."

"I'm so proud of you." His smile filled his eyes.

"It must have been all those books you paid me to read."

He laughed and turned his pants pockets inside-out to show me they were empty. "Aye, Gracie! You cleaned me out with all your reading!"

"Did you know that I'm getting married this August? His name is Stephen Bradford and he's a doctor. We'll be living in Philadelphia until he finishes his residency."

He took my hand in both of his. His eyes searched mine. "Tell me about Stephen . . . is he a good man? Does he treat you with respect? Does he love God?"

"He's very good to me, Father. And yes, he loves God as much as I do."

"Good. Do you and he want the same things in life? Are they things worth working for?"

"He feels that practicing medicine is his way of serving God."

"Do you love him, Gracie? Not the fact that he's a doctor. Are you in love with *who* he is, not *what* he is? Would you love him even if he were poor?"

I thought about how Stephen and I had met, and my face must have glowed. "I loved him long before I knew that his parents were wealthy."

"Does he love you? Not just your outward beauty, but does he know the woman inside? Does he love her and cherish her?"

"Yes," I whispered. "I know that he does."

"Then may our Lord and Savior bless your marriage . . . and your new life together." He squeezed my hand.

"Father O'Duggan. . . ?"

"Yes, child?"

"You've been like a father to me all my life and . . . and I've come to ask if you would be willing . . . if you would be able . . . to walk down the aisle with me at my wedding."

His eyes brimmed with tears until they overflowed. He didn't wipe them but rose to his feet and pulled me into his arms, holding me tightly.

"Aye, Gracie. Aye. I would be honored."

———

1980

"He walked me down the aisle, Sue. He was my father . . . and I never even knew it."

"He loved you. Remember Grandma's words?"

"My wedding day was the last time I ever saw him. We lived in Philadelphia during Stephen's last year of residency—the year Father O'Duggan died. I was eight months pregnant with Bobby, and Stephen didn't want me to travel to the funeral. I wish I had known that he was my father. I wish I had . . ."

"Mom, can we look at your wedding pictures? It's been ages since I've seen them."

They went downstairs, and Grace retrieved the album from the shelf in the family room. They sat on the sofa and slowly paged through the photos. There were the usual pictures of the bride and bridesmaids preparing for the wedding, and a shot of all the attendants lined up at the altar rail beside Stephen and the minister. But Suzanne stopped when she came to a picture of Grace walking down the aisle with her father, her hand tucked securely beneath his arm. Father O'Duggan wore his black clerical suit and collar.

"Mom, look," Suzanne said in a whisper. "Look at the pride in his eyes. His love for you is written all over his face."

"If only I could have told him what he meant to me . . . how much I loved him."

"But you did tell him, Mom. Just look at this picture."

Grace was still sitting in her family room, paging through the photograph album when she heard someone come in through the back door. She thought it was Suzanne, returning for something she had forgotten, but a moment later Stephen walked into the room.

"What are you doing home?" she asked in surprise.

"I came to see how you're feeling. How's the migraine?" He sat on the sofa beside her and kissed her forehead. "There, does that make it all better?"

"Oh, much better. Don't you have a golf game? Isn't this your afternoon off?"

"I cancelled it."

"You didn't have to do that, I'll be fine. Suzanne was just here. She left not even half an hour ago."

"I was worried about you, Grace. I could tell you'd had a rough time sleeping last night. And then you weren't feeling well when I left this morning. . . ."

Grace put her hand to his face. "Stephen, you've always been so sweet to me when I'm sick, starting way back when I had scarlet fever."

He laughed and kissed her palm. "At least migraines aren't contagious. What's with the wedding album? It's not our anniversary, is it?"

"No, that's in August."

"Phew! I was afraid I'd forgotten!" He slumped against the sofa cushions in mock relief and loosened his tie.

"You've never once forgotten, in all these years. Suzanne and I were looking at the album because she has been on this insane quest to find out more about my father. And yesterday . . . well, I haven't been able to talk about what we learned yesterday. I've been in shock and denial. I'm glad you came home because I'm finally ready to talk about it. But you and I need to discuss something else first. Something very important."

"This sounds serious," he said, sitting up straighter.

"It is. Stephen, I know you don't want me to work, but I would like to accept the directorship of the crisis pregnancy center."

Grace paused, waiting for him to rant and rave. Stephen looked very displeased, but all he said was, "Go on."

"My mother sacrificed her own happiness for my father and me. My grandparents made enormous sacrifices for each other. It's what people who love each other are supposed to do. If they don't . . . well, that's why Suzanne and Jeff are on the verge of divorce. Each one is living only for himself, and neither one is willing to budge. Love requires us to give willingly for each other. It's what we vowed to do at our wedding—and we've kept those vows, you and I. You've worked long, hard hours to give the children and me a home and to give them an education. I sacrificed nursing to stay home and take care of you and the children. But you no longer need me to make that sacrifice. We have maid service, we eat out more than we eat at home . . ."

"Why do you need a job, Grace?" he said, frowning. "Don't I give you all the money you want?" The expression on Stephen's face told Grace that he was more hurt than angry.

"This isn't about money. In fact, I plan to donate my salary to the center, so, in effect, I'll still be a volunteer. I'm asking you to sacrifice your pride, your long-held ideas of women's roles, whatever else it takes—and let me do this. Remember the song that made you decide to go into medicine? 'Take my life and let it be consecrated, Lord, to Thee.' I want to consecrate my life too. You don't need me to run your house, Stephen, but God needs me to run this center. I think He's calling me to do it, just as He once called you to be a doctor. Do you understand what I'm saying?"

The angry, troubled look on Stephen's face had softened to one of bewilderment. "I'm trying to understand, but I never knew you felt this way about working."

"I didn't—until yesterday. Now I think it's finally time for me to use the gifts and the training God gave me. From all that I've learned about my father, the right-to-life movement and this crisis pregnancy center are two causes that would be very close to his heart."

"What? *Your* father?"

"Yes, he would have encouraged me to take this job. In fact, the board of trustees has been trying to come up with a name for the center, waiting for some rich benefactor to come along to name it after. When I donate my salary I'll have it named after my father."

"After the man who tried to abort you? You're going to name it after Karl Bauer?"

The image in Grace's mind dissolved, erasing the face of Karl Bauer. She saw her real father striding toward her with his warm smile and his gentle, rolling gait.

"No, I'm going to name it after the man who was my real father—Father Thomas Patrick O'Duggan."

———

Suzanne sat at the kitchen table that evening, trying to glue together the broken pieces of a miniature table from Amy's dollhouse. Her daughter's tears had been dramatically out of proportion over the incident, telling Suzanne that the tears weren't about the tiny furniture at all. There had been too much brokenness in her daughter's life lately, too many changes.

As long as she had the glue handy, Suzanne decided to try piecing her broken dinner plate back together as well. She knew it would never be usable, but somehow it seemed important to try to repair it—in the same inexplicable way that the toy table was important to Amy. As Suzanne worked, the sound of the girls' excited, high-pitched voices drifted in from the living room, alternating with Jeff's low, deep voice. He had flown into town for a one-day meeting and had stopped home afterward to see the girls. He would fly back to Chicago late tonight.

"Do you really have to go away again, Daddy?"

"Yes, Amy. You know that I do."

"But why?"

"I have to go to work tomorrow morning. And I work in Chicago now."

"Will you please, *please* come to the teddy bear picnic at my school, Daddy?"

"That depends. When is it, Melissa?"

"I think it's Fursday."

Jeff laughed. Suzanne had missed the sound of his laughter. She remembered how freely he had laughed in the campus coffee shop the day they'd first met. It had been a long time since they'd laughed together that way.

"That's very funny, Melissa," he said. "You made a joke—a teddy bear picnic on *Furs*day!"

"I did?" She giggled helplessly and Suzanne knew Jeff was tickling her. "So will you come, Daddy?"

Suzanne couldn't bear to hear his answer. She stood and poured another cup of coffee into her great-grandmother's crying cup. She had been drinking from it lately. It soothed her to feel connected with all the women who had lived and loved before her, Eve's daughters, as her great-grandmother had once called them. As she sipped, she wandered to the doorway to watch Jeff and the girls. He sat on the loveseat with his daughters nestled on his lap. He still wore his suit from work.

For some reason, the sight of him in a suit and tie jolted her, as if she'd discovered Bradley Wallace in the living room instead of Jeff. *"A suit is an overpriced straitjacket. A tie is a silk noose,"* Jeff had once told Bradley. Where had that wild, impertinent hippie gone? When Suzanne searched for him beneath the suave exterior, she was saddened by what she saw. He'd been domesticated, tamed . . . like a wolf chained to a doghouse. And he'd first donned a suit and tie for her sake. If only there was some way to cut those chains and set him free.

They had started out their marriage with a willingness to sacrifice for each other, but somewhere along the way, they had started living for themselves. Was that when their marriage had been thrown off-center like flawed pottery on a wheel? *"It isn't too late to put the pieces of your marriage back together,"* Grandma Emma had said. *"But it won't be the same marriage it was before. It shouldn't be. That pattern was flawed. . . ."*

"Jeff? Can we talk for a minute?" she said suddenly.

He looked up, startled to see her standing in the doorway. "Girls, go get ready for bed," he said. "I'll come upstairs to tuck you in before I go." Suzanne heard the wariness in his voice.

As they slid off his lap and scampered upstairs, Suzanne retreated to the kitchen. She felt shaky all of a sudden, so she sat at the kitchen table again and took a sip of coffee from the crying cup, as if for strength. Jeff followed her as far as the door and leaned against the frame, waiting for her to speak first.

"I want you to know that I forgive you for not consulting me before you made the decision to move," she said.

Jeff tensed, frowning, as if suspicious of her motives. "What do you mean?"

"I mean exactly what I said. I forgive you. I don't want to hang on to all this bitterness anymore. It's tearing me up inside. I'm tired of fighting about everything from the antique desk to visiting rights. I want to discuss things like two adults again and see if we can't resolve the matter of joint custody in a way that's fair for all of us. I don't want to deprive the girls of their father."

"Thanks . . . I'd like that too." He looked relieved but still wary. Suddenly Suzanne's heart was too full to talk about visitation rights. It seemed as though all of the people who had lived and loved before her and Jeff had crowded into the room—Louise and Friedrich, Emma and Patrick, Grace and Stephen. They were watching her, rooting for her, waiting for her to make the right decision. But what was the right thing to do?

"You know," she began, "for the past few weeks Grandma Emma has been telling me stories about her life and about her mother's life. My great-grandmother used to play the *Someday* game when she lived in Germany. We did that before we were married, remember, Jeff? Your dream was to be a great artist. Where did that dream go? Do you ever think about it anymore?"

He folded his arms across his chest. "No, I don't. What would be the point of games? I have a family to support."

"But we don't need all of this—expensive cars, a huge house, maid service. Lately I've been wondering if we bought all this stuff just to prove to my father that you could be a success."

Jeff's anger was instantaneous, like striking a match. "What kind of screwed-up mind games are you playing, Suzanne? If you're trying to imply that I—"

"Wait, don't get mad . . . just listen. We loved each other when we had nothing. We were so poor when we were first married it was laughable. But we were so much in love, Jeff. Remember? All we had was a bed, so we spent every spare moment in it. Now we have all of this stuff—and we've lost each other. It's not a fair trade. And somewhere along the way we lost God. Remember when you first took me to the art museums in New York? We were going to tell the world about Christ through our art." She looked down at the crying cup, fighting her tears. She traced the figure of the little girl on the front.

"I've been listening to all these stories—my mother's, my grandmother's, my great-grandmother's—and I realized that the love we once had is much too precious to let it slip away . . . and faith in God is even more precious." She looked up, waiting for Jeff's reaction.

"So . . . go on. . . ."

"I could give up my job for you and move to Chicago. I could make all the sacrifices you're asking me to make . . . but not if we're only going to rebuild the same empty lives we have here—both of us working night and day, never talking. Is that what you really want us to do?"

"No . . . but what's the alternative?"

"What if we went back to the way it was when we were first married?"

He gave a humorless laugh. "You mean live in a firetrap apartment and drive a beat-up Volkswagen?"

"Yes, exactly! You gave up your dream of being an artist to help me go to graduate school. Now I'd like to repay you. We could make the garage into your studio. You wouldn't have to quit advertising cold turkey. You could do freelance work. But at least you'd have a chance to paint again. You're so gifted, Jeff."

He turned away, paced a few steps, then turned back. "I don't think you realize what it would mean to give all this up."

"Probably not. But I wonder if we really like the people we've become, or if we just like the income and the life-style. I have choices and opportunities that my great-grandmother Louise never had. But I've lost some of the good things she had—things like relationships. Other people raise my kids, my husband is a stranger, I don't have time for friends, I don't know God anymore. I've gained a sense of myself, but I've lost a sense of my importance to other people. We've become islands, Jeff, isolated in the busy rush and flow of life. Our marriage slowly went under, and we didn't even know it. So did our faith. God is no longer an important part of our life. What happened to Him? What happened to proclaiming Christ in our work? I'm not doing that in my work, and I don't think you are either. Remember how compromised you felt when you first took an advertising job? You said you were prostituting yourself."

"That was a long time ago. You can't seriously be asking me to be poor again? What about the girls?"

"It won't be any worse for them to be poor than to be shuttled back and forth between two homes. How well-off will they be living on my salary and child support? How well can you afford to live in Chicago after deducting support payments and commuting to see them? Besides, I don't think we'll be poor for very long. I believe in you. You're a talented artist, Jeff. And there are so many other things you could do. A few years ago, the Art Institute asked you to teach part time, remember?"

"Yeah, I remember. I didn't have time to teach." He was thoughtful for a moment, then the sexy grin she had once loved so much danced briefly across his face. "Can't I at least keep my BMW?"

Suzanne smiled. "Not with the enormous car payments we're making! Besides, you won't need to commute if you have your own studio at home."

Jeff grew thoughtful again. "This is an awful lot to hit me with, Suzanne. I have a plane to catch."

"I know. And you're probably going to get back to Chicago and decide that this was just something I cooked up to get my own way. But it isn't. I've been hearing about the sins of my mothers and learning a lot from their lives.

We owe it to Patrick and Grandma Emma to make our marriage work."

"Who?"

"I don't have time to explain. But will you at least think about what I said? We can talk about it some more when you come home in two weeks."

Jeff nodded and turned away. Suzanne heard him trudging upstairs to say good-bye to the girls. He came down a few minutes later, briefcase in hand, and leaned against the kitchen doorframe again.

"Hey, Irish . . ." He hadn't called her that in ages. "I . . . uh . . . I really am sorry for not talking it over with you before I took the job. It was a stupid, selfish thing to do. I can't even imagine why I did it . . . I was just . . . well, I was just thinking of myself." A horn tooted outside. "My cab is here. I'll be back at the end of the month. But I'll be thinking about everything you said in the meantime." He turned to go.

"Jeff?"

"Yeah?"

"You were right all along, you know . . . I really am Irish."

———

Emma stared out of the window at Birch Grove without really seeing the beautifully landscaped lawns, the beds of flowering annuals and perennials. She hadn't heard from Grace since Katie's funeral two days ago. Her silence was more painful to bear than any harsh words or accusations she might have hurled at her. Emma could have more easily borne those. She shuddered every time she recalled the shock and anger on her daughter's face. How devastated Grace must have been to learn that the two people she loved and trusted the most had lied to her to cover their own wrongdoing. Patrick had been right when he described the destructive consequences of sin.

When Emma heard a knock on her door, she wasn't sure if she should answer it. She had been avoiding all the group activities at Birch Grove for two days, too wrung out and depressed to put on a cheerful face for everyone. This was probably one of her new friends at the door now, coming to inquire about her. But when Emma opened it, she faced her daughter.

Grace didn't say a word. She simply opened her arms to Emma, then held her tightly.

"I'm sorry, Gracie . . . I'm so very, very sorry," Emma said when she could speak.

"I know."

"Come inside."

"I can't stay long. I just wanted to see you and tell you that I'm sorry. . . ."

"For what, Gracie? You didn't do anything wrong."

"For judging you and Father O'Du—you and my father."

"No, Gracie. Your judgment was right. We did a terrible, terrible thing. Can you ever forgive me for it . . . and for lying to you all these years?"

"Of course I forgive you."

Emma covered her face and wept. Gracie had been harmed the most by Emma's sin. If Grace could forgive her, then maybe God could forgive her too. Hadn't Papa said that he and their heavenly Father would both be waiting with open arms for her return?

"There was never any question of forgiving you, Mother," Grace said as she gathered Emma into her arms again. "I was shocked and hurt and angry at first, but Sue helped me sort through it all. When you shared your story and Grandma Louise's story, Sue and I both did a lot of thinking. And you may have saved Sue's marriage. She told me she and Jeff are talking again."

"Then it was worth digging up all those painful memories. It was worth it all."

"I came to ask if you have this weekend free. Sue and I would like to take you to Bremenville to visit your sister Vera."

"Vera? Oh my. I don't think she'd want to see me."

"Suzanne and I have been to Bremenville already, Mother. We talked to Aunt Vera and to Karl Bauer's adopted son. That's how we began to suspect that Karl wasn't my father. We promised Aunt Vera that we'd bring you back for a visit. She's eager to see you."

"Do you really think it would be a good idea . . . for me to go back there?"

"I do. It will be like closing the circle. But it has to be this weekend." Grace wore a bemused grin. "Starting Monday I'll be a working woman."

"Working!"

"I'm the new director of the crisis pregnancy center."

"Oh, Gracie! Oh, I'm so glad! Your father would be proud of you!"

"We've been looking for a name for the center, and I'm on my way to ask the board to consider naming it after Father O'Duggan."

"He'd be honored . . . but he wouldn't want it to bear his name. He'd want it to bear yours. . . . He would want it to be known as a house of grace."

She smiled. "Grace House. I like that even better."

———

Grace awoke in the motel room in Bremenville early Sunday morning. Suzanne was still asleep in the bed opposite hers. So much had changed in Grace's life since their last trip here to Bremenville, when she had awakened in this same room to the chilling knowledge that she might be illegitimate. Somehow, accepting the truth hadn't been nearly as painful as she had thought it would be. The important thing was that she had finally found the key to unlocking the door between her mother and God. Now if only Emma would walk through that door.

Coming back to Bremenville had drawn all three women closer together. In the car on the way here, Suzanne had brandished a file folder. "I've been saving this surprise for today. After hearing all your stories, I wanted to learn more about Black Jack and O'Brien. So I did some investigating. . . ."

"No, please don't tell me," Grace begged. "I loved those two characters. I don't want to know anything bad about them."

"But this is good news."

"Tell us, then," Emma said. Her eyes shone with excitement.

"Well, according to my source in Las Vegas, two former small-time gangsters once operated a legitimate, licensed casino known as 'The Black Jack Lounge.' It never amounted to much compared to the big-name places, but as the city grew, the property it sat on slowly increased in value. To make a long story short, twenty years after they bought the place, *Fergus* O'Brien and *John* 'Black Jack' *Doyle* sold it for a cool four million dollars and retired to their private yacht in the Bahamas!"

"Bravo!" Emma applauded. "I'm so happy for those two! But *Fergus*! No wonder poor O'Brien never told anyone his first name!" They had laughed until the tears came.

Emma grew unusually quiet when they finally drove down the hill into Bremenville. "Everything is so familiar, yet so changed," she said. "It doesn't seem real. It's like visiting a movie set for a picture I once watched a long time ago. It doesn't seem as though I ever really lived here."

"Is that the car dealership Gus Bauer owned?" Grace asked as they passed the Ford garage.

"Yes . . . but back then it didn't take up half a block like it does now. Ah, poor Markus . . . such a waste of a handsome young man."

They drove down Main Street and parked near Bauer's Pharmacy, now an ice cream parlor. "Do you want to go inside?" Suzanne asked.

"Are you sure Karl's dead and gone?" Emma asked with a wry grin.

"I saw his death certificate, Grandma."

"All right, then. Let's see if the milk shakes are still as good as they once were." They went inside and sat on stools at the soda fountain. Emma ordered a chocolate shake, and Grace and Suzanne dug into enormous sundaes. "These are all the original fixtures Karl bought years ago. Aren't they beautiful? Poor Karl . . ." Emma said with a sigh.

"According to Aunt Vera, he lived a pretty good life," Grace said. "He married a widow and adopted her son, then they adopted two more boys."

"Would you mind if we drove past the house where you and Karl lived?" Suzanne asked.

"Not at all. I'd love to see it myself." When they finished eating, they drove up the hill to where Bremenville's wealthiest residents had once lived. "It's that big white one with the wrap-around porch and all the gingerbread," Emma said, pointing. "My, such a beautiful home. But the years I lived there were the unhappiest years of my life. You would think that the depression years would be, when we were so poor and lived in that decrepit apartment. But they weren't unhappy at all. We had each other, didn't we, Gracie?"

"Always," she said, smiling.

"Do you want to go inside, Grandma? It's a bed-and-breakfast now. They would probably let you look around."

"No," Emma said quietly. "No, let's not."

She turned away and rolled down the window on the other side of the car. Grace turned, as well, and followed her gaze. "Oh, you can see the river from here! You never told me that you had such a beautiful view."

"That's because I could never force myself to look at it. My bedroom faced the front, you see . . ." Emma's voice grew hushed. "And that little hump of land in the middle of the river there . . . is Squaw Island. . . ."

They drove down the hill and across the bridge, following River Road to Friedrich's church. "I wish I had a dollar for every time Eva and I walked this road into town and back," Emma said. "And now the town comes all the way out here, just as Papa said it would. My, wouldn't he and Mama be amazed at how huge their church is now."

Emma didn't want to go inside it, so they walked around the building to visit the cemetery in back. "See how old I've grown!" Emma said. "These huge trees were only saplings when Papa planted them . . . and I was just a little girl."

All three women grew quiet as they gazed down at the three graves—Reverend Friedrich Schroder, Louise Fischer Schroder, Eva Schroder. Emma's older sister, Sophie Mueller, and her husband, Otto, were buried nearby. Before they returned to the car, Emma stood on the small rise beside the Sunday school addition, where the parsonage used to be and looked out at the river again. "Only the river has remained the same," she said. "There's a lesson there—'Joy and sorrow come and go like the ebb and flow.'"

Suzanne rested her arm on Emma's shoulder. "Would you like us to take you out to Squaw Island, Grandma?"

"No, dear . . . that's one place I'd prefer to always remember the way it was."

Emma was solemn as she climbed back into the car. She didn't look back at the church as they drove away but gazed sightlessly through the window as if deep in thought. Grace worried that this trip was becoming too painful for her. Then they pulled into Aunt Vera's driveway, and when Emma saw her sister, her joy overflowed.

"Vera! Oh, I've missed you so! A lifetime is much too long for sisters to spend apart!"

"You haven't aged a day, Emma! I'd know you in a crowd of millions!"

"I understand that you've already met my daughter, Grace, and my granddaughter, Suzanne."

"Yes. And I'm so glad they kept their promise to bring you home again. You have a beautiful family, Emma."

"Gracie looks just like her father, doesn't she, Vera?" Emma's voice had grown very soft. Her face wore a guarded look. Grace understood that she was asking Vera how much she knew, and pleading with her for acceptance and forgiveness.

"She's the very image of him. And oh, what a handsome devil he was!" Vera's hands suddenly flew to her face as she laughed out loud. "Did I really say *devil*? What an awful thing to call a priest!"

"Then you knew about my father?" Grace asked in surprise.

Vera smiled. "Honey, the biggest mystery of my lifetime was solved the moment you showed up at my door and told me who you were!"

Their reunion with Aunt Vera had been both touching and hilarious. As usual, Emma turned the smallest event into a grand occasion. When the day finally drew to a close, she accepted Vera's invitation to spend the night, while Grace and Suzanne returned to the motel. Altogether, it had been a momentous weekend.

Early Sunday morning when she awoke, Grace felt a small shiver of excitement. Tomorrow morning she would begin her new job as director of Grace House. Too excited to lie still, she rose and began to dress.

"You're up awfully early," Suzanne muttered from beneath the covers.

"I thought I would worship at my grandfather's church this morning. I read on the signboard yesterday that they have an eight-thirty service. I'll wake you up when I get back, and we can collect Mother from Aunt Vera's house."

Suzanne yawned and stretched. "Would you mind if I came to church with you?"

"No! I'd love it!"

Grace hadn't expected the church to be so crowded for the early service. The hallways were fairly bursting with activity as parishioners of all ages packed the sanctuary. She and Suzanne had to sit near the front in order to find empty seats. She recognized the pastor from their previous visit.

"We have a special guest this morning," he announced after the opening prayer and praise service. "A former member of this congregation has returned for a visit and has agreed to play a special number for us on the piano."

Grace's heart began to pound. It couldn't be! She turned and saw her mother striding down the aisle toward the front. Grace's vision blurred with tears.

"This is Emma Bauer. She's the daughter of Pastor Friedrich Schroder, the man who first established this church at the turn of the century and made it what it is today."

Emma sat down at the piano to enthusiastic applause. "Thank you," she said, smiling. "It's so good to be home! You know, I was baptized in this church eighty years ago. Papa preached here, and I first learned to play the piano here. My goodness, so much has changed since those days! But isn't it nice to know that in a world of change, God's grace never changes?

"Papa loved the story of the Prodigal Son. He loved the way it portrayed God as a loving, forgiving father. When the prodigal came to him and said, 'Father, I have sinned against heaven and before thee,' there followed a glorious celebration in his father's house. I'd like to play a song for you this morning. And, Papa . . . if you're listening up in heaven . . . this song is for you too." Emma closed her eyes and began to play, singing the words in her clear, strong voice:

"Amazing grace! how sweet the sound, that saved a wretch like me!
I once was lost, but now I'm found, was blind, but now I see. . . ."

LYNN AUSTIN has authored several works of fiction, including *Fly Away* and the CHRONICLES OF THE KING series. In addition to writing, Lynn is a popular speaker at conferences, retreats, and various church and school events. She and her husband have three children and make their home in Illinois.